MONTAUK

MONTAUK

Nicola Harrison

ST. MARTIN'S PRESS

NEW YORK

MONTAUK. Copyright © 2019 by Nicola Harrison, LLC. All rights reserved. Printed in the United States of America. For information, address St. Martin's Press, 175 Fifth Avenue, New York, N.Y. 10010.

www.stmartins.com

Designed by Kathryn Parise

The Library of Congress Cataloging-in-Publication Data is available upon request.

ISBN 978-1-250-20011-2 (hardcover)
ISBN 978-1-250-20012-9 (ebook)

Our books may be purchased in bulk for promotional, educational, or business use. Please contact your local bookseller or the Macmillan Corporate and Premium Sales Department at 1-800-221-7945, extension 5442, or by email at MacmillanSpecialMarkets@macmillan.com.

First Edition: June 2019

10 9 8 7 6 5 4 3 2 1

For Christopher and Christopher

Acknowledgments

—❧—

I am grateful to many people for their generosity, advice, and guidance while writing this book. Thanks to my incredible agent, Stephanie Kip Rostan, at Levine, Greenberg, Rostan; my brilliant editor, Leslie Gelbman, and the entire team at St. Martin's Press, for their warm enthusiasm and hard work; and to The Writers Room, which provides a peaceful and productive space for me to write.

Many thanks to the talented novelists in my writing workshop, Donna Brodie, Mario Gabriele, Barbara Miller, Mike Pyrich, and Rob Wolf, and especially to Jennifer Belle, who has offered invaluable mentorship along the way.

Thanks also to my dear friends and early readers, Elisa Moriconi, Bethany Raborn, and Suzanna Filip; to Henry Osmers at the Montauk Historical Society; and Montauk local Vinnie Grimes, for telling me stories of the good old days.

Finally, my gratitude goes to my family: my parents, Michael and Jayne Harrison, for their constant love and support; my son, Christopher, who knows Montauk better than anyone, and, above all, my husband, Greg Ray, for always believing in me.

The South Fork of Long Island is like a slender arm extending from New York City out into the Atlantic. And Montauk, the final stretch of land before a drop into the ocean, is a beckoning finger drawing you to her, right to the very end, leaving you with no place to go but back to where you came from.

MONTAUK

1

※

Summer 1938

We left the train and were escorted to our awaiting cars, one for
Harry and me and one for our trunks—packed to the brim for
the summer months ahead. I looked up at the Manor on the hill and saw
it for the first time, silhouetted against the deep orange early evening sky.

As we drove up the tight and winding road, tree branches reached overhead toward each other like lovers' hands desperate to connect, and then
the road suddenly opened up and I gasped. It was just as it had looked in
the brochure, but bigger, grander, even more magnificent than I could
have imagined—a Tudor façade with turrets and spires, more reminiscent
of a vast and dignified English castle than a beach town hotel.

Harry put his hand on my knee and squeezed. "I told you you'd like it
here."

"Oh, you were right, darling; I can already tell I'm going to fall in love
with this place."

Several other couples had taken the same train from the city as Harry
and I, and a caravan of cars followed behind us. We entered through the
carved wooden doors and as I looked around the grand lobby, which

seemed to extend for miles with its enormous exposed wooden beams, stone flooring and three oversized fireplaces, I felt like a guest at the palace.

"Mr. and Mrs. Bordeaux, welcome to The Montauk Manor. We are so pleased you'll be staying with us for the summer," the front desk clerk said. "I see this is your first time."

"First time in Montauk, actually," I said. "Some of our friends have been summering here for the last few years and we've heard such wonderful things."

"It certainly is the place to be." She smiled sweetly as if she were right off one of the posters I'd seen around Manhattan advertising the beach town. "Tomorrow night's the first soirée of the summer; it will be here in the grand lobby."

"We wouldn't miss it, would we, Beatrice?"

"Not a chance." A jazz band played quietly at the other end of the room and I could already feel myself getting into the swing of things.

"Please arrange for the butler to deliver our luggage and unpack our belongings while we dine," Harry said.

"Of course." She nodded, handed us our keys and had us escorted up to our room.

Harry and I first talked about Montauk that April during a pre-show dinner at Barbetta's, our favorite Italian restaurant, behind the Metropolitan Opera House. We were seated at our usual table under the great chandelier when he'd snapped his menu shut. He said he had a surprise for me, then told me we'd be spending the whole summer in Montauk—or rather I would. Harry would stay in the city during the week and take the new express train out to join me on the weekends.

I resisted at first. We'd already agreed on three weeks in Providence, together, it was all planned and I'd been so looking forward to spending time with Harry, just the two of us, away from the hectic, overheated city and his busy work life.

"Cancel it. We'll try something new this year," he'd said, taking a swig of his drink. "It will be good for us, Beatrice, a change, a fresh start. You said we needed that, remember?"

He was right, of course. I had said that. He handed me a brochure and I looked at the illustration on the cover: The Montauk Manor was the focal point and pictured below it were men and women engaging in various leisurely activities: fishing, golf, archery, swimming, tennis, horseback riding. One man, or woman, I wasn't quite sure, was in flight gear. They certainly made it seem that anything was possible. Far in the background a lighthouse stood proudly at the very tip of the island, surrounded by seagulls.

"What will I do all summer long?" I'd asked. "Most women who summer at their vacation home have children to entertain and nannies to help them, and friends with children. What reason do I have to be in Montauk for twelve weeks?"

"What reason do you have to be in the city?"

His quick response felt sharp. Feelings of futility came gushing to the surface and I felt my cheeks burn red.

"Well, I could work again," I'd said, quietly, turning the stem of my glass, making small ripples in the cream-colored tablecloth. But Harry told me, once again, that it wasn't appropriate for someone like me.

"We've already discussed this, Beatrice. You're not a college girl anymore, or a farm girl for that matter. You're a Bordeaux now and you should be proud of that." He reached over the table and placed his hand on mine. "And it's my job to take care of you now, to support you; don't rob me of that, sweetheart."

Something in me hesitated and I couldn't quite tell why. I looked at the illustration again; everyone had a look of strange detachment, each person lost in his own world. Of course it would be a treat to summer all season long; who wouldn't want that? But to be away from my husband four nights of the week left me uneasy. A tiny voice in my head told me it was a precarious situation, and suddenly that was the only voice I could hear.

We dined at the Manor's seafood restaurant that first night in Montauk. The ceilings were high and the sound of laughter, chatter and clinking wineglasses mingled in the air and made me excited for our adventure ahead.

"Harry, let's explore the town tomorrow and maybe even take a boat out; wouldn't that be fun?"

"Not tomorrow, sweetheart, I've got archery, remember?"

"Oh," I sighed, and looked at the menu. Local fluke, striped bass, lobster. "You know, now that I think of it, I remember my brother mentioning the name Montauk years ago."

"Why would your brother have known anything about Montauk? It wasn't even a destination to visit until a few years ago."

"I remember him telling me it was a little fishing town all the way out on the tip of Long Island and that he wanted to go there sometime to fish for bass." I looked out the window; just the mention of him made my chest tighten. I focused on an elderly waiter putting all his effort into opening a window on the far side of the room that looked out into the night sky. I had the urge to get up and help him. Eventually he wrestled it open and I felt relieved by the cool, crisp ocean air on my bare arms.

"Darling, I don't know why you bring up the topic of your brother; you get upset every time," Harry admonished.

The next instant he started waving madly at a couple walking into the restaurant and insisted that they join us. "It's Dr. and Mrs. Sanders," he said in a whisper as they approached. "He knows a lot of people."

It was quite an ordeal for the restaurant manager and another waiter to move a table next to ours so we could sit together and I wasn't entirely sure the other couple was as enthusiastic as Harry about the arrangement, but he was insistent.

"So what do you think of this place?" Dr. Sanders asked once we were situated. "Pretty great, isn't it?"

"It looks lovely," I said, "though we haven't had a chance to take it all in yet; we just arrived."

"We summered here last year," Mrs. Sanders said, touching my arm. "The swimming pool is beautiful—you'll be spending a lot of time there, I'm sure, but wait until you see the beach and the boardwalk, it extends for more than half a mile along the ocean, oh, and the yacht club, it's perfect, it really is, such a wonderful escape from the city."

"We're so lucky," I said.

Harry lit a cigarette. "Have you put any money into this town yet, Doc?"

"Not yet, but I'm considering. We have a few properties in Miami, so I don't know if it makes sense to invest in all of Fisher's schemes. But I heard you're going in big—I'm impressed."

"With the way things are going," Harry said in a hushed voice, "now's the right time to buy in."

Dr. Sanders nodded. I tried to catch Harry's eye so he'd let me in on what he was discussing, but he looked into his martini, swirled it, then gulped the rest of it down.

Back in the bedroom I looked around, opened the drawers and the cupboards and marveled at the attention to detail. The hand-carved drawer pulls, the soft cotton bedsheets trimmed with lace. Harry sat on the end of the bed and untied his shoelaces.

"I don't want you to leave on Sunday," I said. "I'm going to miss you."

Harry sighed.

"Well, what if I get lonely?" I said.

"Beatrice, you'll be a mother one day and then you'll have your hands full and you won't have the luxury of time to lounge and relax."

I nodded, my expression turned serious. I was trying to remain hopeful that we would be blessed with a child sometime in the near future, but the same old fear and questioning about why it hadn't happened yet came rushing back. The thought of being around all the women during the week with their children at the beach and the pool, teaching them to play tennis and build sandcastles, made me feel rather melancholy. Most likely I'd be the only one of childbearing age without a child to care for and everyone would be asking why I wasn't in the family way. My stomach clenched and I suddenly found it hard to swallow.

"But Harry, I'm not a mother yet."

"You'll get in with the women. It's good for business. You'll make friendships here and then back in the city we'll be invited to dinner parties where I'll forge business relationships."

"I hardly think that my making friends will lead to any business," I said.

He shrugged. "It's how my mother and father always worked, as a partnership, and it turned out pretty damn well."

The mention of his mother made me cringe a little—I had never really fit with the Bordeaux family and they knew that as well as I did.

Of course we'd been to all the parties and we'd hosted lots of dinners and I'd done my best to play the part of the perfect companion, but the idea that Harry and I could be more than just a married couple was compelling, that I could somehow be beneficial to his business gave me a sense of purpose and direction, a feeling that had been hampered since we'd married. I twisted the band of my ring.

"Say, Harry, what was that talk with Dr. Sanders about buying into Montauk, and now being the right time?"

"Nothing for you to worry about."

"No, really, I'm interested. If you want me to be more involved with your business life then you must keep me informed."

He took off his jacket and unhooked his suspenders. "Look, Beatrice, I wasn't going to tell you about this yet, not until I had more information, but there're a few of us who are very seriously considering investing out here."

"Really? But you've barely even seen the place. Is that why you wanted to come here, for an investment?"

"It's the real thing, Beatrice. We could be sitting on a gold mine if we are smart about it."

"Who was the Fisher guy you mentioned?"

"You met at the horse races last summer."

"I don't recall."

"Sure you do. Dapper fellow, a bit of an oddball. Carl Fisher, an eccentric dresser. When War Admiral won the Triple Crown and we all stayed until the wee hours dancing on the grass."

"I remember the night, but I don't recall meeting anyone named Carl Fisher."

"It doesn't matter, but he's the one who turned thousands of acres of unpopulated, unwanted mangrove swamp into Miami Beach. You couldn't give that land away before he took an interest in it, and now his fortune is made."

I sat down on the bed next to him.

"He convinced the entire East Coast that it was America's greatest winter playground, and he was right. After Miami he set his sights on Montauk. Same thing, nothing was here, just a rural wilderness, cattle roaming the hills and a tiny fishing village."

"So he's the one who put up all those posters around the city, *Montauk in the Summer, Miami in the Winter;* he wants wealthy New Yorkers to spend their money in both of his worlds," I said.

"Exactly. He brought his construction crew from Miami and built his dream—a yacht club, a bathing club, polo fields, a golf course, prime hunting, a ranch, and this place, the Manor, is his centerpiece, a two-hundred-room castle by the sea."

I laughed. "I suppose it is."

"There are glass-enclosed tennis courts, a beach club and a fantastic swimming pool looking out on to the beach—you heard Mrs. Sanders rave about it."

"You don't even swim," I said, hearing it come out sharper than I'd intended.

Harry stood up and went into the bathroom. "Fine, but you do."

"Darling, it sounds spectacular, I can't wait to see it all and I am not disagreeing with you," I called through the doorway, "but it doesn't sound like there's much to invest in if Mr. Fisher has done all this work already."

"Well, that's the thing." Harry leaned his head out of the bathroom with a toothbrush sticking out of his mouth.

"What's the thing?"

"He's done all this work, well, a lot of it, but there're still some things that are not finished. He's designed and built up this glamorous, luxurious town and now he's broke."

"Broke?"

"Broke, broke, broke." Harry hit the doorframe hard and loudly three times as he said it, grinning. He turned and I heard him spit into the sink; then he reemerged, suddenly perked up.

"Remember that hurricane that hit Miami? It devastated the place and it needed a massive rebuild, which cost him an absolute fortune," Harry said, grinning. "He'd already lost a lot of his money in stocks and he'd put the rest of his money into Montauk."

"So you and your friends will just swoop in and take over?"

"Beatrice, don't you see what I'm saying? He needs people like me to come in and save him so he doesn't go under completely. We're going to help him. And you, my darling, by staying out here for the summer and getting to know Montauk, you'll be an asset to me. We could be spending a lot of time here in the future; it's important to me that you like it." He took my face in his hands and he kissed me. "I want you to be with me on this, Beatrice, in every way; can you do that for me?"

It was the first time I'd heard him say something like that in years, not since we first kept steady company and he had big plans for us.

"I can." I smiled. Perhaps he was right; maybe Montauk would be good for us after all.

Something about the way Harry spoke to me that first night in Montauk gave me hope. We'd been married for five years, but the last year or two had been difficult. I'd felt him pull away, distance himself from me, and I'd seen his eyes wander. But that night it was as if he wanted to come back to me fully, as if he wanted me to be an important part of his life again, for us to go back to the way we were when we first married, when it seemed that nothing mattered more than me and him. We were in love again. I felt this so strongly that I agreed to everything he proposed.

I had his undivided attention for the first time in months and was sure something between us had changed. I slept in his arms that night and convinced myself we had turned a corner. I grasped at the possibility of a transformation, a shift, however small or insignificant, a new place for the summer, a new sense of partnership, something, anything different from our last year of marriage where I'd always felt he was just beyond my reach. A new beginning, I thought. I hoped.

2

---※---

I slipped into the royal-blue silk stunner—elegant, hem to the floor, nipped at the waist with puffed shoulders and a daring dipped back. It was the most beautiful of all the dresses I'd brought with me for the summer and I felt beautiful, too, as I slid my room key into my evening bag, linked my arm through Harry's and descended the stairs of The Montauk Manor. Harry, handsome and clean-shaven, wore his new three-piece pin-striped suit and I felt all eyes on us as we made our entrance.

As we walked through the crowd there was an air of excitement for the first big party of the summer where everyone would see exactly who they'd be spending the next three months with in Montauk. Arms were freckled and cheekbones kissed by the first few weekends of sun, everyone was eager to be sociable and the barmen worked extra hard as the guests sipped champagne and mingled as though they'd been hibernating all winter long. I recognized a few faces from the city. Folk from the same high-society circles that Harry and his business partners moved in would be here this summer, along with other curious souls passing on Providence and Newport for the season, and even hailing from Miami, to see what all the fuss was about.

The jazz ensemble played on in the grand lobby, but no one was dancing yet. Harry spotted Clark and his wife, Dolly, a couple we knew from the city, and we walked over to them arm in arm.

"Hello, old chap," Harry said, slapping Clark on the back. "I hear you did well at the archery tournament today."

"I'm pretty rusty," Clark said. "A few of us are heading out to practice early tomorrow morning if you want to join us."

"I'd love to. Clark, you remember my wife, Beatrice?"

"I do," he said. "It's lovely to see you again.

"Maybe you two ladies will cheer us on at polo tomorrow afternoon." He nodded to his wife, Dolly, who gave a slight shrug of the shoulders.

"Perhaps," she said at the exact time I said, "Of course."

Dolly had attended Vassar College like me but several years earlier. She was closer in age to Harry than me, but she and I really seemed to get along. She was legendary, actually—wildly popular and active in women's service and in promoting the idea of education for young females. The boys had loved her and she'd always worn the most beautiful hats.

Hors d'oeuvres were passed around and the room began to swell with guests, everyone in their finery, proudly making the rounds, the excitement for summer buzzing throughout the room as the music picked up and the singer took the stage. Her flawless skin was the color of polished caramel and her hair was pulled tight on the top of her head where a mass of black curls obediently stayed put. She began her set with a Billie Holiday number, "I'm Gonna Lock My Heart." It made my hips sway. I loved that song and the girl could sing. Her beautiful voice was flowing through me like the long notes of the trumpet. As her last note ended and the sax player took over with an upbeat solo, a few couples started to swing.

"Come on, Harry," I said, tugging his arm toward the dance floor. "Let's go and brush off the cobwebs."

It had been months since Harry and I danced together. Harry was far better at the more traditional styles than swing, but I just wanted to move and I always felt closer to him after a good go-around on the dance floor. My cheeks flushed with color, my pinned hair loosened and my smile was wide and free as he whisked me across the dance floor. For a moment, though, I saw his face looked strained, and when I sensed he wasn't enjoying it like I was I had the urge to suddenly stop. When the song came to an end we exited the floor and made our way back to Dolly and Clark.

"Aren't you two the spring chickens," Dolly said. "You looked fabulous."

"Not me," Harry said, waving to the waiter to bring him a drink. "I'm going to throw my back out dancing like that."

"Oh, Harry, you were wonderful," I said, linking my arm in his, trying to encourage him.

"Say, Clark, we could leave archery for another day and join the fox hunt tomorrow morning. . . . I haven't done that since December in Boston." He plucked a martini off a passing tray.

Dolly rolled her eyes. "Well, if you gents will excuse us I think Beatrice and I will go and admire the view." Dolly placed her diamond-heavy hand on mine and led me over to the lounge. "I hope you don't mind, darling, but talk of hunting small animals just turns my stomach."

"I don't understand the fascination with it," I said. Dolly had rich, dark hair and even on the first weekend of summer she had a golden complexion like that of the Europeans. With her high cheekbones and full lips you could see how her husband had fallen in love. Refined and elegant in the way she carried herself, she exuded something that I admired, envied even, something I couldn't quite place. Her womanliness, or her confidence, or perhaps it was the two together that was rare to see.

"How are the hats coming along?" I asked. Her father was a well-known milliner in the city and she had recently launched a collection of her own.

"Fine," she said. "You should come down to the factory with me sometime; we could make you something special."

"I'd love to," I said.

Excused from the tedious talk of shooting, we settled into lounge chairs that gazed on to the Manor green and beyond that the Long Island Sound. We smoked cigarettes and Dolly leaned all the way back in the deep lounger and swished her legs to the side like a movie star. Though we were three thousand miles east of Los Angeles, it seemed Hollywood glamour was everywhere.

"Heart and Soul" played in the background and I looked around for Harry, but he had his back to me, talking to a woman in a peach gown. Dolly seemed uninterested in the rest of the party and perfectly content to watch the sun go down with no one's company but mine, yet guests constantly stopped to greet her and she introduced me to some of her friends from Providence, where they had summered before Montauk became the place to be. And then Harry came over, approaching me from behind the lounge chair.

"How are you, darling?" he asked. He bent down, draped his arms around my shoulders and kissed me on the cheek. "Can I get you ladies another drink?" I still had half a glass of champagne left, but he took it from me and replaced it with a full glass already in his hand. "You look beautiful tonight," he whispered. That was the line he always used right before he was about to disappear for a while.

"Thank you," I said, feeling a pang of disappointment. I knew it was silly and selfish, but I wanted him to want to stay. I didn't want him to get swept up in whatever parlor game it might be; I wanted him to be by my side, to introduce me to some of his friends' wives so I'd know a few people after he went back to the city for the week. I wanted him to show me off on this first weekend; I hoped he'd feel proud to be with me and happy for us to spend time together. I thought perhaps we'd go upstairs to the room together at the end of the night and I'd feel close to him even after he left for the city. Things were supposed to be different, but they weren't feeling that way.

"I'm going to play cards with the gents," he said. "Be back in time to take you for another spin on the dance floor, maybe a fox-trot this time so I can keep up." His face was next to mine, his mouth by my ear, so he couldn't have seen the look on my face, but maybe he felt my smile drop, my cheek go slack. I knew him. An hour would mean three or four and I'd be asleep by the time he joined me in the suite. "You don't mind, do you, darling? It's just that I haven't seen some of these fellas since winter."

"Of course not," I said, turning back to smile, to convince him I meant it. "Go on, have fun and win some money. I was just about to see what's on offer at the buffet."

He kissed my cheek and left. I didn't look back or let my eyes follow him, but I could feel his footsteps moving farther away.

I should have worn the beige chiffon, I thought. I should have saved the royal blue for another occasion.

We wanted to have a baby right away and as newlyweds Harry and I couldn't keep our hands off each other. It should have been that way anyway, but trying to get pregnant gave us an added incentive, a secret that only we knew. We'd make eyes at each other all evening across our dinner table with ten guests, and as soon as they left we'd dash to the bedroom, Harry tearing off my clothes, ripping at my underwear before we even made it to the bed. There was such urgency. Sometimes as we lay there, after, the sheets tangled at the end of the bed, my head on his chest, him passing me his cigarette, I'd wonder if I was ready for all the passion and desperation for each other to dwindle, for me to become more domesticated, more motherly. I wanted a child, but I wanted Harry, too. I had time. I was only twenty-two when we married, but Harry was already thirty. We wanted two children, maybe three, and Harry was adamant that he didn't want to be an older father. But each month I waited and each month my menstrual cycle arrived perfectly on time.

A year or so into marriage the doctor gave us a chart to follow indicating certain days that we should "indulge" in each other. He called it the rhythm method, a new, scientific way to estimate the likelihood of my fertility based on the days of my cycle. He said it was experimental but that we should remain optimistic. We both felt uncomfortable about it, awkward. Sometimes Harry couldn't get aroused on the particular day that Dr. Lombardi told him to. I started to feel rejected, he was frustrated and the whole thing began to feel like a damned science experiment gone wrong. We stopped talking about having a baby completely. I longed for the day that I'd be with child; then this would stop, his job would be accomplished and we'd have a new focus, a new life to enjoy. But I waited and waited.

3

⁎

The women crammed together at the platform and waved madly as the train pulled away from the station.

"I'll miss you, darling!" one called out. "Hurry back, sweetheart," said another, while the rest blew kisses to closed glass windows already forty feet away.

They were all made up like dolls, giving their husbands one last glance at their loyal and loving faces before the men headed back to the city after the first weekend of the summer, not to return for four whole days. It seemed a little odd and overly zealous to behave so desperately, but I joined the commotion anyway, waving frantically long after the train had left the station.

I watched until it was just a speck in the distance, and when it was no longer in sight I felt a sudden pang of panic. I looked around at all the unfamiliar faces. I barely knew anyone in Montauk; my marriage didn't feel quite as it should. What on earth was I doing here?

"Yoo-hoo, off to the Seahorse," someone cooed in the crowd.

There was a note in the Manor newsletter that after the gentlemen left the women would meet at the nearby Seahorse for cocktails and the season's first "Week in Review" meeting led by Jeanie Barnes, secretary of the Junior League back in New York. I got the impression that these afternoon meetings were to become a regular thing. I needed to get to know some of the other women so that I wouldn't feel like an outsider here and I wanted to make friends soon, since we'd all be in one another's company for the rest of the summer. Not only that, I was eager to have some new acquaintances to report back to Harry, but I felt as though I'd been putting on a show all weekend playing the perfect wife in a perfect marriage and part of me was looking forward to having the evening to myself. I briefly considered sneaking back to the Manor unnoticed. Now that Harry was gone at least I could read my new book by Virginia Woolf. He didn't think I should be reading that kind of "feminist baloney," so I had kept it under the bed the whole weekend.

I admit I had a tendency to get wrapped up in books. Before Woolf I'd been captivated by the romance of du Maurier's *Rebecca* and before that the murder and scandal of Field's *All This and Heaven Too*. I'd spend hours immersed in their worlds, enraptured most by those that felt so far from the prim and proper behavior of our Manhattan crowd.

"Beatrice, darling, we're meeting momentarily." It was Jeanie. Everyone was somebody's darling. She and the crowd of about twenty women were heading left as I was veering right, toward Manor Hill. "I'm really looking forward to your thoughts for the Wednesday afternoon activity."

"Oh, I thought we were meeting at the Manor," I lied.

"Well, what were you going to do, walk up there?" She laughed.

"I suppose not," I said, though I would have quite enjoyed the fifteen-minute walk to the Manor in the fresh, crisp early evening air.

"Of course not," she said. "I've arranged for the Manor trolley to pick us all up in a few hours, after we've had a chance to discuss the social calendar."

"Great." I walked over and, at her suggestion, with her hand on her hip and her elbow pointing right at me, I linked my arm through hers.

"Sit close to me," she said in a whisper, as if she were letting me in on some big secret. "I've been heading up society events for a while now; you could learn a thing or two from me."

"Okay, I will, yes. Harry really wants me to get involved."

"You know just before summer started I organized a wonderful luncheon at the Frick House and we had a private tour of the art collection; next time you should come along."

"I'd love that, thank you."

"Of course it's not that simple to set up a private tour and a private luncheon in the gardens; you have to know people. And my husband's father knew Henry Clay quite well before he passed. So of course we're well connected to the family."

Though I didn't know her well at all, I had a strong sense that one wouldn't want to get on the wrong side of Jeanie Barnes. She and her husband, Cecil, were pictured in the Society Pages almost weekly. Rumor had it they lived in a magnificent five-story brownstone on the Upper West Side and had three live-in nannies for their three children. I'd only seen one of their nannies in Montauk, but they were staying in one of the penthouse suites in the Manor to accommodate Jeanie's brood.

I'd also heard that she had some beef with the President of the Junior League and was desperate to let everyone know how worthy she herself was of such a prestigious position. The higher-ups in the Junior League were treated like movie stars in and around Manhattan, and they were invited to the top soirées in the city.

Jeanie was certainly a well-connected woman—thriving on introducing one acquaintance to another and taking credit for whatever friendship or social success might ensue. Getting in her good graces would definitely be useful.

Sometimes I longed for the close friendships I had with the girls from back home in Pennsylvania. It's funny how the bonds you form when you're young, that tiny window in-between girlhood and womanhood, are often the ones you long for most. It was at that time with those girls when I felt truest to myself, as if they were the ones who knew me most intimately. Now that we were older I wished I could talk to them about life, about marriage, to ask if they ever felt their husbands drifting, to ask for advice on what to do to make sure Harry felt wanted and needed. But when Charlie, my only brother, died, I'd drifted away from so many friendships and I'd retreated into myself and into mourning, cutting ties with old friends and new because I didn't know how to be sad; I felt it was a burden to others, so I extricated myself from just about anyone except my family.

In New York my friends were Harry's friends' wives for the most part, and while they were pleasant enough, it quickly became clear that these women wouldn't be the kind I could speak to in confidence. Since I had stopped working after we married, I was finding it hard to meet anyone on my own who I felt was trustworthy and compatible and not just interested in climbing the social ranks. Part of me hoped this summer in Montauk would help me find my own way a bit more, find my own friends again, not be so reliant on Harry. And at the same time I was invigorated to build friendships that would help him, us, succeed in business.

The Seahorse was a small cocktail lounge with red walls and floral upholstered barstools. People came here and drank while they waited for the trains to come in. Dolly caught my eye and nodded toward the bar. She looked magnificent in a fitted gingham dress, a matching belted jacket and an electric-blue hat at an angle. Into one of the creases on her hat she'd pushed a large cluster of purple hydrangeas likely plucked from a bush outside the Manor. I admired how she always looked so put together in an effortless way, unlike Jeanie, who looked as though she'd spent most of the afternoon squeezing her post-baby tummy into a dress far too tight. Why not let your body recuperate after such a transformative experience, I thought, instead of trying to force it back to the way it used to be? Of course I knew nothing of how the body really reacted after having a baby; I could only imagine.

I ordered a gin fizz and Dolly a mint julep. She drank it down in less than five minutes and ordered another. By the time Jeanie started clinking her glass with a fork, all the seats at the long table were taken, so Dolly and I stood in the very back near the exit by a woman who introduced herself as Martine. Jeanie glanced back at me with a glimmer of disappointment. I shifted my feet and looked again for an empty chair up front, but there was nothing and Dolly looked perfectly relaxed as she leaned against the wall, so I tried to emulate her ease.

"Ladies, I hope you all have a cocktail in your hand and have had a chance to mingle." Jeanie finally stopped the glass clinking and set it down on the table in front of her. "Now that everyone's settled, let's get down to business and go over the week's exciting events. Tomorrow, we'll meet at ten a.m. at Gurney's Inn on the great lawn for a game of croquet and immediately following there'll be a luncheon hosted by Mary Van de Coop, to raise money for the Tail Waggers' charity." She went on, giving a rundown of the activities for the entire week. "And Wednesday afternoon I've arranged for archery lessons." There was a gasp and Jeanie clapped her hands. "Well," she said, "I don't see why the men should have all the fun."

"What about rest and relaxation?" Dolly whispered toward me and Martine. "Isn't that what we came for?"

"Apparently not if Jeanie has anything to do with it," Martine said.

"Well," Dolly said, "if she doesn't pack our schedules, and hers, then God forbid, she might have to take care of her children." The three of us giggled like schoolgirls in the back row.

"Do you ladies have something you'd like to add?" Jeanie asked.

"No," I said quietly, shaking my head.

"Ooh, I do," Dolly said, adjusting her hat to an even more tilted angle. "Don't forget, ladies, I'll be hosting a trunk show for my hat collection in a few weeks at the Manor. You can place orders for the fall and I may have a few ready-to-wear summer hats, too."

"Wonderful, Dolly, I'll be sure to add it to the newsletter. Okay, moving on to the End of Summer Masquerade Charity Ball, I know the summer has just begun, but it's going to be here sooner than you think and we still need committee leaders for raising funds."

"What is it?" I asked Dolly.

"Yes, Beatrice?" Jeanie called out. "Questions can be directed to me."

"Oh." Everyone turned to look toward me. "I was just asking about the charity ball?"

"Of course; I almost forgot," Jeanie said. "For those of you who are joining us in Montauk for the first time, the End of Summer Masquerade Charity Ball is a wildly fun evening held on Labor Day weekend where we each invite, and pay for, a member of the Montauk community to attend the party."

I squirmed at the way Jeanie announced that we newcomers were joining her in Montauk, as if she owned the place just because she'd summered there before.

"It's always quite a mixed crowd and it's a wonderful chance to thank the locals for making our summer so comfortable," Jeanie continued. "From the porters at the Manor, to the lifeguards at the beach, to the tennis coaches." She fluttered her eyelashes and got a few giggles from her audience.

"We need to form a costume committee so that everyone at the ball will have a mask to wear; that's what makes it so much fun. Of course we'll need to find inexpensive options for the locals and I'm sure some of us will be sending out to the city to have our own masks custom-made."

"I'll donate the masks," Dolly said, raising her hand. "No need for a costume committee, I'll have them made in the factory in the city and I'll have them delivered."

"Wonderful," Jeanie said. "But I'd hate for you to go to so much trouble. Perhaps you needn't bother with such elaborate masks for the locals?"

"No, I'll do fabulous for all; it's easier that way." Dolly took a sip from her mint julep and the matter was closed.

Jeanie hesitated a little awkwardly, then moved on to form a fundraising committee.

"Clarissa, you and I will be in charge of the fundraising. If anyone has any issues with that raise your hand. No? Okay, moving on." And that was that. "As the secretary of the Junior League in Manhattan it is my duty to continue our charity and volunteerism even when we are on vacation, so that we can fulfill our mission—to put to good use the opportunities afforded to us, and to enrich our members' lives by improving the living conditions of those less fortunate."

"She is really going hard for that President position this fall," Dolly whispered just a touch too loud. "She's been passed up four years in a row; there's no way she's going to get it this year. Everyone knows she's just in it for the fame and social aspect—she couldn't care less about the less fortunate." Martine laughed and I was petrified that someone would hear what Dolly was saying. Soon the women began to chatter among themselves and everyone started to mingle.

4

⁂

Tuesday morning was laundry day, so I emptied the laundry hamper, gathered Harry's dirty sporting clothes and rang downstairs for a pickup.

"I'm so sorry, ma'am, but the laundry lady has already left," the front desk clerk said.

"What do you mean left?" I asked. "I thought the laundry was taken care of right here at the Manor."

"No, it's picked up and taken to the village."

"Oh dear, Harry's going to be furious with me if his clothes aren't ready for the weekend. When did she leave? Maybe I can catch her."

"About five minutes ago," he said. "She'll be halfway down the hill by now."

I left through the service entrance at the back of the Manor partly because it was closer to the hill that led down to the village and partly because I knew Jeanie and the rest of the women would be meeting up front for their jaunt to Gurney's Inn any minute. I didn't know what would get Jeanie worked up more, seeing me with a bag of laundry slung over my shoulder or seeing that I wasn't ready to join the party.

I hurried toward the hill as best I could and had to slow down a little when I reached the steep and winding slope. About halfway down I caught sight of her, a petite woman about my age, in a grey smock, attempting to control a top-heavy metal cart full of stuffed laundry bags. When I approached her I saw she was sweating like a man.

"Excuse me, I'm sorry, can I give you one more bag?" I asked, but as I did so I saw the ridiculousness in my question and I flushed with embarrassment. She looked at the cart, then at me.

"Of course, ma'am." She wiped her forehead with the back of her hand, then kicked a metal stand that held the cart in place while she reached for my bag. I considered retracting my request—there was no way she could manage all this laundry by herself—but as she outstretched her hands I let her take it, my mind jumping back and forth between not having clean clothes for Harry and letting this poor woman battle with the overloaded cart. "You're a guest at the Manor, right?"

"Yes," I said. "Sorry I missed you. I'm Beatrice Bordeaux."

"Nice to meet you, ma'am. I'm Elizabeth." She took the bag, but as she did the cart started to roll down the hill, the metal stand making a terrible screeching sound on the road. We both reached for it, but instead of stopping it, we tipped it slightly, and the whole thing crashed to the side, sending bags tumbling down the hill a little way. Mine, which I had tied in haste back in the room, spilled out dirty laundry all over the road.

"Oh no, I'm so sorry," she said, scrambling to collect the clothes.

"It was my fault," I apologized as we hoisted the cart back to an upright position and began to pile everything back onto it. "Why don't I help you down the hill with all this? It would be terrible if it overturned again and you were all alone."

"Oh no," she said, "I couldn't possibly accept your help. I can manage from here."

I stood and watched her walk away, the cart pulling downhill and the woman struggling to keep control, my conscience telling me that I shouldn't have let her leave. I felt my mother's eyes on me, a gentle but disapproving look. "That's not how we raised you, Bea," I heard her calm yet confident voice in my head.

Back at the Manor I hurried to select a luncheon-appropriate outfit that wasn't too warm—I was already perspiring from my trek up the hill and it wasn't even ten thirty. I opted for a short-sleeved, star-print dress with a wide collar. I belted it but immediately removed the belt when the cotton of the dress stuck to my skin. I asked the chauffeur to drive fast to Gurney's Inn, which was four miles away on the other side of town.

It was not good form to show up late and slightly disheveled, but my only alternative was to not show up at all and I was determined to make a good impression at the first luncheon of the season. Luckily, when I arrived guests were still mingling on the lawn and had not yet been seated. Jeanie was talking to a small group of women and I hurried over and stood next to her like a disobedient child waiting for a break in conversation. But there was no break. No one looked at me or opened up the circle and I felt like an intruder, attentive, waiting until someone acknowledged my existence. I smiled at one woman and hoped she'd bring me into the conversation, but as my eyes met hers she quickly turned her focus back to Jeanie. I should have just said something the minute I approached. Jeanie knew I was by her side, she must have, but she remained intently locking eyes with the woman she was talking to until the conversation was completely over, punishing me for my tardy arrival and waning social etiquette.

"Where have you been?" Jeanie asked, finally, turning toward me. "We waited almost ten minutes for you to come down, I even sent the driver to look for you."

"I'm terribly sorry, Jeanie; I took an early morning stroll and lost track of time."

"Obviously." She looked me up and down then settled her eyes on my hair, which I'd pulled hastily into a loose side bun. At the time I thought it looked rather modern, but now I was starting to regret my decision. "Well anyway, let me introduce you to Mary Van de Coop." She took a step back to present me to the woman next to her. She was stunning—tall, towering above me, and curved, with a full, glamorous demi-wave. She had perfectly shaped eyebrows, a flawless complexion and rose-colored lips. She looked like a movie star. "Mary, this is Beatrice Bordeaux. Beatrice, this is our luncheon host today, Mary Van de Coop, the head of the Tail Waggers' charity."

Mary Van de Coop described the organization's mission to expand the charity's reach from New York City all the way to Hollywood. She spoke quickly about the national "Be Kind to Animals" campaign but then rapidly moved on to talk about her own business aspirations.

"So the idea is to open a hotel for dogs, a trailer of sorts that would allow vacationers, like us here in Montauk or Miami, to bring their dogs along for the adventure without having to actually keep them in the hotel or walk them." I saw Dolly across the way sitting on a lawn chair, alone and carefree, smoking a cigarette, and I had to force myself not to make my excuses and join her. When I looked back to Mary Van de Coop she had stopped talking and was waiting for my response.

"So the hotel for dogs is part of the charitable organization?" I asked.

"Oh no, that's just my pet project." She giggled. "I'm an animal lover," she said. I didn't quite believe her.

Jeanie was starting to make her way toward the tables, so I excused myself from Mary Van de Coop and caught up with her.

"Jeanie," I said. "Thank you for introducing me to Mrs. Van de Coop; she seems very"—I stumbled a little—"concerned, about the dogs and whatnot."

"And beautiful, too," she added.

"Yes," I said, "a real showstopper." I imagined, for a moment, Mary Van de Coop wearing a ball gown and parading a beautifully groomed poodle around the ring at the Westminster dog show and thought that seemed more likely than opening up shelters. "Actually, Jeanie, I'd love to sit at your table, if there's space." The words almost didn't come out, since the idea of it, with her disapproving glares just moments earlier, was starting to sound positively frightful, but I felt it was right to make the effort.

Jeanie knew everyone and if I was to find a group of women who would make Harry's work life a little easier back in the city it would be worth putting in the time now. I wanted to show him I was capable and worthy, that there was more to me than he'd seen in the last year or so—which was little more than a lonely woman who waited for his attention. Harry still loved me, I thought, but he seemed distant, drifting too far out. I knew as well as anyone that when the wind took you it was easier to keep going with the current rather than swim against it.

After we lost Charlie I had drifted further and further out until it seemed impossible to get back to the way things used to be. I'd ignored my new college friends, made them feel unwanted and shallow for their socials and dances, which had seemed frivolous to me then. Harry had been my life raft. Though he may not have known it, when he found me I was bobbing away in the swells and he pulled me back to a sense of normalcy, to New York society, to love, to life. I owed it to him to show him the same courtesy he had shown me after I had lost my way and to reel him back in any way I could.

"The seating arrangements have been made already," Jeanie said.

"Oh." I tried to look disappointed. "It's just that I took to heart what you said the other day about how I could learn from you and your socializing skills." My stomach felt unsettled and a wave of nausea came over me. It was hot and I was speaking half-truths, but with ladies like Jeanie, I knew flattery would get me where I needed to be.

"Really?" She didn't seem convinced.

"You are just so graceful at these events." I laughed a little, nervously. "You seem to know everyone."

"Well," she sighed, "we can probably squeeze you in," and she put one hand on my shoulder like a schoolmistress and led me to her table.

There were six of us seated at the Star Fish table: Jeanie, Mary Van de Coop, me and three others who looked like they were in their late twenties. Everyone except for Mrs. Van de Coop and I wore sun hats, and being the latecomer to the seating arrangement, I had to sit with the sun shining directly into my eyes.

"I hear you're a Vassar girl," the brunette named Clarissa said across the table after introductions were made.

"Yes. I attended, but I left before graduation," I said, holding a menu up to the sunlight so I could see her face.

"Well, yes, you probably met your husband and he swept you off your feet; why would you stay?" Clarissa said. I didn't correct her and tell her I left of my own accord because I couldn't concentrate on my studies, I couldn't act normal around people anymore, I felt too guilty to have the opportunity to graduate when Charlie's life was cut short. "But we must have mutual friends," she continued.

She went on to list some names, many of people whom I'd known briefly at some point but hadn't made the effort to stay in touch with. There were exceptions, of course, where I'd bumped into a few of those girls and their husbands around the city and made promises to meet for tea.

"Of course," I said, putting my menu down hoping that my squint in her general direction would put an end to the discussion. "Unfortunately, I haven't seen many of them since our Freshman year."

She gave me a puzzled look. "Most of the Vassar gals I know moved to the city; you don't see them?"

"You know how it is—married life just keeps me so busy."

Jeanie spoke up and took control of the conversation. "Look at this." Jeanie gestured toward the ocean several feet below the grassy hilltop where we sat. "It's so beautiful here, isn't it?" There were nods of agreement all around.

"It sure is," Mary Van de Coop said, "but I can't help but miss the city a little, too."

"I miss having Harry around," I said, feeling that was the wifely thing to say among women. It wasn't entirely true. While I missed having some- one to wake up to, Harry and I didn't spend much time together during the week at all. He was out for work dinners most nights and didn't come home until late, often intoxicated and bumping into things before I'd get up and guide him into bed. One night, late, he fell directly onto our glass cocktail bar and it shattered into pieces around him. I leapt out of bed at the thunderous noise and found him sitting in the middle of it all, laughing, thick jagged chunks of glass surrounding him sticking up at all angles. I was terrified that when he stood up there'd be a piece speared in his side and he'd bleed to death right there in our dining room, but he didn't even get a scratch. He'd stumbled to the sofa and fallen into a deep, snoring slumber while I carefully picked up the glass, boxed it up, then swept the entire apartment. I found tiny splintered remnants for months after.

"Yes, but I mean the convenience," Mary said, bringing me back to the conversation. "I miss the luxuries we are so used to in the city. Like when my maid makes my favorite frozen fruit salad. They try hard out here, but it's just not the same."

"Oh, I agree," Jeanie chimed in. "I mean the laundry ladies from the village, they just don't come close to my gal back home, not even close. Cecil has been complaining about his shirts for the past few summers; one is far too starched, the other not starched enough," she sighed, and the others agreed. "And I told him, 'Cecil, I have three children to take care of. I cannot manage the laundry lady as well; I simply can't.'"

"And don't get me started about diapers . . . ," Mary Van de Coop said in a loud whisper.

"Ugh." Jeanie took a gulp from her champagne. "Agreed. They really have to sort out a better system. It is such a pain to pack up those dirty, stinking diapers and get the nanny to drop them at the post office."

"The post office?" I realized as soon as I said it that it had come out too loud and with more than a tinge of disgust. The table went quiet and all eyes turned on me.

"Yes, Beatrice, the post office," Jeanie said.

"Why on earth would you send dirty diapers to the post office?"

"Must be nice not to have to think of such things." Jeanie laughed and a few others joined in, as if I were the crazy one for not being in on the joke.

"But why?" I asked, more quietly, a little softer this time.

"To send them back to the city. Who else is going to do it? The laundry girls in the village claim they don't have time, but personally I think they are just too darn lazy."

"They don't want to get their hands dirty." Mary Van de Coop rolled her eyes.

I thought of Elizabeth carrying that enormous mound of laundry down Manor Hill in the heat, with the added humiliation, not to mention the stench, of having to wrestle with a week's worth of someone else's child's dirty diapers. That would be horrific, to have to launder some other family's soiled diapers. I almost asked Jeanie to clarify how exactly they sent those diapers to the city, in a bag, in a box, were they sent on the passenger train or on the Fisherman's Special? But my God, they must stink out the entire train car. How repulsive. If you chose to have a child, surely you should have to deal with the nasty and the nice instead of shipping the unpleasant parts back to some poor house girl in the city. I realized I was having this argument in my head and I had to bite my tongue not to speak out loud, knowing it would be bad form to discuss such things any further at a luncheon.

Besides, the conversation quickly moved on to nail colors and matching them to your lips. Mary Van de Coop held up her perfectly manicured fingernails to her lips to show a match. "It's tea rose," she said.

"Divine," Jeanie said.

"Thank God for Cutex!" the blonde, Kathleen, called out from her seat next to Clarissa. She didn't impress me much, this Kathleen woman; she seemed prepped and primed as Jeanie's first lady, agreeing with and echoing anything that she said.

"I don't care for the matching look," Clarissa said. "I think it's garish." Then she looked across the table to me. "What do you think, Beatrice?"

I looked from Mary Van de Coop's nails to her matching lips and didn't want to say the wrong thing.

"I don't wear nail polish very often; I'm terrible at doing it myself—"

"Darling, you must go to the salon; they'll do it for you!" Mary cried out.

"But I do like the tea rose color," I said.

I couldn't help it; I was judging these women for their lightweight conversations and their material obsessions, just as I had judged everyone
after the accident, everyone from my dearest friends from high school to
my newfound friends in the dormitories. Looking back, I could see they
were doing the best they could, trying to entertain me, to talk about anything that would take my mind off Charlie, but I resented them for it.
Anything they spoke of seemed childish and petty. I seemed to have been
thrust into the world of adulthood overnight. How could I relate to these
people anymore? I'd thought back then. How would they ever know how
it felt? We'd never be able to go back to our gushy conversations about
boys and first kisses and possibilities. My mind was already drifting just
like it had all those years ago, and to a painful place.

Officer Johnston had shown up at my parents' door in Pennsylvania with
his hat under his arm. It was an accident. Charlie and the other apprentice
at the mechanic's shop had been fixing the starter crank of Mr. Holden's
car, the dairy farmer from the other side of town. When they were done it
had been my brother Charlie's job to squeeze his bicycle in the back seat,
drop off the car with Mr. Holden, then ride his bike back to the repair shop
to finish up the afternoon. It was one of Mr. Holden's farmhands who saw
the black smoke erupt from the winding road behind the haystacks. The
police said they thought Charlie had taken the turns too fast and that one
of the wooden wheels had become loose, causing the car to flip over. He
was unconscious when they found him trapped inside the overturned car,
and by the time he got to the hospital he'd stopped breathing altogether.

5

I'd only been away at college a few months when Charlie died. The Dean was sympathetic and allowed me a three-month leave. When I returned to school it was for a few days at a time; I'd go to my classes, then take the train back home to take care of my parents. I was terrified of leaving them alone. My father threw himself into his work. He owned a chain of warehouse-style grocery stores in Pennsylvania. They weren't anything glamorous; there was very little shelving and structure, mostly boxes piled on top of boxes, which required less stocking shelves, and less space, but because of that he'd been able to keep the prices down and he'd continued to be very successful even after the economic crash because so many people shopped at his stores instead of the fancy ones to save money.

Being home without my brother walking through the door at the end of the day was too painful, so my father started spending all hours at the stores, negotiating deals with vendors, keeping items affordable, working among it all in the warehouse. People loved him for that and remained loyal. Those stores gave him something to do, a purpose, and he knew he was making a difference in people's lives when the loss of jobs and industry was crippling to so many families. But my mother was a different story. She couldn't speak, couldn't eat and couldn't sleep. Within two weeks she had withered to skin and bone and I was scared that if I wasn't around to keep an eye on her and distract her from her thoughts, then she might simply give up on living.

When Charlie and I started school my mother volunteered in the school nurse's office, so all the kids at school knew and liked her. As we got older she volunteered at the elderly persons' home, too. One day she took me with her to visit the old folks. She mostly just rewrapped a bandage or asked the men and women how they were feeling and made sure they were comfortable, but I remember how surprised I was to see her with her patients, how confident and knowledgeable she seemed. I also marveled at how soothing she was to these strange old people and how grateful they were for her help. I desperately wanted to help her, but there was nothing I could do.

When I finally returned to college my classmates didn't know what to say or how to act. Their sympathetic eyes, their silence when I approached them after class, the extra kind behavior because they were too embarrassed to say anything real—it made me go numb, pretend it wasn't happening.

They tried to help me. They invited me to parties, they tried to get me to the socials and arrange a date for me for the formal, but I had changed. I wasn't the person they'd met a few months earlier. I regretted those last few months I'd spent away from my brother with these new friends, and all the time we had wasted talking about the boys at Yale and Harvard. I'd thought I was so accomplished, being one of a handful of girls from back home who went to college. I'd thought I was better than him for going when he chose to stay in our hometown fixing cars, but after the accident I wished I had never left home and part of me blamed those girls for taking up so much of my time. They all wanted me to go back to the way I was when they first met me, but that would have been impossible. Every smile felt forced; every laugh felt like a betrayal. I was mourning for my brother but also for my parents.

I tried to bury myself in Shakespeare and Dickens, Melville and Poe, as a distraction. I rushed into secretarial classes at the last minute and was the first to leave when the bell rang. I learned to type faster than any of the other girls, but while I stuck it out for another year, I just couldn't stay.

I tried to go home, but my father insisted that I not move back to Pennsylvania. He made excuses—they were preparing to sell the house, to move to a smaller, more manageable home; there would be no room; I'd be in the way but I knew what he was really doing. He didn't want me dragged into their continuous cloak of grief.

So I took the Greyhound to New York City. I was determined to start fresh, meet new people who would only know the new me, the way I was now, people who would not expect glimpses of my former self. My father gave me enough money to rent a small room in a girls boardinghouse in the West Village off Fifth Avenue. The room was barely big enough for a bed, a dressing table and a small armoire. From a tiny window in the living room I could just see a corner of the arch in Washington Square Park.

I took a job as a secretary at *Forbes* magazine answering the phone and typing memos for a grumpy old editor called Mr. Savage. When he conducted interviews in his office I brought coffee for him and his guest. One spring morning I delivered coffee on the silver tray and set it down on the desk.

"You must be the lovely secretary I've been hearing so much about," the guest said.

Mr. Savage grunted and shuffled his papers, a sign that he was eager to get started.

I asked if there was anything else I could get for them and after I glanced at the guest I had to force myself to look away. He was devastatingly handsome, a little older than me but not too much, tanned, smiling and dashing, with perfect white teeth. His face looked chiseled, and the chalk stripes on his suit gave him a long, lean look.

I had also felt quite fresh that day. Daddy had sent me a card with a little money and I'd spent the weekend shopping at Macy's. That morning I was wearing, for the first time, my brand-new red suit and my mother's fur stole.

I busied myself at my desk straining to hear the interview. It was about the economy, again, and what was being done to help the banks get back on their feet. The handsome man was a banker, it seemed, and his responses were optimistic and cheerful. From what I could hear I believed every word.

On his way out he stopped by my desk and thanked me for the coffee—saying it was some of the best coffee he had ever tasted in his entire life. I told him I didn't believe him, that it was regular old office coffee. He smiled an enormous smile and placed his card on my desk. *Harry J. Bordeaux.* "May I call on you," he asked as if it wasn't even a question.

"Oh, I don't know; I'm still quite new to the city and getting acquainted," I said. It had been almost a year.

"How about this," he said. "I'll call on you and you can decide then whether you'll turn me down." He tapped my desk twice, turned and walked out through the big glass doors.

Three days later he took me to dinner at the 21 Club. We sat in a private dining room in the wine cellar with a group of fifteen of his work friends and their wives. I had been adamant when I left Vassar that anyone who knew me now would only know the new me, the hardened, reserved, cynical me. But that night among strangers, I had such a wonderful time I must have smiled the whole time. I smiled so hard that my cheeks hurt when I got home. I felt like a grown-up, not the child I'd been the two years prior, the child who'd been hiding and scared of everything. Harry introduced me to his friends proudly and awakened something in me that I thought had died along with Charlie. My New York life suddenly felt alive and full of promise. As the weeks went by I found myself falling in love with this astonishingly seductive man, his world, his friends, his life, and soon I began to envision this as my life, too.

Everything happened so fast. Harry took me out on a date every Wednesday and every Saturday for three months and then he proposed.

"Darling Beatrice," he'd said one night when he was walking me home after a few too many gin martinis, "we have a good time together, right?"

"Of course we do." I kissed him.

"And I think I make you happy," he went on.

"You do."

"Well, good, because you make me happy, too. And I'm not getting any younger; there should be a Harry Junior running around and we'd make fine-looking children."

"Oh, Harry," I said, steering him along the sidewalk, thinking he was drunk. "You'd better get me home before you get yourself arrested."

He stopped in his tracks and after walking a few more steps I turned to check on him. He was down on one knee.

"Harry!" I said.

"Marry me."

"What? Are you joking? You can't ask me like this, here! It's almost one o'clock in the morning!"

"Well, I'm an unconventional kinda guy, and I'm asking. So is it a yes or a no? Please say it's a yes. Oh . . ." He felt around in his inside pocket and pulled out a ring, holding it up to me. "I almost forgot. I've been carrying this around with me for the past few days and if I don't give it to you now I'm going to lose it, and I can't do that because it was my grand-mother's, one of a kind, an antique."

I stood there stunned, looking from the beautiful ring to his grinning, shinning face.

"*Oui* or *non*? *Oui* or *non*."

"*Oui*, of course, *oui!*" I said. "*Oui, oui, oui!* Now get up, you great fool." I pulled him up to standing and we kissed right there on the sidewalk.

There were times during our engagement that I questioned why Harry had picked me, out of all the girls in New York City. He could have had anyone and they would have been far better suited to the Bordeaux family than me. Harry was raised in a town house off Park Avenue and summered in Providence. I was a country girl, he knew that, but I sensed he wanted something different from what he knew. He seemed to enjoy taking me to dine in expensive restaurants, introducing me to powerful businessmen and educating me on this brand-new world. I think he enjoyed making me happy, where perhaps another woman with his social standing may have been less impressed, less enthused, because she'd seen it all before. I can't honestly say I loved all the extravagance all the time, but I always let him think I did because I was sure it made him feel proud to offer me that life.

Harry's mother insisted on taking me to the bridal salon at Bergdorf Goodman to select a wedding dress.

"Now Beatrice," Harry's mother said, shaking her head when I got excited about a simple but elegant white column-style dress. "This is going to be a spectacular day and we'll have hundreds of guests who want to see who our dear boy is choosing to marry, and to see you in all your splendor. You have a duty to look the part." She let her eyes drop and linger on my pale pink day dress; then she abruptly signaled for us to regard more designs. A beautiful older woman directed a younger woman to try on the dresses for us while we sipped tea and Harry's mother shook her head at each one, brushing some away as if the mere sight of them offended her. I loved all of them and was more excited and surprised at the idea of our own private showing.

"Yes." She finally clasped her hands as the bridal associate and the younger model carried out and struggled to hold up a huge, showy gown with a tight-fitting bodice and a full, wide skirt that could have swallowed ten of me whole. "Would you like to see the model in this gown, Mrs. Bordeaux?"

"This one is far more suited to the occasion," his mother said.

"It looks very heavy," I said. "Can I help you?" I began to stand to assist the two women, but his mother wrapped her hand around my wrist and eased me back to my seat. "I'm not very tall; isn't this style too much for me?" I said. "I thought perhaps the more simple dress would be a good choice because I could wear it again."

His mother closed her eyes and rubbed her temples. I knew I'd disappointed her. Or maybe her son had disappointed her by choosing to bring me into his family. But when my mother married my father she wore a dress she already owned, and she wore it many times after, too. I'd dressed up in it for years as a child, until it was filthy on the bottom, and I had envisioned my own daughter doing the same with mine, but I couldn't picture that happening with this piece of art that Harry's mother had her eye on.

"We'll see the dress," his mother said.

"Of c–c–course," I stammered. "You have far more experience in this sort of thing than I do." This seemed to please her.

I ended up with the gown she selected. It took four months and eight fittings for it to be ready and it used thirty-eight yards of satin and twelve yards of tulle.

I was so excited for the day to finally arrive and the morning of the wedding flew by so fast, various people dressing me, fussing with my hair, my face, while others scurried around setting up the grounds for the reception.

We married at Harry's family home in Providence. A white tent was erected in the garden and over 250 guests were in attendance. I knew it was an honor to have such a wonderful celebration for our wedding day, but I couldn't help but feel terribly nervous in front of all those strangers, all eyes on me as I walked down the aisle and danced at the reception.

Every table was dressed with white linens and white roses and then there was my enormous white gown. When I tried to sit at the wedding table to eat a few bites of food I was so nervous that I'd spill on myself and embarrass the family that I didn't eat a thing and sipped champagne instead to calm my nerves.

My parents had never been to anything so extravagant in their whole life, and I couldn't help but notice how my small family seemed out of place among all of Harry's family and friends. I caught a glimpse of my mother as I walked down the aisle toward Harry, who was standing under an archway of roses. My mother looked so petite and frail, and the pale yellow color of her dress made her look a little unwell. I felt a pang of regret as I continued down the aisle, wishing I'd spent more time with her prior to the wedding and helped her find a brighter, more lively dress for the occasion.

It may have all been for show, but part of me hoped the excitement of the wedding day would bring my mother back to life, even if just a little. For years she'd struggled to get out of bed and face each day, but now we had Harry. Having him as part of our fragile family, I hoped, would somehow help in filling a void. And I was sure that when we had a baby it would help matters even more, bringing new life into my family's home again.

6

❖

W e were only a week into summer, but it was already the day of
the Golden Cup Regatta.

Harry and I were invited to Winthrop Aldrick's yacht, an enormous
vessel that fit at least fifty partygoers, and with more luxurious amenities than most would have in their home. Dolly and Clark were also
guests aboard the boat, as were Clarissa and her husband, Mitchel, and a
few other faces I recognized from the Manor.

The town was packed. *Montauk Mae,* one of the yacht club's own, had
won the previous year's trophy in Detroit, which meant that Montauk now
had the privilege of hosting this year's races. Hundreds of yachts lined up
and anchored down around the perimeter of Lake Montauk, providing
party boat after party boat. They had entered through the opening to the
Long Island Sound that Carl Fisher had blasted when he first bought the
land a decade earlier. He had used dynamite to open up a channel from
the freshwater of Lake Montauk to the Atlantic Ocean, giving the town a
bay to keep its boats and access to deep-sea fishing, as well as a yacht club
for the well-to-do. No one could have imagined then that his foresight
could lead to an event as magnificent and popular as this.

Jeanie had been making a big show of telling people all week how she and her husband would be dividing their day between Mayor Fiorello La Guardia's yacht and that of banker and businessman Harvey Dow Gibson. "Our presence has been requested at both soirées and we simply can't choose one over the other," I'd heard her say repeatedly to anyone who would listen over breakfast at the Manor, while practicing her swing on the tennis courts or while lounging at the Beach Club. "It's really quite a to-do! How could we possibly turn one down? We just don't want to insult them."

The sloping hillsides on three sides of the lake meant that even the locals would have a good view of the races. They set up picnics and laid down blankets and made a family day of it.

We boarded the yacht at eleven o'clock and immediately the champagne began flowing. I'd seen horse shows; I'd been to football games, big ones with pride and rivalry fueling the atmosphere in the stadium. I'd even been to an opera attended by royalty, but I had never been to an event so charged with energy as this Gold Cup race day.

Some of the outfits were so outrageous you'd swear we were all attending the wedding of a dignitary, not a motorboat show. The women wore silk scarves over coiffed hairdos or huge, wide-rimmed straw hats with all sorts of embellishments. Dolly brought me a hat to wear and I was grateful because it made me feel the part. Some allowed their swimsuits to peep out from sweeping chiffon dresses that were daytime appropriate due to the pastel colors of yellow, blue or pink. It wasn't apparent, until later that afternoon, that the relentless sun and libations would persuade us to strip down to nothing but swimming costumes and lounge around on the deck chairs.

About forty-five minutes into the party I finally met the host. Dolly and I were sitting at the back of the boat away from all the cigar smoke, debating how long it would take for the first drunken fool to tip over the side of the boat, when Winthrop Aldrick emerged from the water and climbed up the ladder.

"Much better," he said as one of his servants appeared by his side with a folded towel, a tray with a cocktail, a cigar and a small bowl of fruit.

"Where have you been?" Dolly laughed.

"Away from those pills up front. Some men are so shortsighted, they can't envision a world beyond the one they live in today. Need a refresher, ladies?" he asked; then without waiting for a response he nodded to his servant, who disappeared and reappeared just as quickly with two new glasses of champagne and a small cheese plate, fresh-cut fruit and crackers. He set it down on a folded table he had brought out with him.

"Winthrop," he said, holding out his hand to Dolly and then to me. He was about fifty with a full head of silver hair but in impeccable shape for a man of his age. "I'm so glad you are enjoying my boat, ladies." He turned to Dolly. "You're Clark's wife, if I remember correctly."

"Correct," she said. "Thank you for having us on board. I hope he's not one of those shortsighted fools you're speaking of," she said. "He's up front with the others."

"Not at all. Actually, we've been trying to get him on the World's Fair committee," he said. "We need a few more people with his knowledge on the transportation division."

"I know. He's had several meetings with Mr. Bel Geddes." Dolly looked to me. "From General Motors. They're planning a simulated airplane ride through the American countryside made to look like it might thirty years from now," she said, laughing slightly, as if she thought the idea of it, or perhaps the gumption they had at thinking they could pull it off with less than a year to go, was something to be chuckled at.

"People will wear special goggles and they'll feel like they're flying over express highways, radio-controlled cars, massive suspension bridges and high-rise buildings all without the plane even leaving the ground," Winthrop said excitedly. "It's going to be quite a spectacular ride and vision of the future."

"They want Clark because of his investment in and knowledge of the railroad systems," she said, again to me. "He might do it, but I keep warning him about his health; he can't take on too much. He got very ill a few years back from working too damn hard; now I try to get him to take it easy."

"Try to persuade him, Dolly," Winthrop said. "This is the chance of a lifetime to be involved with such a visionary project."

"He's a man of his own mind," Dolly said.

There had been a lot of chatter about the World's Fair slated for the following year just outside Manhattan in Queens. Everyone was beginning to catch on to Roosevelt's talk of hope and optimism for the future despite all the hardship going on around us that no one on this boat wanted to even tip their hat to, and this enormous effort was supposedly going to display the most promising developments of ideas, products, services and social factors of the day. There were to be scientists, inventors and some of the world's best thinkers in attendance, giving the public a glimpse of what they thought the future had in store for us. It was, admittedly, quite exciting, albeit hard to fathom. There was talk of a dishwashing machine, a television, a xerographic photocopier, a jet-powered airplane, a mechanical computer and even a walking, talking robot, but I would have to see it before I could believe any of it. It all just seemed a little far-fetched.

"You know what I'm most excited about?" Dolly asked. "The time capsule. They're going to put all sorts of things from our time inside this metal container and bury it, not to be opened for five thousand years."

I raised my eyebrows. "Oh really, like what?"

"Thousands of pictures and articles on reels of microfilm," Winthrop said.

"And fashion from our time," Dolly added. "Say, who can I talk to about getting one of my designs in?"

Winthrop smiled. "I'm sure it's all been decided, but I'll find out for you."

"This is one of Dolly's designs," I said, doing a little twirl to show off the hat. "But wait a second; who's to say all the artifacts won't just rot, buried underground for so long?"

"They've thought of all those things, Bethany," Winthrop said, looking pleased with himself.

"Beatrice," I said.

"I stand corrected, Beatrice. They are going to make it with a special metal that resists corrosion and it's going to be filled with a gas that prevents things from spoiling."

He seemed like the kind of person who didn't have to work for any of the beautiful things that he had, as though he'd had everything handed to him his whole life. He was the kind of person whom everyone agreed with, whether they believed him or not.

"I wonder what life will even be like five thousand years from now. What if the English language has been replaced? How will they read all the articles on microfilm? And what if no one even knows to look for it? It could be a big waste of time and money."

"Darling." Dolly reached over and gave my arm an uncomfortably tight squeeze. "The man has just gotten out of the water; give him a chance to get dressed before you pepper him with questions."

"Oh, it's quite all right," Winthrop said, turning to me. "I like a lady with such an active mind." He took my hand and held it for a second. I quickly pulled it away. "And such a quick spirit," he said. "It's not often you see beauty and brains in one package. How very refreshing." His stare lingered and I felt the need to cover myself up. He wrapped his towel around his waist and smiled. "And who are you here with today? Am I fortunate enough to have a single lady among the crowd of couples?"

"Hardly," I said, lifting my hand to make sure he saw my wedding band. "I believe you invited my husband, Harry Bordeaux."

"Lucky man," he said. "Well, I must excuse myself, to attend to my guests and to find Mrs. Aldrick, but I'll seek you both out later," he said, fixing his eyes on me, then winking before disappearing to a lower deck.

"Well, he sure took a liking to you," Dolly said, lighting a cigarette. "Despite your tone."

"He's a bit disrespectful," I said. "Going on like that when he knows I'm a married woman."

"I wouldn't call it disrespect; I'd call it flattery. Enjoy it. Besides, he's very influential; you should indulge him a little."

I shook my head and took one of Dolly's cigarettes. "And he's married?"

"Of course," Dolly said. "To a very 'understanding' wife. But it's okay to be feminine, you know, and to allow men to admire you." She sat back in her deck chair, propping her feet up on the side of the boat. "It's what you do with that admiration that can get you in hot water. But you mustn't be so cold; it won't get you anywhere and you'll get yourself a bad name."

"I wasn't cold."

"Just learn to say 'thank you' now and again, and say 'yes' sometimes, too. You have to know when it's okay to take pleasure in a man's advances."

"I don't know about that; he rubbed me the wrong way," I said.

"Goodness, just enjoy the moment," she said. "That's all."

An announcement came over the loudspeaker to signal the beginning of the races.

"Ladies and gentlemen, we are pleased to announce the commencement of the Gold Cup Regatta, held for the first time on Lake Montauk. Fifteen of the fastest boats ever made will be racing three thirty-mile heats—these boats are the handiwork of the country's finest naval architects and boatbuilders. . . ." The announcement went on and everyone turned back to his or her present company, and so the day unfolded.

There was a funny feeling in the air that evening at the Star Island Yacht Club casino night, a mix of weariness and exhilaration. Two back-to-back parties were too much really, but *Montauk Mae* had won the race and everyone who had even the tiniest connection to Montauk, be it a local or a summer guest, somehow felt responsible and proud of its success.

Apparently millionaire real estate owner Vincent Astor and aviator Charles Lindbergh were among the guests at the soirée, mingling briefly before making their way to the gambling tables. Many others were in attendance, too, faces I didn't recognize and hadn't seen in Montauk over the previous week, important-looking people who'd come in just for the races. Harry and I were making the rounds when he got pulled into a poker game. I turned and saw Dolly engrossed in conversation with some gentleman she'd introduced me to earlier who owned department stores up and down the East Coast, so I excused myself and made my way to the powder room.

When I returned, Harry was nowhere in sight, Dolly was still talking to the department store gentleman and the only other women I recognized were standing around Jeanie Barnes looking fascinated as she told an animated story about her "exhausting day" between two luxurious yachts. I couldn't bring myself to join them, so I sat down, alone, took out my cigarettes and placed one into its holder. A man with small, round glasses flipped open a lighter and held it to my cigarette.

He was short, bald on top except for a few wispy hairs, with a full speckled grey beard. He wore a cream-toned three-piece suit.

"Adam Rosen," he said. "Pleased to meet you."

"Beatrice Bordeaux."

"Are you visiting for the races?" he asked.

"Oh no, I'm staying for the whole summer."

"Really." He nodded thoughtfully. "What do you do with your days out in Montauk?"

"Well, it's only been a week, but a little bit of everything really, social gatherings, sunbathing, swimming." He nodded, waiting for more. I felt self-conscious about my response and how trivial it sounded. "Oh, and reading," I added, relieved to come up with something else to add to the list. "There's something very satisfying about sitting under the big tree at the Manor in the afternoon and getting lost in a good book."

"Yes, fresh air and nature have the same effect on me."

"My husband thinks reading can turn a person into a recluse!"

"Well, it sort of does for a moment in time," he said. "But isn't that the whole point, to lose yourself in a world that's different from your own?"

"I agree; sometimes I'd rather be in the presence of fictional characters than real people." I laughed but then looked around; speaking out of turn like that to a man I'd just met wasn't going to do me any favors in this crowd. "I'm joking, of course."

Mr. Rosen nodded. "So, so true," he said, pulling at his thick, wiry beard as if he wished it were just an inch or two longer. "So where do you stay in Montauk?"

"At the Manor. I'm staying through Labor Day," I said.

"Really, that long? Do most people stay the whole season?" He was asking a lot of questions for a first meeting, but I didn't really mind; if it weren't for him I'd be smoking alone.

"The women do, and then everyone clears out after the summer's over. And, forgive me if this sounds rude, but may I ask why you are so interested?"

He shook his head and smiled sheepishly. "I'm a writer, a newspaper editor actually, and I have this strange compulsion to turn every conversation into an interview. It unnerves people apparently." He took out a cigarette of his own.

"Ah, that makes sense." I laughed. "I was starting to wonder."

"The truth is," he said, "I'm out here on an assignment, looking for a story angle."

"Oh, how exciting. It certainly has become a very popular spot; people love it out here."

"They sure seem to. By chance do you now know of anyone who might be a good interviewee, someone who's pretty involved socially?"

I thought of Harry and his fellow investors.

"I might know some folks who are considering putting some money into Montauk," I said, unsure how much Harry would want the attention and publicity or if they'd want to keep things quiet for fear of others reading about the opportunity and jumping in ahead of them. "I could ask around and see if any of them might want to talk."

Mr. Rosen put his hands in his pockets and shrugged. "Fisher going bankrupt? We've covered that already. This is for the leisure section. What our readers really want to know is what people are doing out here and what they're wearing."

"You're right," I said. "I'm guilty of spending a disproportionate amount of time on the social, fashion and leisure pages. It's addictive."

"Morbid fascination, more like. Have you read Hedda Hopper?"

I shook my head.

"She's an actress turned what they're calling a 'gossip columnist' for the *Los Angeles Times* and she's becoming quite popular, more than she was on stage or in the films. So now all the publishers are scrambling to do something similar. I'm more of a newshound myself. I'm addicted to the goings-on in the city. I really don't get out of town as much as I should, and when I do my family and I weekend in the Catskills." He shrugged. "It's what we do."

Jeanie and Cecil Barnes were walking past as if they had somewhere to be, but for some reason, probably because Mr. Rosen had been talking about gossip and society, I reached out and touched her arm as she went by. "Oh, hi there, Jeanie, great party, isn't it?"

"Hello, Beatrice," she said, barely slowing down as she kept walking, and then a few steps past she did a double take and tapped Cecil on the arm. They slowed and turned slightly toward us, looking from Mr. Rosen to me.

"How's Harry this evening?" she asked.

"He's fine, off gambling, I imagine. You must meet Mr. Rosen; he's a newspaper editor." I turned to him. "Mr. and Mrs. Barnes are often in the papers," I said. "In the social pages; they are very well connected."

"Great to meet you both." Mr. Rosen held out his hand, but Cecil began to pull Jeanie away.

"We have to dash," Cecil said, tipping his head to him instead of shaking his hand. "Good night."

Mr. Rosen and I both looked out to the room not quite sure what to say.

"Gosh," I said, embarrassed by their behavior. "Sorry about that. They seemed terribly hurried this evening."

He just shrugged. "That's okay. I'm used to that sort of thing. Thanks for trying."

7

❦

"Harry," I whispered; he was snoring next to me. I wrapped my arms around him, trying to wake him gently. "Harry, I've got something exciting to tell you."

He opened an eye, then closed it. I don't know what time he came in. I'd searched for him in the smoky room of the yacht club, but he was nowhere to be found. He must have gone into one of the high-roller rooms in the back. After parting ways with Mr. Rosen I mingled briefly with a different group of women who were staying at Gurney's; then, feeling somewhat accomplished in socializing, I called it a night and took a car back to the Manor.

"Harry, I met some ladies last night who invited me to play billiards this week—"

"Oh, for God's sake, Beatrice." Harry abruptly shoved my arm off his chest and turned to face the wall, pulling the covers tight over his head. "It's the middle of the goddamn night." A thick, rotten mix of whiskey and cigars hit me when he spoke. I looked at the sun streaming through a gap in the curtains, then to the clock on the mantelpiece. It was past eight o'clock.

"It's later than you think," I said, sitting up against the headboard, hoping that he had still been half-asleep and hadn't really meant to speak that way. "I just wanted to tell you about my night, that's all, since I barely even saw you yesterday."

"What, that you were hanging around with a Jew last night? Yes, I heard."

"What are you talking about, Harry? Mr. Rosen?"

"Don't be a damned idiot, Beatrice. Spend time with whoever you goddamn please, but not Jews for Christ's sake; that doesn't exactly look good for me."

"Mr. Rosen was a lovely person, Harry." I couldn't stand to hear him speak of my newfound acquaintance in such light. "You're all wrong about him. He was very interesting and smart; he's going to interview Albert Einstein at the World's Fair—"

"Oh, leave me alone," Harry groaned. "Hell, I've got a headache and you're not helping."

I didn't want to breakfast alone among all the other couples, so I dressed quickly and quietly in the bathroom and walked fast and angrily into town. It was a good thirty minutes by the time I arrived at the Main Street and I was famished. I walked into the first place I came to, Loftus and McGunigal's General Store. I looked around: it was part general store, part diner. There were fishing boots on one shelf, homemade bread on another and canned food on another. Three men in white aprons worked behind the counter serving coffee, eggs and toast to men who looked like they were either on their way to work or coming off a night shift. I should probably move on to the next place, I thought, a spot suited more for summer visitors, but I saw an empty stool at the counter and my eyes stopped on the back of a man shorter in stature, with a polished bald head.

"Mr. Rosen," I said, approaching him, happy to see a familiar face in the unfamiliar store.

He had a coffee, a fried-egg sandwich and a notebook opened to a blank page. "Good morning."

"Is this a good place to do research?"

"Ha, no, just has good cheap coffee and breakfast, and I'm about to head back to the city. Here take a seat, please." He moved his satchel from the stool next to him.

"How's the article coming along?"

"Actually, I'm coming up dry. I thought I'd get some inspiration being out here, but I'm not so sure I've made much progress. The locals are nice enough, but summer guests have been . . ." He looked at me as if to gauge if he should proceed. "Well, it's been quite difficult to break in. As you saw, I didn't really get anyone to open up to me."

"People can be a bit stiff." I cringed, thinking of Jeanie and Cecil and how word had traveled back to Harry.

"I'm not sure I'm the right person to write this, to be honest. I feel I'd be missing the real story. I need someone who's out here for the summer and knows what's going on behind closed doors."

"The problem is, Mr. Rosen, all the gentlemen go back to the city during the week and I don't know if any of them would be willing to give up their weekend hours to pen an article for you. Most of them are banker types or business owners. You could try the East Hampton paper; maybe one of their reporters could help—"

He nodded, but he was staring out the window, shaking his head. "No, no, that's not what I need." The intensity was back in his voice. "What I need is someone immersed in the life out here, someone who's involved in the weekend co-ed activities and galas as much as they are in the day-to-day goings-on. That's what people back in the city want to read about, not an outsider's superficial observations of a Saturday afternoon." He seemed excited all of a sudden. "It should have a little scandal, a touch of gossip, and if I'm truthful with myself it should be about the fashions, too. Everyone out here is decked out to the nines. People would read that; I know they would. And I think it should be weekly, ongoing. Yes, that's it." He turned to me as if about to make a big announcement. "I need a woman."

"A woman?" I said, a little more high-pitched than I intended. "Writing a weekly column for a newspaper?"

"Yes, Mrs. Bordeaux, a woman. A lot of females are making their way into the field now."

"I can't think of a single woman out here who'd take on that job."

"Surely someone wants to be heard and get paid; it's a paying job, you know."

"Heard, maybe, but no one here cares about getting paid." I laughed.

He shrugged and went back to his fried-egg sandwich. I ordered a coffee and looked out the front door of the store. The sun had come out: it was going to be another beautiful day. I put my hand to my head and realized I'd left my room in such a rush to get away from Harry's foul temper that I'd forgotten to wear my sun hat. Mine was grubby these days from several recent nature walks. I'd ask Dolly to bring one back from the city next time.

"That's it!" I said excitedly. "I know exactly who you could interview for your first column." I clasped my hands. "Oh, it's perfect. If you really want to write about what people are wearing out here, sprinkled with a bit of gossip here and there, you should talk to my friend Dolly. She's a milliner, her father owns a factory in the city and she's very well connected."

He nodded again but not as enthusiastically as I'd expected.

"I'm telling you, she'd make a perfect introduction to the column."

"I don't doubt that."

"So then why aren't you writing down her name?" I pointed to his notebook, but he was grinning. "What's so amusing?"

"Why don't you give it a try, Beatrice? Would you be willing to pen a weekly article?"

I looked at him for a moment, shocked. Surely he was kidding.

"I'm serious, Beatrice. You seem to know the right kind of details that our readers would latch on to, but you're not so wrapped up in things that you can't see the forest for the trees."

"Mr. Rosen, I am flattered that you would ask, but for one thing I can't write—"

"Really? I thought you were college educated. What did you study?"

"English literature, but I didn't even finish my studies and I can't write the type of thing you are suggesting. I don't even know how."

He scoffed.

"And secondly, my husband wouldn't allow it; he'd think it a very unladylike profession, I'm afraid."

"And you," he asked, "what do you think?"

"Well, what I think is irrelevant."

"Is it . . . ?" He paused and for a split second my mind jolted back to Harry, so cold and abrasive, not even giving me a chance to speak. I stared into my coffee. "Well, if you really believe that, Beatrice, then maybe you're right; maybe you're not the person for the job," he said.

Mr. Rosen didn't take his eyes off me, reading me, I imagine, the way he probably did all of his interviewees, taking notes in his mind of how a person tensed up, wrung their hands or hunched during difficult questions, observing facial expressions.

"You could always use a pen name," he said quietly.

"A pen name? You mean write it anonymously?"

"Why not? You'd have far more freedom if it were anonymous."

"I couldn't possibly," I said. "It would mean risking everything, absolutely everything that my husband and I are working toward. I couldn't betray Harry's trust, and that of the people out here, many of whom are dear friends, potential clients or colleagues."

"Well, that's good. You seem like a very loyal friend and wife." He slurped his coffee. "But I have to say you didn't seem so dear to them last night when they snubbed you because you were talking to me, a Jewish man."

"Oh, Mr. Rosen, they didn't mean anything by it—"

"Maybe they didn't. You certainly know them better than me."

"No, it's really just about my husband; he . . . he needs me to focus on other things, and spend time with him."

"Sure thing, Beatrice, I just recall you being all alone yesterday evening, that's all. I didn't see your husband once."

He was one observant newspaperman, and his facts were spot on. What would I even write about? I thought. I was no gossip columnist, and certainly not a fashion writer. I was no writer at all and I felt so awkwardly far out on the outskirts of our social group that I was the last one to know anything about what was going on.

"I'm sorry, Mr. Rosen, I can't."

"It's your choice. But please." He reached into his inside jacket pocket and pulled out a thick white card with raised black lettering. "Let me know if you change your mind."

8

❧

On Monday I waited by the service entrance with my laundry bag properly tied up. Several of the staff offered to take my bag to the back room for pickup, but I told them I'd rather hand the laundry over myself, as I had almost missed her the previous week.

I decided to skip out on the beach day that the ladies were planning. It was to be very informal and no one would notice that I wasn't there. Besides, Dolly and I planned to meet up and head to the beach later that afternoon when it wasn't so hot.

The service entrance looked on to the tennis courts and beyond that out to the Long Island Sound. At the bottom of Manor Hill across the train tracks and right on the edge of Fort Pond was the fishing village, and I knew Elizabeth would be making her way up that hill anytime. I pulled my laundry bag across the grass, receiving offers, again, from the staff to assist me, and I sat on the grass, under a tall oak tree that I knew would be on her path to the Manor. I leaned back and began to read.

I was half a chapter in when I caught sight of her hauling the metal cart toward the Manor.

"Nice to see you again, ma'am," Elizabeth said.

"So glad I caught you this time," I said. "Must be quite exhausting pulling that cart all the way up the hill."

"Some weeks I come up with the car, but my husband had to use it today for a special delivery to East Hampton. If I didn't get started on the washing this morning, I'd never get through it all by Thursday."

"What does he do, your husband?" I asked as I walked alongside her.

"He's a fisherman and he works for the post office."

"How interesting."

"Yes, and it's been quite busy and exciting these last few summers when all the guests arrive. The mail service is ten times busier than the rest of the year. We're very grateful for all the work."

I told her I'd give her my laundry bag once she'd gathered the rest of the bags from inside.

"Mind if I tag along?" I asked when she came back out.

She shrugged. "If you like."

I walked with her down the hill, crossed over Edgemere Street and kept walking all the way along Industrial Road, across the train track and to the fishing village. The walk and the fresh air felt good.

"You really don't have to come all this way with me," Elizabeth kept saying. "I'm fine now that we're on flat land." But I liked to hear her talk. It was comforting to imagine people living in Montauk year round, even in the winter months when it was quiet and snowing families stayed there, lived there, their kids went to school—it reminded me of home. Elizabeth told me that she and her husband had moved to Montauk from New London, Connecticut, several years earlier with her brother and his family when the channel opened up between Lake Montauk and the Atlantic Ocean. They were some of the first families to settle in the "new" fishing village, along with others who came down from Nova Scotia for the deep-sea fishing and because of the high demand for seafood in the city.

"We don't have much," she said, "but with a fishing fleet right at our doorstep I know me and my boys will never go hungry."

After we crossed the railroad tracks I thought maybe I should go back. I'd never had reason to go to the fishing village until that point and I had a strange feeling I was trespassing. But since I'd come so far, part of me wanted to see Elizabeth to her front door. I was curious about how and where she lived. The houses were more like wooden shacks, lined up in a row less than one hundred feet from the shoreline of Fort Pond Bay. A single gated fence ran along the front of all the houses, making a feeble distinction between the fishing bay and the residential area. I held the gate open for her as she wheeled the cart into a dirt-filled yard.

"Can't get the grass to grow here, what with all the salt from the ocean, and the boys bringing their bikes in and out all the time," she said.

"What a nice view," I said, quickly turning to look at the bay.

"Waterfront property," she said, laughing awkwardly, standing at her door. "Can I pour you a lemonade or something?"

"Really, there's no need," I said.

"You must be thirsty, though," she said. "I know I am; here let me fetch one for you." She walked into the house, hesitating for moment as to whether she should invite me in; then she decided it would be best not to. "I'll bring it out," she said, gesturing to a lawn chair. There was nothing dividing one person's yard from the next, and the small lots of land surrounding each shack seemed to be filled with junk. On closer inspection, though, they were large metal lobster traps and fishing rods that the fishermen must use, stacked up against the house. Two men walked up from the dirt road and along the side between Elizabeth's house and the neighbors'. They were chatting and laughing, but when they saw me they went silent and glared.

"Can I help you?" the shorter of the two men asked.

"I'm fine, thank you, just waiting for someone." They waited as if for more explanation. "My friend Elizabeth lives here. She's getting me a lemonade."

He nodded slowly and they continued on. I felt out of place, intrusive and uncomfortable standing there alone, so I pretended I was searching for something important in my pocketbook. When I looked up they were almost out of sight, walking around the back of the house.

Elizabeth returned with two glasses of lemonade in one hand and a baby on her hip.

"I think I just saw your neighbors walking up here," I said.

"Oh, that was Patrick, my husband, and his friend Thomas, from the lighthouse; they came in the back door," she said. "They've been working on our car. We're really lucky to have one, but it breaks down all the time. We can't afford to keep taking it in to the mechanic, so these two end up spending most of their days off fixing it up."

"Oh," I said. "They were probably wondering why I was hanging around outside his house like an interloper."

Elizabeth blushed. "We're not used to having summer visitors down here in the village. I hope Patrick wasn't rude to you."

"Not at all!"

A young boy no older than nine peeked out the front door.

"This is my son Gavin. Say hello to the lady."

"Hello," he said.

"And this one here is Jake," she said, nodding to the baby in her arms.

"Can I go now?" Gavin said. "Billy and Johnny are at the train tracks already; I was waiting for you to get home. He's had his milk."

"You know I don't like you and your brothers playing on those tracks," Elizabeth said.

"We won't be on them; I promise."

"Okay, go on then, but send your brother down to the docks to wait for Ted London's boat to come in and bring back a mess of cod, and tell your brothers that you all need to be back here for dinner at six o'clock."

"Yes, ma'am."

"And make sure you keep an eye on little Johnny."

Gavin ran off and Elizabeth shook her head. "I have my hands full with four boys, but they do take care of each other when we need them to."

"Such lovely children," I said when I caught the baby looking at me. "How old is he?"

"Four months, last week."

"Do you mind if I hold him?"

"Please do," she said, handing the baby over. "This one's a real mama's boy. Never lets me put him down."

I hadn't held a baby in a long while. I'd purposely avoided the opportunity. For a while when Harry and I first started trying to have a child it had been all I could think about, what he or she would look like; would he have Harry's blue eyes, my mouth or my button nose, as my mother used to call it? Would she be fair like me or have the tanned complexion of my husband? Would she have red hair like I did as a baby, or would it be blond like Harry's? I imagined what it would feel like, the weight of a baby sleeping on my chest, how its hair would smell, what its cry would sound like. I once woke up from a dream where I had been nursing a baby; it was so vivid that I stood up from my bed and took a few steps toward the nursery before I realized it had all been a figment of my imagination. But after having no luck month after month I'd begun to put the idea of a family out of my head almost completely. Almost.

"You don't have any children?" Elizabeth asked.

"No," I said. "Not yet. But we're trying," I added, because that's what people liked to hear, and that usually ended the conversation.

"Trying?" Elizabeth said as if she'd never heard that expression before. Maybe it was just us city folk who said things like that. "How hard are you trying, because I can tell you I do not try, I resist, and somehow I ended up with four boys under the age of eleven!"

I blushed, then burst out laughing. "I guess we're not trying very hard at all," I said, giving the baby one last little squeeze, then handing him back to his mother. "I should get back. Thank you, for the lemonade."

9

———✦———

Dolly picked up the dress I had hanging on the back of the hotel room door and hung it back in my closet. She flipped though my dresses and pulled out a long all-white, flowing dress with cap sleeves and a jeweled empire line.

"Dee-vine," she said.

"I can't wear that," I said. "That's a weekend dress for dinner with Harry; he hasn't even seen me in it yet."

She raised her eyebrows. "It's a Tuesday dress now! Wear it," Dolly said, plugging in my electric curling iron. "Come over here," she said, and when I walked into the bathroom she sat me down on the edge of the bathtub and started curling my hair.

"My pins are in the bedroom," I said, standing up to get them. She put her hand on my shoulder and gently nudged me to sit down again. "Let's try something different," she said. She took a few curls from the right side and swept them away from my face with a sparkly silver and pearl comb from her handbag, leaving the other side to drape slightly across my left eye.

I looked in the mirror. No one wore their hair down, especially when it was long like mine, it was always curled and pinned up, but Dolly's instincts were right—I felt pretty and young like this. The red hint to my hair got lighter and blonder in the summer months and the slight golden tan on my face from being outside so much made my hazel eyes look more dramatic, a deeper brown, not so plain and boring. Lately I'd been feeling older, as if I weren't just twenty-seven, as if I were middle-aged already, past my childbearing years, past my prime, but when I looked at myself in this beautiful dress that I'd never worn before, with my hair loose and a few freckles on my nose, I didn't feel that way; I felt youthful and attractive.

"You don't think it's too . . ."

"Too what? Womanly, feminine, beautiful? Yes," she said. "Now, to the Surf Club let's go."

We sat at a cocktail table and had barely finished our martinis before an announcement came over the loudspeaker that the entertainment was about to begin. We settled up with the barkeep and made our way toward the activity. Chairs were set up in a large rectangle around the swimming pool and a fenced-off grassy area next to it. The crowd was a curious mix of city folk from the Manor and Gurney's Inn, men in tuxedoes and women in pretty, elegant dresses, as well as locals in their canvas work pants and shirts and women in cotton frocks. But the two crowds stood apart, the locals standing behind chairs, while the dressed-up summer guests, like Dolly and me, took seats in the front row.

"The first event will be the much-anticipated greasy pig contest!" the announcer said with great enthusiasm over the loudspeaker.

"Oh my," Dolly said. "This should be fun."

One by one, the announcer called the names of eleven boys between the ages of ten and eighteen and they walked out into the fenced-in area, took a bow and lined up. The final boy, no more than eleven, looked familiar, his hair shaved, his body skinny, and when he turned in our direction to take a bow I got a good look at his face. He looked exactly like Elizabeth's younger son Gavin, whom I'd met in the fishing village, but taller with more chiseled features. I was sure he was her eldest son. I searched the crowd for Elizabeth's face on the other side of the lawn but didn't see her.

"And to do the honor of greasing the pig, please give a grand round of applause to one of Montauk's most loved business owners and employers, Mr. Dick White!"

A man walked out onto the lawn in a white pharmacist's jacket as the crowd roared with applause.

"Who's that?" I asked Dolly.

"He owns White's Pharmacy and most of the other shops in town."

He held a large can of Mazola oil in his hand and waved it around in the air creating even more applause, while another man walked a smallish pig, on a leash, to the center of the lawn. The pig received even more attention than Mr. White, who then covered the animal with oil and rubbed it in. The boys took off their undershirts, taking their positions and clapping their hands with anticipation.

"On your mark," the announcer called, "get set. Go!" The pig was released from its leash and after trotting a little in one direction, then another, it seemed to pick up on the excitement and began running furiously. The boys chased it around the lawn like a bunch of lunatics, leaping for it and hitting the grass on their bare bellies as if they were playing a game of competitive football. The crowd was screaming with delight and the pig looked like it was in on the fun, too. About ten minutes into the spectacle one of the boys took a dive for the pig and crashed into the temporary fencing that had been erected for the event. A flurry of tuxedoes and chiffon clambered to get out of the way as the pig made a run for the downed fencing, away from the green and straight toward the pool. The crowds were no longer separated as the entire audience left their chairs and standing posts behind and swarmed, en masse, to follow the boys who were following the pig. I grabbed Dolly's arm and joined the chaos, both of us howling with laughter.

There were suits up against fishing slacks and caps, ball gowns rubbing with work clothes, all chasing the action. The pig was fast—a horde of sweaty, dirty boys behind it. The pig was running for its life and the boys were running for their dinner. It kept heading for the pool and the boys followed. I didn't think the pig knew what it was getting itself into—it just kept running. Its little legs took it straight over the edge of the pool, splashing into the water, and the boys leapt in after. The water splashed back onto all of us who were at the front.

"Catch that pig!" cried one man who looked like he'd come straight from a fishing boat. "Get him by the back legs!" called out another. A few men even jumped in to be part of the madness, and even the women were giddy with excitement.

A couple of the boys swam to the edge of the pool and caught their breath while the others ducked and swam and chased until one successfully grasped the swine around its chest right under its two front legs and swam, like a lifeguard saving a drowning child, to the stairs at the corner of the pool and struggled to hold the pig up to show his victory. The crowd roared.

"And it looks like we have a winner!" the announcer called out.

I strained to see if it was Elizabeth's son who'd won the prize. I pushed my way through the crowd to get a better look, desperately hoping he'd won, but I couldn't tell.

"Come on," I said to Dolly as I worked my way toward the front to get a better look, but I'd lost her in the hustle.

By the edge of the swimming pool the winner was being announced, drying off and getting ready to receive his cash prize, as well as the pig, which a local family nearby seemed particularly excited about. The winner wasn't Elizabeth's boy, though. I searched the crowd and saw him and two other boys; one of them was Gavin, Elizabeth's nine-year-old whom I'd met at the fishing village, standing with a tall, slim man who had his arm around the boy's shoulder. I inched my way closer. My martini had given me a warm feeling of confidence and courage, so I walked around the edge of the pool toward them.

"Congratulations, that was wonderful entertainment," I said to the boy.

He looked at me a little oddly. "I didn't win, miss; he did," he said, pointing to the winner.

"Yeah, he didn't win," the younger boy chimed in.

"Oh, but you were very close," I said.

"No I wasn't."

"Okay, that's enough, lad," the man said. "No need to be rude to the lady." He looked at me as if waiting for me to move on.

"I'm Beatrice," I said. "I know Elizabeth; you must be her husband, Patrick?"

"I am," he said, still skeptical.

"I know her from the Manor," I said. "She does our laundry."

"She does, yes."

"She's wonderful; I mean she does such a fantastic job taking care of our clothes." I knew I should stop talking, that it wasn't exactly customary for me to walk with Elizabeth and the laundry cart the way that I had, but I couldn't seem to find the right words to justify it so I kept trying to come up with something better. "Actually, I visited the village yesterday and I think I may have seen you and your friend walking up to your house."

"I remember," he said. "She mentioned there was a guest at the Manor who was being very kind to her."

"Oh no," I tried to object. "She's the one who's been kind. . . ."

A man approached with two beers in his hands, giving one of them to Patrick.

"Who's this then?" he said. He was taller than Patrick and muscular, with tanned skin. His hair was chestnut brown, speckled with grey, and he desperately needed a shave.

"She's a summer guest; she's been very good to my wife."

"Hello," I said. "I'm Beatrice Bordeaux."

The man stared at my face intently and gave me a strange look. His eyes were quite shocking—an uncommonly bright shade of blue, so intense it made me glance away for a second.

"And you are?" I said with a forced laugh. He continued to stare; it began to feel uncomfortable, and with those eyes I didn't know where to look.

"Thomas," he said quietly, his expression unchanged. He ran his free hand through his hair, sweeping it back from his face.

"Oh, that's right. I saw the two of you walk by Elizabeth's house yesterday; you called out to me and asked if I needed any help." I looked to Patrick to confirm this and he took a drink of his beer. "She mentioned that you work at the lighthouse."

"Yes, I'm the keeper. But why are you . . . what are you doing here?" he asked.

It was an odd question and Patrick seemed surprised by it, too.

"Tom." Patrick nudged his arm.

Thomas shook his head. "Sorry, I thought for a minute, I thought I recognized you."

"Oh, I don't think so." I shrugged, trying to act normal, but his intensity was unsettling. I should move on, I thought, go back and find Dolly—yet I rambled on, strangely rooted to the spot, intrigued by his fascination. "That must be exciting, to work at a lighthouse. I was just telling Patrick his boy put in a great effort with the hog, really great." I saw him glance down to my dress and I instinctively brushed out some imaginary creases. "I'm a bit too dressed up really; I didn't know there would be a pig."

"No, you look very . . . grown-up."

I felt my cheeks blush and I looked to Patrick again.

"He means, you probably don't have greasy pig contests in the big city," Patrick said, stealing a sharp look at Thomas.

"We don't." I realized that the rest of the crowd had separated again into city folk and locals and I was definitely on the wrong side of the club. When I looked back, the keeper's eyes were on the ground; he looked saddened all of a sudden. It was all quite odd.

"Well, I'd better get back." I nodded to them both. "It was a pleasure to meet you." Then I made my way back through the crowd looking for Dolly.

I couldn't find her anywhere, but I felt a wave of strangeness. The interaction with the lighthouse keeper had been so peculiar and yet I couldn't pinpoint what I had said to make him act that way. The pig contest had been such a wild and unexpected treat, but then that conversation had had a sobering effect. I walked past the bar, waited a few minutes, then turned and walked the other way looking for Dolly. I didn't want to wander aimlessly alone or to be seen wandering alone, so I gave up and took a car back to the Manor.

That night I wrote my first article for Mr. Rosen—the way the pig was ceremoniously greased, the way these boys, some of them just a few years from manhood, had bared their chests, chests different, perhaps, from those of well-bred New York City boys. These were arms that had been pulling up lobster traps from the ocean floor since they were old enough to swim, backs that knew how it felt to shovel snow from the pathways in winter just so they could get outside and make the mile-long walk to school. Boys who, rather than learning how to sit quietly and read in the library, had been told to get outside and amuse themselves for hours, to navigate the docks, to untangle fishing nets for their fathers, to rip out the mussels and seaweed and anything else caught from the day's catch. In the summer the beach was their playground, they'd surf on anything that would float, they'd swim until they were ravenous and of course they'd work. They were ball boys, they were skippers, they were caddies and at night they chased greased-up pigs around a fenced-in green to make a buck and maybe they'd win and enjoy the pride of feeding their family a whole pig for a week.

I wrote about the contrast of tuxedoes and work clothes, simple cotton frocks against embellished gowns. Many summer guests had enjoyed cocktail hour at the Surf Club followed by dinner and dancing. The greasy pig contest had been a brief source of entertainment. For the locals it was the main event. I wrote about the flurry of excitement as the pig escaped and the sudden blurring of high fashion and hopeful fishermen moving together toward an unknown outcome.

Most likely this wasn't the Montauk Mr. Rosen was after, but it fascinated me; it sent my imagination soaring, to picture these lives, filling in the missing pieces with snippets Elizabeth had told me and glimpses I had seen. I scribbled it all down fast, put it in an envelope and sent it to Manhattan.

10

---✦---

Harry and I ate an early dinner with a small group he'd sat with on the train ride to Montauk. It was Winston, his college friend, and his wife, Betty, and two other couples whom Harry knew from the business. We dined at The Claw, an outdoor deck overlooking the water next to Duryea's Lobster Wholesalers, near the fishing village, before you crossed the train tracks. We ate lobster dipped in drawn butter with napkins tied around our necks. We watched the sun set over the Long Island Sound, the seagulls circling overhead waiting for scraps. Harry ate the coleslaw from my plate and still had the glistening of butter around his lips when he reached over and kissed me.

"I missed you, Beatrice," he said, toying with my freshly curled hair, pulling one ringlet down to my shoulder and letting it bounce back up to my chin. He topped up my wineglass, then sat back, draping one arm around my shoulders, tapping a cigarette out of the box with the other.

I can't honestly say I missed him through the week, but I did need him on weekends. During the week I started to enjoy the freedom of staying up until the early hours of the morning reading, and wearing loose frocks and nightgowns around the room for as long as I wanted, no rushing to dress. And yet when the Friday evening train arrived I felt relief. Even after just a few weeks in Montauk it was becoming too easy to forget how it felt to be part of something, part of a couple. Alone among acquaintances who felt like strangers, it was easy to wander aimlessly from luncheon to afternoon tea. When Harry arrived on the weekends it gave me purpose again, a duty to be dressed and ready to attend this function or that, to be made up for my husband, to accompany him to dinners.

I'd taken a fancy to wilderness walking on the weekday mornings before many of the women were up for breakfast. Some might call it hiking, but I didn't seek out the trails that had been cleared and labeled. I liked to push through the brush, climb over fallen trees, wrestle my way through branches and come back with brambles in my hair. Sometimes I'd find blackberries or raspberries and fill myself up on them. I saw wildlife I didn't even know the names for, things that I knew none of the other women would see. I marveled at the contrast of wooded areas so close to the sea; I could be staring down a family of deer in one instant and picking up sand crabs in the next. I'd never been to a place so alive with a kind of nature that could be so different.

Harry would have thought I was crazy going out there alone, but there was something serene about being alone in nature when the rest of the Manor was still sleeping. It reminded me of being a kid when Charlie would wake me up early in the summer and we'd go down by the train tracks with buckets and come home hours later with more blueberries and blackberries than Mom could ever use. We'd eat cobbler and pie for weeks and jams for months after that.

There were others in the Manor, of course, who were early risers, but they were mostly the nannies, getting up with the kids and taking them to breakfast while the ladies still slumbered. Gossip traveled fast at the Manor, between nannies and the other ladies, so I made a point of carrying extra change in my pocket to tip the waiters and busboys as I came and went through the service exit in my long trousers, Wellington boots and tousled hair.

After our lobster dinner and after the gents each had a whiskey and cigar downstairs back at the Manor, Harry and I went up to the room, turned on the radio and listened to Roosevelt's fireside chat. Even in the heat of the summer Harry liked to light a fire when we listened to the President talk. I could tell the bellboys thought it absurd when they came to the room with kindling and logs. It was something his father liked to do and now Harry was adamant about it, a tradition of the previous six years of FDR's presidency that he felt he needed to uphold, as if it were a superstition that if he didn't light a fire things would a take a turn for the worse, a turn in which the depression would not just affect the farmers and the laborers and the middle class and the working class but ruin us all.

"Hear, hear," Harry said, when Roosevelt spoke of "a restoration of confidence," raising his double old-fashioned to the flames dancing in the fireplace.

"It is because you are not satisfied, and I am not satisfied, with the progress that we have made in finally solving our business and agricultural social problems that I believe the great majority of you want your own government to keep on trying to solve them," the President spoke to us in his elegant, down-to-earth tone. "In simple frankness and in simple honesty, I need all the help I can get—and I see signs of getting more help in the future from many who have fought against progress with tooth and nail in the past."

And that was what I loved about him, this President of ours; he needed us, he needed our help and our feedback and our optimism and our get-back-to-work attitudes, to pull this country out of the trenches. We felt good when we listened to him speak; we felt his confidence; we believed in it. We all just needed a little hope.

"He's a good man," Harry said, the way he did after most of the chats we listened to, "a good man indeed. You know he could have just coasted through this second term; that's what some people in politics told him to do."

"But he didn't," I said, feeling Roosevelt's power to unite us, me and Harry, us and the rest of the country. "He's making changes for the better."

Harry changed out of his clothes and into a robe and started brushing his teeth in the adjoining bathroom.

"So I was thinking I might pop into the city on the train this week with Dolly," I said, lingering at the bathroom door. "She has a few meetings at the factory and, well, it would be nice for us to spend our anniversary together," I said, not entirely certain that he remembered. "Just for the night, or maybe two."

He didn't speak right away, but his body tensed as he brushed remnants of tooth powder into the sink and rinsed. He stood up straight and ran his hands through his hair, noticing a few greys and pulling at them.

"Unless you're busy with work," I said.

"It's a hectic week, so I won't have much free time. It's probably not worth the trouble." He kept on with his bedtime routine and I let the silence be, feeling utterly rejected. This time in Montauk didn't feel like it was good for us, as Harry had promised; we weren't getting any closer. Being here made me feel like we were moving further apart.

"But we can arrange something, I suppose," he said finally. "I'll make a reservation."

"All right," I said, clasping my hands together, trying to seem enthusiastic.

"You don't know how it is in the city when the women are gone. You'd think summer months would be carefree, but there are business dinners set up left and right; everyone's getting their work obligations in now while their children and women are out of the way and they can concentrate."

I resisted the urge to backtrack, to say, of course, we should just celebrate the following weekend in Montauk. I had to actually hum a little song in my head to refrain from talking myself and him out of it, but I had been looking forward to the idea of going to the city ever since Dolly mentioned it. A glimpse at glamorous Dolly at work in her factory had sounded like fun.

"So we'll make it work," he said, and then almost as if he had to force himself to say it, "That would be nice."

It had been months since we'd been together as man and wife should be. I remember when it had all changed, back in February. It was cold. I had lain awake staring at the ceiling waiting to hear the front door creak open. He'd stumbled in drunk long after midnight and he fell heavily into bed. He didn't say anything, just fumbled around beneath my nightgown, clumsily feeling my body with his hands, cupping my breasts and pulling at them, reaching down between my legs, then pushing himself into me from behind. He didn't kiss me on the lips. He didn't look at me or speak to me. I didn't see his face and when he finished he groaned into my ear, then he rolled over and went to sleep.

We didn't speak of it in the morning. I didn't even know if he remembered, but that's how we made love from then on. When he spoke about going to Montauk that first time, saying we should start fresh, I thought he wanted to start over with love and tenderness. But now I wasn't feeling so sure. He'd made no attempts to woo me into his arms. I hadn't tried either, to be fair. The lack of intimacy began to feel strangely normal, but I knew it wasn't right; it wasn't the way a husband and wife should be.

I decided to go to the city that week and make it special, to remind him of what we used to have. I'd get Dolly to help me.

11

---❖---

Dolly and I settled in on the train. Her assistant, Sally-Jane, traveled with us. We'd barely left Amagansett when Dolly called to her to fetch the lunch box.

"You know, I don't even think I'm hungry yet. I just finished breakfast an hour ago."

Dolly raised her eyebrows and smirked. "Who said anything about lunch?"

Sally-Jane took a small rectangular tablecloth out of a picnic basket and draped it over the table between Dolly and me. On it she placed two wine-glasses, two small white china plates and two rolled cloth napkins. From another bag she pulled a small silver bucket engraved with Dolly's and Clark's initials.

"I'll be right back with the ice, ma'am."

"When I travel I like to travel in style," Dolly said.

I laughed. "Where will she find ice on a train?"

"The gents in the fish cars love her; they have boxes and boxes of ice back there."

At the back of the passenger train, she told me, were several cars that the Montauk fishermen had loaded up with fresh catches from their early morning trips, and they were sending them off to the city to sell.

Sure enough, Sally-Jane returned to the first-class passenger car with a bucketful of ice that she placed on the table's edge closest to the window; then she opened a half bottle of Champagne Montrachet, filled our glasses and rested the bottle in the ice bucket.

Dolly put her nose in the glass and took a deep breath. "Oh, that's good, Clark sure does know a good bottle when he sees one. Go on, Sally-Jane; you pour yourself a little glass, too," she said.

"No thank you, ma'am; you know how the good stuff goes to my head, even the tiniest sip." She untied several brown paper parcels and placed a selection of cheese slices, cured meats and breads on a serving plate in the center of the table.

"I have mixed feelings about trains," Dolly said. "On the one hand, they saved us; on the other hand, they almost killed us."

"What do you mean?"

"Well, remember at the Golden Cup I told you Clark had suffered a heart attack; that's because he invested all his money in the railroad business. It worked out very well for us in the end, financially, but the stress almost killed him."

"Oh goodness, Dolly," I said. "How terrible."

"He's fine now, thank God. But I'm convinced it was the railroad that did it to him, the stress of so much of his money tied up in one industry. He should have diversified." She took a sip of her champagne and leaned back into her seat. "But that's how my Clark is. He has a one-track mind; when he's got his heart and mind set on something he'll go full force until he gets it. That's how it was with me."

Clark and Dolly had the kind of relationship one should envy, although you wouldn't necessarily know it from a distance. They'd been married for six years, but they had that kind of relaxed composure about them that made it seem as though they'd been together all their lives. They both married later in life, Dolly told me, she in her late thirties and Clark heading toward fifty, and they agreed right away it was too late for children.

"I never wanted to get married," Dolly said, looking out the window, watching the trees fly by. "Not even as a little girl when that was all my friends could think about. I never wanted to be under someone's thumb, trapped, stuck with the same person for the rest of my days. It sounded like torture to me."

"So then why did you?" I asked.

"Because I had my fun first." She smiled and tucked an imaginary stray strand of hair from her immaculately set curls into her hat—a vibrant shade of purple sitting about eight inches tall, with various points and peaks like a bird flapping its wings about to take flight. Only Dolly could wear that headpiece with such ease and confidence.

"I had lovers," she said, leaning across the table. "I had a lot of lovers," she said, louder this time, with a look of excitement in her eye.

"Dolly," I said, blushing, looking around the train car for anyone we might know.

"Oh, Beatrice," she said, sitting back again, picking up a slice of cheese, "I'm not ashamed, and neither is Clark; that's why we work so well together. We've experienced life; we've tasted lust and sex and maybe even a little love in all of its forms. We've come together having lived, ready to share, without resentment or regrets or repression."

"So Clark knows?" I wished we weren't having this conversation in the first-class train where people were sure to overhear us.

"Of course he knows." She laughed. "And I'm assuming by the color in your cheeks that Harry is the only man you've ever been with, am I right?"

I nodded and she waited for me to go on. "I didn't have steady company with any gentlemen before Harry."

"You were so young when you met Harry, it's perfectly normal."

"It's more than that, Dolly. I haven't told many people this, but I had a brother who died in an accident soon after I started at Vassar."

"I'm so sorry, sweetheart." She leaned in and placed her hand on mine.

"I never really got over it and I don't think I ever will, and for a few years after the accident life just stood still. I couldn't be around people, let alone consider romantic interests. It wasn't until I met Harry that I began to feel alive again."

I took several sips of champagne. I wanted to relax; despite the age difference and the apparent difference in experiences, Dolly was the first person who'd spoken to me candidly and I wanted to be honest with her, too.

"Harry and I—" I stopped, I wasn't sure if I should do this, confide in another woman, an older woman, about our personal life, or lack thereof. Dolly smiled, waiting. "Well, we, we aren't as close as we could be," I said, feeling I owed her some glimpse of truth, since she'd just been so revealing with me.

"You mean you don't have sex."

"Dolly!"

"Sorry," she said in a mock whisper. "So you don't make love then?"

"I didn't say that," I said, regretting my decision to confess. "But no, not as frequently as we once did, and . . ."

"And?"

"And not as lovingly, or passionately." I liked Dolly a lot and I admired her frankness and her ability to speak of such things, but I found it very hard to talk openly in a place like this. I looked around for Sally-Jane, perched in the back of the train car on a large trunk. When she caught my eye she immediately stood and walked over to top up our glasses.

"My dear, you are like a chameleon," Dolly said, leaning over the table and taking my hands in hers. "One minute you are red as a beetroot; the next you are the color of ash. Is all this talk of frolicking making you ill?"

"Of course not," I said, finishing my wine and picking up a piece of cheese from the plate. "It's just that I worry sometimes, that's all, that he's lost interest or something."

She looked at me kindly and she seemed to understand.

"Sometimes it can be quite . . ."

"Quite what?" Dolly asked.

"Well, it's been a while, but the last time it was as if I could've been anyone, just a warm body." I looked out the window embarrassed that I'd said too much but relieved also for getting it off my chest. "I don't know; maybe it's just what happens after being married for a while."

"The thing is this," she said. "Men are like animals; they have basic needs. If those needs are not being fulfilled at home they will find gratification elsewhere."

"Dolly, I'm not suggesting that he's—"

"I'm not saying you are, but just be aware that your husband has certain primal needs."

She called to Sally-Jane and tapped our glasses. "Would you mind, darling?" she said. Even though Dolly was always polite and Sally-Jane certainly didn't seem to mind, I couldn't help but cringe at Dolly's gesture. I was raised to roll my sleeves up and get the job done and I could have easily retrieved the bottle and poured it myself, but within seconds our glasses were full again.

Dolly and I had made plans to visit her father's hat factory together as soon as we arrived in the city. She was going to show me the milliners at work, the wooden molds they used and the new colored wool felts she'd be using in the upcoming season's line. I was going to have just enough time to freshen up, drop my bags at the apartment and meet Harry for a late dinner. But Dolly changed our plans.

"Let's see the factory tomorrow. You seem worried about your marriage and I think I can help. Today our first stop will be Regine Brenner's on Fifty-Seventh Street. It is the best and the only place you should shop for lingerie from now on. And let me assure you, once Regine Brenner is finished with you, your man will never take his eyes off you again."

I smiled gratefully and suddenly had complete faith in Dolly and this Regine woman. I'd been weighed down with uncertainty about Harry recently, even though I tried to remind myself it was probably all in my head, and I felt relieved to know I was going to do something about it.

"We'll call Harry's secretary and make up some excuse why he needs to stop by the apartment this afternoon before dinner, and you can surprise him," Dolly said. "In nothing but your Regine Brenner."

"Before dinner?" I asked.

"Yes, sometimes you need to change the routine, shake it up a little. Then, after . . ."—she paused as if to ensure I understood where we were going with this—"send him out for a martini while you freshen up for dinner. I'll send Sally-Jane over around six so she can do your hair."

A doorman greeted us from the taxi, took our luggage and led us to an elevator inside 50 West 57th Street. We rode up seven floors and the elevator boy pulled back an ornate steel gate to reveal a large showroom. Cloth mannequins were draped with silks and lace in various shades of pale pinks, whites and beige. There was a chaise longue in the center of the room and decorative mirrors reflecting beautiful fabrics from all angles. As we walked into the room to meet Regine Brenner, I caught a glimpse into the back room where ten women worked at sewing machines. Dolly took my hand and squeezed.

"It is wonderful to see you again," Mrs. Brenner said to Dolly with what sounded like a Russian accent, or maybe it was German. Dolly kissed her on the cheek, then pulled the short, slightly pudgy woman in for a hug. She wore small, round glasses and her hair was pulled into a low bun that was too severe for her face. It was summer and Dolly and I were dressed in cotton day dresses, but Mrs. Brenner wore a dark green skirt suit with a hem that almost touched her ankles and a high-necked blouse.

"This is Mrs. Beatrice Bordeaux, a dear friend of mine, and she's in need of some extra special lingerie for an extra special occasion." Dolly winked and clasped her hands.

Mrs. Brenner remained straight faced. "We measure first," she said, snapping her fingers. She led me into a dressing room the size of my bedroom with long silk curtains, plush carpeting and pale pink roses in tall glass vases on three wooden tables. Once inside she started to unbutton my dress and unfasten my belt, then handed them to a dark-skinned woman who appeared in the dressing room holding a tape measure. I felt naked

standing there in nothing but my girdle and panty briefs, and my instinct
was to slouch my shoulders and cross my arms over my midsection.

"Stand up straight," Mrs. Brenner said as she wrapped the tape measure around my hips, my waist and then my chest. I watched her in the
mirror feeling like a child being fitted for a school uniform. I had always
felt so awkward in front of mirrors, so skinny and boney. In the last few
years I had developed a few more curves, but they were slight.

"Why you wear this?" Mrs. Brenner asked, pulling at the fabric of my
girdle. The Sears catalogue had promised it would "do wonders for a
woman's hips."

"To improve my hips?" I said, asking her approval for something I'd
been wearing for weeks.

"You don't have hips," she said. "You don't need to flatten; you need to
make more voluptuous." She ran her hands around two imaginary beach
balls as if to replicate the perfect, full-figured hips. "You're not a boy; you
are a woman; you need to dress like one."

She scribbled my measurements down on a piece of paper and spoke in
what sounded like a combination of Russian and Spanish to the woman
standing behind her, who scurried away to pull some styles from the showroom.

"Yoo-hoo." Dolly walked into the dressing room with a cigarette in
an ebony holder in one hand and a glass of champagne in the other. "Here,"
she said, handing me the champagne.

"I put a call out to Harry's secretary and I've arranged for him to be at
the apartment at four thirty."

"What did you tell her?" I asked.

"Oh, something about the landlord, who needs to meet him immediately due to a possible leak in the apartment."

I frowned; Harry would be furious if he was called out of work for
something ridiculous.

"Don't worry," Dolly said. "Once you surprise him in something very
special he won't even remember why he's there. Regine." She turned her

attention to Mrs. Brenner. "She needs something very, very seductive, none of those old-lady gowns I like to sleep in. Also, Beatrice needs some silk slips, ooh, maybe one of those that lace up in the back," she said, "and short to show off her legs."

Mrs. Brenner squinted her eyes and stared at my body, turning me around. She sighed. "Not easy," she said. "She needs meat on her, especially in bosom. And buttock. But legs and waist, good."

"Oh, honey, I think you look amazing," Dolly whispered encouragingly as if she didn't want Mrs. Brenner to hear. "It's like what Wallis Simpson said in the papers: 'A woman can never be too rich or too thin.'"

"My mother always said I was like a bean pole," I said.

"Well, some say thin is in."

Mrs. Brenner's assistant returned with an armful of silky slips, nightgowns and robes. Mrs. Brenner closed the curtain on Dolly and began to dress me.

"This one cami-knickers, all in one combination," she said as I stepped into a soft pale pink slip that turned into shorter shorts than I would ever wear in public. She pulled it up over my torso and placed the straps on my shoulders. It felt light as air, as if I were wearing nothing at all. The ruching on the hips and the gathered fabric on the chest created an illusion of slight curves on my otherwise straight up-and-down figure. She pulled the fabric tighter at the back. "This better," she said. "Small waist, so I ask the girls to alter for you."

The silk against my skin felt even more luxurious than the lingerie Harry bought me for our wedding night, and something about the way it draped in some places and accentuated my figure in others made me feel more womanly than ever. I looked at myself in the mirror and imagined myself standing in front of Harry in this expensive, decadent silk.

Dolly pulled back the curtain, took a long look at me, then turned to Mrs. Brenner. "Do you have it in black?"

"Black?" I asked.

"The pink is too innocent," she said.

"Only good on some ladies," Mrs. Brenner said. "You, Mrs. Dolly, yes, black is good; you got the sex for it. But Mrs. Beatrice, I am not sure; we try." She went out to the showroom and Dolly rummaged through her handbag and pulled out a lipstick in a silver case. She rolled it up, puckered up her lips, instructing me to do the same, then painted my lips a bright, daring red. She then took out some of my hairpins, pulled my hair around my shoulders and left it long and wavy and wild. She stood back and raised her eyebrows in approval.

I left Regine Brenner's with four beautifully packaged boxes full of camisoles, underwear, slips and robes, a decadently embroidered corset that made my waist even smaller and gave the appearance of hips, and several lace bras in my exact cup size. Mrs. Brenner had even altered several of the garments in the sewing room while Dolly and I waited in the showroom. I received strict instructions not to use Ivory Flakes on the silk, and instructions from Dolly on when to wear each item. She even slipped her half-used red lipstick into my handbag, to be worn with the black silk number later that afternoon when Harry got home from work.

The elevator was all the way up at the twelfth floor, so I left my luggage with the doorman and carried only my lingerie boxes up three flights of stairs to our apartment. I heard a door slam and when I reached the second floor a woman passed me on the stairs. I knew almost everyone in our building, but I was sure I hadn't seen her before. She caught my eye for a second, then looked away and hurried down the stairs leaving a trail of Shalimar perfume behind her.

Our apartment was like a large three-pronged fork. The front door opened into a rectangular living room/dining room, and shooting off that main room was our bedroom, the kitchen and an office/extra bedroom, which we thought would be a nursery one day. The rooms were without doors when we moved in and we had intended to add them at some point, but we both grew to love the openness of the apartment, how light from the bedroom windows streamed into the living room and bounced off the pale yellow walls, so we left it that way.

I hadn't been home in three weeks and the smell hit me the moment I opened the door. Fresh cigarette smoke and Shalimar. I held on to my bags at the door and I spotted two martini glasses on the coffee table, one with a single olive left in the bottom, the other with jarring pink lipstick smeared on the rim. Harry hadn't been expecting me to arrive until after six o'clock and Doreen, our cleaning lady, usually came on Wednesday afternoons. He must have thought she would get there before me.

That nervous excitement I had felt in my chest all the way from Regine Brenner's to my front door suddenly vanished and a sickening dread took its place, tightening my throat, my chest, and winding down into the pit of my stomach. On several occasions over the past year I had wondered, privately, if Harry had been unfaithful, but I'd pushed those thoughts to the very back of my mind. I never dared to acknowledge my fears. I knew deep down that our relationship was in trouble. I thought he might feel he was failing as a husband, unable to impregnate me, but could that really drive a man into another woman's arms? One comment from Dr. Lombardi that it could very well be Harry's fault that I wasn't yet with child and he had to go out and prove that he was still a capable lover. Was that what this was about? Or was this just par for the course? Was this how he envisioned marriage, a wife at home, mistresses on the side? A new, more interesting, different-looking woman when I became too familiar? I felt sick. I had to sit down.

Harry had always been successful, as a child and as an adult. He had prospered, running a successful trading company when many in the financial industry had failed. With help from his family, and especially from his father, who passed his trading company down to Harry, he had been a success his entire life. And here he was unable to perform the one duty that almost anyone could do—rich or poor, successful or down and out. Any man could make love with his new, young wife and impregnate her. I understood how this could cut a deep emotional wound, especially coming from a family where there was an expectation that he carry on the family name. But of course we never discussed it. To speak of it would have made it real, and if it were real we wouldn't be able to go on; the resentment would be out in the open. So we kept on with the game and acted as if it still might happen. I still held out hope for a child, however unlikely it sometimes seemed, but Harry had clearly given up on us.

I remembered our first night in our new apartment. We lay in bed, he stretched out on his back, with me leaning on his chest, my face inches from his.

"God, I'm glad I love you as much as I do," he had said, putting one hand behind his head.

"Well, I should hope so," I said.

"I've seen so many couples, friends of my parents and such, who just seem so unhappy in their relationships. More than that, they seem to despise each other, but they stay together because they have to."

"No one has to stay together if they are not in love," I said, so sure of myself, so sure back then that love was more important than anything else.

"Beatrice, people like us don't get divorced."

"People like us?" I asked.

"Okay, people like me, my family, who are now also your family, so yes, people like us." He reached for a cigarette. "It's not done in our circles."

My people—grocers, steelworkers, even business owners like my father—we could divorce if we really wanted to. But the idea had never come up, my parents had been so devoted to each other. Besides, everything had happened so fast and so urgently between Harry and me, there wasn't even room in my mind for the thought that we might not last.

"I don't think it's anything that we will have to worry about," I said, playing with the hairs on his chest.

"I don't either," he said, "and that's why I'm so goddamn happy I met you." He lifted me up and sat me on his toned stomach. "I knew you were something special when I first saw you, sitting at your little desk, in your pretty little frock, scribbling down notes for that editor, Savage."

I remember thinking that I had felt more important than that when I was Mr. Savage's secretary. I liked working and making my own money, and thinking I was making a difference in that grumpy editor's day. I even had a little game with myself every morning when I brought him his coffee. I'd be determined to make him smile, and I'd keep track of it in a little notebook. Even if he just curled one side of his lip in recognition, I'd count that as a smile. If I got four smiles out of a five-day workweek, I'd treat myself to tea at Lady Gray's on the weekend. In some small way I'd convinced myself I played a part in getting the magazine out the door each month, but maybe I had just imagined that sense of being part of something.

"I'm glad I don't have to work there anymore," I said. And then Harry kissed me, holding me a little too tight around my chest, but I didn't stop him; it was as if he needed me more than anything. I was so sure then that I had been given this gift, this man whom I loved so much and who loved me, I was sure it was some kind of consolation from God for taking my brother away from me.

But now to see firsthand the remnants of his affairs, left like a sloppy criminal, spilled out across our apartment, made me feel physically sick. How foolish I'd been, only now to be confronted with cold evidence, not in some hotel room, not in some other woman's bed, but in my own home, which I had created for him, where I had picked out the colors for the walls, I had gone to Macy's and selected the fabrics for the curtains and I had selected sheets and pillows for our bed as finishing touches to what I hoped would be a perfect home.

The doorman knocked at the door and delivered my weekend bag from downstairs. I asked him to send Doreen away when she arrived; I didn't want her here cleaning when I felt like this and I was convinced that Harry believed she would come and clean up his evidence. If I hadn't arrived early to surprise him she would have known that there had been another woman in my apartment while I was in Montauk, she would have washed those martini glasses, she would have washed those sheets, and then I'd have to face her again and again and she'd be burdened with this secret. I carried my bags into the bedroom and set them down on the floor.

The bed was a tangled mess of sheets. I stripped it, placing the sheets in the hamper and making the bed with a fresh set from the linen closet. I emptied the ashtrays on the dining table into the garbage, noting the same horrific pink lipstick stamped on the tips of at least five cigarettes and feeling the heat from one of them. I washed the martini glasses and set them upside down on the kitchen counter to dry. In the bathroom I dusted off our lace demi-curtains and put a bottle of setting lotion, not mine, in the cupboard under the sink. I straightened the pillows on the couch, swept crumbs and dirt from the floor and wiped down the dining table.

I thought of another woman's skin on our cream-striped couch, her hair in the shower, her bare feet on the floor, and I felt the sudden desire to wander the rooms of our apartment the way some other woman had, as if I too had no care for another woman's marriage. I wanted to feel that kind of freedom, confidence and power that some other woman had felt just hours earlier, probably opening the drawers and looking inside, free to roam her lover's home while he was at work and his wife was summering in Montauk. It was then, after I imagined what it would be like to be the other woman, the woman I'd passed in the stairwell, or the woman at the Manor or the woman in Palm Beach, it was then that I walked back to the bedroom and took the black silk slip from the lingerie bag.

Slowly I unbuttoned my dress and hung it on the back of the door. I removed my girdle and put it in the garbage can as Mrs. Brenner had advised. I stepped out of my underwear and stood naked among the wreckage of our apartment, our marriage, our life. I turned to the long freestanding mirror in the corner of the room and unpinned the rest of my hair, letting it fall around my shoulders any which way it pleased. I stepped into the slip, the one with lace detailing and corset-like ribbon that zigzagged all the way up from the small of my back to my shoulder blades; then I took Dolly's lipstick out of my bag and painted my lips, big and red and bold. At Regine Brenner's I had felt beautiful, empowered, as if I were the one who would be the success this time and I would bring Harry up with me. But as I stood there in my own bedroom, amidst his trail of careless, vulgar deceit, I felt like nothing more than one of his whores.

I wanted him to see me dressed that way, even if just as a reminder of what could have been, of what he could no longer have. I knew then that everything had changed between us. Things could never go back to the way they were before.

I wanted to lie on the couch and imagine I were her, whoever she was that day. As I walked past the mirrored wall surrounding the fireplace I saw a smeared handprint. I placed my fingers against the print; it was smaller than Harry's but ever so slightly larger than mine. I picked up the cleaning rag and was about to wipe it away when the front door swung open.

Harry stood in a pale grey suit, white shirt and the baby-blue striped tie I had given him for his birthday. I'd always thought it made him look so handsome.

"Beatrice, my God, what are you doing here?" he said, stunned. I stood there, barefoot, clad in black lingerie with the cleaning rag in my hand. He looked around the room, his eyes searching for the glasses, the cigarettes, maybe even the single stocking I had found entwined with the bedsheets. His eyes seemed to settle on the kitchen counter, on the upside-down martini glasses.

"Is Doreen still here—"

"I told her not to bother," I said, my throat dry as if I'd swallowed a box of matches.

He looked at my outfit and I think I saw a look of horror cross his face. "What are you wearing? Why are you—"

I cut him off; it was all too terrible to let him go through with it and finish his sentence. He'd been caught, in our own apartment, on our anniversary. Another failure.

"I thought I'd surprise you."

His eyes darted to the bedroom, to the made-up bed. "I thought you were on the later train," he said in almost a whisper.

"Well." I pressed my lips together, forcing myself to remain composed. "Happy Anniversary, darling."

He didn't take one more step toward me; he didn't even let go of his briefcase. I'd never seen him so crestfallen, so caught out and tangled in his own game. Charming Harry, the one who always remembered everyone's name and the names of their children. Harry who knew a little about everything in the news, in history, in politics, enough at least to join in every conversation at a cocktail party. This time Harry couldn't think fast enough to lie.

"So the landlord?" he asked.

"It was all just a lie."

"Can we talk about this at dinner tonight?" he said, looking for a brief moment as though he needed to lean on the doorframe for support. I had to resist my instinct to run to his side, take the briefcase from him, steer him to the couch and pour him a drink. "I have to get back to the office."

"Okay," I said, turning, setting the dirty rag on the end table. "I'll get changed."

"I made reservations at The Hurricane Club," he said, his face serious and his forehead furled.

"I know," I said. "I'll be there."

He made a couple of awkward steps toward me. I shook my head. "Don't bother," I said, and I looked at the ground. He stopped, turned slowly, then walked out the door.

Sally-Jane came over and fixed my hair as planned. I had been crying and my eyes were red and puffy. She went to the kitchen and returned with ice wrapped in a cotton cloth; she placed it on my eyes and had me lie down on the couch, my hair hanging over the side. She brushed it for a good fifteen minutes, humming a little song. I wondered if this was part of Dolly's daily hair routine or if it was just something that she knew I needed. When I got up, Sally-Jane set me with curlers and started pow-dering my face, penciling in my eyebrows and rouging my cheeks.

That night Harry arrived at the restaurant before I did. When I walked up to the table he was sitting with another couple. He stood and kissed me on the cheek as if nothing had happened. "Beatrice, darling, you don't mind if Putman and his wife, Bess, join us, do you? I bumped into them at the bar."

"Of course not," I said, thankful that I didn't have to sit through an eve-ning of dinner alone with Harry, even if it was our wedding anniversary.

12

---❖---

The next morning I had to force myself to open my eyes and face the day, but once awake I wanted to get out of that apartment. Harry had already left for work; he must have tiptoed around, because I hadn't heard a thing. I quickly dressed, repacked my bag and left.

I had promised to meet Dolly at the hat factory. She wanted to show me her father's empire as well as her fall collection in the works, and she had offered to design a hat for my return to the city that September. When we made the plans on the train in from Montauk I'd been excited, but now everything had changed. I was sure she'd ask me about the night before, and though part of me wanted to tell her the truth, I knew I couldn't. How could I sit at a dinner table with her and Clark and know that they knew what was going on behind the scenes in my marriage? If I told her, I'd never be able to keep up the façade; I'd crack. My head was throbbing from all the wine I'd allowed myself to drink at dinner and my body felt like a lead weight, but I knew that if I canceled on Dolly she'd be sorely disappointed and she'd suspect that my evening with Harry had not gone as planned.

I took a taxi to 39th Street and Fifth Avenue and walked toward Sixth.

It was only ten o'clock but it was already hot and muggy, the heat warming up the garbage cans left out on the street and filling the air with a sour, pungent smell. The sidewalk felt sticky under my shoes and a worker from a delicatessen poured a bucket full of soapy water on the sidewalk and scrubbed with a wide broom. The stream of dirty water ran into the littered street, picking up cigarette butts and scraps of old newspaper along the way. I walked past a vacant lot with a row of makeshift houses built from sheets of cardboard and bits of wood. Two men sat on wooden milk crates smoking; another read a newspaper and two children in filthy clothes played in the gutter. I gave them each a nickel and they ran into the lot, kicking up dust behind them. I crossed to the other side looking for 63 West 39th.

The tiny elevator opened directly into the factory and I stepped inside. It was loud in there; the sounds of a large, whirring fan, the tapping of a hammer, filled the large loft space. It felt like a furnace. Metal shelving lined the walls, stacked with wooden hat molds of different shapes and sizes. There were shelves dedicated to crowns—rounded bowlers, indented fedoras—and others stacked high with large circular molds for brims: some wide, some narrow, some burned black from use, others fresh and white and newly carved. Workbenches piled with sheets of wool felt blocked my view as I took a few steps into the space and looked for Dolly.

To the far left, seven men, silhouetted by the light coming in from the windows, stood in a line at a workbench with their backs to me. Across from them, where heat seemed to be emanating from irons and what looked like a small kiln, I saw Dolly with a pair of goggles on her head. She was working shoulder to shoulder with an older man, the sleeves ripped off his shirt, his ebony skin glistening from the heat. As I approached I saw that Dolly was wearing culottes, a blouse and a bandana wrapped around her hair. She looked dangerously modern.

"Darling," she said, pushing her goggles onto her forehead. "You made it."

She kissed me on the cheek and her skin felt hot and damp. Taking me by the hand, she led me to where she'd been working. "This is Blue—he has a workshop downstairs." The man nodded his head in my direction. "Blue is our mold maker. He carves and shapes the molds, so we can literally dream up any shape and style we want here and he turns them into tangible reality."

Dolly took me around the factory showing me where they steamed the fabric onto the mold, ironed the crown for smoothness and stiffened the brim. She was so knowledgeable and comfortable in the factory, and, even in a workroom full of men, she fit right in.

"You certainly know your way around," I said.

"Oh, I practically grew up here. Daddy would run the show and work with the guys over there"—she pointed to the back corner—"and my mother would sew and trim." She looked around and I could feel her sense of pride. "These are my uncles."

"Really?"

"Well, not really my uncles, but they feel like family. I grew up with them."

"Is your father here?" I asked.

"He doesn't come in too often these days. It's hard for him now that he's older."

"Oh, I would have liked to meet him."

"We do mostly men's hats here, as you can imagine, in fact, Daddy used to do only men's until I got involved, but these gents are working on my fall collection." She walked us to the corner where the men were standing at the workbench.

"Max, here, is our top-hat maker," Dolly said. "He's made hats for the last seven Presidents, isn't that right, Maxi?"

"That's right, ma'am. Mrs. Dolly's father and I personally delivered a midnight-blue silk style for President Roosevelt's inauguration. Seven and three-eighths is the size of his head if I remember correctly. A good-shaped crown that man has, a good-shaped crown."

Dolly and I smiled.

"How long have you been doing this?" I asked him.

"All my life, ma'am."

"And Max's nephew is learning the trade, too," Dolly jumped in. "Daddy set up an apprentice program to train the next generation. I'm trying to get some girls in here, too, to help with my women's line," she said in a quieter tone as she led me away from the men, "but the men are so hungry for jobs they'll do anything, work long hours, anything."

The factory was fascinating; it was such a busy and different world from what I was used to. Though my mind kept jerking back to the previous evening, to Harry's face and to that horrible dinner I had to sit through, being in the factory was a comforting distraction. Taking in so many details and sounds helped me fill the painful emptiness I felt inside, even if just for a few moments.

We walked around a corner into another room altogether, this one long and skinny with a window at the far end, filled from floor to ceiling with fabric and trims on one side, horsehair braid, crinoline, buckram, straw, wool felt and silk, Dolly pointed out. On the other wall were hundreds of small numbered wooden drawers, most with an inch-long piece of trim tacked to the outside, and a sliding ladder allowing one to reach the very top drawers.

"My mother's doing," Dolly said as I peeked inside a drawer labeled with a delicate green feather. "This is her room." Under the window, a sewing machine sat next to a neat, organized table stacked with reels of thread in every imaginable color. "She still comes in once or twice a week, but we have some young ladies working in here mostly."

"You must have learned a lot from her," I said.

"Everything," Dolly said, looking at the chair and the sewing machine. "So, your hat. Do you want safe, daring or middle of the road?"

"Probably middle of the road."

Dolly nodded. I wanted to let her take the lead, since she clearly had the fashion sense and the expertise, but I was not one to wear anything outrageous.

"Okay," she said, already holding several fabric swatches up to my face, then standing back and giving me either a crinkle of the nose or a squint of the eyes. She held up numerous wooden blocks while switching out brims of various widths to get a feel for which shape and style suited me most; then she ditched the brims altogether and settled on an oversized and slightly exaggerated netted pillbox, tall and two-tone in black and candy pink.

"I like the contrast of the masculine military shape against the hot-pink felt," she said. "You'll turn heads."

That fall would be Dolly's third season. She'd started with a small collection and she named it Dolores Ann, her full first and middle name. The response had been incredibly positive and, since she'd only had a small number of hats made, the demand was high. Over the spring and early summer her designs were often seen in the papers on Dolly's friends and on celebrities. Bergdorf Goodman had picked up the entire collection and there was to be a fashion show in September for Dolly's collection, paired with designs by a luxury fur coat maker, that I had promised to attend, and of course I would wear a Dolores Ann original.

I wondered what it must feel like to walk down the street and see someone wearing a design that you had created in your mind. What must it feel like to know that women, old and young, would walk into a store and fall in love with something that you had dreamed up, something that had started as just a whisper of an idea, developed in your mind, then actually created into a real thing?

"How did you know you could do it?" I asked.

"Do what?"

"This, working here in a hot factory alongside all these men? You look so happy here, but how did you know you would be?"

"Sweets," she said. "I was never really interested in making my debut and then shuffling quietly into married life, never to be thought of again, except as someone's wife. If that had been the case I never would have married."

I nodded. So many women, me included, did just that. "It must be amazing," I said, "to know that you're creating things that are real and that are being worn and loved and cherished by complete strangers."

Dolly looked at me and smiled.

"You know what," she said, walking over to the window and forcing it open, then turning on a small electric fan. "It does feel magical; it really does. I look at things differently now; I look for ideas everywhere I go. Those intolerable luncheons and socials and ball games, I may look like I despise them, sitting on the outskirts watching it all unfold, but I actually enjoy them because I see things with different eyes. I see all those abominable events as an opportunity."

I envied Dolly's calm spirit, her confidence and her contentment with the world. Her ability to find positives in the driest of situations. I wanted to take the goggles off her head and wear them—actually see through her eyes and claim the world the way she did.

"One night Clark and I were at dinner at Minetta Tavern with one of his bosses and his duller than dull wife, Edith. All she wanted to talk about was the household chores and cleaning products and I just couldn't understand her fascination with it all because it's not like she'd ever picked up a cleaning rag in her whole life. She was probably a nice enough person deep down, but she just wouldn't stop and she kept twirling her spaghetti on her fork, twirling and twirling and twirling, while she talked about vinegar versus lemon juice for tackling lime buildup in the bathtub, and then the whole thing would slip off her fork and she'd have to start twirling all over again. I just stared at her fork, the pasta forming these beautiful glistening piles on her plate each time the strands fell, every time a slightly different spiral formation. I was mesmerized." Dolly stood up and slid the ladder to the corner of her mother's trim room and climbed to the very top where there were rows of hatboxes. After pushing some to the back, pulling a few to the front and peeking inside, she climbed down with a box and set it on my lap.

"Open it," she said, grinning.

Inside was a black wide-brimmed hat with a mass of velour strings organized into two piles of what could only be described as spaghetti. One in deep red, the other a slate grey. She took it from the box and held it to the left side of her head on a deep slant.

"It's magnificent," I said, and it truly was.

"Around the factory we call it the spaghetti hat, but when I sold it to Bergdorf's I named it 'Edith.'"

I thanked Dolly for showing me around and for the hat she was going to have made and told her I had to get back to catch the train. On the way out I saw a small stack of soft crocheted baby bonnets.

"Oh, how sweet, you do baby hats, too?"

"It's just an idea I was playing with; these are just some experiments. I was considering expanding into a children's line, you know, for girls and boys, not just babies, but I don't really know enough about it, about them!" She laughed.

"They are ever so delicate and precious. You have a good thing here, Dolly, really; I would buy these as gifts for friends' children. In fact, I would love to buy one for a friend now; are they for sale?"

"Oh, you flatter me. Beatrice, take one, please."

"Let me pay you," I said.

"No, no. Take it. I need to get organized here and decide which hats I'm going to bring for the trunk show at the Manor. Say, will you work with me that day? I could use a helping hand and some moral support."

"Of course," I said. "I'm helping Jeanie set up the women's fair first thing in the morning, but I'm sure working with you will be much more fun."

Dolly rolled her eyes. "Why do you mix with her?"

"She's not so bad when you get to know her."

"I don't know why you won't stay one more day, head back to Montauk with me and Clark tomorrow. Maybe Harry will be on the same train and we can all sit together; it will be fun."

"I can't," I lied. "And besides, Harry will be on the late train. He's terribly busy with work." I had no idea what was going on with Harry's work or which train he'd be on. But I knew he'd be on one of the trains out to Montauk the next day and our life would go on as before, both of us pretending that nothing had happened.

"Oh my God," she said, pulling my face in close to hers, "I almost forgot to ask." She lowered her voice to an excited whisper. "How did it go last night?"

I paused briefly. Maybe it would feel better to tell just one person and not harbor such a huge, crushing secret.

"You were right. . . . Regine Brenner was exactly what we needed."

When I stepped out onto the street the sun was hotter and the smells were stronger. I quickly walked to Sixth Avenue and flagged down a cab.

"Pennsylvania Station, please," I said, checking the time. If we hurried I'd just barely catch the one o'clock train. The next one wouldn't be until four and part of me wanted to get back to my room at the Manor, lock the door and shut out the rest of the world. But another part of me felt unsettled, jumpy and fired up. Seeing Dolly in the factory, excited, eager, grubby, sweaty and glowing all at the same time, something about that left me agitated. I seemed to be failing at much of my personal life and I yearned for Dolly's sense of pride and accomplishment.

I tapped my feet on the floor of the taxi and looked out the window. Two women pushed baby carriages on the sidewalk. Among them, weaving in and out and up and down Sixth Avenue, were men dressed in suits, suspenders, fedoras and pocket squares, walking with purpose, all heading somewhere important, I imagined, to make something of themselves, to make a deal, to make money so they could earn their drink at the end of a long day. So they could order a second one and send a round to the group of secretaries gathering for a birthday celebration at the end of the bar.

I opened my handbag to make sure I had enough cash for the taxi driver; then I reached around in the small compartment in the lining where I had placed a business card a few weeks back at the yacht club.

Adam Rosen
Executive Editor
The New York City Reader
820 Eighth Avenue

We were already heading uptown, but something inside of me, some racing feeling in my chest and in my stomach, was telling me to stop.

I hadn't heard anything from Mr. Rosen about the greasy pig article I sent in and it was just as well, because Harry would be furious if he knew I'd sent something to an editor, especially to a Jewish editor. He told me, firmly, when we first married that it wouldn't be appropriate to earn a paycheck, that none of the women in his family worked after they wed, except in the home, and that it would send the wrong message. I had happily conceded, but now my home life was a shambles, a baby seemed an impossibility and I didn't know where that left me. Maybe it would be smart to inquire about the piece I'd sent in, just make sure Mr. Rosen had received it.

"To hell with Harry," I said.

"What's that, ma'am?" the taxi driver said.

I leaned forward. "I said forget Pennsylvania Station. Take me to Times Square."

I got out of the cab and stood at two enormous doors with the gold numbers 820 perched above them like a crown. The sun was in full force now and it reflected off the glass, forcing me to shield my eyes. Four women in almost identical uniforms of white blouses with patterned skirts, probably secretaries, exited the building in single file and turned to the left for their lunch break, I thought. I watched them and envied them. Then both doors swung open and a group of gentlemen walked out, tipping their hats against the sun, a sense of urgency in their stride. I quickly stepped out of the way.

This place was big and towering and intimidating and I hadn't even stepped inside. I felt a trickle of sweat run down the side of my face. I couldn't do this. Who was I to think I had any business being here? Maybe when I first moved to New York City, once I got used to working for Mr. Savage, I could have worked my way up to one of these big office buildings and this would have felt normal to me, but now it was as if I didn't fit in anywhere, and certainly not here in the midst of the lunchtime rush hour.

I turned from the building, walked to the edge of the sidewalk and saw a taxi approach. As I lifted my hand to hail the cab a tall, heavyset man in a suit far too dark for the heat of the summer blasted past me.

"Taxi," he blared out, and he knocked into me so hard that my handbag and all of its contents spilled onto the ground and into the gutter.

"Good God," I said, scrambling to the ground to pick up my belongings.

Dolly's lipstick, my purse, keys to the apartment, a key to the Manor, a swatch of fabric that Dolly had given me to remind me of the pillbox hat—I collected it all and stayed crouched, scanning the street and the sidewalk to see if there was anything left.

"Miss," I heard behind me. "Is this yours?" I looked up, but the sun was shining right in my eyes. All I could see was the business card right in front of my face.

"Oh, thank you," I said, and when I took it the man gave me his other hand and helped me to my feet.

"I hear he's a real piece of work," he said. He was wearing dark glasses and a narrow-brimmed fedora.

"Who is?"

"That guy, Adam Rosen." He motioned to the card still in my hand.

I looked to the card and then to the man. He took off his glasses and I instantly recognized him.

"Oh, Mr. Rosen," I said. "How nice to see you!" I brushed my hair back from my face, took the card and quickly shoved it back into my handbag. "What a coincidence. Is this where you work?"

"It is indeed. I received your article."

"Oh." I pulled my handbag into the crook of my elbow and straightened out my dress. "That . . . Oh my goodness, I don't even know why I sent it." I stopped. I was suddenly horrified that I'd actually mailed it to him.

"And here I was thinking you'd come by to bring me another article. I loved it—such a great angle, to talk about the local boys and put the spotlight on them instead of summer guests." I couldn't believe I was hearing him correctly. "It ran in yesterday's paper; your check's already in the mail. You really didn't see it?"

"What? No, I . . ." It ran in the paper? A check was in the mail? I couldn't believe it.

"Listen, I'm running to a meeting, but if you go to the front desk they have copies of yesterday's paper." He motioned inside. "I knew I'd found the right girl." He put on his dark glasses and tipped his hat. "I do hope you'll be sending me more like that. Good day to you, Mrs. Bordeaux. You know where to find me."

On the train, as I left New York City behind I read the piece over and over and realized that Mr. Rosen hadn't changed a word. There it was, the night of the greasy pig contest captured in words in print. Now it couldn't be changed. I had seized a moment and made it permanent, indisputable. It was a strange and incredible feeling to see my words, my thoughts, on the page.

It might have been just a glimmer of hope that I felt on that train ride back to Montauk, a flash of confidence that I could do something if I really wanted to, a kind of confidence that I hadn't known I'd been missing until I felt it. Maybe Harry didn't have to be my whole world, the way it was expected when I married. I was certainly not his everything. Maybe I could do something worthwhile, be something more, something small but significant. I don't even know who I am, or who I'm trying to be, I thought as I watched the city zip by outside the windows. For years now I had been bumbling around, not even trying to figure out what was important and necessary. But seeing my recollection of the evening with the local boys in Montauk, my view of a moment in time when there was excitement, energy, competition and thirst for life, smelling the ink of my words, that felt good.

I laid my head back and closed my eyes. The events of the past two days played in my mind like a picture show—the train ride with Dolly, Regine Brenner, the dirty martini glasses, the hot cigarette, Harry's face, the sickening shock, the hat factory and now this, my words in print. I felt a rage and a hot determination side by side and that was something. That alone gave me hope. Something was better than numbness. Something was better than not caring, not dreaming, not daring.

13

---❖---

I could have simply called and had the bellboy pick up my laundry like everyone else, but for the past few weeks I'd adopted the habit of taking it down myself. After that first time, when I'd walked all the way to the fishing village with Elizabeth, she'd seemed reluctant for me to accompany her again, so I hadn't. Maybe she thought she'd get into some kind of trouble with the Manor patrons for accepting my help, or maybe she'd been embarrassed about her house and neighborhood. One other time we'd walked down the hill and then parted ways before we reached the fishing village. I thought it was more dignified for her that way.

Some of the guests from the Manor were at the Beach Club, it was a beautiful summer's day, but I just didn't feel like going there. I sat under the oak tree and read the first paragraph of my book three times, getting to the end each time and realizing that I hadn't been paying attention. I'd barely slept the night before; I couldn't get my mind to stop thinking about Harry and what would happen next.

He had come out on Friday night on the late train with not a word of remorse or acknowledgment about what had happened in the city, and then he spent the weekend hunting. Up at the crack of dawn, shooting for hours, then recuperating with his hunting fellows with drinks and cigars at the Lodge, a mansion near the Carl Fisher house. He bathed and dressed for dinner while I was at a pre-dinner floral arrangement class in the social lounge. Jeanie insisted I attend and I hadn't objected. I was avoiding him as much as he was avoiding me.

When we reunited with the men in the cocktail lounge, Harry pecked me on the cheek and we moved arm in arm from one group conversation to the next as if everything were as it should be. It was as if he were punishing me, making me question everything. His denial forced me into silence. My body felt stiff and uneasy and my stomach churned every time I envisioned his guilt-ridden face when he had walked into the apartment and seen me there in my lingerie. On the one hand, I didn't want to revisit the exchange we had at the apartment and confront him, but on the other hand I wanted him to acknowledge his mistakes, take responsibility for his behavior. I wondered how our marriage could go on. Would I always cringe at the sight of him? A sight that at one point had made me smile until my cheeks hurt. Would we succumb to it and live separate lives, be strangers sleeping under the same roof for the rest of our days? Or would I forget his affair in time and eventually forgive? I wondered if he'd be able to move past the humiliation of getting caught or if he'd be cold toward me forever. Harry had made it clear that divorce was not an option. His family would be shamed and I would be disgraced and destitute.

I drank quite a bit when I was with him and then my thoughts would run off again, infuriated that he would get away with it all so easily, without so much as an apology. He should be begging for forgiveness, promising that he would never do it again, even if we both knew he would.

He left on Sunday evening after the fireworks even though it was the Fourth of July weekend and he could have stayed an extra day if he'd wanted to. Most of the gents weren't working on Monday, but I felt relieved that he left. I didn't want to be around him any longer and I could tell he didn't want to be around me either.

I heard someone walk across the lawn, the sound of twigs breaking underfoot. I began to stand, ready to deliver my laundry and accompany Elizabeth down the hill a little, but it was just a worker from the Manor.

"Do you need help, ma'am?" he asked, rushing to help me up.

"No, I'm just waiting for someone. Thank you."

"Would you like me to call anyone for you, ma'am?"

"No," I told him, "I'm fine here."

He nodded and walked toward the Manor. I started to worry that I'd missed Elizabeth. Aside from the laundry, I looked forward to the walk to the village. I'd ask about her boys and hear snippets about life in the fishing village, what time the boats came in the evening before, what they cooked for dinner; it reminded me of home and my childhood.

Since I'd been back in Montauk after my visit to the city I'd felt paranoid that everyone already knew about Harry's philandering. How could they not? Women talked and Harry, apparently, was about as discreet with his affairs as a pack of rats going through a dumpster.

I walked briskly across the lawn to see if Elizabeth was coming up the hill; then I quickly came back to the tree, sat, then stood again. Agitated, I pulled my bag to the service door and left it there, asking one of the workers to keep an eye on it. I couldn't very well pull it through the hotel lobby.

The truth was I didn't have anywhere else I wanted to be, but I started to think about this "laundry meeting" as if it had been prearranged and I was being stood up. Jeanie was holding a meeting that afternoon about activities for the upcoming month, but I had a few hours before I was needed there. Nevertheless, I felt my temperature rise as I marched into the hotel lobby.

"Has the laundry girl been?" I asked the butler, rather hotly.

"Yes, ma'am, just a few moments ago." He extended his arm toward the front door. "She went that way."

"But I've been out back. . . ." I stormed toward the door, not even bothering to finish explaining myself, and when I got outside I saw Elizabeth, bent over, loading bags into the back seat of the car.

"What are you doing?" I asked, not even saying hello. She jumped and bumped her head on the roof of the car.

"Oh, good morning, ma'am," she said, standing, squinting in the sun and rubbing her head. "Would you like me to collect your laundry?"

"You're late!" I said. "I was waiting for you out back; my bag is out there."

"I'm sorry, ma'am. My husband isn't working for the post office today; it's his day off."

I looked at her perplexed, still angry. This was no explanation. "And?" I said.

"He's out fishing, so I brought the car." She smiled slightly, as if she wasn't sure if she should. "It's much easier with the car than coming up the hill with that cart," she said.

I let out a deep breath trying to calm myself; I wasn't even sure why I was worked up and Elizabeth was getting the brunt of it. I walked back to the front door and asked one of the bellboys to bring my laundry bag from the service door; then I made my way back to Elizabeth's car. I stood there unsure what to say. Elizabeth kept loading the car, filling up the back seat. She stood up and stretched out her back.

"Is everything okay, ma'am?" she asked.

"Yes. Fine. I'm just a little out of sorts today." I felt disappointed. I'd planned to walk all the way down to the village with her today. I wanted the fresh air, I wanted to feel helpful and I wanted the company of someone outside of the Manor. The bellboy lifted my bag into the back seat and forced the door shut.

"Where are you off to now?" I asked Elizabeth.

"Home to drop off the bags, then up to the lighthouse to pick up."

"The lighthouse?" I asked.

"Yes, remember Mr. Brown, the lighthouse keeper? I do his laundry—he's a family friend and he helps us out a lot, especially with the car."

"I remember." I nodded. He had seemed so familiar to me, yet so intense and inquisitive. It had felt nice, if slightly unnerving, to have someone notice me so much. I wanted to get away from the Manor and take my mind off things. "Do you mind if I come along? I've never seen the lighthouse."

Elizabeth looked around as if she was worried someone had heard me ask. "Ma'am, I don't know if that's a good idea."

"Why?" I asked, but before she had a chance to respond I started talking again. "It's not a bad idea. I would really enjoy the drive. I go to all the same places, Gurney's, the Yacht Club, here, the Beach Club. I'd love to see the scenery." I made my way around to the passenger side and put my hand on the door. Elizabeth hadn't moved. She was looking at the ground. "Unless you don't want me to accompany you," I said.

"It's not that, ma'am. It's just that . . ."—she paused and looked up—"I might get in trouble. People might talk."

"Oh, for goodness' sake, Elizabeth, you're starting to sound like the women at the Manor," I said, opening the door and climbing in.

She stood there, hands on her hips, running her foot along the edge of the wooden-spoked wheel. I watched her for a minute, then stared straight ahead through the windscreen. Eventually she took her foot down from the wheel, reached into the car, flipped the coil box switch, then walked to the front of the car. She bent down and pulled the hand crank toward her a half turn. Nothing happened, so she cranked it again, this time with force, and the engine began to roar.

We rode in silence and out of the corner of my eye I saw her push a long lever forward, release her foot slightly off one of three pedals and pull the throttle down. I'd always sat in the back of the car whenever Harry and I went anywhere, and we always had a driver take us where we wanted to go. At one point Harry had talked about buying the Model 48 and I was rather excited at the prospect of learning to drive one day, but in the end he decided against it and was happy with Albert or José driving us around town. With the exception of a few rides I took in college, I wasn't used to being driven around by a woman.

We wound our way off the Manor driveway and toward the hill where

Elizabeth usually wrestled with her laundry cart, and we started to bounce in our seats from the uneven road. The engine was loud at first, but as we made our way down the hill it started to smooth out.

"It's a beautiful day," I said.

"Yes, ma'am," she said, keeping her eyes on the road.

The breeze from the open windows felt good, but the tension in the car made me clammy and uncomfortable—I'd been too forceful; it wasn't like me. A laundry bag from the stack in the back seat fell forward between Elizabeth and me and I pushed it back in place, wondering whose laundry that might be. We reached the bottom of the steep and bumpy hill, then turned left onto the main road and right toward the village, the same route we'd taken when we walked there a few weeks earlier. We crossed over the train tracks and turned into the fishing village, which, to me, even though it was no more than five minutes from the Manor, felt like another world. Just as before, I was amazed at the beauty of the water and all the docked boats catching the sunlight just a few feet from where the row of small, run-down wooden houses began. We pulled up outside her house. She put the car in neutral, pulled on the brake so that the engine came to a sputtering stop.

"Elizabeth," I said. "I hope this is not too much trouble." Her fingers tightened on the steering wheel and she sighed but said nothing.

"Look," I said, feeling that ugly, irritable streak surge once again through my veins. "If you don't want me to tag along I can get out and walk home." I was defensive and embarrassed for forcing myself on her this way when I clearly wasn't welcome, and yet every time I spoke I seemed to make things worse.

"Ma'am, I really can't afford to lose this job. If the hotel management saw me giving you a ride they'd think I was bothering you or asking for something. After all, when you summer guests leave in September there's no more work. Things are really hard for the families out here. I have to make enough now to get us through to the next summer."

I opened my mouth to speak, but she kept on going.

"There are a lot of laundry gals who would kill for this job. I only got it through my husband's connection to the Manor. He's been delivering mail and special packages to the patrons since it first opened. . . ." She paused, looked up at me for a second and then back to the steering wheel. "My husband doesn't think it's a good idea. I'm sorry, but my boys are always hungry and they don't stop growing. This is not a game for me."

Part of me just wanted to get out of the car and run back to the Manor, I was so embarrassed and ashamed. Was this a game for me? Was she some distraction from the petty realities of my upturned life? I hadn't thought about the possibility of jeopardizing her job just because I felt angry and frustrated and in need of a change of scenery. I could go back to the Manor and everything would go on as before, I suddenly realized, but this little scene that I had caused could cost Elizabeth her livelihood.

I reached into my handbag and felt around for the tiny baby's bonnet that I'd brought from Dolly's factory. I considered giving it to Elizabeth now as a peace offering, but the moment wasn't right; she was angry and I deserved it. I felt the soft bobbles of crocheted wool and held it between my thumb and forefinger; then I ran my fingers along the bonnet slowly as if I were worrying the beads of my mother's rosary, all the way to the silk ribbons that Elizabeth would tie, gently under her baby's soft, fleshy chin. I suddenly had a deep desire to hold the baby close to my chest and smell the powdery, milky smell of his hair. My eyes filled with tears. I looked out of the window and blinked them away.

"I'm sorry," I said finally. "You're right; of course you are. It's just that I've so enjoyed the brief moments we've spent together. I'd like to be a friend to you if I can." Elizabeth turned back to the steering wheel. "And I'm sorry I was so brash with you before."

"That's all right, ma'am," she said. "You seemed upset over something."

"Well, yes," I said. "I had a rather nasty weekend back in the city." I looked out to the bay and the water somehow calmed me. "My husband seems to have other interests," I said, as matter-of-factly as I could, "interests that don't include me, if you know what I mean."

She looked confused.

"Women, probably several of them. It's probably been going on for a while; I was just too foolish to see it."

"Oh," she said, glancing toward me, then away, then back to me again. I didn't want to make her feel uncomfortable and I shouldn't be telling her my business, but I felt I would go crazy if I kept it inside and all to myself.

"I suppose I should have known, or maybe I did know, but I just couldn't bear to admit it, and now that I've seen it, and he knows that I know, I can't go back, I don't believe. I can go forward, but things will be different, you see, and I don't know how to live like that."

The tears welled up again. I took a Kleenex out of my handbag and dabbed at the corners of my eyes; then I placed both my hands in my lap, feeling a sense of relief and remorse all at once.

Elizabeth placed her small hand on mine and left it there. "You're a strong woman," she said gently. "And different from the others. You'll find a way."

We sat like that for a while, with the salty smell of just-caught fish and ocean, and the noise of the village all around us—men calling from the boats to the crew onshore, seagulls squawking overhead for scraps, someone hammering away in the yard by the houses and kids running on rocks and laughing at the water's edge.

"This is for you," I said finally, pulling the tiny bonnet from my bag. "My friend is a hat designer and she's toying with the idea of a baby's line. It's one of a kind."

I handed it to Elizabeth and she opened her hands, palms up like she was holding a prayer book, and she held it, as if it were a fragile, ancient document that might crumble if she so much as breathed.

"Do you like it?" I asked, picking it up from her upturned hands and placing my hand inside to give it shape. "It's crocheted and it's got a little lace brim, which I thought might shade baby Jake from the sun." I turned it around so she could see it from all sides.

Her hands were on her chest now, one on top of the other. "I've never seen anything so beautiful in my whole life," she said. "It's so delicate and lovely; thank you." She picked up one of the silk ribbons and it slid though her fingers. "But why?" she asked.

"Why not?" I said, feeling exceptionally relieved that she had liked it and that she seemed to have forgiven me, for now. "Come on," I said. "I'll help you unload."

The car moved a little faster without the weight of all those laundry bags shoved in the back seat. Elizabeth and I had tied scarves around our hair and the air rushed around us. I tilted my head out the window a little, holding on to my scarf, feeling invigorated and miles away from the city.

The road was paved and smooth under the wheels of the old Ford and Elizabeth controlled the car just as well as any man I'd seen. It was thick with greenery on both sides and the trees reached over our heads toward one another, creating a shady canopy. I saw the rooftop of one, maybe two houses on the short drive up the hill, but this part of Montauk was populated mostly by birds, squirrels, and a few deer grazing at the side of the road. We passed a horse and cattle ranch and I thought how lovely it was that Montauk hadn't been overdeveloped; there was still so much greencry and open space, with beaches that went on for miles on both sides of the hamlet. Only two vehicles passed us on the way, a state trooper and a school bus.

"Mind if I stop and pick up a pie for dinner?" Elizabeth steered the car into a parking bay near the top of the hill. She gestured toward a small trailer parked off to the side of the road. "She's an old friend of ours, Mrs. Barrow, makes the best steak pies. I buy one once a week when I come up this way. You should try one."

I looked over and saw an elderly lady in a floral apron waving from a drop-down window.

"Oh no, I'm fine, thanks," I said, knowing I would eat at the Manor later but certain that if my mother were there she wouldn't think twice. Elizabeth returned moments later with a brown paper package that she set carefully in the back seat.

"It may not look like much, but she's one of the best cooks in town; my boys go crazy for her pies. She's hoping to open up a proper pie shop in town someday."

"I'm sure she'd do very well," I said.

"I hope she does. She lost both her sons to the war. So it's just been her and her husband for the last twenty years. She deserves some kindness and some luck."

"Terrible. How would you even go on if your child didn't come home from war?" I said. "It's not like an illness that at least you can try to cure, or understand, or even an accident; you'd be wondering for the rest of your life what happened, where they were and what you could have done differently."

"I can't even imagine if my boys had to go to war. . . ."

"They won't; that won't happen again." I thought about Roosevelt and his voice coming over the radio. Being able to hear him made me feel like I knew him, and I trusted him.

"It could," Elizabeth said, steering the car back onto the road. "Patrick says that German leader, Adolf Hitler, is foaming at the mouth to invade Czechoslovakia and he says once people start fighting it spreads; it's infectious."

"But we would never get involved. The United States would never send their own men and boys to fight Europe's battles again. Honestly, we would never do that, not after the last time."

"Men are crazy when it comes to fighting, though. It's as if they want to do it."

"Not Harry. God, he would come up with any excuse to avoid joining the troops."

The trees whizzed past us as we continued up the hill, and they opened to vast meadowland when we reached the very top. Elizabeth slowed down and I knew we were close to the cliffs because the air changed—salty, fresh and dewy. And then I saw it, first the steel and glass enclosure high in the sky, then the white tower with the red stripe around its midsection and, at its feet, a grey, modest home with two front doors. Elizabeth parked at the bottom of a pathway that led to the lighthouse.

"Wow, it's magnificent, isn't it?"

Elizabeth smiled. "Do you want to stay in the car while I run up?"

"No, I'll come with you, if you don't mind," I said, getting out of the car and walking around to Elizabeth's side. "Do you need those?" I asked, pointing to a couple of white button-down shirts on the back seat.

"Oh yes, please, can you grab them?"

"So how long have you been doing this man's laundry, the keeper?"

"Thomas? As long as I can remember," Elizabeth said. "His wife never took to life at the lighthouse; she left him," she whispered, "so he needs a little help with those kinds of domestic things."

"Goodness, it must be awfully lonely up here."

"Well, there's the assistant keeper and his family; they live on one side of the keepers' dwellings." She pointed to the grey house at the top of the hill. "And Thomas lives on the other side, but he's alone. And in the summer a lot of visitors come through, but for the most part he keeps himself to himself."

As we climbed higher, the lighthouse looked even more beautiful, with the summer sun catching it like a picture postcard.

"Thomas!" Elizabeth yelled, and I just about jumped out of my skin. "Sorry, ma'am, didn't mean to startle you," she said, pointing halfway up the lighthouse tower where a man stood on scaffolding painting the exterior wall.

"I swear, every time I come up here I spend about an hour just trying to find him. He's either inside the tower, at the very top cleaning the lens or in the engine room around the back or God knows where. At least he's where I can see him today. I just have to get his attention." She yelled his name again.

"Need help?" I asked.

On the count of three we yelled at the top of our lungs, "Thomas!"

"Do you think it's appropriate that I am shouting his first name like this?" I asked. "I mean I haven't been formally introduced at his place of work."

Elizabeth looked at me, then started laughing. "Ma'am, there is nothing formal about this place, but if you prefer we can use his surname."

I laughed a little, too. "Okay, if we're dropping formalities don't call me ma'am; call me Beatrice."

Elizabeth smiled and dropped her glance. "Ready?" she asked. "One . . . two . . . three. Thomas!" we yelled in unison. Still nothing. The wind had picked up at the top of the hill and it seemed to carry our voices out to the ocean. "Let's try the house," she said.

We walked around to the front of the house where two identical navy-blue doors stood side by side under a white porch. I looked at them both as if it were some sort of game.

"This one," Elizabeth said, knocking on the door on the left. "This side is where Mr. Milton lives, the assistant keeper," she said, then added in a whisper, "Apparently they don't get along all that well."

A plump middle-aged woman opened the door in a housecoat with an apron tied around her waist.

"Sorry to bother you, Mrs. Milton," Elizabeth said, "but I'm trying to get Mr. Brown's attention. He's up at the top of the tower painting and it's laundry day."

She nodded her head. "One minute," she said, and she walked into the house, returning a few moments later with a small brass bugle horn. "Here you go," she said, handing it to Elizabeth, then nodding to me. "This is what I use to let my Milton know that dinner's on the table."

"I can never get this thing to work," Elizabeth said as we went back to the base of the lighthouse tower. She stood at the bottom of the scaffolding and blew into it, but no noise came out. She tried again.

"Let me try," I said, taking it from her. I pursed my lips and blew into the horn, letting out a loud, high-pitched howl. Elizabeth clapped her hands. "Nice work," she said. The keeper immediately looked down at us over the scaffolding and acknowledged us; then he began to climb down.

We watched him carefully maneuver from one level to the next with what seemed like relative ease. He was pretty high up and it was going to take some time to climb all the way down. "It's really beautiful up here," I said, looking around us. It was all ocean, cloudless sky and greenery no matter which way I looked. The road we drove up on cut a line through the thick trees, but it seemed as though we were miles away from any-where.

Elizabeth followed my gaze. "It is, isn't it?" she said. "It's funny, the more time you spend in a place, just getting on with your life, working away, the less you look around and appreciate it."

When he approached he looked surprised to see me there with Eliza-beth.

"Did you forget it's laundry day?" Elizabeth asked.

"No, not at all." He ran his hand across his forehead and wiped it on his undershirt. "Hope you haven't been waiting long?" His skin was speck-led with paint and his undershirt had a damp V down the front of his chest with wet rings under his arms and a slight salty odor.

He briefly glanced my way again, then turned to Elizabeth.

"I've been up there for hours and lost track of time."

"It's fine; we weren't waiting long," Elizabeth said.

"We borrowed a bugle," I chimed in; then I cringed at the sound of myself saying something so ridiculous.

He laughed. "Nice to see you."

"Oh, where are my manners?" Elizabeth said. "This is Beatrice Bour-deux; she's a guest at the Manor."

"We've met," Thomas said. "At the pig contest."

"Oh, I didn't realize," she said. "Here." Elizabeth handed him the shirts, folded neatly. "I still had these from last week. I sewed on the missing buttons."

"You're good to me, thank you," he said. "I could have done that."

"I know you could," Elizabeth said, "but I don't mind, and you bring our car back to life almost weekly." She turned to me. "Thomas worked on the armored cars in the war, so he knows a bit more than my Patrick when it comes to engines."

He put his hands in his pockets. "How are the kids?" he asked.

"Good, good, trying to keep them busy and out of trouble for the summer."

"And Pat?"

"Same as the kids." She laughed.

When I watched them talk I had a strange pang of jealousy. They seemed so familiar, so friendly. That night at the pig contest he'd acted so peculiar yet interested in what I had to say, his eyes had locked on mine to the point where it made me want to leave, but however uncomfortable that had been, I suddenly wanted his attention again.

"Do you have to paint that whole thing?" I asked, pointing up to the lighthouse.

They both looked at me. "Eventually," he said.

"How long will it take?"

"A couple of weeks, at least."

"I think I would be terrified of being up so high," I said, and my eyes fixed on a white scar across his eyebrow where the hair didn't grow. I wondered if he'd gotten it from a fall. He rubbed it and I looked away.

"I'm pretty used to heights," he said. "The tower's open to the public a few times a week. You should come back and climb the steps, give it a try. I'm sure you did more adventurous things than climb a lighthouse growing up in the country."

"That's true," I said, thinking of the adventures I'd gone on with my brother, running away in the woods one day after he had an argument with our father, swinging across the river on rope we found in the garage, trying to keep up with the boys and climbing the trees, then needing Charlie to rescue me because I'd gone higher than I thought and frozen when I saw the ground.

"Where did you grow up?" Elizabeth asked. "I assumed you were born in New York City."

"Oh gosh, no, Pennsylvania," I said. "I moved to the city after college." I looked at the lighthouse keeper, perplexed. "How did you know that?"

"You told me; you must have told me the night of the contest." He looked a little sheepish and I laughed. I was pretty sure I hadn't told him, but clearly it was a dead giveaway that I wasn't a born and bred New Yorker. I wasn't a Bordeaux by blood.

"I'll get the bags then," he said to Elizabeth.

He glanced back toward me when he walked up toward the grey-shingled house.

I wondered, for a brief second, if he had asked about me. But who would he ask?

"He's a bit odd, isn't he?" I said quietly as we stood watching him walk up the hill.

"He's not usually, he's always very sure of himself, but you must make him nervous." She laughed.

"Nervous?" The idea sort of excited me. Lately it didn't seem that I'd had any effect on anyone, except perhaps that Winthrop man. "Why on earth would I make him nervous?"

"I don't know, because you're a summer guest, or maybe because of your beauty."

"Ha," I laughed, brushing away the idea with my hands. "Have you ever been inside?" I asked, changing the subject.

"The house?" Elizabeth shook her head. "Never. The grounds and the tower are open to the public on weekends, but the house is strictly off-limits; no one goes in there."

We waited in silence for a moment.

"Sorry I didn't introduce you properly," Elizabeth said after a while. "I should have said something right away. I didn't realize you'd met already."

"Oh, that's okay," I said. "But you know I could just be a friend. I don't have to be someone from the Manor."

She nodded. "It's just, I've never really known any of the summer guests before."

"They can get tiresome sometimes."

"I think you're very lucky," she said, trying to be cheerful for me, despite what I'd told her in the car earlier about Harry. She must have thought

I was ungrateful for all that I had, and I had the feeling that she'd never be able to understand how I felt. How could I expect her to? She didn't have a minute to herself. After picking up this last load of laundry she'd go back to her house, set up the wringer and the tub and start scrubbing complete strangers' clothes and undergarments with her bare hands, run them through the wringer, then hang them out to dry, iron them, pack them back up into their bags and return them to their owners for $1.50 a bag, at which time it would almost be time to do it all over again. All the while she'd be caring for her baby, keeping her older boys out of trouble and getting them to do their chores, cooking for her family and getting the boys all washed and into bed each night.

I had no responsibilities, no one to care for and love and keep safe. Nothing that needed to be accomplished by any certain day or hour. Not even much of a marriage to tend to. I looked at her, her plain face and blond wavy hair pulled back into a bun, frizzy pieces curling at her hairline, and I envied her.

"You're lucky, too," I said, and I wanted to say more, to explain how alone I felt, even surrounded by all these people, to tell her that I'd spent hours imagining my life any other way than it was right now. I wanted to tell her that in my daydreams I pictured what my life would look like if I'd married Jimmy Wilkes, the kid who lived one town over from us and helped my father with deliveries. Or what it would be like in the bedroom if I'd married Denny Goodman, the quarterback of the local college football team who'd asked to take me to the picture house my second year in college but who I'd turned down because it felt wrong to entertain the idea of being happy so soon after my brother died. I wanted to tell her all these things, but I was afraid I'd be misunderstood.

As I stared up at the house I tried to think if I'd been happy as a kid, growing up. I had; I was sure of it. I thought about how different dinnertime was at my parents' house from dinners with Harry. My mother used to mix white margarine with yellow food coloring and set it in a small glass dish on the table to resemble butter. It was special when Daddy brought home a real stick of butter from the store. Mama would fry up a whole plate of bacon, nice and crispy the way Daddy liked it, and Charlie and I would spread white bread with real butter and eat bacon sandwiches for dinner, and then again for breakfast if there was any left over. As a kid I never wanted more; I didn't lust after decadent foods or expensive clothes. I felt lucky because Daddy would sometimes bring home treats like that, or milk with cream on top, even when things were scarce. We never went without food or clothes; we may have had to make things last longer, but we didn't go without. There were always kids worse off than Charlie and me at school wearing pants with holes in the knees and shoes with their toes peeking through the front. We didn't have much, but it always seemed to be enough; in fact, we seemed to be doing quite well compared to some of the other families I knew.

At Vassar the incoming freshmen were a mixed bunch. There were the rich Park Avenue, New York, girls, but there were also girls like me from more humble families and others from even more humble families, farm girls who'd won scholarships. We all sat in class together all the same, rich, poor or in the middle, and when we graduated it was fair game. We could go back to our farms and our small towns or we could go out into the world, to New York City or to Paris. It was as if we'd been handed new credentials. But maybe I wasn't ready for it; maybe I'd been naïve about what that world entailed and how I'd have to sacrifice love and happiness for the sake of luxury and money. It was never something I felt I needed or sought out, but once you had it, it seemed hard to relinquish.

The keeper returned with a bag full of clothes, and two pairs of overalls hung over his arm. "Sorry about the grime," he said. "We had a leak in the engine room and my overalls are filthy."

"I'll do what I can, Thomas," Elizabeth said.

"Thanks," he said. "I'll bring these down to the car." He picked up the bag and threw it over his shoulder and walked ahead of us.

"Nice to meet you again," I said as I got into the passenger seat.

He looked at me and nodded. "It certainly was."

❈

On the drive down toward the village I leaned my head back against the seat and closed my eyes. I wondered what he must have thought of me, a summer guest tagging along with the laundry girl. I didn't know what I was thinking forcing Elizabeth to take me up there the way I had. I just wanted a distraction. I kept thinking of Harry and what would become of us now. Had he seemed sad? Had there been a glimpse of remorse that I'd missed this past weekend? Maybe he realized now that he'd made a terrible mistake; maybe he'd try harder now to be the loving husband he had once promised to be. I felt sick reliving it all over again.

I forced myself to think of something else and pictured the lighthouse. I imagined sitting on the grass up on those cliffs and reading, away from the rest of the world. Maybe Mr. Rosen might like to know about this side of Montauk, the rough-around-the-edges keeper against the backdrop of all that natural beauty, the old lighthouse, the surrounding meadows, even the old pie shack at the side of the road. Maybe Rosen should interview these locals for a fresh perspective, a look at this resort town from a different angle? But then I recalled him talking about the gossip columnist Hedda someone or other. He said his readers wanted glamour, money, gossip and fancy clothes. I started to imagine what I might write. I closed my eyes and let my mind drift from day dress to day dress, evening gown to evening gown, seafoam chiffon next to layers of purple silk, next to golden satin. Just as I began to relax imagining the luxurious fabrics, I began to picture the women's faces, serious and severe, judging me, staring at me like the faces of a Matisse painting, harsh eyebrows, long noses, from one lady to the next, Betsy to Mary Van de Coop to Clarissa to Jeanie. I suddenly jerked my body upright and gasped.

"What is it?" Elizabeth said, startled.

"Dear God," I said, "Jeanie's planning meeting!" I sat up straight in the passenger seat and felt my hair, a wild mess. I hadn't bothered with the head scarf on the way home; I'd let the wind run around me like crazy. Jeanie had asked me to act as her secretary for the meeting, taking notes as she rounded up ideas and requests for our afternoon activities for the

upcoming weeks in July. She was allowing me into her planning circle as
a favor, she told me, to give me a little visibility and to help me weave my
way into her circle. I'd been counting on this opportunity. I debated about
heading straight to the Seahorse, but I knew I needed to freshen up, and
what would the women say if they saw me getting out of Elizabeth's car?
I considered for a moment what would be worse, arriving late but respectable or arriving on time, disheveled and with the laundry gal. Late was
better.

"Elizabeth, can you drop me at the Manor?" She looked over, concerned. It was one thing for her to allow me in her car that morning for a
quick tour of the town, she must have thought, but quite another for anyone at the Manor to notice that I'd spent almost the entire day with her.
"If you drop me round the back by the service entrance, no one will see
me get out."

"Okay, ma'am," she said. "If you're sure."

In my room, I rushed around taking a clean dress from the closet, brushing the tangles out of my hair and powdering my face. I checked the clock.
It was five minutes past three. I looked through the newsletter Jeanie had
handed out with the schedule for the week and I scanned the column for
the planning meeting. Four o'clock. I checked the clock again. Oh thank
God, I wasn't going to be late after all; I had almost an hour before the
meeting. It would only take fifteen minutes for me to tidy myself up. I
took a deep breath and sat down at the bureau to compose myself and drink
a glass of water. I was tired from not sleeping the night before. I didn't
feel like seeing all those women. And why was this even important? The
effort was for Harry. Did I even care about helping him anymore? He
surely didn't care about me.

I pulled my journal from the drawer. After Charlie died, writing in a
journal was my only way to let my thoughts out. I couldn't speak to my
parents; they were in their own cloud of grief. This time I started jotting
down notes while they were fresh in my head. For what? I didn't know.

For Mr. Rosen, for a story, for my dreams, for my imagination, for company? I wrote about the lighthouse, standing 111 feet tall, the red daymark around its middle, the widow's walk barely visible at the top and the ragged cliffs below. The specks of white paint in the keeper's hair and on his forearms. The way he'd rolled up the sleeves of his shirt. The strange detail he'd known about me, where I'd grown up. His mysterious, inquisitive nature. My impulse to walk up to the house with him when he went to get the laundry, to peek into the windows of the grey house at the base of the light tower.

I laid my head on the desk and closed my eyes for a second. How did he know anything about me? I imagined a return visit to the lighthouse, a reason to speak to him once more. I could set up a tour for the women perhaps—maybe I could suggest that at the planning meeting for a July activity. No, I changed my mind; I wanted to pretend the lighthouse was my secret. Maybe I would write something for Mr. Rosen after all; then I'd really have a reason to go back and ask questions. I began to feel calm, not rushed. I had time, no need to feel stress. My hair was brushed; my dress was on the bed. I'd be ready in two minutes. . . .

I awoke to a knock on the door. My neck hurt and I felt the imprint of my wedding ring pressed into my forehead. There was another knock, louder this time, and I jumped to my feet. What time was it? It was pitch black outside. I smoothed down my hair and the dress I'd been wearing all day, catching a glimpse of the clean "meeting" outfit still lying on my bed as I rushed to open the door.

"Well, well, well. Aren't you a naughty girl?" It was Dolly, all dressed up and slightly tipsy in an elegant evening gown with a plunging neckline and a cape draped around her shoulders. "You're not going to be in Jeanie's good books anymore." She laughed and walked into my room. "My God, you look like you've just woken from a nightmare," she said with a laugh and a look of concern. She tilted my chin upwards and looked in my eyes. "Are you okay, Beatrice?"

"I don't know what happened!" I said. "I must have fallen asleep. I was planning on coming to the meeting and I just fell asleep. Dear God. What time is it?"

"Darling it's two a.m. Don't worry; the meeting was an absolute bore as usual. But you missed a party at the yacht club casino; I even won some money." She took some notes from her pocket and waved them around.

"But, Jeanie—"

"Oh, Jeanie can shove it up her enormous—"

"Dolly!" I said.

"Oh, for God's sake," she said in more of a whisper this time, "Jeanie will find another poor young woman to order around and you should be grateful you got out before you got in!"

I shook my head. Maybe I wasn't going to succeed in having Jeanie as a friend, but I certainly didn't want her as my enemy.

"Cheer up, darling," Dolly said. "You look like you need to get out and have some fun. There's music and entertainment at the Surf Club tomorrow evening." She blew me a kiss, then turned toward the door, stumbling a little. "I'll come by around six to pick you up."

14

I loved to be near the ocean. Growing up in the middle of Pennsylvania, Charlie and I never had the luxury of the beach at our doorstep. For a few years, though, starting when I was around age eight or nine, Daddy would drive the four of us down to New Jersey and we'd stay for a week at a little inn just a few short blocks from the beach.

On the beach my brother and I would play for hours and hours and hours. We'd be running, swimming, collecting, digging and building. And he indulged me, too, letting me play girly childish games.

"This one, Charlie, was given to me by an emperor," I would say, holding up my newly found shell, brushing off the sand, rinsing it in the salty water that licked our toes.

"That's a keeper," he'd say, nodding to the buckets we carried. "Add it to the collection."

I wished I could be back there on the sand with him holding our treasure chests in one hand, collecting jewels with the other.

We'd collect and collect until our arms were stretched out behind us as we dragged our full buckets back up the beach to the lounge chairs. I always liked the end of the beach day best, when most of the full-dayers had packed up their parasols and headed home. Daddy let me stay longer when I was with Charlie. The dogs were out then, past six, and we would try to pet them as they bounded by, leaping in the air, barking gratitude for freedom. We'd sit on the sand and line up the shells and rocks, watching the early evening swimmers glide into the lavender horizon.

Sometimes I yearned for that forever feeling—those hours that stretched into days and days into a week, without a thought for tomorrow. It was simple then. We wore swimsuits all day and we slept long and deeply at night, eager for it all to start again the next day, never thinking for a second that another day wouldn't come.

Whenever we got home and back into our normal lives, Charlie playing with the neighborhood boys and me back with my friends or at home with my mother, I missed him. Even though we were under the same roof, eating meals at the dinner table together, it was different from those forever days at the beach.

Dolly and I sat at the bar that looked out on to the beach and sipped our martinis, listening to the waves behind us and the guitarist strumming away softly at the end of the bar. Dolly was in a mellow mood and I was spinning the stem of my glass thinking about Charlie, wondering what he'd be like now as a man, what advice he might give me about the sad state of my marriage.

The place was fairly busy for a weekday night. I'd been avoiding Jeanie and her minions all day. Ever since Dolly left the night before I'd been in a panic about the repercussions of missing Jeanie's meeting. I'd heard stories of her, and women like her, in the city. They might seem petty and irrelevant in the grand scheme of things, but their ability to ruin your reputation if they felt betrayed or disrespected in any way could cripple a person's place in society. And if that happened Harry would be furious. I would get back into Jeanie's good books, I told myself as I glanced over to their table on the terrace, but not today. I simply didn't have it in me. Harry would be arriving in a few days and a strained weekend would unfold—fake conversation at group dinner tables and the rest of the time him finding ways to avoid me, busying himself with hunting and fishing and smoking cigars with the men, all so we wouldn't have to be alone together. The whole idea sat like a lead weight in my stomach. That and the thought of who he'd been waking up next to in our bed that week in the city.

I turned to Dolly. "How many of these women's husbands do you think have cheated?" I asked.

"All of them," she said, nonchalantly, taking a sip of her martini.

"All of them! That's a little extreme, don't you think?"

"No," she said. "All men cheat."

"Why do you say that?"

She looked at me as if I had a few screws loose. "Because they do. Men cheat, and women, God bless their little hearts"—she looked over to the table with Jeanie and Clarissa and Kathleen, who were all laughing over something—"women put up with it or pretend it's not happening. Most women think that if they are good little wives that run the house, keep themselves beautiful and nurture their children, then they can will their husbands to remain faithful."

I opened my mouth to say something but closed it again. "Well," I tried, but nothing followed.

"Honey, men are simply made that way. They need to be fulfilled or they look elsewhere; I've told you that already." She tapped a cigarette out of the box and offered one to me. "And," she continued, "if most of these women knew what was good for them they would have their affairs, too; it evens the score."

"Evens the score?" I repeated, horrified but intrigued that Dolly actually believed this.

"All good relationships are based on balance and harmony and if only one part of the couple is having some excitement then the balance is off."

She inhaled deeply from her cigarette, then lit mine. "Anyway, why do you ask? Who are you worried about?" She looked over to Jeanie's table again.

"Oh, no one in particular, I was just curious. So are you saying that Clark cheats, and you? Do you cheat?"

"Honey, don't sound so troubled by it all, and please stop calling it cheating; it sounds so criminal. We've had our share of affairs, darling; of course we have. How do you think we've stayed in love for so long?"

I took a gulp from my martini and set it down.

"Another round?" Dolly asked.

I nodded and Dolly snapped her fingers for the barkeep. I'd never considered for a moment that all men strayed, and the thought of it sickened me. Why bother with any of it, the big ceremony, playing house, having children, if you'd rather be with other people? I thought I was one of the few unlucky women stuck with a cheating bastard and the idea that I wasn't alone in that, strangely, didn't give me any sort of comfort. In fact, the idea of other husbands being unfaithful to other women only added fuel to my rage against Harry. It was them against us, those slick, moneymaking, city-dwelling, train-taking men in their suits and hats and suspenders, against us, the women who had been shipped out to this quiet little beach town out of the way so they could have their fun. I was furious. I considered Dolly's point and wondered if one affair really could cancel the other out.

On Friday evening the women stood three deep at the platform and buzzed with excitement as the train pulled in. Once the men arrived the weekend would officially start and the party could begin.

"Here they come!" someone called out. "Gee, I really missed him this week," I heard one woman say. "It's so hard to be away from him for so long." I wondered how much of this display and chatter was intended to give off the image of the perfect marriage, the perfect life, the perfect wife.

I felt a sense of obligation to be there and that was it. Each woman found her man in the crowd and walked arm in arm with him to their chauffeur.

I was one of three women left. Still a trickle of men emerged from the train, one or two obviously drunk, but Harry wasn't one of them. He hadn't even bothered to let me know.

I skipped dinner and had already changed into my silk nightgown by nine o'clock. I lay in bed and read. Either he'd show up or he wouldn't, I thought and at that moment I rather preferred that he not show up at all.

A little after 4:00 a.m. I heard the door unlock and clank against the chain bolt I'd put across it. The bedside lamps were still on and my book was lying across my chest. I got up to unlock the door in a sleepy daze.

"Beatrice," Harry whispered, smelling of liquor and kissing my unresponsive mouth. "I'm so sorry, I had to work late. Thank goodness I was able to get on the late train. Fisherman's Special, left at one a.m."

I shook my head and climbed back into bed.

"Oh, don't be sore with me, sweetheart," he said, taking off his brown loafers and throwing his suit and tie on the chair.

"You didn't even leave a message for me," I said into the pillow, my eyes closed, hoping that I would be able to return to sleep as quickly as I'd been woken from it.

"I wanted to surprise you," he said. "Look, you're tired; we'll talk more in the morning."

I squeezed my eyes tightly shut, but I knew I wouldn't be able to sleep again. My muscles felt tight beneath my skin and my stomach clenched. I didn't move. I faked sleep until I heard snoring from Harry's side of the bed; then I lay on my back and stared up at the ceiling until the sun came up.

Harry was sitting in bed reading the newspaper and drinking coffee when I returned from an early morning swim.

"Morning," he said. "Nice swim?"

"Fine," I said.

"That's fabulous, darling." He slurped his coffee and gave the newspaper a flick to make it stand straight at attention.

"Beatrice, I've invited the Turners to join us for lunch today at Gurney's; you don't mind, do you?"

I flipped my head over and rubbed my hair roughly with the towel.

"Oh, and this evening there's a bit of gambling going on at the yacht club and I told the men they could count me in. You know I don't indulge in that too often, so I assumed you wouldn't mind, give you a chance to do something with the ladies."

I stood up and brushed my hair straight down my back.

"As a matter of fact, Harry, I do mind," I said, standing in front of him in wet swim clothes and a robe. "I haven't seen you all week; I barely saw you last weekend while you were here. You show up at four a.m. with no valid explanation and now you're telling me you're leaving me alone again tonight and you've crammed our only time together with the Turners?" I flung my hairbrush on the dresser, where it slid over and crashed into the mirror, creating more drama than I had intended. But I held strong, hands on my hips.

"Darling, you're upset. Don't be. You know how I like to see everyone when I get out here."

"Yes, everyone but me," I said.

"I want to see you, too."

"I'm your wife, God damn it. You should want to see me, but instead you use up all your free time dallying around with other women in the city while I'm out here." I held my breath, staring him down. I couldn't believe I'd said it. It was out there now, acknowledged, verbalized. I might have just ruined everything. I didn't dare breathe. Or blink. Or move.

His face was one of total shock. He knew of course that I was aware of his philandering, but he seemed genuinely stunned and unprepared for me to confront him in this way. We were both frozen until his face softened and he rubbed his forehead with his hand.

"Come here, Beatrice, please." He stretched his arms out to me, reaching for me. I sat on the bed next to him and he wrapped his arms around me, pulling my head to his chest. "I've been such an idiot, such a fool. I have this beautiful woman, my beautiful wife, right in front of me and I've taken you for granted; I haven't given you the attention you need and deserve." He kissed the top of my head and talked into my damp hair. "All that's over now. I promise you, it's over. It's just you and me, I swear to you."

I was tempted to leave it at that. The more we spoke of his infidelity, the more it could become etched in my brain and harder to forget. I wanted to let it go, but I couldn't.

"But why?" was all I could muster, and it came out like a tiny mouse-like squeak.

He sighed a heavy-hearted sigh. "I don't know." He said, "It was stupid; there's no explanation for it. I just . . ."

He paused and I looked up at him. "You just what?"

"Well, you've been unhappy; I know you wanted a baby and it's made you quite melancholy. And you complain when I go out, but you don't understand, these are business dinners. Who else is going to make the money for us to live the life we live?"

I felt scooped out from the inside. Hollow. I was unhappy, he was right, but I hadn't always been. It made me unhappy that he was out sleeping with other women. And yes, I was sad that I wasn't with child, but I thought I'd kept that to myself for the most part. Had I really driven him to step out of our marriage? I felt sick and guilty and angry.

"I'm not unhappy," I said, wiping away the tears.

"It would be good for us to have a baby. I think it would be good for you. It would give you something to do. You'd feel more useful; you wouldn't have all these ideas in your head. You'd have more to talk to the other women about, don't you think?"

"But we've tried," I said, sitting up. "I've tried so hard. We even saw Dr. Lombardi, remember."

"But we should really try this time. We'll go to the best doctors; whatever it costs, we'll pay it. We'll spend more time together. It will be just about you and me, no one else."

He squeezed me tighter into his chest and I couldn't breathe. I could no longer see his face nor he mine, so I nodded. I wanted a baby more than anything. I knew I had enough love inside of me to make a happy life for a little child; I just knew it. Harry was not the perfect man and I had spent hours lying in bed alone, staring at the ceiling waiting for the click of the door to open or for the crack of light to shine into the bedroom to show that he was home, and in those hours I'd thought about how I could leave him, how I could experience true happiness, if that was even a possibility or just a fantasy. If I walked away I'd probably never have a baby. I'd be shunned, I'd be disowned and my chance at motherhood would pass me by forever.

"Okay, sweetheart?" he said. "Let's really try this time."

I nodded just a little, not sure what I was agreeing to.

15

❖

The waiting room was cold and devoid of color except for a thin bottle-green carpet. White walls were bare, with no hanging pictures of babies or happy families, or any other image that might help one think positive thoughts during her visit. I sat bolt upright in a metal chair in the opposite corner from the only other people, a concerned-looking couple, huddled together, he holding her hand in both of his. They looked thin and frail, especially the woman, the skin under her eyes a bluish grey, giving the impression that you could see everything going on under the surface of this woman. Maybe she wouldn't even need to disrobe; the doctor would simply take a look at her pale, almost transparent skin and would know immediately the solution to their problem. Perhaps he'd tell her she needed to take more sun or to eat more iron-rich chopped liver, cooked kidney or tripe and then she'd become impregnated.

The husband glanced up at me, perhaps feeling my gaze, and I quickly looked away, picking up a medical journal from the side table and flicking through the pages, wondering what they thought of me, in the waiting room alone.

I had been to the lady doctor before; in fact, it was a group outing in the first two weeks of college. One of the girls got a steady boyfriend and the talk started about taking "the natural next step." So a few of us went with Cat Fowler, big bosomed and wide hipped with a tiny waist and a confident smile. She made as if it were no big deal, four of us walking into the Birth Control Clinic, stuffing pamphlets into our bags that described everything from sponges to pessaries to coils to thimbles to jellies, while she asked for the name of a doctor. We hovered nervously in the waiting room, until we were kicked out for whispering too loudly, and out she walked with a small plastic box in her hand, holding the magic contraption that would allow her to engage in sexual intercourse freely without fear of an unwanted pregnancy.

Back in the dormitories we crowded into her room, sitting on the bed, the desk, wherever there was a space to see, while she removed her undergarments, took out the round plastic cap dusted with talcum powder, folded it the way the doctor instructed, then crouched down and stuck it between her legs while we all looked on in wonder. She then stood up and walked around the room, even did a little dance just to prove it was firmly in place.

Intentionally or not, I saved myself for my wedding night and never had the need for a diaphragm or contraceptive jellies or a douche bag that hung on the back of the bathroom door.

But this was an entirely different visit. I was not trying to block the happily swimming sperm from making their voyage to my ovaries with some rubber dam; I wanted instead to help them on their way, find out why they were getting lost or distracted or just lazy before they reached their destination. To save my marriage and to give myself a chance at motherhood I needed to expedite the process, and lately I had the feeling that time was running out.

Harry and I were trying to go back to normal, I suppose, but things still felt tense and distant between us, despite our talk about having a baby. We tried to be close before he went back to the city, but my body didn't loosen up and cooperate. It felt as though we didn't fit each other anymore.

And yet after he left, when alone at night, my mind wandered freely and my body seemed womanly and just fine. Falling asleep, I'd drift into different scenarios, my body relaxing into each chance encounter. I wondered what life would be like if I lived in a small town like Montauk, working hard to make ends meet, sitting down at the end of a long day with a big, busy family around the kitchen table, everyone ravenous. Hungry but happy, me cleaning the dishes as the kids got washed and changed into pajamas, putting them to bed one at a time, except for the older ones who put themselves to bed, dog tired, their long, awkward limbs hanging over the sides of the bed. After the kids were asleep, falling into bed tired but satisfied. The man beside me in the wood-framed bed, tired after working all day but eager for me. I imagined his body without his damp undershirt, the salt, the taste, the scent of him, and my body worked just fine.

They were silly thoughts, fantasies, but I needed to put an end to them if I still wanted to bring Harry back into my life and back into our marriage. Giving him a child would remedy everything, a child for him, for us and for his family. It was the missing piece and it was the thing that had sent our relationship into this awkward state of uncertainty for too long. If I could just get to that point, I was sure everything else would fall into place.

"Mrs. Bordeaux," the middle-aged woman with small, round glasses called my name, and I felt relieved that I'd be seeing a woman about this matter. But my relief was short lived.

"Take it all off," the woman instructed. "The brassiere, the girdle and the stockings," she said, handing me a robe as if this were the most ordinary thing in the world.

After she took my vitals and measurements in the examination room she introduced me to the doctor. He was completely bald except for a thin ring of wiry-looking grey that wrapped around the back of his head from ear to ear.

"Name?" he asked.

"Beatrice Bordeaux."

"Age?"

"Twenty-seven."

"Any pregnancies? Stillborns?"

"No."

"So," he said finally, peering at me. "What seems to be the problem?"

"Well." I shifted uncomfortably, pulling my robe around my body and crossing my arms over my chest. "My husband and I are trying to conceive a baby and we are having no luck."

"How long have you been trying?"

"Since we were married five years ago," I said.

"Ah," he said, pulling at the longest parts of his moustache on either side of his downturned mouth. "And how frequently do you engage in sexual intercourse?"

I blushed, then swallowed hard. This was, after all, the whole reason for my visit, so I had to be honest.

"Well, we used to engage quite frequently. . . ."

"How frequently?"

"Gosh, I don't know, two times a week." I was horrified to be telling this perfect stranger about my marital relations and I suddenly pictured him imagining them. I squeezed my arms tighter across my chest. "But lately it's been significantly less. Just once in a long while."

"Well, there is your problem," he said. "Lie back."

I did as I was told and felt all the muscles in my body tense up as he opened my robe and surveyed my body.

"You mustn't limit your sexual activity," he said. "In some women the cervix is too tightly closed and the only way to train the body to do its reproductive job is practice." He pushed down on my stomach with his cold hands, glanced at my breasts, gave them a little squeeze and a lift and told me to cover up and sit up.

I wrapped the robe around me tightly and once again crossed my arms over my chest. What did my breasts have to do with getting pregnant? He looked concerned, remaining silent, tugging on his moustache again and scratching the back of his shiny head.

"Are you an anxious woman?"

"Anxious?" I repeated. "I'm a little concerned about why I can't get pregnant. I'd like to have children, like every married woman."

"No, I mean in general, do you consider yourself to be a highly nervous person?"

I hadn't thought of myself in that way before, but I suppose I did feel anxious quite often, especially given the state of my marriage, my inability to become pregnant, and it was true that I didn't particularly enjoy the company of most of the women out at the Manor. I tended to avoid them, and my run-ins with Jeanie Barnes and her group left me somewhat unsettled, going over in my head what they had said and what they meant by it. Did that make me a highly nervous individual, I wondered, or did that just make me human?

"I wouldn't say highly nervous," I said, "perhaps moderately so, at times."

"Your body is very tense, under stress perhaps. Do you engage in relaxing activities? Do you knit or crochet? I often tell nervous patients to take up crocheting or knitting or needlepoint."

"Do you think there's something wrong with me?" I asked. "Or with my husband?"

The doctor gave me a puzzled look. "Is there reason to believe there's something wrong with your husband? Has he had mumps or chicken pox?"

"No."

"Has he been injured?"

"No."

"And does he fulfill his duties and perform during sexual intercourse?"

"You mean . . ."

"Does he climax?"

I cleared my throat. "Yes. Usually, I mean he sort of forces himself to, I think, unless he's drunk and falls asleep."

"Well, then clearly there are no problems with your husband. And you, do you climax?"

This was awful; I wished I had never set foot in this office.

"It's very important that you do," he continued. "The male sperm can only travel to the desired location if the woman reaches an orgasm and opens up the interior passages."

I looked to the floor and suddenly felt filled with grief. I couldn't remember the last time I had climaxed with Harry. It had been at least a year, maybe two. I didn't think it mattered and now I felt filled with shame and responsibility. This had been my fault all along.

The doctor must have sensed my disappointment, because he softened slightly. "What's important in situations like these is that you find a way to relax and nature will most certainly take its course. My suggestion for you is to take up relaxation in any way that feels right to you; rest, sleep in the afternoons before your husband arrives home, sew and at night relax with a small glass of brandy, every night." He jotted these thoughts down on a prescription pad, tore off the page and handed it to me. "Take this seriously," he said. "It's your duty to your husband and to America."

I nodded.

"And if it still doesn't work after you do all these things then you may just have to face up to the reality that you waited too long, that the opportunity has passed you by. How old are you again?" He looked down to his chart. I couldn't even remember my own age; the thought of missing my chance to become a mother just swallowed me whole. "Almost thirty!" he said with zest. "You're really getting on, maybe it's just too late, but try, really try. If nothing else do it for the sake of your husband and try to give him a son; the father always does better with boys."

As I walked out of the doctor's office and into the bright daylight outside on 34th Street I thought of President Roosevelt and his announcement that voluntary childlessness was an unpatriotic act. Had I been unpatriotic in my failure to climax? In my failure to conceive in my early twenties? I was light-headed and felt as if I needed to lie down. I went into a bar next to the Empire State Building, feeling miniature and insignificant. I sat down at the bar and ordered a brandy, double, knocked it back in one shot and ordered one more.

At the train station there was a commotion on the platform of the incoming train. Everyone was hurrying away from the last car and there were sounds of disgust and repulsion coming from passengers. I was on the opposite platform, but I could see that there was a general feeling of dissatisfaction from everyone who had been on board.

Eventually I saw a postal worker emerge from the train car covered in what looked like dirt, carrying two large cylinders. Everyone stepped away and clearly wanted nothing to do with him. Two men in suits next to me started laughing. "Poor bugger," one said. "Wouldn't want to be going home to him tonight," said the other.

"What happened?" I asked.

"Miss, you don't want to know," said one man.

"I do. I do want to know; please tell me. Is he okay?"

"This is the third time it's happened in a week. The diaper tubes exploded again 'cause of the heat. That poor fella just got sprayed with crap that came all the way from Montauk."

I put my hands over my mouth and gasped.

"You said you wanted to know."

The next few days I took the doctor's "prescription" seriously. I lounged at the Surf Club; the combination of sun and breeze felt good on my bare shoulders and legs. I kept going over in my mind what the doctor had said and it gave me alternate feelings of disappointment and newfound resolve. If all I needed to do in order to have a baby was relax and enjoy sex more, then I would do just that. Harry was planning to take a few days off work that week and come out on the Wednesday night train. I was determined to have some kind of metamorphosis before he arrived.

At the Beach Club on Wednesday Clarissa wowed us all in a printed linen halter top and swimsuit bottoms showing an inch or two of her midriff while Jeanie remained covered up in a floor-length hooded cape that looked more appropriate for the bathroom than the beach.

Clarissa was reading out loud from a dating advice section of *Parade* magazine and the others were chiming in.

"'Don't drink too much, as a man expects you to keep your dignity all evening,'" Clarissa read.

"Tell that to Betty's cousin Susan!" Kathleen shouted out, referring to a games night they'd attended at the yacht club where the woman in question had vomited on her way to the ladies' room from too much rum punch.

"'Don't use the car mirror to fix your makeup. The man needs it in driving, and it annoys him very much to have to turn around to see what's behind him.'" The ladies laughed.

"Oh, I use the car mirror to put on lipstick every time we go somewhere." Jeanie laughed.

"Me too," Kathleen chimed in.

"Oh, speaking of driving, Harry's taking the rest of the week off work. He and I are going to drive around and explore Montauk this weekend, just the two of us," I said. I was really trying.

"How lovely," Jeanie said. "Saturday, I hope, not Sunday; don't forget the golf tournament."

"Saturday," I said. "I thought I might order a picnic lunch from the Manor to surprise him; there are some beautiful trails up on the cliffs for walking."

The ladies all thought this was a wonderful idea and started chatting about how they should do that, too, sometime, and for a moment I felt that I was fitting in quite well and this prescription for relaxing was working.

"Yes, usually Harry doesn't take time out for himself to just relax and take in the beautiful surroundings, he's always going, one thing to the next to the next to the next, so I thought it would be good for him to slow down a little."

"Oh, Lord," Mary Van de Coop said. "My husband is such a lazy slug, I wish he'd get off his backside and do some more activities; all he wants to do is lie on the beach chairs and be waited on."

Everyone chuckled because it was so true; we'd all seen it.

"Okay, here's a good one. 'Do your dressing in the boudoir to maintain your allure,'" Clarissa continued to read. "'Be ready to go when date arrives; don't keep him waiting. Greet him with a smile!'"

"I agree with that," Jeanie said from her spot in the shade. "I didn't let my husband see me dress or get made up until we had been married for several months already. Even now I try to get dolled up in private; it keeps the mystery alive."

"And 'don't talk about clothes or try to describe your new gown to a man. Please and flatter your date by talking about the things he wants to talk about,'" Clarissa read.

"Well, that doesn't make sense," I said. "Why couldn't you describe a new gown to your husband? Especially if you plan to wear it in his company."

"Because that's boring to men," Jeanie said. "Fashion doesn't appeal to them."

"Oh, I don't know. Dolly works in fashion; I'll bet she talks to her husband about style."

Jeanie rolled her eyes. "Her husband's old, ancient; he probably can't even hear what she's saying." She laughed and the other women joined in.

"He's not old," I said, feeling protective of Clark. "And Dolly is anything but boring."

"He's got to be at least fifty," Jeanie said, "and she's no spring chicken either; she must be pushing forty. I don't know how her husband stands it. No children, she's out at work making those ridiculous hats while he's left to take care of himself. And now we find out she talks to him about nothing other than herself and fashion. What a horrific bore."

"She's the furthest thing from a bore." I couldn't stand to hear Jeanie talk of Dolly that way. I sat up and pulled my cover-up around my shoulders. "That's what makes her interesting," I said, "the fact that she has something else going on in her life besides parties and gossip."

"No children, though," Clarissa chimed in, almost absently, flicking through the next pages of her magazine. "It's so sad."

"Having a child doesn't make a person interesting," I snipped. I had liked Clarissa, but now she seemed as mean as the rest of them.

"I'm sorry, sweetheart." Jeanie sauntered over to me and put her hand on my shoulder. "I didn't know that childlessness was such a sensitive subject for you. You must feel quite a lot of pressure seeing all of us with our little darlings. Let's drop it, shall we? I don't want to see you upset."

"I'm not upset," I said, feeling the blood pump through my veins. "I just think you can all be terribly rude sometimes."

I stood up, grabbed my beach bag and walked to the concession stand. Once there I ordered a Coca-Cola and felt all eyes on me. After a few moments I heard the conversation start up again. I didn't look back. I drank my Coca-Cola down in one sitting, threw the bottle in the waste can and headed to the pickup area, where I flagged down George the driver.

"Back to the Manor, ma'am?" he asked.

"Yes, please, George," I said as he closed my door and walked around to the driver's side of the car. "I can't be around these people all the time; they drive me mad."

He nodded his head, turned back to the steering wheel and started the engine.

I made a beeline for the elevator. I didn't want to see anyone in the reception room or get pulled into any afternoon activity, but the front desk receptionist called my name.

"Mrs. Bordeaux, telephone message for you!" she called out, rushing over to me. "Your husband called. He said he's terribly sorry, but he won't be able to make it out to Montauk until next week due to work commitments."

"Oh," I said.

"Such a shame he'll miss the golf tournament." It was one more punch to the stomach. The doctor, the women and now this, after all that Harry had promised. "Perhaps you'll join the synchronized swimming class tomorrow, since you'll have more time on your hands without your husband to care for," she said, in an apparent attempt to cheer me up.

"I doubt that." I turned and made my way to my room.

❊

I sat down at the bureau, took my journal out of the top drawer and flung it open. I stared at the page for a moment and then closed it. I placed it back in the drawer and instead took out a piece of stationery and began to write.

There was an explosion at Penn Station on Monday, July 11th, involving a postal worker and a train attendant working in the last carriage from Montauk to New York City. Thankfully no one was seriously hurt, but the cause of the explosion is of unlikely means. The culprit was a cylinder packed to the brim with dirty diapers that New York City families, staying in Montauk for the summer, send back to their housekeepers in the city for cleaning and disinfecting, to be returned to them via the postal service.

As you can imagine, the stench and filth as a result of the explosion was quite unpleasant for all involved and it caused angry commuters to ask the question: Why do these wealthy families not take care of their own children's feces?

The women involved have reported that they simply do not have the facilities or the wherewithal to clean such things and the postal service and train is the best option available.

That's bad news for the postal train workers.

I signed it with my pen name, Jonathon Hubert, and slipped it into an envelope, attached a stamp and addressed it to Mr. Rosen. I then walked it down to the front desk and asked that it be sent out with the next mail collection.

16

—◦◆◦—

The next morning I went down to breakfast as usual, but as I descended the stairs I heard the noise of children and chatter, clinking glasses and plates. It was funny how during the week the children ate in a different room accompanied by the nannies with the doors closed separating the ladies from the children, but on the weekends, as if for show, some performance of how a family should look and behave, they sat together with their mothers and fathers in their Saturday and Sunday best.

I approached the buffet and picked up a plate, but nothing looked appealing, so I sat down at a small table by the window and picked up the morning papers from the table next to me. Nothing jumped out at me on the front page of *The Wall Street Journal,* so I glanced at *The New York Times.* "Construction Still Booming in Manhattan Despite Financial Hardship." "Winston Churchill Stays at the Waldorf–Astoria." "Howard Hughes Sets New Record in Flight Around the World." "Mayor Vows to Shut Down Hardlucksville on East 10th Street." I turned to the international pages: "European Countries Refuse Jewish Refugees at Evian Conference; US Accepts 30,000." "British Steam Locomotive 4468 Mallard Sets New Speed Record." I sighed. I didn't want real life.

Soon the nannies would start getting the children ready for a day at the beach or at the pool and the mothers would be preparing for their day's activities: tennis, golf, lounging in the cabanas. I couldn't face another day at the Beach Club.

I'd actually been excited to show Harry some of the Montauk that Elizabeth had shown me, a different side of the village he hadn't seen before. I thought he'd be impressed that I knew about some nature walks and trails that hugged the bluffs and took you all the way down to the water's edge at the very tip of Montauk Point. I felt rejected. And foolish. Harry had been so convincing. I'd almost believed him when he said he wanted to try harder, with our relationship and to have a baby, but I could already sense he was back to his old ways. It hurt to know that something else, someone else, was more compelling than I, more interesting, more worthy of his time and his affection.

I thought about the lighthouse keeper, how he'd stared at me with such interest, how that unnerved me. I wasn't used to being looked at that way, as if he wanted to know my innermost thoughts. It had made me uncomfortable at first, but now I craved it; I needed to feel that my company was worth something. I'd ask Elizabeth to take me with her again. But I couldn't, not really; I needed to be more careful for her sake. If people saw her spending too much time with me she could lose her job. I needed to respect her privacy and not jeopardize her livelihood.

I wavered back and forth, but in the end decided I'd go up there alone. I collected the lunch basket that the Manor kitchen staff had prepared for Harry and me, took out the wine and a sandwich and flagged down the driver.

George peppered me with questions, not content to let me go wandering off alone.

"Is there a gathering up there, ma'am?" he asked.

"No, I'm just exploring," I said.

"Will anyone be accompanying you?"

"No, just me," I said.

"Up at the lighthouse?" he asked, finally opening the door.

"In that general direction, yes," I said, exasperated, handing him a nickel as I climbed into the back seat.

"I'm sorry to badger you about your choice, ma'am," George said as he drove toward Montauk Road. "I just want you to be safe, and, well, I thought you'd want to be involved in all the commotion at the Manor, that's all."

"It's funny, George, but when the place is heaving with life and energy and families, that's when I feel lonely." I was finding it incredibly hard to forgive Harry, to forget what he'd done to us, especially when he didn't even bother to show up. It was what I didn't have that I yearned for. George caught my eye in the rearview mirror. "Harry was supposed to come out early for a few days this week, but now he has to stay in the city to work. And he'll miss the big golf tournament this weekend."

George nodded. "Ah yes, that's a real shame."

George stopped the car at the base of the pathway leading to the lighthouse. He climbed out of the driver's seat and opened my door.

"Should I come back in an hour?" he asked. "I'd wait, but I'm needed back at the Manor."

I stepped out and took a deep breath. The air felt cooler up here, fresher and cleaner; it immediately settled me.

"I might be a while," I said. "I need the fresh air. Can you pick me up at one?"

"But it's just past ten o'clock, ma'am," George said.

"I need some time; one o'clock would be wonderful."

"What should I say if anyone is looking for you?" he said, as if I were doing something wrong by not joining the group en masse and following along like a sheep to whatever activity might be planned for the day.

"George, really, tell them whatever you want; tell them I wanted to go for a walk. Believe me, no one will notice that I'm gone."

From the top of the cliffs I saw the white sailboats leaning with the wind, fishing boats and their guides taking the tourists to try their hand at catching striped bass, fluke and bluefish—the serious fishermen would have left hours ago and would be well out to sea or on their way back by now. The view from up there was clear and crisp and expansive. This wasn't the side of Montauk that the newspaperman had originally thought about capturing, but this was the part that took my breath away. All the chiffon and the headpieces and the small talk could be found in the city on any day of the week, but this place was alive.

I walked across the bluffs quite a way and followed a narrow pathway that had been cleared through the long grass and led down to the pebbled beach. There were boulders peeking out of the ocean not too far from shore, and on top of one lay a large, fat seal posed on its side, one flipper reaching up to the sky, letting the sun warm its enormous round belly. Another grey head bobbed in the ocean and that seal launched itself up onto a neighboring boulder. It let out a bark and the fat seal barked back.

I took out the half bottle of wine that I'd taken from the picnic basket and took a swig right from the bottle. I hadn't even bothered to bring glasses. It felt good going down—clean and crisp and cold. I took another gulp.

When you remove yourself from the chatter and the clutter of life, I thought, you can actually hear yourself think. The seagulls were talking in squawks overhead, the seals were barking, the ocean waves were rolling onto the pebbles and they were responding with a melodic crackling as the waves pulled back. I lay back on the beach and let the sun warm my skin.

It was still quite early when I made my way toward the lighthouse and when I stood and started walking I felt woozy from the swigs of wine. George wouldn't be back to pick me up for two more hours and I began to get a sickly feeling in my stomach that I'd made a mistake in asking him to leave me there for so long. I looked down the hill just to check that he hadn't changed his mind and decided to stay, but the car was out of sight.

There was no sign indicating when the grounds opened for visitors and I didn't want to seem like someone who showed up in places I wasn't supposed to be. Perhaps it's best to announce myself, I thought. If I'm here I should at least pop in and say hello to the keeper, I justified to myself; after all, I'd met him twice and he might be pleased to see a familiar face. I wanted to see him, think of a reason to talk to him. Momentarily I felt brave and adventurous, or defiant and tipsy. I gathered the nerve to go up to his door.

I looked around and didn't see anyone outside, so I knocked on the door to the right where Thomas lived. There was no answer. I tried it again, but no one came, so I stepped over and tried Mr. and Mrs. Milton's door on the left as Elizabeth had done. Still no answer.

I circled halfway around the tower past a small white shed, an engine room or storage space perhaps, but the doors were closed and there was no sign of anyone working, so I kept going around the base of the tower until I was in the very back, on the water side, close to the edge of the tall cliffs. Turning back toward the lighthouse, magnificent and tall, I saw a single seagull soaring high overhead. Green grass surrounded the lighthouse, and from where I stood, looking out at the hills rolling away from the tower, I felt strangely empowered, as if I had just discovered the most beautiful place on earth and it was all mine. I breathed it in, the fresh ocean air, the bright sunlight, the sound of seagulls, and I looked up to the top of the light, elegantly rising into the cloudless blue sky.

After a while I walked back to the front of the house and knocked again; then I placed my hand on the brass doorknob and turned. It clicked open. I stepped back, the door slightly ajar—I hadn't really expected it to open—then I looked around and stepped inside into a narrow corridor.

I shouldn't have been there, in that house. I was astonished at my own behavior, but something compelled me to stay, getting further and further away from all sense of familiarity. The walls, the floors, the shutters on the windows, everything was made of wood and either painted white or varnished. There were two small doorways, one opened to a living room with several pieces of wicker furniture, a rocking chair, an upright piano and a small center table with an oil lamp and a radio. A second led to a dining room with a few boxes stacked in the corner and a desk against one wall. It was neat and tidy but sparse.

"Hello!" I called out quietly.

There was a large door at the end of the corridor with a stained-glass depiction of the lighthouse in the center, but it was closed, so I turned and took a few steps up a wooden staircase. They creaked and I froze, my heart racing, waiting for someone to appear.

I climbed the stairs and stood on the landing. Another smaller, steeper staircase wound around and went into what looked like the attic of the house. On the floor where I stood there were two small bedrooms. A damp, musky smell filled the space and everything about the house, the colors, navy and white, and the textures, polished wood and wicker, seemed masculine, as if a woman hadn't lived there for a long time.

I stepped into the first bedroom. All I could see out of the window was the green grass that dropped off at the cliffs and beyond that the surf breaking against the rocks in the ocean. I could spend hours admiring that view. The bed was made up with crisp white sheets, clothes folded neatly at the foot of the bed and a picture of a young boy, age seven maybe, in a picture frame on a small desk across the other side of the room. I picked it up and looked into his eyes—he looked just like Thomas. Growing up in a lighthouse would be strange and lonely, I thought, and I was suddenly back in Pennsylvania, holding my mother's hand, walking the long walk to school, down the gravel pathway, alongside the lavender fields. My socks and sandals and halfway up my legs covered with dust by the time I got to school.

I placed the picture frame back on the desk and ran my hand across a large, well-worn leather book with the cream pages curled at the edges. I opened the front page and saw black neat handwriting, *Property of Thomas M. Brown*. Suddenly I heard the front door open, then close, and I gasped, slamming the book shut. Heavy footsteps climbed the stairs and I looked around for a place to go. There was nowhere; the only way out was the staircase. I looked around quickly, nothing was out of place, then I rushed out of the bedroom with a start, running straight into him as he was taking the final step onto the landing. He started to fall backwards, grabbed the handrail with one hand, and the other hand shot forward to balance him, whacking me right below my right eye.

I fell back against the wall and put my hand to my eye, feeling the blood rush to my skin.

"Oh my God," he said. "Are you okay? You almost knocked me down the staircase. What the hell are you doing up here?"

The back of my head began to pound where it had made contact with the wall. I suddenly felt dizzy as if I might pass out and closed my eyes, leaning back.

"Sorry," I said in a whisper. "I was . . . I just wanted to say hello." Even in my state of shock I realized how ridiculous that sounded. I opened my eyes and saw a look of confusion cross his face. I giggled. It was the wine. He was wearing a navy-blue uniform with brass buttons. "I like your outfit," I said.

"Are you okay?" he asked again. "I think you're going to have a shiner. I was just trying to . . . I swear, I didn't mean to . . ."

"I know." The dizziness was subsiding a little and my words were coming back to me.

"We'd better get you some ice," he said. "Can you stand?"

"I think so."

"Come on then." He steadied me. "Come down to the kitchen."

He took me by the hand and led me down two flights of stairs to a dark, dingy basement, which, when he lit a kerosene lamp, I realized was the kitchen. Even with the lamp it was damp and dark and dismal down there.

"Sit down," Thomas instructed, pulling out a chair from a kitchen table. As it scraped across the tiled floor it made a horrible screeching sound that hurt my head.

He pumped water into a glass from a black iron faucet and set it down in front of me, standing over me as I took a long sip.

"Listen, sorry about the eye," he said. "You could have gotten yourself shot, you know. We take intruders very seriously around here."

I nodded feeling terribly embarrassed.

He lifted my chin and examined the spot under my right eye where I could feel the blood throbbing violently. He looked so serious I thought

I might start laughing again. He let go gently and walked into another dimly lit room. I took the opportunity to fix my hair, straighten out my yellow day dress and untangle the gold necklace that Harry bought me when we first began keeping company.

"Here," Thomas said, returning to the room with a hunk of cold red meat in his hand. I scooted my chair away from him, but he walked right up to me, lifted my chin again and placed the meat on my skin, covering half my face. "This will make the swelling go down faster than ice and if we're lucky it might not go black." He took my other hand and placed it on the meat. "Hold this in place," he said.

I cringed at the smell and the drop of blood I saw on the floor where he'd walked over to me. "But I . . ."

"Don't worry; I'll fix something else for dinner."

"I need a napkin or something; it's going to drip blood all over my dress."

"Oh," he said, going to the kitchen cabinet and returning with a kitchen rag.

I felt a trickle of blood running down my hand and then my arm. He wiped it for me, then pulled up a seat opposite me at the kitchen table.

"Anything else I can get for you?" he asked.

I shook my head, though I was quite enjoying being taken care of.

"So what in God's name were you doing sneaking around the house anyway?" he asked. "I kid you not, this house is property of the United States Coast Guard and trespassers are taken pretty seriously. You could have gotten yourself arrested if you'd been breaking and entering in the other house." He nodded toward the wall of the adjoining house. "And thank your lucky stars I didn't have a shotgun in my hand; you could have wound up dead!"

"I know, sorry for all this commotion, I just . . ." I couldn't possibly say I was just popping in for a chat after I'd caused all this fuss. My head started to spin about how I would have explained any of this to Harry if I had been arrested and returned to the Manor in a police car, or if Harry had received a phone call at work that I was being held at the station. I looked up at him and realized he was waiting for an answer. "Well, it's just that I'm, I'm a journalist, actually," I said, feeling myself blush even more. "I write a column for *The New York City Reader* and I was thinking perhaps I could interview you about life at the lighthouse."

He looked confused. "You're a journalist?"

"Undercover," I said, and realized that sounded wrong. "I mean anonymous really; I use a pen name. You know how it is; people prefer to think they are reading from a man's mind rather than a lady's."

He nodded but looked unsure. I couldn't tell if he was buying it.

"I wrote about the greasy pig contest," I said, suddenly remembering we had that in common and I had published proof. "I could show it to you. But please don't tell anyone it was me; I'd be in a lot of trouble."

He looked very confused.

"So anyway, if it's not too much trouble I could certainly come back another time, or skip the interview altogether if it's not convenient."

"Well, I feel bad about the eye," he said, leaning over, moving the slab of meat from my eye, coming in close to take a peek, then quickly setting it back in position. "Keep it on there," he said. "It's definitely going to turn purple, I'm afraid. So what do you need to know?"

I gave him a blank stare.

"For the article?"

"Oh," I said, suddenly flustered, fishing around in my handbag for a scrap of paper and a pencil, but I couldn't seem to think of a single thing to say. "Well, um, I was wondering how long you've been a lighthouse keeper." I felt like a fraud and a fool.

"Eighteen years."

"Okay," I said, scribbling it down, trying to keep the paper still and write with only one hand, the other still pressing the meat against my eye.

"Eleven years here in Montauk, though I took a year off, as you may know. . . ." He paused waiting for a reaction.

"Okay," I said.

"I did about four years at Stratford Shoal, and another couple years at Race Rock," he said. I frantically tried to think of what to ask next, but luckily he kept going.

"I got the job at Stratford Shoal as a favor, mostly; they liked to help out the vets right after the war." He stretched and leaned back in his chair, putting his arms behind his head. He'd taken his jacket off and was wearing just a white T-shirt. His arms were strong and muscular when he sat like that, no wonder my face was throbbing so much. My mind started to drift to the day when Elizabeth and I had seen him climb down from the scaffolding.

"And then I moved around some from there," he continued.

I held on to the meat, trying to keep it from dripping on my dress. "And what are your primary duties here at the Montauk lighthouse?" I asked, looking at my pencil and wondering if I could manage to balance the hunk of flesh on my face if I tilted it back slightly while taking notes with the other hand.

He followed my gaze to my notebook and pencil. "Um, this seems difficult for you; why don't I show you around a bit?" he said, standing. "And then I'm really going to have to get back to work."

He led me up the stairs to the ground floor of the house, then through the large white door into another passageway. It was a small space that connected the keeper's house with two other rooms.

"This here is the oil room," he said, "and this one"—he motioned to the left—"is the radio room."

I peeked inside the first room and against the right wall there were large silver tanks with all kinds of pressure gauges, oil canisters and tools hanging on the wall. On the other side was another door.

"And that's the entrance to the tower," he said. I walked toward it so curious, wanting to ask to go inside, but he had already turned and was leading me back to the house. "We work in twelve-hour shifts, me and the assistant keeper and another assistant who lives away," he said, leading me out the front door and standing once again on the porch. "We work the lights, the foghorn, cleaning, polishing the lens, painting, cutting the grass, general maintenance, you know." He put his hands in his pockets and I sensed the interview was over. "How's the eye?"

"Good, I think," I said, lifting the now warm meat away from my skin and dangling it back toward him. "Maybe we could finish this another time when you're not so busy," I said.

He looked amused. It was the first time I'd seen anything resembling a smile since the night I talked to him at the Surf Club. "Maybe," he said. "But generally free time is a bit of a luxury for me. And I'm surprised you'd want to set foot back up here again after getting knocked down like that."

"I'll take my chances," I said, and walked down the pathway to wait for George.

17

The next morning was Sports Day on the village green. I'd tried to conceal the purplish-red half-moon under my right eye, but the cosmetics barely made a difference, so I put on a hat, pulled it down at an angle and wore my favorite sunglasses.

The children lined up excitedly wearing their name tags and numbers, each having signed up for his or her sport of choice: the relay, the wheelbarrow race, the egg-and-spoon race, the jumping sack. It was a frenzy of activity as nannies and mothers got every child in place, while the few men sat in deck chairs on the edge of the green sipping Pimm's Cups.

I hadn't expected to see Dolly there, but she was at a table set up near the finish line, looking fabulous as usual in a sporty jumpsuit and a white fedora with a green ribbon.

"What are you doing here?" I asked.

"Oh, how wonderful to see you," she said. "Come, sit." She pulled up another chair to her table. "You can help me give out the rosettes to the winners."

On the table in front of her was a large assortment of ribbons and rosettes in reds, greens, blues and yellows, decorated with jewels and feathers as well as more boyish options in navy and white stripes, adorned with twill and miniature anchors.

"These are so beautiful," I said. "Where did they find them?"

"Oh, I put them together with old scraps from the factory," she said, sorting through them. "I did it last year for the kids; this is one of my favorite events of the summer. This and the masquerade ball, of course."

"Really?" Dolly was one of those people who, just when you thought you had her figured out, did something that surprised you, showed you another facet of her personality. She was the last person I would have imagined seeing at Sports Day giving out handmade rosettes.

I sat at the table and pulled out my compact, lowering my sunglasses on my nose to see how I looked in daylight. Though it was ugly, something about it fascinated me. I touched the skin and felt a smile waver on my lips.

"Good Lord, what on earth happened to you?" Dolly said, horrified, pulling my sunglasses completely off my face.

"Oh, I know; isn't it terrible?" I said, reaching over and grabbing the glasses back from her. "I went for a walk yesterday by the bluffs and I tripped and fell. Thank goodness it was just below the eye."

"You fell? And that's how you got a black eye?"

"It's just a bruise. I bruise easily, that pale skin of mine."

"You should get that seen to," she said with great concern, having another good look.

"It's fine," I said, sliding my sunglasses back up my nose and pulling my hat down a little more.

The children were making a ruckus and the mothers seemed to be having a whale of a time, too. Jeanie had actually climbed inside a sack and pulled it up to her waist and was hopping across the lawn attempting to teach her son how to do the race without falling flat on his face each time. Clarissa was racing with her two daughters back and forth down the racetrack with an egg balanced on a spoon and her girls were winning every time. When the whistle blew they all quieted down and were told to arrange themselves by sport and age.

"I love to see the children like this," Dolly said. "All energized and allowed to be kids for a while. They are expected to act like little grown-ups half the time."

"Why did you never want to have children, Dolly?"

"Oh, Clark and I were too old when we met and married. Well, I suppose if we'd gotten right down to business we could have had one child, but we just wanted to have fun. And we did have fun, lots of it; we still do." She absently smoothed the ribbon tails of a rosette. "It's far too late for us now, but it's probably for the best."

I nodded, watching the first set of children get in position for the relay race.

"What about you, darling?" she said. "Any improvements in the bedroom and the baby making?"

"Oh." I tried to be upbeat, but it sounded false and tiresome. "Not really."

"Honey, it's so hard to make love if you're not in love." I tried to protest, but I ended up just shaking my head. "Unless, of course, he's a dashing young thing." She laughed. "Then it's somehow easy as pie."

The relay was in full swing and Dolly gathered up her first round of ribbons. "This is the fun part."

That afternoon while the children took naps and played at the pool and the adults lounged at the beach or out on the boats, I sat on the green overlooking the Long Island Sound. It had been twenty-four hours since I had broken into the lighthouse and the embarrassing incident had been constantly on my mind. Without pausing to question why, I found myself devising ways to go back. I should apologize for barging into Thomas's house; I wanted a chance to explain myself and not come off as some crazy intruder.

Not more than an hour later I borrowed a bicycle from the Manor and rode through town and along the Napeague Stretch almost all the way to Amagansett. I leaned it against a tall oak tree at the farm's roadside stand, which I'd seen on my first drive into Montauk from the city. My legs burned from the bike ride and I still had to make the return journey, but I felt compelled to make this right. Thomas probably thought of me as just another one of the Manor folk and I felt an overwhelming need to prove him wrong. I don't know why I cared what he thought of me, but I did. I'd drop off a peace offering, a basket of food perhaps, just to smooth things over.

The farm stand was spilling over with vegetables, red tomatoes on the vine, bunches of slim, green asparagus tied with twine, yellow and green zucchini, baskets of spinach and strings of herbs hanging from the slanted wooden roof. In a separate cart there were cheeses, and preserves and all sorts of baked goods. It would almost seem a shame to disturb anything, displayed so beautifully.

"Good mornin'." An older woman's cheery plump face peeked out from behind the vegetable cart.

"Hello there," I said.

"What can I get you? The corn was picked this mornin'; the strawberries are ready to eat. I've got fresh-baked bread 'round here and pies, peach cobbler, berry pie. . . ."

"Thank you, I need to make up a basket," I said.

"A picnic basket? Lovely," she said. "It's the perfect evening for it."

"Oh n-n-o, it's nothing like that," I stammered.

"I know just what you need," she said. "I'll be right back."

The lady returned with a wicker picnic basket and placed it in the front carrier of my bicycle to make sure it fit; then she took her time selecting the ripest box of strawberries, then tomatoes, arranging them carefully, next looking about her for what else to add.

She wrapped a small Pullman loaf in brown paper and cut an assortment of cheeses from a tray that she had brought from the farmhouse.

"How about one of these?" I said, pointing to a small blackberry pie.

"Perfect."

She finished off the basket with a small bunch of sunflowers, tied in place with string across the top.

As I opened my change purse, she placed a hand on mine. "What will you be drinkin'?"

I hesitated.

"My husband makes his own wine. We sell a few bottles."

She turned before I could think what to say, and when she bustled back from the house she was grinning and carrying a small jug of something; two jelly jars tucked under her arm. After taking the payment from me, she followed me back to the tall oak, where she helped me place the basket and myself on the bicycle.

"Good luck," she said.

"Oh really, it's nothing like that. I don't need luck."

"I meant on the ride back." She nodded toward the bike. "You've got some extra weight on there now, miss."

"Right, right, I'll be fine," I called back as I rode away slightly un-steady, wobbling, but managing to straighten up and gain my balance after I pedaled a few times. When I eventually felt sturdy I raised one hand to wave.

I arrived at the foot of the pathway to the lighthouse a little after six o'clock in the evening.

"A peace offering?" I said, holding up the picnic basket when Thomas answered the door. "For breaking and entering." I had rehearsed what to say blindly, not knowing if this visit was something I needed or instead a reckless mistake. Thomas looked startled by the sight of me and I had a sudden sinking feeling that it was a terrible idea and I should quickly turn around and leave.

"I should be waving the white flag," he said. "I was the one who al-most knocked you senseless. How's the eye?"

I lifted the sunglasses, completely unnecessary at this time of day, but which I'd been hiding behind since morning. "Not too bad." I smiled uncertainly.

"Not too good either," he said, lifting my chin and touching the pur-

ple moon shape gently with his thumb. "Geez. . . ." After a moment's pause
he opened the door all the way and stepped back to let me in.

I walked in slowly and felt my stomach drop as I passed him; what was
I even doing here? Yet I kept going down the hallway, hearing him close
the door and follow behind me.

"Have you already eaten?"

"No."

"Would you like to?"

"That's very kind. I usually eat in the kitchen," he said, "but it's not
often that I have company and it's hot and muggy down there today.

"Follow me," he said, taking the basket and leading me down the corridor that connected the house to the base of the lighthouse. I swallowed
hard and rubbed my sweaty hands together feeling grateful for his warmth
and kindness toward me. We kept going out a back door, down a grassy
pathway, past the oil room and toward the bluffs. A lone wooden table
and chairs sat a few feet from the edge of the cliff and we walked toward
it. His hair was wet and brushed back from his face, his clean white undershirt tight against his body and now and then I got a hint of lemon-scented
soap as if he'd just bathed. He looked rugged and outdoorsy, weathered,
not polished and artificial like Harry sometimes looked in his freshly
pressed suit, his hair slicked with brilliantine.

"This was kind of you," he said when we reached the table.

"Well, I actually owe you a steak, since you wasted yours on my eye."

"Oh, that?" he said. "I cooked that up." He grinned and I couldn't tell
if he was joking.

We arranged everything on the table, I cut up the tomatoes and laid
out the cheeses and bread. I set the strawberries and blackberry pie at the
other end of the table for dessert. I was pleased with the selection. Thomas
picked up the jug of wine and unstopped the cork.

"We don't have to drink it, obviously," I said.

"Why waste a good bottle of wine?" he said, pouring two servings
into the jelly jars. He raised his to mine, then took a swig.

"So what's all this about?"

"What I said earlier, a peace offering."

"You want more information? For the article?"

The article. I hadn't even thought about it since our conversation, nor had I thought about any further questions. I'd been so taken aback by the events the previous day that I'd almost forgotten about my claim to be a reporter.

"Well, you did say I should come back and climb the steps," I said, suddenly remembering his suggestion.

"Yes, during visitor hours." He laughed.

I shrugged. "I thought that was right now."

"Persuasive. What else do you want to know?" he asked. "For the interview?"

"Oh, we don't have to continue the interview now; we can finish it another time," I said, trying to buy myself time. I couldn't believe I was in this situation again, totally unprepared. He looked at me, waiting, and all I could think of were questions that I personally wanted to know the answer to. I wanted to ask what it was like to be alone up there at the lighthouse all the time. What had happened with his wife? I wanted to ask about the picture of the boy in the bedroom, how long he'd known Elizabeth and her husband, how it had been in the war, but nothing seemed appropriate or relevant to the supposed article.

I racked my brain for more predictable questions, but nothing suitable came to mind.

"Have you always lived here alone?" I asked finally.

He seemed serious, as if he had seen more than most, and hardened somehow. Small creases formed in the corners of his eyes, and a single shallow line ran across his forehead, the brown-grey beginnings of a beard, and a mouth that intrigued me.

"I don't really like to include personal information in these types of things," he said. "I just work here."

"Of course," I said.

"I don't mind talking to you; I just don't want it in the news."

"I understand completely," I said. I wanted to tell him to forget about the article, nothing was going in the newspaper. I had probably horrified Mr. Rosen with that diaper explosion story and had no idea if he would want a story about life at the lighthouse. It was hardly fashion and gossip. I wanted to tell Thomas he could talk to me about anything and I wouldn't tell a soul.

"How about you?" he asked.

"Me?" I realized I was holding my breath.

"Yeah, did you marry? Any family?"

I looked up at him and forced a smile, hoping he wouldn't push me to explain. "It just hasn't happened yet. My husband is . . ." I stopped myself; I didn't want to talk about Harry.

"Injured?"

"Oh no, nothing like that. He's just not around all that often."

He nodded and took another swig of his wine.

"He's busy, you know, with work and such. . . ."

"Is he good to you?" he asked.

"Yes, of course," I said; then, shrugging my shoulders, "In some ways 'yes' and some ways 'no.' But isn't that how it is for married people?"

"Sure," he said, "sometimes, but not always."

We sat for a while and both looked out to the horizon. I felt him glance at me from time to time.

"Do you ever get used to it, the ocean? Do you ever stop hearing it?" I asked.

"There's not one day that I don't marvel at that sea, and admire her power. Those waves are a constant rhythm in my mind; they're part of me. I left the sea once for about a year, thought I needed a change, a break from all this solitude." He looked up at me as if to check if I was listening. "But I missed the ocean. I can't imagine ever leaving her again."

We sat for a while and listened. Too often I felt a need to fill silence with some nervous banter, but I found myself letting go.

"What draws you to the world of writing?"

"Oh gosh, I'm not a real writer. I just like to remember the details of everyday life. If I don't write things down I forget them, they lose significance somehow, but once they are on paper they are preserved; they'll be remembered."

"I don't trust myself to remember the things I want to remember either," he said.

I had frantically written down every detail I could remember of Charlie's life when he died, terrified that I'd forget things he'd said and done. I even wrote down all the bad things, the things I wished I'd said, the fights I wished I hadn't started, the times I'd chosen to do something other than spend time with him, the look of disappointment on his face when I stole a bag of candy from his room, the one and only time I pushed him off his bike and the look of shock on his face when I did so and the silent treatment after that stung the most. But I had ripped up those pages, wanting to preserve only the good.

"The tricky thing about the mind is its ability to hold on to the times you want to forget," I said.

"A lot of soldiers came back from the war perfectly intact, you know, all four limbs attached," he said, "but it's their mind that kills them in the end; they can't get the horrors they saw out of their heads." He took a sip of wine. "It's a hard thing. Anyway, how did we get on to such somber talk?"

I laughed. "No idea."

He looked at me and smiled. "Maybe I could take you up to the top of the light later, if there's time."

I felt a jolt of excitement run through me. "I promise I won't tell anyone it was after hours."

But we didn't move. After a while the orange and pink sunset lit up the horizon and then everything around us turned a brilliant deep blue, that final transformation as day turns into night. It only lasted a few minutes and then everything deepened, turning hazy grey; the horizon began to disappear, the ocean merging with the sky. I knew I should have left already, but I couldn't bring myself to end the evening. Within minutes darkness enveloped us, the grass looked black beneath our feet, the only light came from the moon and the stars in the clear Montauk sky.

"We should have packed up before it got dark," I said.

"I should have brought a lamp," Thomas said, starting to put everything back up into the basket. "But we'll manage."

When we walked up toward the house it was pitch black and I realized how long we'd been sitting out there, enjoying the summer evening. The light towering above us was sending a beam nineteen miles out into the ocean, but not even a glimmer of that was lighting our path. He placed his hand gently upon my shoulder, leading the way for only a moment, along the wall of the lighthouse; then he walked a few steps ahead. My eyes fixed on the glowing white of his shirt, and if my hands had been free I might have reached out and grabbed the shirt, letting it lead me back to the house. If someone had seen me then, walking in the darkness, alone with a man who wasn't my husband, whether it was in innocence or not, it would have been a scandal, a black mark on my reputation and on Harry's, but in that moment I really didn't care.

We kept walking and all of a sudden there was a thud and the sound of plates crashing into pieces as the picnic basket spilled open. Thomas's white shirt was gone from my line of vision, and when my eyes followed the sound I saw Thomas lying in a dirt ditch about six feet deep, surrounded by shards of white porcelain.

"Jesus Christ," he moaned. "Damn it."

I dropped to the ground and saw that he'd fallen into a trench of some sort that was half-dug near the outer wall of the lighthouse.

"Damn it, damn it," he said. "God damn Milton. We weren't going to start the foundation check until after the weekend."

"Are you hurt?" I asked.

He stopped cursing and glared at me. "No, sweet girl, I'm not hurt; I'm just making a hell of a fuss about nothing."

I grimaced. "Fair point. What hurts?"

Pulling himself up to standing, he was still deep in the ground, only his shoulders and head at grass level. "My ribs, oh hell, it hurts to talk, and my ankle, God, I hope it's not broken, but it's surely sprained."

"Should I go and get help?"

"No," he said firmly. "If you get injured out here, you get replaced." He put his hands on either side of the ditch and tried to heave himself up, but it caused him more pain and he wrapped his arms around his rib cage.

"Wait," I said, getting down on my knees and attempting to hook my arms under his arms, to hoist him up, but it was no good. The feel of his strong arms and shoulders under his thin shirt made me realize there was no way I could help him out of there. He shook himself free of me.

"I can do it," he said. "Stand back; we don't want you falling in here as well." But a second attempt failed; the combination of his inability to put weight on his foot and the painful bruised or broken ribs left him stuck.

"Wait, before you do any more damage, what if I could find something for you to stand on so you don't have to pull yourself up so much?"

"There's a ladder in the shed over there by the outhouse," he said, pointing to a vague black outline about one hundred feet from the house. "Keys are hanging up just inside the front door of the house."

"Okay," I said, determined and focused. "Stay right there. I mean, just, don't move."

He tried to laugh, then bent over holding his ribs again. "I'm not going anywhere, darlin'."

I grabbed a few of the biggest pieces of broken porcelain and dropped them in the picnic basket, threw in the empty wine jug and glasses and walked briskly up to the house.

"I'll be right back," I called over my shoulder.

The keys were lined up neatly and labeled on hooks just where he had said they'd be. I took down the one that said "work shed," noting the "outhouse" key next to it and hoping I could wait until I got back to the Manor before I had need of it. I'd read in a tourist's guide in the Manor lounge that they'd only electrified the keepers' dwellings earlier that year, so it seemed that this remote lighthouse was one of the last places to get up to date with modern amenities.

Thomas pointed toward the shed as I walked back down the hill. "That way," he said. "Watch your step; the ground's uneven over there." I took small steps with my hands outstretched in front of me, scared that I'd be the next one to fall. I unlocked the first shed and stared inside the pitch-blackness waiting for my eyes to adjust. Finally, I could make out the shape of a medium-sized wooden ladder and I wrestled it out of the shed onto the lawn. Then I pulled a rake from a collection of shovels and hoes, thinking it might work as a temporary walking stick; then, stopping every few minutes to wipe the sweat from my brow, I dragged them back to where Thomas was. I lowered the ladder down to him.

First he tried to hop up the rungs so he wouldn't put pressure on his ankle, but this seemed to cause excruciating pain in his ribs, so he tried a different approach, climbing very slowly, hooking his arms over the top rung, then pulling himself up. I wanted to help, but I didn't know how, so I just held the ladder steady and gradually he made his way to the top, climbed out and held his leg.

"It's not broken," he said, sitting up. I carefully helped him up to standing. He seemed to be in a lot of pain but trying not to show it; then he attempted to put weight on his right foot but couldn't.

"I'm not going to be able to walk on it for days. God damn. Once Milton gets word of this he'll be writing to the board for my position and they'll send me back to some remote location like Redcliffe. Unbelievable."

"Then don't tell him," I said.

"I can't work like this," he said. "I can't even walk, let alone climb up the tower."

"Can't someone help you?" I said. "How long will it take to heal, a couple of weeks?"

"At least."

"I'm sure someone can help you out."

"They can't; everyone's got their own business; this is a round-the-clock job."

"I could help you."

He let out a snort and shook his head.

"I could," I said, more determined. I steered him to the side of the light-house, where he could lean his weight on the wall, then went back to get the rake. "Here," I said, handing it to him upside down, "a walking stick." He was holding his right foot off the ground, so I placed the rake in his right hand and arranged myself on the left side of him, swinging his arm over my shoulder and wrapping mine around his waist.

"I can manage," he said, switching the makeshift walking stick to his other arm and using the wall instead to steady himself.

"Don't be ridiculous," I said, positioning myself back at his side and taking the first cautious step. "I'm here, so let me help you; put your weight on me."

His side pressed closely against mine, which felt warm and strange to be so close to another man like that, and within minutes we were both perspiring. I concentrated on getting him up the steep hill using only one leg, a rake and me as support. I could tell he didn't want to put his full weight on me, so it made for slow going. We didn't speak; we just walked, focused, determined. Finally, we hobbled through the front door and into the living room, where he collapsed into the armchair, beads of sweat dripping from his brow. I set the makeshift walking stick next to his chair, removed my cardigan, then went to the kitchen to fetch us some water and to give him a minute to catch his breath. When I got down there I had to sit and catch my breath, too. I felt so guilty. This was all my fault. I shouldn't have come, selfishly trying to fill my need for company. I had just felt so lonely, even being around all those people at the Manor, and I had a strange compulsion to trust this man. But now, by imposing myself on him and by staying past nightfall, I had complicated his life. I had to try to fix it.

Back upstairs I slid a footstool across the room, propped up his injured leg and rolled his trouser leg to his shin. Carefully loosening the laces of his boots, I removed his boot and sock slowly. Even the slightest movement made his whole body tense. Holding his foot and ankle gently in my hands felt so personal. I tried to channel the detachment a doctor would have while delivering a baby, or a surgeon cutting into someone's flesh for a lifesaving operation or my mother applying cold compress after cold compress to a sick child's forehead in the nurse's office when a fever wouldn't break.

"Oh, that's not good," I said, pressing gently on the outer side of the ankle and the top part of his foot, which was already swelling and had the beginnings of a purple bruise. "There's been quite a bit of damage here."

He peered down at his swollen foot. "I felt a pop when I went down."

"You must have torn some ligaments. There's already a lot of fluid buildup. If you can, try to move it slightly so the fluid doesn't accumulate."

"What, are you a doctor and a writer?"

"My mother volunteered as a nurse." I stood up. When I was younger, I'd thought that I could be and do anything, naïvely switching goals and ambitions week by week, day by day—a nurse, scientist, or even a doctor, a professor. As a kid anything seemed possible; in the real world, though, nothing was. Youth gave us an inflated sense of possibility, that you could achieve anything if you really went for it, but it felt as if you'd have to fight your whole life to get there, and most of us just got married and had children.

"Now what about your ribs?" I didn't know much about how to heal those. He lifted his shirt and tried to take a look, but even that seemed to hurt and he put his head back against the armchair and took a deep breath. I laid my fingers gently where a large bruise was already taking shape. "How do we know if it's broken?" I asked.

"I have no idea."

"Don't move. I'm going to get ice."

"There's an icebox in the pantry in the back of the kitchen."

"I remember." It had been one full day since I'd taken those rickety wooden stairs down to the basement kitchen and been sternly told to drink water and hold cold steak to my eye, and now here I was, tending to this man's injuries. If it weren't so painful for him it would almost be comical.

I turned on the light in the kitchen and after a few moments the room glowed tentatively. I took two kitchen towels to the icebox and filled them with ice, gathered the corners and looked for something that could secure them. The kitchen, like the rest of the house, was immaculate, nothing left out, as if no one actually lived there. I unbuckled the narrow fabric belt from my dress, tied it around one of the ice packs and took them back upstairs.

"I think we should move you to the settee," I said when I got back to the living room. "You can lie down and elevate your ankle."

"I'm fine here," Thomas said.

"You're not; you're going to need to sleep eventually," I said, helping him up and leading him to the settee on the other side of the room. "You'll never make it up and down those stairs to your bedroom, at least not tonight."

I rearranged the cushions, one for his head and the rest stacked at the other end to raise his ankle. "The bruising is the blood pooling from the damaged ligaments inside, so you need to keep it elevated." I placed his leg atop the cushions, held the belted ice-filled kitchen towel on his swollen ankle and placed the other on his rib cage and told him to hold it in place. "If we can't get this swelling down you'll have to see a doctor."

"No need for that, I'll be all right, just need a few days."

"You want to be sure it's not broken."

"It's not broken," he said with a sigh of exasperation.

I sat at the far end of the settee holding the ice in place on his ankle. I remembered from my mother tending to sprains and twists that my brother and I had endured growing up that the first few hours were the most important to reduce swelling.

I looked around at the sparse and functional decor. The keepers' dwellings were closed to the public, but he kept his looking like a museum, nothing out of place, not even a book lying open on the wicker coffee table.

After fifteen minutes or so the ice had melted and was dripping through the towel. Thomas had his eyes closed and I wondered if he might be drifting off to sleep, so I removed the wet towels, took them down to the kitchen and wrung them out; I could fill them again later. Quietly, I walked up the stairs to his bedroom.

The single bed was made up. The sheets folded over a blanket that had been neatly smoothed out with not a single crease. I peeled back the blanket to take downstairs and tried to leave the rest of the bed as neat as possible. On the desk across the room where the picture of the young boy stared back at me I saw several leather-bound books, one labeled "Inspections," another labeled "Duties and Schedules" and the same unnamed one that I had noticed the day before. I opened the "Duties and Schedules" book and looked for the day's date. Each day's duties were organized under three names, Head Keeper: Thomas Brown, First Assistant: David Milton and Second Assistant: Bill Worthington. I knew that Milton lived in the attached house next door, and Thomas had said the other assistant lived somewhere else, perhaps in town. They worked twelve-hour shifts in rotation to man the light and the foghorn and an additional six hours of maintenance duties every few days. Milton had begun his shift at 6:00 p.m. and would conclude at 6:00 a.m., at which time Thomas was expected to hold a meeting with the three keepers, assign duties for the day and then take over from Milton and begin his twelve-hour shift.

As I walked toward the door I noticed that hanging on the back was Thomas's uniform, pressed and pristine, navy like an officers', buttons polished, the creases in the arms and legs sharp. The formality of the uniform alone commanded attention and respect. I took it from the peg and carried it downstairs.

Thomas's eyes opened when I placed the blanket over him and he looked a little startled.

"I checked your schedule; it looks like your shift starts at six," I said softly. "Please don't object," I said when I noticed his surprise. "I'll sleep upstairs and help you to your station in the morning. Where will you be, manning the light?"

"No, the foghorn, no need for the light in the day."

"Of course," I said. "I'll get you situated."

"You can't; if Milton or Worthington sees you I'll get reported, and word might get out to your folk as well. It won't go down well."

"I'll stay upstairs. Besides, I have no way of getting home tonight; it's too dark." I thought for a minute about how I'd get back in the morning. "I'll ride the bike back; I'll leave early in the morning after your meeting."

"Elizabeth comes tomorrow; she'll probably have Patrick's car," he said.

"Good, then I'll get a ride back to the Manor with Elizabeth. I'll just explain what happened."

He looked out the window to the black sky. "Why are you doing this, Bea?" he asked.

Only my family back home called me Bea; I felt a wave of familiarity and comfort when he said it. "Doing what?"

"It's dangerous ground you're treading on, you know. I don't think your husband would like it."

"I want to help," I said, feeling determined at the thought of it, "and I feel responsible for all of this. If I hadn't come over here, bothering you, in the first place you wouldn't be in this mess." I walked to the windows and drew the curtains. "I'll get more ice."

"And a whiskey if you don't mind."

Upstairs in the bedroom I stood in front of his single bed. My throat burned with the peaty taste of whiskey I had swigged in the kitchen. I took off my shoes and placed them at the foot of the bed, then sat down on top of the sheets in my dress, now beltless and dirtied with mud at the hemline. After smoothing my hand across the sheets I lay down on the bed. I wouldn't be able to sleep here, in this strange room, thinking of Thomas downstairs, thinking of my bed standing empty at the Manor. I picked up a pillow and Thomas's work boots from behind the door and made my way back downstairs.

"Probably best if I sleep down here," I said, setting the pillow on the armchair. "In case you need anything."

"Suit yourself," he said, "but you'd be far more comfortable upstairs."

"I'd feel better here. Can I get you anything for the pain?" I asked. He picked up his whiskey glass and gave it a little shake. "Good idea," I said.

I came back a few minutes later with the bottle and an extra glass.

"It's easy to drink your head off out here," he said, "especially in the winter when no one comes by. I've seen it happen, lost good keepers to booze."

"Even during prohibition?"

He laughed, then grabbed his ribs. It was a stupid question; everyone drank who'd wanted to drink regardless of the law. I'd seen that every-where.

"We had boats come around and anchor off Scott's Cove. They'd come in at high tide: the old assistants would run a fishing boat out to them, row in several crates of booze, store it in the basement until the next morn-ing when someone would come pick it up and they'd get paid in bottles and cash."

"You were rumrunners?" I asked, fascinated.

"I got paid for keeping my mouth shut and turning a blind eye. Could have lost my job, all of us could, but it paid a pretty price, too good to pass up. I'd never make that kind of money again in my lifetime."

I felt the warmth of the whiskey flowing slowly through my body, and I hoped it was loosening his muscles and easing the pain.

"I got it all saved for a rainy day, but the others drank it all away." His eyes were closed now and his voice was getting softer and softer. "Some-times you just have to take the opportunity that's in front of you, even when you know it's not the one God would want for you."

Eventually he stopped talking. I watched him for a moment until his breathing got deeper, less pained. And soon I closed my eyes, too, falling deeply into what I had thought would be an impossible sleep.

18

⸭

It was light out when I blinked, looked around the room and took a moment to remember where I was. My neck was stiff from sitting upright in the armchair and a soft brown blanket covered me. There was no sign of Thomas; his cushions had been rearranged to their original order on the settee. I jumped up to check the grandfather clock in the hallway and on my way out the door I noticed Thomas's uniform was gone. It was a quarter to six. I rushed to the stairway and heard movement in the room down the hall. I tiptoed back into the living room and hid behind the door unsure if it was Thomas or if it was one of the other keepers. A door opened and I heard a step, then a clunk, then a step and I knew it was Thomas using his makeshift walking stick. I peeked from behind the door and he half-smiled, all dressed and clean-shaven.

"I didn't want to wake you," he said. "You looked peaceful."

"How did you manage to get dressed?" I asked, suddenly aware of the fact that I hadn't brushed my teeth or my hair since the morning before.

"It's taken me about half an hour to get this far," he said, standing barefoot. "Those tower stairs are going to be a real son of a bitch tomorrow night." He sat on the edge of the settee and carefully tried to pull a sock over his ankle. "Actually, would you mind?" He nodded to his socks. "Damned humiliating that a man can't even get his socks on."

I knelt down and felt around the ankle and foot. "It's still very swollen."

"I'm never going to get my boots on," he said.

"We should wrap it; that will help with the swelling."

I went to the linen closet upstairs and brought down a sheet. "Mind if we cut this up? It will work as a bandage until I bring something more suitable from town."

He took it from me and tore it into strips, which I carefully wrapped around his ankle. "The other one looks fine," I said, lifting his trouser leg and noticing his muscular calf and tanned skin.

"Why, thank you," he said, chuckling. "The other one is fine." I quickly dropped the trouser leg, felt the blood rush to my cheeks and went back to the wrapping. "I'm just teasing," he said.

I smoothed my hair, mumbled something about needing a hairbrush and hoped the tingling sensation that spread all across my body wasn't showing itself as a nervous rash.

We came up with a plan. I'd help Thomas get to the breezeway early, the little room that connected the house to the oil room and the radio room, where he'd conduct the morning meeting and assign duties; he'd already be standing when they arrived and then he'd send them on their way before he would head to the fog tower so they wouldn't notice the injury or his limp. I would wait for him in the downstairs office behind closed doors and when the others left I'd help him to the fog tower; then I'd go to the upstairs bedroom and watch from the window for Elizabeth to arrive.

I listened for my cue from the office, and when Worthington tried to lollygag in the breezeway after the brief meeting Thomas told him firmly to get on his way, something about an inspector coming that month and things needing to be in top shape. When everyone had gone I tiptoed out of the office and brought Thomas his walking stick and helped him to the engine room. Everything went according to plan; then I went up to the bedroom and waited.

It was almost noon when Elizabeth finally pulled up at the bottom of the hill. I had dozed in an upright wooden chair from seven until about nine o'clock but hadn't dared to close my eyes after that in case I missed her. The night before it had all seemed so practical, to stay and care for an injured new friend, but as the morning started to bloom, the sun starting to burn the fog off Turtle Hill and making everything look clear and bright, my stomach began to tighten. My foot twitched nervously against the chair leg and I picked at my cuticles until my thumb began to bleed. Late last night, with darkness everywhere, no one around except for us, I had no choice. What good person would leave in such circumstances? But now spending the night seemed reckless, dangerous. I was disappointed with Harry and still hurt no matter what my intentions were to forgive and forget, but I was suddenly scared of being caught in this situation. He would absolutely not approve and I didn't want to crumble whatever chance we had left of salvaging our marriage and having a child. I waited for Elizabeth to approach the front porch before I ran down the stairs to meet her.

"Thank God you're here," I said, hugging her, so relieved that I'd made it through the night and those early morning hours without being seen; if anyone caught sight of me now they'd think we arrived together.

"Oh my God, what happened to your eye?" She looked at my face and then at my muddy dress.

I'd completely forgotten about the black eye. "It's nothing. It was an accident."

She stood stiffly as I hugged her. "Beatrice, what are you doing here?" She looked around anxiously.

"It's fine, it's fine; don't worry," I assured her. "Thomas fell and got hurt, but he's going to be okay. I helped him," I said in a whisper.

"What do you mean? Why are you here? Did you fall, too?"

"No, no."

I explained about the food basket and the trench that Milton had dug prematurely and the sprain and the ribs and the necessity to keep Thomas's injuries a secret, but Elizabeth still didn't seem to be hearing me. I told her I had the laundry bags tied up and ready by the door. "Would you mind dropping me off at the Manor on your way home?" I asked. But she still looked confused and slightly angry.

"I know it's a little unusual, but I really had no choice," I said, willing her to understand. "Will you walk to the fog station with me? I just want to tell Thomas that we're leaving." She hesitated. I pulled at her hand gently and she followed me out the back door.

The fog signal had been emitting a blast every fifteen seconds or so since 6:00 a.m. The morning fog had been thick and dense but had finally cleared up and the signal had become less and less frequent.

"Well, we're off then," I said.

Thomas was sitting on a chair, ankle propped up on a pipe with six or seven glass lanterns on the floor around him, one in his hand that he was busy polishing. He looked up at Elizabeth sheepishly. "I went and fell down a godforsaken trench," Thomas said, nodding to his propped foot. "Bruised or broken a rib and then this stupid ankle."

"That's terrible," Elizabeth said. "You should have sent for help; you know Patrick would have come up and helped you out."

"Appreciate that," he said. "But your friend here has been very helpful. A real Florence Nightingale." He laughed dryly and I looked at the ground feeling I was being made fun of.

"Well, I saw the laundry bags by the door," she said. "Is there anything else I can help with?"

"No, no, I'll be all right. It's a pain in the neck, but I should be back on my feet in a few days, with a bit of luck." He nodded in my direction, a nod of acknowledgment, I thought.

"I'll be back around dinnertime," I said, "with something to eat. And I'll ice and rewrap the ankle."

"You don't have to," he said, looking away from me and focusing on polishing the glass on the lantern.

"It's fine," I said. "I'm happy to help." I turned and walked toward the exit. Elizabeth lingered a moment, then followed. We walked through the house, picked up the laundry bags and headed to the car in silence.

The engine roared, but we remained quiet. I had so much I wanted to tell Elizabeth. I wanted to tell her about the previous evening, but also about the fear and anxiety sitting in the pit of my stomach from what I had committed to. I wanted to confide in her, but she just seemed angry.

"I was so glad to see you pull up," I said. "I had my fingers crossed that your husband would let you use the car today, otherwise I would have taken the bike back, but I borrowed it from the Manor and I didn't want them noticing me returning too early in the morning." I waited. Elizabeth had kept her eyes on the road, but when I stopped talking she looked over to me.

"What are you up to, Beatrice?"

"I know it's not ideal, but who else is there to help?"

"Me, my husband. You could have contacted us; we would have helped."

"You have kids to take care of, you have work to do and so does your husband. You said yourself this is your busy time of year. Thomas needs assistance at odd hours; he needs someone to wait around so he can get up and down the stairs, continue his work shifts as if nothing happened. I can do that; I've got nothing else to do. I'm glad to be able to help."

"And if you get caught, then what happens?"

"Well, it's not as if I'm doing anything wrong!" I felt like a kid being reprimanded by her mother. "Where's the harm in helping out someone in need?" I said. "A man, whose job it is to prevent ships from crashing into the cliffs, is injured. If he can't work people could die." I needed to stop talking and justifying; it was making things worse.

"There are livelihoods on the line here," she said. "Thomas is a good man, for God's sake; he's been the head keeper for years. This isn't a game."

The excitement I'd felt the night before had come to a silent halt. "I'm not trying to cause trouble; I'm helping. You don't understand. They can't know that Thomas got hurt; otherwise they could replace him."

She said nothing, just drove. "Do you have any laundry?" she asked flatly.

"Not much really, Harry didn't bother coming out this weekend, so it can wait."

We pulled up to the back entrance of the Manor and Elizabeth sat still, killed the engine and turned to me. "I know you're trying to help, Beatrice, you are a kind person, you're not like the others who summer here, but you're different from us whether you want to be or not." I shook my head; I didn't know what to say. "Please just be careful, for your sake and for Thomas's. It might be a kind gesture, but you don't want it to spiral into something more than you can handle." I opened my mouth to correct her, dispute what she was saying, but there was nothing I could say that I hadn't already. "But if you are going to do this, to help, and I can tell you are, no matter what anyone says, then you need to be smart about it. You can't be spending the night up there. You just can't."

"It wasn't like that . . . ," I said.

"It doesn't matter. You need a way to get back here when your work is done."

"I'll borrow the bicycle from the Manor again."

"Well, I doubt you can keep doing that without raising suspicion. I have a bicycle you can use. Come by the house later and you can take it."

I leaned over and hugged her. She patted my back twice and I felt her thin frame heave into a big sigh.

"Thank you," I said through the window as I closed the car door. "That means a lot."

I walked in through the service door and took the back stairs to my room. Once inside I closed the bedroom door and leaned against it. I ran a hot bath, took off my filthy dress and wrapped myself in a towel. Then I called down to the front desk.

"Are there any telephone messages for me?" I asked.

"No, Mrs. Bordeaux, no message, I'm afraid."

"Not to worry," I said, feeling a deep sense of relief that no one had been looking for me.

"Oh, but Mrs. Bordeaux, you have received a letter."

"Oh," I said. "Thank you; does it say who is the sender?"

"Yes, ma'am, it's from a Mr. Rosen in New York City. I'll have a porter deliver it to your door."

"That's all right," I said, remembering, with a shiver of embarrassment, the hastily scribbled article about the dirty diapers I'd sent him a week earlier. "Don't bother; I'll collect it from the desk when I come down."

Now, I thought, as I stepped into the steaming water, what to make for dinner?

19

―❈―

I didn't have much experience in the kitchen. Harry and I dined out at restaurants often and on many occasions he had business dinners, so I didn't bother to cook for just one. My repertoire was still mostly what I'd learned from my mother growing up. Chicken soup was served, or any soup, for that matter. In my mother's house most meals I could think of were created to use up leftovers—stews, casseroles, soups, creamed anything on biscuits—and I could barely remember the original meals that the leftovers came from.

When Harry and I had dinner parties we had a maid come to cook and serve; it was the way his parents had entertained. Harry made cocktails and my job was to make sure our guests were comfortable, taking their coats, making small talk. I always made a point of whipping up dessert—people liked to compliment the hostess on the dessert—but the maid always served it.

For Thomas, I decided to buy fresh local fish from the fishmonger and make a tomato and peppers sauce from a recipe I'd seen in a magazine at the Manor. It seemed simple enough, and with the full kitchen at the lighthouse and several hours before Thomas's shift was over, this seemed the perfect time to try it.

The fishmonger packed the striper in ice and I rode Elizabeth's bike to the local grocery store, where I bought ingredients for the sauce and my absolute favorite, Chocolate Cherry Fluff Pie. It was always a crowd pleaser, but as I placed the items in the basket of the bicycle and began to ride up to the light, I wondered if I should rename it something a little more sophisticated—Choc-Cherry Supreme or Cherry and Chocolate Delight.

I let myself in through the front door and found him in his downstairs office, at the back of the house.

"I didn't hear you come in," he said, startled. "Did you knock?"

"I didn't want you to get up to open the door," I said. Things seemed suddenly formal between us. The air of familiarity, of drinking whiskey until we fell asleep across from each other in the living room, and our morning plan to get him to his station without anyone noticing seemed far from where we stood now.

I took a deep breath. At the Manor I'd been excited to return. It was the thrill of being helpful and needed, I think, probably heightened by the fact that it was this man who needed me—a man who seemed very much in control and confident in so many other ways. But there was also something about him that had me feeling out of sorts. I was a married woman and I respected that of course, but I couldn't deny the rush I felt when I was near him and able to be useful. I supposed most women felt satisfied by cooking and caring for their families, but with no children and a husband who was rarely around, an injured patient had seemed an ideal and rather interesting distraction. Yet returning here things seemed tense and I wondered if I'd made it all up in my mind.

"Well, I'll start on dinner. I've got work to do if this is to be ready for this evening." I nodded and turned, walking back through the house.

"Very kind of you!" he called out softly as I took the stairs down to the basement kitchen.

—✦—

There were no windows and a single overhead lamp glowed. I set out all the food I'd purchased on the long wooden table in the middle of the room and stared at it as the light warmed up and spread in an otherwise pitch-black room. I didn't know where to begin; suddenly the idea of cooking a meal and dessert felt daunting. I decided to start with dessert, as it would need time to set.

It took me about three times as long as it should have just to navigate my way around the kitchen. I opened every cupboard and drawer to see what utensils were at my disposal. I took out a glass bowl and began crushing the chocolate wafers with the end of a rolling pin; then I mixed in the butter, now perfectly softened from the sun on the ride up. I looked around for a piedish, but there wasn't one anywhere in the kitchen. How could I make a Chocolate Cherry Fluff Pie without a piedish? And then I remembered seeing a china cabinet in the dining room the night before when I'd checked Thomas's logbook.

The cabinet was more like a hodgepodge of knickknacks with some mismatched china dishes and serving bowls, nothing close to a complete set. I opened the glass doors and removed a decorative piedish and held it to my chest with relief. The Chocolate Cherry Fluff Pie could go on. A medium-sized bowl, similar to one we had at home, with delicate blue painted daisies forming a chain around a matching lid, would be ideal to serve the fish, I thought. I looked for matching bowls, but we'd have to make do with the dishes on the drying rack downstairs.

I pressed the chocolate wafer and butter mixture into the piedish to form a crust, melted the chocolate in a pan, drizzled it over the crust, then put the whole thing in the icebox to chill for a few minutes while I worked on the filling—marshmallows melted in milk, Jell-O and cream whisked in, chopped cherries added—which I poured into the pie crust and put on ice to set. When I was done I sat down relieved for a second that I'd succeeded with the dessert—but I still had to make the fish. I was sweating down there in the basement and had a terrible feeling that I'd have nothing to serve but Chocolate Cherry Fluff Pie.

I quickly chopped up the ingredients for the sauce and left it on the

stovetop to simmer while I ran upstairs to set the table, pouring two glasses
of wine while I was there. I considered drinking one down quickly to calm
my nerves but decided against it when I heard Thomas's slow and careful
footsteps upstairs, where he was probably changing out of his uniform.

"Dinner's almost ready," I tried to sing up the stairs as breezily as possible, feeling at once domesticated and womanly and at the same time ri-
diculously fake. Who was I to run around acting as if cooking and nursing
came naturally to me?

"Ten or fifteen minutes," I added in case he thought I was suggesting
that dinner was imminent; then I bolted back down to the basement. The
sauce was boiling angrily, not simmering at all, so I quickly removed it. It
looked more like a thick spread that was stuck to the bottom of the pan
than a smooth, silky sauce as the recipe had described, so I added some
water from the pump and stirred.

In a separate pan, I managed to cook the fish in butter without burn-
ing it; then I placed it in the bowl with the lid, poured the sauce on top
and hoped for the best. I had just placed it in the center of the table when
I heard Thomas approach the top of the stairs.

"I'm all right," he said as I hurried to the bottom of the stairs to help.
I went up anyway and he put one arm around my shoulder, the other on
the banister.

"It's why I'm here," I insisted, wondering if he'd feel the perspiration
on my skin from all the running around in the kitchen.

Once at the bottom of the stairs he began to make his way around to
the basement.

"Oh, it's all ready," I said, stopping at the dining room and indicating
that the table was set for dinner. He looked in, then looked to me, quite
puzzled. Then back to the dining room. And then he burst out laughing—
quickly stopping himself and holding his ribs.

"What on earth is all this?" he said, still chuckling. "You've got my
mother's soup tureen out. Why aren't we eating in the kitchen?"

"Oh." I felt the blood rush to my cheeks—a soup tureen? "Well, you shouldn't be going up and down all these stairs for one thing. And your mother would be quite offended I'm sure, as mine would, if you let her good china do nothing more than collect dust." I walked briskly into the dining room and pulled out his chair. "Now would you please sit down before it gets cold?"

He sat down still smiling. I took the lid off the fish.

"That's not soup," he said.

"No, it's fresh striped bass from Jean, the fishmonger in town," I said, spilling some of the sauce on the table as I served it onto his plate.

"You paid good money for striper?" He shook his head. "I can catch that out back for you anytime you want."

"Well, not when you're injured you can't." I finished serving Thomas, then served myself, glancing back at him. "Why are you still smirking?" I asked, exasperated.

"I'm smiling, not smirking," he said, looking serious for a moment, then smiling again. "This is all very kind of you. Very fancy but very kind."

"Thank you," I said.

He raised his glass. "Cheers."

It occurred to me, the minute the fish touched my lips, that I hadn't even tasted it. "It needs salt," I said quickly. I had completely forgotten to salt. I stood up.

"It's delicious," he said.

"I'll get the salt." I flew down to the kitchen, grabbed the salt, took a minute to dab my forehead and smooth my hair, then walked in a more ladylike fashion back up the stairs.

He salted. I salted, and then I stared at the fish on my plate.

"I forgot to even buy rice; I think this dish is supposed to be served with rice." I looked up and a small, very kind and sweet grin was beginning to form on Thomas's lips. He looked as if he was trying not to laugh. And then I couldn't help it; I started laughing myself and couldn't stop.

"I don't know why I did all this," I said between gasps. "I'm not much of a cook. I spent about two hours just figuring out where things were down there and trying to guess how and where you eat dinner." I shook my head. "I suppose I should have just asked."

He started laughing, too. All of a sudden everything about the last few hours seemed hilarious and ridiculous. "I even made a Chocolate Cherry Fluff Pie!" We began laughing hysterically.

"I haven't had a Chocolate Cherry Fluff Pie for years," he said. "Did you really make it?"

"Yes!" I couldn't stop laughing. I actually felt tears of laughter drop down my cheeks at the thought of introducing it as Cherry and Chocolate Delight or Choc-Cherry Supreme. I covered my face with my hands, but I just kept on uncontrollably. He pulled one hand away from my face and held it in his until I was finally able to take a breath.

"Oh God, this is all just so silly."

"It's lovely." He didn't let go of my hand. "Thank you."

Though I was the one supposedly helping, it was as if he had just given me an enormous gift. I couldn't remember the last time I'd laughed so much at myself or otherwise. It was lovely. I felt lucky to be there.

"And yes," he said, letting my hand go and gently placing it on the table. "I'm sure my mother would be very proud. Although I don't think she ever used this tureen herself. I remember always seeing it sit in the cabinet on display."

"Well, at least we're putting it to good use now."

"Cheers to that." He raised his glass again.

I tried a few bites of the fish and was relieved that it wasn't terrible, which helped me relax into conversation. He told me about his family—both his parents had passed and he hadn't any siblings.

"Were you lonely growing up then?" I asked, wondering if being a single child had steered him into a solitary career.

"Not at all," he said. "The boys in my neighborhood were like one big family. How about your family, your parents?" he asked. "How are they holding up?"

"They're fine," I said, squinting at him. "What do you mean by that?"

"Oh, nothing, I didn't mean anything. . . ."

I hadn't meant to be rude or accusatory. This obviously wasn't an everyday occurrence for him, dining with a married woman and using his mother's soup tureen. He probably wasn't as familiar with socializing and conversing. It had taken me months to be able to converse in a way that Harry approved of at his social gatherings.

"No, no," he continued. "Just that it must be hard for their daughter to leave the town where the family is."

"Oh," I said. "Yes, a lot of people do stay; most do, actually. I was only one of three girls from my high school who went to college. Most were married and in the family way by seventeen. I always wanted to see more than my hometown and experience new things."

After dinner we had dessert, which, I realized when I brought it to the table, was large enough to serve ten guests and gave us another chuckle. We finished the bottle of wine.

"Well, I'll clear this off and get you situated for the evening," I said, looking out the window. "I'll tidy the kitchen and then I'd better head back to the Manor before it gets dark." For a second I thought I sensed a hint of disappointment in his face.

"Would you like to stay for a snuff of brandy?"

Yes. I wanted to stay longer. Not one part of me wanted to leave so soon. I was enjoying his company and conversation and feeling brazen and warm from the wine, but I knew I should go. If the sun went down I wouldn't be able to see to get back. There was no lighting on the road back to the Manor. And I needed to remember my duty to Harry. It wouldn't be right to stay up here again, even if I was helping. "I've got to ride that old bike back," I said, reluctantly, "but at least it's downhill."

He nodded. "I appreciate you doing this," he said. "But you shouldn't ride at night. It's dangerous."

"It's fine, really. I'll head out before the sun goes down. What time does your shift start tomorrow?" I asked.

"I can manage in the morning," he said. "But climbing the light is going to be a challenge tomorrow evening."

"Okay. I'll be back for you then."

20

Tennis mornings at the Manor courts were always well-attended and classy affairs. I arrived right on time decked out in my green tennis dress, white lace-up shoes and matching green visor.

Dolly was stretching on the lawn. She had a mean serve and was one of the most aggressive female players I'd seen. Not the best by a long shot, but she gave her all to smack the ball to her opponent.

"Hello, Dolly," I called. "Ready to play?"

"Always. You're glowing. You must have had a good night's sleep."

"I did," I said. "I'm pleased it's such good weather for tennis; a nice breeze, that's what we need so we don't drop dead out here in the heat."

"Sweets, I'm heading into the city early next week; I need to go to the factory. Care to join me?"

I wanted to; I really did. Being around Dolly made me feel that my feet were planted firmly on the ground; she had a stabilizing quality to her, a commonsense attitude toward life that I wanted to absorb and emulate. But I'd committed to helping Thomas out for at least another two weeks until his injuries healed. "In a few weeks I probably can, I'd love to in fact, but I'm a little busy next week, I'm afraid."

She gave me a skeptical glare. "The fundraiser?"

I nodded to the party committee sitting on the bleachers. "They've got me roped in," I said. I'd managed to avoid Jeanie since my outburst at the beach, but I sensed she'd been giving me the cold shoulder, too.

"Well, it's Monday or Tuesday that I have to go, need to select the final pieces for the trunk show. And don't forget you agreed to help."

"Of course."

A waiter walked past with a tray of lemonades and I took one for me and one for Dolly; then I grabbed one more. At the other end of the court Jeanie was in a cloud of commotion with her kids and her nanny. One was clinging to her leg screaming as Jeanie tried to break free and the older child was stamping her feet and swinging her arms so much that Jeanie reached over and slapped her on the rear end, which sent her running off toward the Manor. The nanny pried the crying child from Jeanie's leg, easing his hands apart, and hurried back in the direction of the Manor with the child screaming in her arms. It was a perfect time to approach.

"Good morning, Jeanie," I said, walking over to her. "How lovely to see the children. How are they?" I handed her the extra lemonade and she gulped it down in a most unladylike fashion.

"Hello, Beatrice," she said sharply; clearly she had not forgotten my behavior. "The kids are fine."

"Gosh, I wanted to say I'm so sorry for my outburst last week," I said, knowing that I didn't need any extra attention from Jeanie or the other women while riding up to the lighthouse every day. "I think I'd had too much sun; it just seemed to send me into a tizzy. I hope you'll forgive me."

"Yes, well," she said, an air of snobbery emanating from her highly coiffed hair all the way down to her pleated white long shorts and polished shoes. "We were all rather shocked. But I suppose it was a particularly hot day, and the heat can turn any one of us into a nasty piece of work, can't it?"

I squeezed my lips together into a long, thin smile, not allowing myself a chance to snarl back at her. "It can," I said, nodding. "Well, good luck in your game; I'm sure you'll be great." I reached over and patted her

arm and then took a seat on the bleachers near the other women. I'd be
heading to the lighthouse around four o'clock to give myself enough time
to ride the rusty bicycle up the hill before dinner and help Thomas start
his shift at 6:00 p.m., so I wanted to make sure I was seen at the tennis
match and that I'd made my presence known.

"Oh, and Beatrice," Jeanie called out, tapping her racket against her
hand, "don't forget to stay after the match. We're having a meeting for
the fundraiser and we need all hands on deck!"

"Great," I said, nice and loudly, "count me in."

The staircase was too small for Thomas and me to climb up side by side
so I could provide support, so I followed closely behind him. Each step
narrowed where it joined the center pole that ran all the way from top to
bottom. A single handrail spiraled up the wall of the tower. He went first,
one painful step at a time, each movement seeming to hurt a different part
of his body. The moment he stepped off with the left foot he winced from
the pain in the right ankle, so he put his body weight on the handrail to
relieve the ankle, then cringed from the broken rib.

"Honestly, Thomas, I don't know how much I help—if you lost your
balance we'd both go flying down the stairs."

"Even so," he said, "I feel better with you here. At least I won't go down
alone." He attempted to laugh.

It took close to half an hour to climb all 137 steps. He, on the one hand,
didn't say much once we got going, just flinched and made quiet groans
and the occasional one-word response to let me know he was listening, or
trying, but I could tell he was remaining stoic through the pain. Me, on
the other hand, I talked the whole way up. I'd done the same with my
parents when I went back home to visit. They'd go about the house silently, the way they'd become accustomed without my brother there, the
way they'd learned to silence their pain, and I went in there chatting about
anything and everything that entered my mind: my teachers, my assign-
ments, stories about the other girls at school even though I'd grown dis-

tant from them. I just talked and talked, thinking I was some kind of cheerleader.

"This is not my first experience with a lighthouse, you know," I started up around step forty after I'd told him all about my morning of tennis and complained about the ridiculous things some of the women at the Manor did. "I climbed my first lighthouse when I was seven or eight, in New Jersey. I begged my dad to let me go inside. We climbed all the way to the top, I remember complaining the whole way that my legs hurt, and when we finally reached the top I was too terrified to step out onto the balcony."

"And now look at you," he said, with some effort between deep exhales. "You're just about running the place."

"Yes," I said. "Put my name down in case one of the keepers pops off, or if someone suddenly falls down a trench. I'll be the first female lighthouse keeper."

"Ha," he said. "So what happened at the top of the light?"

"Daddy loved it up there, I remember the wind sending his hair in all directions, even though it hadn't seemed windy at the bottom, but I burst out crying when I realized just how high up we were and that there was no easy way to get down."

A tiny window in the wall of the stairwell let in some light; the wall was three feet thick. Thomas stood for a minute or two and leaned on the windowsill, as if he were taking in the view, but I knew he'd seen that view a thousand times before. This was taking everything he had just to get this far. I put my hand gently on his back.

"You all right there, Tom?" I asked, walking around him, standing a few steps ahead so I could see his face. He looked ashen. "You've lost your color," I said. "Do you want to sit for a minute?" He shook his head and paused another minute, then turned back toward the stairs, one hand still on the windowsill; the other hand he reached over and placed on my hip.

"I'm all right," he said, and I wondered if he realized where his hand was, or if he was too exhausted from this climb to notice. I pretended it was the most normal thing in the world for his hand to be resting there, that it didn't send warm shivers down my legs and make my heart race.

"So you're afraid of heights? Is that what you're telling me?" he asked, dropping his hand and taking another step.

"No, no." I tried to remember what story I'd been telling, but all I could think about was the touch of his hand. I could still feel where it had been as though it had scorched an imprint through my clothes. "I'd been so consumed with whining about my tired legs that I'd forgotten how far we were from the ground, and from my mother down below."

When we reached the small circular room at the top Thomas sat on the floor for several minutes, his back against the wall, catching his breath. It had taken all of his energy to get there. I tried not to draw attention to his discomfort. I looked around the small room and set a flask and a notebook on the small desk he had pushed against the rounded wall. The corners of the desk were shaved off so it would fit flush.

The men spent hours in that tiny room below the light. The ceiling was just tall enough for Thomas to stand with space for a small writing desk and chair, a trunk that held supplies and a heating lamp. An easel was folded and stashed next to the trunk, along with a set of paintbrushes wrapped in a rag, and a few rolled-up canvases.

A door led out to the iron gallery that wrapped all the way around the tower and a ladder went up to the light.

"Can you get that door for me, please?" Thomas asked. I knew it pained him to ask me such a basic favor.

As I unlatched it the wind pushed the whitewashed door back against me. Thomas leaned against the wind and went out, checking some gauges and apparatus, and I followed him out.

"Whoa, we are high up!" I said.

"Gets you every time, doesn't it?" he said.

I walked all the way around the widow's walk and breathed in the fresh evening air. Thomas limped back in to the desk and made notes in the logbook and I stayed out there for a while. The sky had turned a purple color, and the setting sun seemed to be reaching out to me, stretching its reflection from the horizon all the way to the lighthouse across the silvery ocean.

The following afternoon when I walked back through the Manor lobby after lunch in the main dining room I stopped and picked up my mail from the front desk. I sat down at the big open fireplace.

Dear Mrs. Bordeaux,

Thank you for the article about the diaper explosion from Montauk. I was not surprised to receive more from you; I had an inkling that once you started writing for the paper and got settled in you'd be compelled to write more. But I will say that the topic was not what I was expecting from you. It was indeed amusing and really exposed those women. Bravo. Between this and the greasy pig contest piece that was published last week you really have captured our hearts. The diaper piece will be published in this week's paper and I look forward to more of your unique take on this town and the people in it. I give you autonomy to choose whatever topic you feel appropriate for our readers and I truly look forward to working with you. Please submit as frequently as you wish and I will of course respect your wish to use the pen name Jonathon Hubert.

Sincerely,

Mr. Adam Rosen.

P.S. I have enclosed a check for $2.30. This will be your weekly rate going forward.

I had to read the letter four times over to make sure I was reading it correctly. He had actually liked it. Not only did he like it; he also wanted me to write more. The idea that he enjoyed my writing, and that I would be published, me a woman, my thoughts, my words, in a public place for others to read, thrilled me. My mind raced at what else I could write about. Ideas sprang into my head, interesting local characters, the woman who sold pies from the back of the van by the lighthouse, Dolly's trunk show, a day in the life of a deep-sea fisherman, swimsuit fashions. I should talk to Elizabeth, I thought, and see if she had any suggestions.

I gathered my belongings and my letter and was about to head up to the room when I felt a trickle between my legs; my underwear felt damp. I had to get upstairs quickly. Once again my period had come. I had done as the doctor had asked: I had relaxed, I had drunk a little brandy, I had tried to encourage Harry to bed to the best of my ability when he was with me, without any luck. In one instant I was elated by the letter; the next I was filled with disappointment. Another month gone by. Another month without the hope of a child. But then I thought of my wish after seeing Dolly working in the factory, to be good at something when everything else was failing.

I rushed up the stairs and put my key in the lock as fast as I could to change, but as I did the door opened by itself. Had I left it unlocked? I wondered. I went inside and knew I had not. My clothes and Harry's were strewn across the room, my jewelry thrown all over the bed, pillows and sheets knocked to the floor, drawers pulled open, cabinet doors swinging wide.

In jarring red lipstick across the mirror on my dressing table someone had written: "Your husband is a lying cheat and a whore—I'm not the only one—neither are you."

I took a deep breath; I was shaking. I set my letter and check on the dressing table and walked into the bathroom and locked the door.

By the time I bathed, dressed, cleaned off the mirror, organized my disheveled bedroom and walked down the back service stairs, it was well past eight o'clock at night. I went around the back where the Manor staff parked their bicycles and found the small, rusty one that Elizabeth had loaned me. On the pathway alongside the tennis courts and toward the hill that led to the fishing village the first evening star glimmered in the sky, but when I turned left down Manor Hill the trees on either side of the road reached overhead, forming a darkened canopy. I focused my eyes on what I could see in front of me, trying to make it to the bottom of the hill without hitting a fallen branch or rock and tumbling over the handlebars. I crossed the main road at the bottom of the hill and pedaled on to the fishing village, turned right after crossing the railroad tracks, then leaned the bike against a stack of lobster traps.

Elizabeth's small house glowed—an orange warmth illuminating the shack against a darkened sky. A dirt road separated the narrow sandy bay from Elizabeth's front yard and doorstep and the Long Island Sound lapped, quietly, at the bay, light from the houses flickering on its smooth glassy surface. It was strange, I always thought, that the sound could be so calm and gentle in the cove here at the fishing village when just one mile across the narrow hamlet of Montauk the ocean waves were crashing on the beach and at the farthest point, the tip of Montauk where the lighthouse stood, the sound joined the ocean, swirling around the cliffs with wild abandon.

I stood on the doorstep and heard a gentle humming coming from inside and the low chatter of male voices. Everything about her home at this time of night seemed peaceful and calm and I considered for a brief moment sitting on the front step and waiting for a break in the quiet conversation. But as the thought crossed my mind a shadow appeared at the window, the curtain moved and the handle on the front door turned.

"Hello?" It was Elizabeth's husband, Patrick. His voice was accusatory and he looked shocked to see me on his doorstep. "Something you need?"

"I'm Beatrice," I said, "Elizabeth's, um . . . acquaintance. I met you at the pig contest."

"I remember."

The humming stopped and Elizabeth appeared at the door by her husband, holding baby Jake in her arms. She looked as if I'd woken her from an incredibly pleasant dream. Her eyes were heavy with sleep, her face looked relaxed and her baby, almost asleep, snuggled into her shoulder. Behind Elizabeth the chair still rocked and one of her boys, Johnny, the eight-year-old, was at the table building a model car.

"Is everything okay, Beatrice?" Elizabeth asked. I nodded. "Your eyes are red," she said.

"I'm fine," I said, and then, in a slightly hushed voice, "Could I have a word?"

Patrick looked from me to Elizabeth. His eyes held her gaze and seemed to ask a question.

"It's okay, love," she said. Patting his arm and nodding once, a communication they must have mastered, because he turned slowly and walked back to his spot at the table, glancing back at me twice.

Elizabeth stepped out onto the front porch and pulled the door closed just a touch, all the while gently rocking Jake from side to side.

"What is it? Do you need help?" She lowered her voice even more. "Is it Thomas?"

"I was wondering if you might be able to drive me there," I said. "I was supposed to be there at the start of his shift, help him get up to the light, but something happened; I couldn't get there on time. It's too far and it's getting too dark to take the bike at this time."

Elizabeth shook her head. "Patrick would never let me take the car and drive so late at night; it's too dangerous. There are no lights yet on the new road; I could steer that clunker right off the road and into the trees."

"Could I try driving?" I said, terrified at the thought of it. I'd only driven a car twice, in broad daylight and on a wide-open road. "I'd bring it back early, before anyone would even know it was gone."

"Lord no, Patrick would never let you," Elizabeth said, just a touch too loud.

"Patrick wouldn't let you what?" He poked his head around the door.

Elizabeth sighed and looked at me, shaking her head slightly as if to tell me she had no choice. "Beatrice has been helping Thomas out up at the lighthouse," she said.

His forehead wrinkled and he looked from her to me and back to her.

"He took a tumble a few days ago, cracked a rib and sprained his ankle pretty bad. You know how those two goons up there Milton and Worthington are out to get Thomas." She turned to me. "They don't like that Thomas gets to keep the main house as head keeper even though he's got no family living there with him no more and never really did."

"How bad is it?" Patrick asked. "He should have let someone know."

"He did," Elizabeth said, flicking her eyes to me.

"He should've let one of us know, someone who can help him."

"I've been helping," I said, "as much as I can; in fact, I am trying to get up there now to help him start the night shift."

Patrick rolled his eyes and pushed past us to pick up his mud-caked boots from outside the front door. "Don't know why nobody didn't tell me," he said.

"What are you doing, Pat?" Elizabeth asked. "It's almost nine o'clock at night."

"Well, someone's got to go, I guess."

"For God's sake, you've got to be at the docks at three in the morning."

She turned to me, "He's on a tuna boat tomorrow. They go seventy miles out sometimes, so they leave really early.

"Come on, Patrick; be serious."

The baby started to whimper and Elizabeth rocked him and reached inside the front door for a blanket. "If you want to help Thomas," she said, "take Beatrice up to the light, then come home and go to bed for a few hours."

"Her?" he said.

"She's able to help him; it's worked out so far," Elizabeth said, quietly, perhaps aware of the awkwardness of speaking about me as if I weren't there but unable to avoid it. "It's not ideal; I'm clear on that. I'd be much happier if it were one of our folks up there"—she motioned to her neighbors' homes—"but no one here can afford that right now." She turned to me and added, "No one here has a spare four or five or six hours, not one person I know; between kids and summer work, every minute is accounted for." She turned the conversation back toward her husband. "Beatrice has the time and she's willing."

Patrick and Elizabeth seemed to continue their conversation through slight nods and thoughts passing between them. I stood there waiting for their silent conversation to come to a conclusion and at last Patrick sat down on the step and began tying his laces.

"I suppose you'd best get in the car, then," he said.

"Thank God you're here," Thomas said when I walked into the living room. He was in his armchair waiting.

"I'm so sorry I'm late," I said.

"Don't worry; I got Worthington to light up before he left, but I just need to get up there now to keep an eye on things. I was about to call on Milton, but you came just in the nick of time."

"I'm really terribly sorry I'm so late. My room was broken into, I thought I'd been robbed, but it seems they didn't take anything; they just messed everything up."

"What? Why would they break in but steal nothing?"

I sighed; I didn't want to talk about it or talk about Harry. He had obviously trodden too close to home this time and ruffled some feathers, which meant that he was involved with at least one woman at the Manor, and probably more knew about it. It was humiliating to think that it could be anyone. And to think I was trying to make friends with all these women. I felt horribly ashamed, but I couldn't talk about it. Besides, Thomas needed to get up those stairs to the light.

"It doesn't make sense; they must have been looking for something," he persisted.

"Who knows." I shrugged. "Come on; let's get you moving."

I gave him my hands and gently eased him out of his chair.

He looked at me, his eyes serious. "I've become completely reliant on you."

"What do you mean?"

"I don't even dare to attempt the stairs alone."

"Really? I wasn't even sure if I was helping, coming up here," I said. "In fact, I was worried I might be more of a hindrance than a help."

"Hardly," he said. "You're a godsend."

"So who's the artist?" I asked when at last we were settled at the top of the light.

"Artist?"

I nodded toward the easel and canvases.

"I dabble," he said. "I'm no good, but we have to do something to keep ourselves from nodding off up here."

"I'm sure you're better than you're letting on."

"I'm okay with landscapes, but there's only so many times you can paint the view from up here," he said. He reached over to the rolls of canvas and began to unravel them. "I've painted it at sunrise, sunset, dusk, facing east, west, north and south." He peeled each painting back, allowing me a quick glance. One canvas remained in the back of the pile, but he rolled them up again.

"What's the last one?" I asked, reaching over to take a look.

"Oh, it's no good, just an experiment."

"Different scene?"

"No. . . ." He paused. "I was attempting a portrait, but it's much harder. Can't get the expression quite right."

"May I?" I asked, trying again to take a peek. He paused a second. "I could give you a critique? I'm no artist, but I am honest."

He considered it for a moment, then unraveled the paintings, slipping the last one out from the pile. It was a half-finished image of a young boy's face, looking off the page, into the distance. I thought of the picture I'd seen in Thomas's bedroom. It could have been the same boy, but in this image he looked a little older.

"It's beautiful," I said.

"It's not finished."

"But I love it like that." I could see the pencil lines under the paint and something about the incompleteness of it tugged at my heart.

"Is it the boy from the picture in your room?" I asked.

"Same boy," he said. A look of sadness fell across his face. The way he kept himself, his brown hair mixed with grey, shaggy and falling into his face, his facial hair scruffy, not quite a beard but enough to conceal some of his expression, I wondered if that was intentional, an attempt to hide his feelings. But his warm eyes now revealed his emotions.

"Your son?" I asked, quietly.

He nodded. "Tommy."

"Where does he live?"

"In Connecticut with his mother." He rolled up the paintings and put them back behind the easel. "I came back from the war a very different person from the man I was before I left," he said. "I saw things and did things that were difficult to live with in the real world. I was mixed up"—he tapped the side of his temple—"in the head, you know. A lot of men were in a tough spot when they got back from the war and Louise, she had a hard time with that. We'd married just months before. I was drafted for the tail end of it, the last year, but it was enough to do some damage."

"You probably saw some terrible things." He nodded, but I really had no idea what he might have seen. "So she left you, just like that?"

"No, no. We were technically man and wife for another six or seven years, but we didn't live as man and wife should. My fault in a lot of ways. I took a job as the assistant at the Stratford Shoal Light, a crooked, just about uninhabitable place. No land, just a pile of boulders and this rickety, small lighthouse. I lived there, coming home only one day a week. It suited me fine then, thought it would allow me to phase back into my old life gradually, but it just cut me off from her even more."

"You must have been lonely," I said.

"I needed some time."

His life fascinated me, so very different from mine. I wanted to know everything about him; I didn't want him to stop talking.

"I needed to learn how to live with everything that had gone on during the war. But it gave Louise time and reason to distance herself."

He tried to stand but couldn't, his ribs causing him to suck in air. I helped him up as best I could and he climbed the few metal steps to check on the enormous lens turning rhythmically above us.

"So then you came here?" I stood on the bottom rung of the ladder and watched him.

"I did another gig at another light, taking the boat home when I could; then I managed to get transferred here. It was a very desirable assignment, a family light, because there are keepers' dwellings and a whole family can live here. I thought it would be good for us, together again. Thought we'd try to have a baby and live a normal, simple life. She agreed at first. We packed up everything; I bought a car. We drove from Connecticut to here; it took twelve hours because most of the roads you see now weren't done then. She stayed three months, then said she couldn't do it anymore, the marriage, the lighthouse, me. She was fed up and wanted out, so she packed up and went back to Connecticut. She'd already wasted so many years on me. Three weeks later she wrote and told me she was pregnant."

I watched him in the metal gallery encircling the giant lens that pumped the ocean with its steady, rhythmic light like a heartbeat. Instinctively I put my hand to my chest. I wanted to reach out and touch his hand, to let him know that I was listening, and that I cared, but he turned to climb back down the ladder and I moved out of the way.

"Do you see him much?" I asked. "Your son?"

Thomas moved to the desk and shuffled some papers, keeping his eyes downcast; then he sighed. "She hasn't made it easy on me, that's for sure. I go out there when I can, but he's thirteen years old and he barely even knows me. I can't risk losing this job or I'd have no money to send for him. I write, but I don't think he sees the letters. I'm pretty sure she keeps them from him."

I stood next to him at the desk and placed my hand gently on his shoulder. "It must be very hard, knowing he's so close."

"He's starting to get more curious; he's been out here a few times. But

I know he doesn't feel close to me—it's like he doesn't trust me; I don't blame him."

He opened the desk drawer and took out a cloth bag: then he removed a rounded piece of wood the size of a potato from the bag and a small whittling knife.

"I'm carving this for him." He handed me the smooth sculpture.

"What is it?"

"The handle to a pocketknife. He might never see it if I send it, but I feel good making something for him. I like to think of his hands holding it, out in the woods exploring, cutting down branches, carving his name in tree trunks."

"He'll love it, I'm sure."

"Yeah, well, I have to do things to keep busy up here on the night shifts. Don't tell anyone I told you, but Milton knits when he's up here!" We both laughed.

"You should give it to him in person, go over there and make sure you get to put it in his hands."

Thomas looked down at the handle and shaved it slowly with the knife, carefully, not speaking.

"I should do that," he said; after a while, he looked up and nodded. "If it turns out all right I'll take the boat over and give it to him. He'd like that."

There was a silence between us as he whittled away at the carving. I felt I owed him something, some hurt of my own, some secret.

"The doctor as good as told me that I've missed my chance to have a baby," I said.

"Really?" He looked surprised.

I nodded.

"But you're so young."

"Not according to the doctor."

"I'm really sorry to hear that, because you'd be a damned good mother, a fine one."

It was sad to say it, to admit to another human being that I would be childless; it made it feel more real, more hurtful. I knew he was trying to be kind. He was a kind soul. But nonetheless I felt deeply, deeply sad and tears formed in my eyes. I willed them not to roll over onto my cheeks. I refused to blink and my eyes started to burn until finally he put down the carving and pointed to a rickety old wooden chair against the wall.

"Why don't you pull that over here and come sit by me," he said, putting the pocketknife back in the drawer. "It won't stand up for us keepers, but I'm sure it will hold your little frame."

I brought it to the side of the desk and sat down. Our knees touched for just a second; then I moved slightly to the left.

"So, what are you planning to do with your day tomorrow?" he asked.

"I don't know," I said. "I've become quite fond of my time up here, but I'm sure I'll find something to occupy myself with on your day off. Sunbathe at the beach perhaps." I smiled.

"It's a tough life you lead."

"It is. And what will you do?" I asked. "Stay in bed and rest, I hope."

"I've got the keepers' dinner tomorrow night; we do it every two weeks in the main house. It's supposed to be good for morale, time to discuss any issues at the light." He rolled his eyes. "But I always cook."

"How are you going to do that in your state?"

"I'll be fine," he said.

"Thomas, what's the point in me helping you all week if you're going to go and run yourself into the ground the first chance you have?"

"I'm not completely useless," he said. "I just have to find a way to get to town and pick up groceries."

"I can do that—"

"I'll send Worthington in the morning."

I wanted to be needed. I had been feeling indispensable and hated the idea of it fading even a little.

"If you're worried about me, maybe you could come anyway. Keep an eye on me while I cook."

I pinched my lips together, hiding the smile from spreading into the corners of my mouth. "I could help," I said. "I'd be happy to."

"So are you any good in the kitchen?" I said, turning to him.

"I'm all right," he said.

"Better than me, I hope."

"You're a fine cook," he said, "and even better company."

"So what's on the menu?" I asked.

"I'll surprise you. Actually, I wish you could stay for dinner."

"With Milton and Worthington, I don't think that would go down well."

"You've done so much for me. My constant companion these last few days, helping me in so many ways. I wish I could do something to thank you."

I smiled. "You are, actually. It won't make sense to you, but coming up here, helping you, it is helping me, too."

He paused and looked at me inquisitively. "Have you always done things like this?"

"Like what? Playing assistant to an injured lighthouse keeper?" I laughed.

"Walking into someone's life and doing something remarkable. A lot of people want to be that way and to think of themselves that way, but few can actually live up to the way they think they ought to be. You're just good by nature, aren't you?"

"No, I'm not one of those people. Sometimes I look at my life and I think what am I doing here? What am I even doing with my life? When I meet people who are doing important things, like you, you save lives by doing your job, and my friend Dolly, she's not saving lives, but she's creating things, and working to carry on and expand her father's business, and she's a woman! And Mr. Rosen, the newspaper editor, he interviews people like Albert Einstein and spreads the word about the amazing inventions and discoveries. People are doing remarkable things. Sometimes I wish I was doing some good. I don't know if that makes sense."

"You are doing more than you know," he said. "And you're doing the best you can; you've had a tough road." He took my hand in his, surprising me, and looked into my eyes. "You've always had a good heart, you're an incredibly strong person and somehow you've ended up with someone who doesn't see you for who you really are. . . ."

He stopped, looked down at my hand and squeezed it.

"You don't know enough about me to say all that," I said quietly. In one instant I felt that he understood me, he knew me better than anyone had ever known me, and then it was as if he got lost in his thoughts and was thinking of someone else. "Are you feeling okay?" I asked, but he didn't look up, just shook his head.

"Bea, there's something I need to tell you." As he said it the door to the widow's walk flew open and whacked against the wall, making a loud crack. We both jumped and Thomas cringed in pain as he did so.

"Oh my God," I said, feeling my heart pound. For a second I thought it was a gunshot.

"It's okay," he said. "We mustn't have fastened the latch right; it's just the wind."

We got up and pushed the door tightly shut and he secured the bolt firmly in place.

"That really scared me," I said.

When we sat back down he took up carving the wooden pocketknife again. I rested my head back against the wall and watched him, letting my eyes linger a fraction too long on his face, on the deep blue color of his eyes, and the left eyebrow that grew slightly different from the right, as if he'd gone over the handlebars as a kid and had a scar where the hair didn't grow back quite right. I had a strange urge to reach over and touch it.

"What are you looking at?" he asked. "My raggedy hair? I know it needs a cut."

"No, although, yes, you could do with a trim," I said. "How did you get that scar on your eyebrow?"

"What scar?" He set the carving down on the floor and touched his brow.

"That one," I said as I reached over and ran my thumb over the white skin.

He put his hand on my hand and held it there on his face for a moment, my palm resting on the side of his cheek. I felt a ripple run under my skin throughout my whole body, a longing to stay in that moment. Then he dropped his hand slowly, and I sat with my back against the wall.

"What are you hiding from?" he asked. "Anyone who wants to spend time up here is usually escaping something in real life."

I shrugged.

"Come on. I've had rumrunners; I've had dogs; I've even had one village kid run out from school and hide out up here for days before we knew it. But I haven't figured out what you're running from yet."

"Nothing," I said quietly.

"So anyway, it's from jumping out of the crib," he said.

"What's is?"

"The scar." He pointed to his eyebrow. "I got it from jumping out of the crib. Apparently I used to jump and jump and jump as a baby, getting higher and higher and higher, and then I'd propel myself over the rails and land with a thud on the floor, never wanted to be caged in, I suppose." He laughed.

"A wild one from the start."

"That's right. I'd cry until someone came and got me off the floor and put me back in. One day I catapulted myself right out onto a wooden rocking horse that was next to the crib, cut my forehead right open." He rubbed the scar.

"And here you are," I said. "You don't feel caged in here?"

"Never," he said. "With the ocean surrounding me, I feel free and at peace with the world."

I nodded and in that moment I knew exactly what he meant.

21

Elizabeth and I sat on the pebbled beach looking out on to Fort Pond Bay. Baby Jake lay on his tummy on a blanket and he was picking up stones and pebbles one by one, occasionally trying to pop one in his mouth. Elizabeth kept reaching down, taking it out of his hand and setting it back on the beach, and he would pick up another one. This happened over and over. Sometimes she wasn't even looking; she just calmly moved it out of reach and he found another, rounder, smoother. That's something you learn, I thought, or maybe it's just something that develops in a mother, this innate knowledge and connection with your child to know what he'll do next, what he'll be drawn to, what could harm him and how to protect him. It was hard to imagine ever having that kind of intuition. I wondered if all mothers had it or just some, and once you became a mother did you have this intuition about children in general or just your own? It was as if Elizabeth was part of some mysterious, imaginary club that I might never be invited to join.

Down by the water's edge Johnny and his older brother Billy were skipping flat stones on the water's smooth surface. They were waiting for the last of the fishing boats to come in so they could see the catches for the day. Elizabeth could recognize the fishing boats already on the horizon as they returned from sea.

"Here comes Tom Joyce!" Elizabeth called out. "Go to the dock and see what he's got," she said.

Patrick was working at the post office that morning and we were waiting for him to come back with the car so I could get a ride to the lighthouse. The bike was good for getting back when I had no other choice, but it took me almost an hour to ride up there and by the time I arrived I was pretty tired already. We'd squeeze the bicycle into the back seat of the car and I'd use it to get back to the Manor at odd hours—thankfully the ride back was downhill. Besides, Elizabeth said Patrick had warmed to the idea of me helping at the lighthouse. I knew it was risky for them to help me, it was risky for all four of us, but it was a risk that we all decided was worth taking so that Thomas wouldn't lose his job.

I was tired from all the back and forth over the past few days. I hadn't felt that way since the first week my father's grocery store business expanded into a warehouse store and took off overnight. He hadn't expected so much business to come his way in such a short time and he hadn't hired the help to unpack deliveries overnight to be prepared for the morning shoppers. He, my mother and I stayed up three nights in a row unloading deliveries until he finally hired some permanent stock boys. But just like those nights, my time at the lighthouse left me dog tired but happy. Useful and purposeful.

When I ran up and down those tower stairs several times a day, to get the logbook, to bring polish for the lens or to bring some food up for Thomas and me to eat when all was calm, I'd feel myself perspiring. I was a teenager again, active and engaged with the world, working so hard that by the end of the day, or whatever hour I returned, I'd fall into bed, needing sleep so I could do it all again the next day.

Elizabeth sat Jake up and placed a few white shells in front of him, just a little out of reach.

"Look," she said. "He can sit by himself now." He reached for the shells and almost had one of them clenched in his tiny, pudgy hand before he spilled over to the side, lay there for a second, silent, then cried. "Oh, my poor baby," Elizabeth cooed. "You can almost do it," she said, "almost."

She picked him up, gave him a kiss, then handed him to me, "It's okay, Jakey," she said. "Get a snuggle from Beatrice; that will make you feel better." His cry slowed to a snuffle, and a whimper. I held him to my chest and breathed in the smell of his hair, baby powder and salt air.

"You're a beach baby, aren't you?" I said. "Going to grow up with your toes in the sand and the salt in your hair, just like your brothers, and your mama."

"Please," Elizabeth said, "I don't remember the last time I had salt in my hair."

"You live less than thirty seconds from the water."

"I know. I used to love swimming. When I was pregnant with my Billy I would spend hours in the water, just floating, like the whale I was." She laughed. "I just don't have time now."

Her boys ran past us and up to the house laughing. "What did you get?" Elizabeth called out as they shot past.

"Cod!" they shouted back, laughing.

"What's so funny, boys? What else is in that bucket?"

"Nothing." They were in her front yard now.

"Johnny and Billy, get over here and bring me that bucket," she said firmly.

They scuffed over. "It's cod; I told you," Billy said.

"And blowfish," Johnny said, bursting into a fit of giggles.

"Oh, Lord." Elizabeth shook her head.

Johnny reached into the bucket and pulled out a fish about the size of my hand, laughing hysterically. He crouched down onto his knees and laid the fish down in front of us; then he tickled the fish's belly and the thing puffed up to a hideous spiky round ball about twelve inches in diameter. I jolted back from where I was sitting.

"Go put that cod in the icebox please, and don't make a mess of the place before your father gets home."

"Okay." They were still giggling.

Elizabeth shook her head and the boys ran off. Once they were in the front yard I saw them kicking around a deflated old soccer ball.

"Those boys," she sighed. "It's a good thing Billy's old enough to work this year."

"Really, he seems so young still. Where does he work?"

"At Dick's in town, he works the soda fountain and puts the newspapers together, whatever they need him to do. It's good that he can bring some money in over the summer, but they need to be back in school. I hope they get the building in order before September."

"What's wrong with the school?"

"It's falling apart. The roof is caving in at one end of the building; the shingles need to be redone—God forbid we have a bad storm this winter; they'd fly off like flower petals. You know, several classes had to move out of their classrooms to other locations," she said. "One moved to the church; literally the kids were sitting in the pews and the teacher stood up front like a priest! A few other classes doubled up."

"That doesn't sound very productive," I said.

"It's not. The problem is so much money has gone into making this town a tourist destination, they've forgotten about the bread and butter—us. And then the developer lost all of his money I heard, so now what?"

I felt ashamed of being one of those "tourists."

"Well, it's not that they've forgotten about us," she went on, perhaps trying to put me at ease. "Actually, part of the school is beautiful, really a good place, and when they first started building it up they brought in some good new teachers. They even have a theater teacher, which is something we never would have imagined out here; guess they wanted to train the kids to grow up to work in showbiz, entertain the summer guests maybe."

I shook my head, hoping these kids' education wasn't being shaped by the city folk.

"Don't get me wrong," she said. "It's great; the kids love it. It's brand new for them. I support it, even if I know that my lads are going to end up out on the ocean just like their father."

I nodded.

"It's just that they brought in all these fancy teachers, but we don't have the space to put them anywhere. We've fifth and sixth grade squeezed into one classroom. The kids in fifth grade are bored to death by the time sixth grade comes around; it's the same stuff they learned the year before."

Elizabeth turned back to the water, relatively unfazed by the squealing going on behind us. "Anyway, it'll all work out."

"I'm sure it will. Your boys seem like they'll thrive no matter where they are."

She nodded, her thoughts elsewhere. "What's it like?" she asked. "Living in the big city?"

"Where? Manhattan? It's like living anywhere really, except there are a lot of cars and everyone's in a hurry to get somewhere."

"I'd love to go," Elizabeth said, looking dreamily out to the horizon. "I just want to see what it's like."

"You mean you've never been?" I couldn't believe she lived only a few hours away and had never seen the city.

"No. Someday I'd love to see the Radio City Rockettes. They are so glamorous." The idea that Montauk was her whole world still shocked me. I didn't know why, it wasn't as if we left our small town all that often when I was growing up, but this town just seemed so infused with New Yorkers now, it didn't seem fair that Elizabeth hadn't seen the city they all sprang from. "Do you feel like you are in the center of it all?" she continued.

"Sure, it's exciting, when you have a big night out at the opera or some party, but sometimes it's as if we're all just being carried along." My apartment, my life with Harry, the dinners, it all flashed into my head for a minute. I didn't miss it.

"I'm sure that life pulses around you when you're in the city."

"Goal!" the boys called out from behind us.

Elizabeth ignored them with the skill of a seasoned mother to three boys. "Oh, and the skyscrapers, to see the Chrysler Building and the new Empire State in real life, so tall and magnificent."

"They are pretty spectacular. One of Harry's clients had a party on the observation deck at the Empire State when it first opened and Fred Astaire was there, taking in the views with his lady friend just like the rest of us. I was so struck by him, all the way up in the sky with us."

Elizabeth was mesmerized. "Wow."

"There's always somewhere to go and someone to see, if that's what you want. But I don't always want that. It's too much sometimes."

"Do people dress up just to go out, even in the day?" she asked.

"No. Well, actually yes, I suppose they do, but it's the same as here. No one comes down to breakfast at the Manor without being fully dressed and made up for the day."

"Sometimes there are leftover newspapers from the city at the post office and Patrick brings them home for me to read."

"I could take you sometime," I said, believing at that moment that I meant it but not really knowing how that would work, the two of us in the city together, or how we'd explain it. She smiled and brushed the baby's fine, wispy hair back from his face.

"I'll get there one day," she said. "Maybe when the boys are a little older."

Later that afternoon I kept Thomas company in the lighthouse kitchen as promised.

"I'm making my famous stew," he said, placing five pork chops on the kitchen counter.

"That's a lot of meat for three men," I said.

"I usually take a plate up for Milton's wife when I cook for the men. She usually has a friend over to play bridge when we have our keepers' dinner, so it's one less thing that she has to worry about."

"That's thoughtful of you," I said, wondering what it would be like to have a man cook for me.

"Oh, it's no trouble, I'm cooking anyway and besides, she's fed me plenty of times."

I'd dressed in an outfit completely inappropriate to cook in, but I wanted to look nice, even if I wasn't actually staying for dinner.

"The butcher in town gets the chops from Fink's Farm in East Hampton," Thomas kept on. "When he's got time he delivers them up here. Between the meat and the potatoes and the biscuits, it keeps us going for a while."

"I wish I could stay."

"Milton and Worthington are always ravenous when they come over here, as if they haven't eaten for days! But I know they have. At least Milton has; his wife is a fine cook."

The darkness down in the kitchen made me forget it was only mid-afternoon. I felt as if I were in a different world, just the two of us, cut off from everything.

"You up for peeling some potatoes?" he asked.

"Of course," I said. He brought a paper bag over to where I sat at the long wooden table.

As the water came to a simmer in the saucepan he dropped in the chops, letting them poach gently, then Thomas sat across from me and attempted to chop the celery and carrots, stopping every few seconds and rubbing his ribs.

"Want to switch?" I said, passing him the potatoes and taking the wooden chopping board and knife.

"So, from what you've told me it sounds like you're spending more time in the fishing village with Pat's wife and the boys than you are up at that fancy castle of yours."

"Well, first of all, it's not a castle," I said, "and secondly, the reason I am spending so much time with Elizabeth and Patrick is because I need a ride up here to help a certain someone, who fell down a trench, to do his job."

"Hold your horses," he mocked. "I think you are starting to enjoy yourself up here."

"Oh, you think so?" I grinned. "I am actually very active in my community at the Manor. In fact, tomorrow night I am attending a planning party for the end-of-summer masquerade ball, which, by the way, you are all invited to as you should know, because it's a locals and city folks soirée, and I'm on the planning committee."

"Fancy," he said.

"I'm quite important, I'll have you know," I said.

"I'm sure you are."

"No. The truth is," I said, "this place reminds me of home, looks nothing like it, but the feeling I get when I'm here at the light or in the fishing village, it's just natural, friendly, comfortable. No pretenses. It reminds me of my childhood, the open air and the nature."

I started on the green beans, snipping off their tops and tails. I put one in my mouth and when I looked up Thomas was watching me. "I guess I just like being around you and Elizabeth; I feel comfortable."

"And your husband? What's he like?"

The reminder of Harry made my body tense up. I kept on chopping. "Let's just say he gets comfortable in other places." I didn't meet his eyes, but something about telling Thomas made me feel as if I were giving myself permission to be there at the lighthouse. "Apparently he has other lovers, more than one, maybe even women that I know or interact with, and I've been so naïve."

When I looked up he had stopped peeling and was studying me.

"What?" I said. "Why are you looking at me like that?"

"You're different, that's all. And you don't deserve that."

After a while he got up and tested the pork again.

"How do you know when it's ready?" I asked.

"When it's falling away from the bone like it is now." He took it out of the pan, cut it into pieces and put it back in with the potatoes, carrots, celery and some diced onion as well as a bouillon cube.

"That needs to simmer for an hour or so. Now for the biscuits." He opened the flour and cracked an egg.

"Oh, you should use Bisquick," I said. "Add half a cup of milk. It's the modern way. Much easier and faster. All the women use it now."

"I like it the old-fashioned way," he said, measuring out the ingredients and stirring, but as the dough thickened he had to pass it across the table to me.

"What about you?" I asked. "I think anyone who chooses to spend their life out here on the light must be a particular kind of person. Don't you go crazy in the winter when it's freezing cold and all the tourists are gone?"

He laughed. "I have Milton and Worthington to keep me company."

"Yes, but you're also a man; don't you have needs for companionship, that kind of thing?"

"You get used to it. I read a lot, I paint and honestly there's not a whole lot of free time; we work constantly."

"You do work a lot."

"Even on my days off I'm still working around the light. We have the garden to maintain, we grow a lot of our own food up here you know, and then there's the damned bird cemetery, oh, and the erosion. We're always trying to reinforce that cliff; it's creeping back year by year."

I stopped mixing and looked up to see if I'd heard him right. "The bird cemetery?"

He shrugged. "Well, that's what I call it. There's a spot over in the woods where I lay them to rest, en masse if you know what I mean."

He sprinkled a handful of flour on the table and began lightly rolling the dough into small, round balls.

"Migrating geese mostly, they're attracted to the light; they get blinded and fly right into it or crash into the tower. Must have buried a hundred this past spring."

"What? That's so sad."

"It's not so bad," Thomas said.

"But they were on a journey, migrating; their mission was cut short."

"They couldn't help themselves; they were drawn to the light. They went for what they wanted; it's not a bad way to go." Thomas dusted the doughballs with flour and placed them neatly onto a baking sheet.

"So you made a burial ground for them? That's very sentimental."

"I can't very well just leave them there to rot, and if Milton has anything to do with it he just throws them over the cliff. The fresh ones, the ones that are intact, he cooks them up. I think they should have a better send-off than that."

"You're a softy," I said.

"You'd better be joking. Or at least keep it to yourself."

It made me laugh, thinking of him burying these geese, cooking the keepers' dinner the old-fashioned way. Somewhere along the way, I had lost this feeling of being happy, laughing; it seemed new again. Thomas got up to stir the stew and I got up, too, walking over to the stove.

"Smells delicious," I said.

"You want to try it?"

I nodded. He spooned some out of the pan, blew on it, then put the wooden spoon up to my lips.

"Delicious."

"Fresh herbs from the garden, makes all the difference. And a little bit of goose." We laughed. Then he took the spoon from my hand and placed it on the counter, looking at me as if he were about to ask me something serious. "He's a damn fool, that man of yours," he said. "A damn fool."

He held my hands in his for a moment; then he ran his hands slowly up my arms to my shoulders and up to my bare neck, to my face, cupping my cheeks as if I were a picture he was admiring. My legs went shaky. I didn't say a word. I could barely think. There were just inches between us. I considered stepping back, turning away. He pulled my face to his and kissed me gently, his lips softer than I had imagined, his intentions clear and strong.

"Thomas," I said, pushing him away, gently. "I'm a married woman. . . ."

"I know; I'm sorry," he said. "I shouldn't have done that."

We stared at each other. I froze, unable to think or move. Then he drew me toward him again, one hand slipping around to the small of my back, our bodies like magnets, pulling into each other. My mouth moved with his and I placed my hands on his chest, then ran my fingers up his back and into his hair. Then he stepped away abruptly, putting his hand to his forehead.

"We can't do this. . . . I'm sorry; I shouldn't have started this. I'm a weak man. You're a beautiful, smart, married woman. Forgive me."

He took my hand and kissed it, a soft, gentle, thoughtful kiss; then he led me back to the table. "So," he said, exhaling deeply, "these biscuits need to go in the oven."

"Thomas," I whispered. "That can never happen. . . ."

"Agreed," he said. "I don't know what came over me. You have just done something to me. I didn't know I could feel this way ever again." He looked down at the table. "I don't want to hurt you, or cause you any trouble; you've had enough of that."

I suddenly realized how much I cared for this man, how much he seemed to understand me after such little time. This time I reached for him, pulling his body toward mine tightly, letting him lean me back against the flour-dusted table and kiss me some more.

22

He could have managed without me, but I was back at the light the next afternoon. I wanted to be near him. We had a secret between us.

"Are you sure you don't need help with anything?" I said, sitting on the sofa while he was at his work desk. "I feel like a spare part."

"Just having you here is making me feel better," he said. "Actually, if you could bring the small logbook down from the desk in my room that would be very helpful."

"Right away," I said, and skipped up the stairs.

Being in his room again made me smile. The glass of water by his bed, the pen next to the inkwell, his clothes folded on the chair. I picked up the picture of the boy again; he had Thomas's eyes. I closed the logbook and put it under my arm.

"Beatrice, could you bring down the stationery box, too?" Thomas called from the bottom of the stairs. "It's a metal tin, actually, on the shelf above my desk. I have to reply to a few letters."

"Okay, I see it," I said, reaching up to grab the square tin on the shelf with envelopes peeking out, but my fingertips barely grazed its side. I stood on my tiptoes and tried again, then looked around for something to nudge it closer to the edge of the shelf so I could reach.

I slid open the small drawer under the desk. A pair of glasses—I hadn't seen him wear glasses before—a set of keys, a notebook. I picked up the notebook and it was perfect; I used it to slide the tin toward me and picked it up with the other hand. As I did so, a newspaper clipping slipped out of the notebook and fluttered down into the desk drawer. I picked it up and saw announcements for silver, golden and diamond anniversaries. Next to them were personal announcements. Congratulatory births and marriages and also deaths. Below headlines read "Pennsylvania Poet Reaches a New Audience" and "Calling All Embroiderers." A feeling of strange familiarity and dread hit my stomach as I read them. I had read those exact mundane headlines before; I'd read them over and over. I'd marveled at so many beginnings of life running into endings of life running into irrelevance. My skin chilled and goose bumps ran up my arms; my hands began to tremble. Before I even turned the clipping over I knew what was there. Something I had stared at and read over and over for hours, days, months. My heart beat fast knowing who I'd see staring back at me when I turned the paper over.

It was Charlie, the last photograph taken of my brother when he graduated from high school, smiling, handsome, young. My palms were sweaty; I was unable to catch my breath when I got to the part that said farmhands battled to free him, but when he reached the hospital he was already dead. Seeing the words printed on the page again made my legs go weak. I sat on the edge of the bed and stared at it, reaching for a reason for it to be there, in Thomas's house. Why would this be in his drawer? I felt my body turn cold with shock and then almost immediately that turned into anger.

I raced down the stairs from the bedroom and into the living room. By the time I reached him hot angry tears streamed down my cheeks.

"I found it," I said, throwing the logbook toward him.

"Whoa, whoa, what's going on?" He stood up gingerly, walked over to me and put his hands on my shoulders, trying to calm me, but I shook him off.

"Don't touch me!" I cried. "Why do you have this?" I held the clipping up—it was shaking in my hand. "How do you know about this?"

His face dropped and he brought one hand to his forehead. "Bea, please listen to me for a minute; let me explain."

I suddenly felt scared; here I was in a house, up on a hill, no one knew where I was, with a man I'd only known a few weeks who I now found out had information about me hidden away in his bedroom, information about my brother, my family. I backed myself closer to the door feeling completely disoriented. "You'd better explain fast."

"I should have said something earlier. I tried, but it was never the right time. I thought at first maybe you recognized me, and then I realized that you didn't, that maybe you were too young then and too distraught at that time, but I recognized you the minute I set eyes on you."

"What are you talking about?" A strange feeling came over me, as if the blood were draining out of me, as if I knew what he was going to say.

"I knew Charlie," he said. "I was with him the day he died."

I slid down the wall and sat on the floor. My eyes filled with tears all over again, making my vision blurry. "What do you mean you knew Charlie?" And yet as I said it, something inside made sense; there had been a familiarity about him, something that I hadn't been able to grasp. "How? When?"

"I briefly worked at Hicks McGowen's repair shop in Morrisville; he's a friend of mine from the war. Charlie and his friend Tim were doing an apprenticeship and I worked with the two boys. Hicks asked me to train them."

I put my hands over my mouth. I remembered Charlie talking about him, his mentor. Charlie called him Tom. He looked up to him and liked him. It had always haunted me that no one from my new adult life would ever know Charlie, that the only people who knew him were back home in Pennsylvania and that he'd never make new friends, find a wife, have a child, that I'd never be able to share him with the people I knew, with family I'd married into. Thoughts were spinning around in my head; I could barely speak.

"Why didn't you tell me? Why didn't you say something when you first met me?"

"I should have, I'm sorry, but I was so shocked when I first saw you, I froze. I never would have imagined I'd see you again. I remembered you from the funeral; you were just a kid, sixteen or seventeen, right? And you were so composed, so strong in the midst of all that sadness. It's very vivid in my mind, seeing you there, your life forever changed, forever saddened, and yet you were a light among all those devastated faces. And then at your parents' house—"

"You were at my parents' house?"

"No, I didn't feel right coming to the reception after what happened, but I did bring Charlie's things to the house that he'd left at the garage and some money he would have been owed. I left it by the back door."

"His toolbox, with an envelope of money inside. I brought that in."

"I saw you through the kitchen window wiping tears from your eyes as you made tea for everyone else. I remember thinking how you were the one who should have been sitting down, being consoled, and yet you were making sure all the guests in your home were comfortable with tea in their cups. I thought, that day, what a wonderful woman you would grow up to be, so strong, so caring, and then when I saw you that night, here in Montauk at the pig contest, a well-to-do guest at the Manor, it was all very disorienting. I was stunned."

I rarely spoke of Charlie, because people didn't know him; I feared they'd feign interest and that would feel like the biggest insult to him, so I kept my memories to myself. And here was this man, someone new who had spent hours, weeks, working with my brother, teaching him, helping him. Someone I could talk to. Just the fact of Thomas knowing him gave me hope that I could bring a small part of Charlie back to life. I wanted to grasp on to that. But I was still angry.

"But the picnic, the dinner I made, up at the top of the light, you've had so many chances to say something!"

"You have every right to be angry."

"You let me take care of you. You kissed me."

He shook his head. "I'm so sorry."

Everything felt so confusing, and yet it made sense. "You worked with him," I whispered. "You knew him." I began to feel strangely light-headed and suddenly I couldn't stop yawning.

"Are you okay?" Thomas said, coming toward me. "Can I get you anything?"

"I'm just very tired; please, just leave me. I need some time to myself." I walked up the stairs to his bedroom, lay down on the bed and curled myself into a ball, squeezing my eyes shut, overcome with exhaustion.

I don't know how long I was there, but when I woke there was a blanket over me. Thomas was sitting on the chair in the corner of his room.

"You slept for a good long while," he said.

I sat up and stared at him.

"When I was seven or eight and Charlie was nine or ten, we ran away. Charlie had this chocolate bar that he'd been saving. We almost never had chocolate, but there'd been a new shipment at my father's store. We were up really early for some reason on a weekend and Charlie was cutting it into pieces on a plate so we could share it but still make it last. But every time the knife hit down on that plate it made this loud clunking noise and my father came downstairs and yelled at him for waking him up at five o'clock on a Sunday morning." I stared at the wall and could see it all happen as if I were still in the room in my parents' house. "Charlie said we should run away, so we put on our hats and gloves and coats and we packed a bag and we left. I didn't know where we were going or even why really, but the thought of running away with him was enough. I remember the cold air hitting me as we left the coziness of our house and how he walked ahead fast and when we got to the big hill before the big road I froze. He slid down the icy grass on his feet, but I was too scared I'd fall, so I crouched down and slid on my bottom. It was wet and cold after, but I was worried that if I couldn't keep up he'd send me back. When I got to the base of the hill he held my hand and we ran across the road and into the woods."

I closed my eyes; I could feel my hand in his. I remembered that feeling—a little bit scared that I'd miss my parents but mostly proud that my brother had chosen me as his runaway partner. "We walked in among the trees for what felt like hours, and when we stopped for a break at some point Charlie gave us each a square of his chocolate bar for energy. He asked me if I was okay and I told him my feet were cold. I didn't mention my freezing behind. He thought about it for a bit, then said we should go back but only because he didn't want me to get chilblains."

I looked at Thomas and he nodded and smiled. "He was a good kid."

"When we got home Mom and Dad just carried on in the kitchen as if nothing happened and I remember Charlie being so disappointed that he got no reaction at all. He refused to eat breakfast and stormed off into his room. I felt a little guilty staying in the kitchen and devouring my oatmeal. After that it was as if it didn't happen. We went back to our own worlds, he went back to his friends and I was back to being his annoying sister."

Thomas came over to me and gave me his hand. "You've had a shock to your system," he said, helping me up. "Let's get you some fresh air."

We walked out on the bluffs in silence and sat on the old picnic bench. It was getting late and the sun was starting to set on the horizon, orange and pink shapes glowing through patches of white and grey clouds.

"Why did you keep the article?" I asked.

He shook his head. "I don't know. After I saw you out here in Montauk I went home that night and dug it out of a box in the back of my closet. I already knew it, but seeing his picture again confirmed that it was you."

My chest tightened to hear him say it; everyone used to tell us we looked so alike.

"I still can't believe you knew him." I turned toward him and placed my hands in his, feeling a strange sense of gratitude and sadness at once. Gratitude that he'd worked with Charlie side by side, that he'd actually known his personality, his mannerisms, his passion for cars and engines, and sadness that none of that could bring him back. Thomas pulled his hands away, pushed them into his pockets and looked out to the ocean. I reached for them again.

"Don't," he said quietly. "There's something I have to tell you. I think it's even why I couldn't bring him up before."

"What's wrong? I'm not angry; I'm just having all these thoughts, reliving things."

"Bea, listen—"

"No, Thomas, you have to understand I was just so shocked, it was just so unexpected. . . ."

"I was supposed to drive the car, Beatrice."

"What are you talking about?"

"The car that we fixed for Mr. Holden. I was going to drive it back. Charlie was supposed to follow behind in the truck from the garage to take me back to the shop, but we were busy that day and he said he could go by himself; he could fit his bicycle behind the seats and ride it back. At first I said no, I didn't think it would fit, but he made it work, so I let him go."

That deep, sinking, wretched feeling rose up from the pit of my stomach. Not because I thought that Thomas was to blame, but because I'd gone over in my head a hundred times all the things that could have gone differently, all the things I could have done differently, the tiny actions or words that could have led to a different outcome. What if Charlie hadn't taken his bicycle to the shop that day, what if he had caught the cold that I had the week before and stayed home sick, what if he'd taken a lunch break earlier or later, what if a part hadn't come into the shop on time and the car still needed work, and here I was being given one more reason. It was overwhelming.

"I should have been driving. It should have been me."

"It's not your fault, Thomas. We could all blame ourselves; we could all come up with reasons for him to still be here with us."

He wrapped his arms around me and held me tightly until the sun disappeared and the sky turned a deep, dark blue. The clouds cleared and the moon lit up the rocks on the cliff like spotlights.

I don't remember much about the funeral. What I do remember comes to me in fragments, like shards of broken glass shattered on a kitchen floor. I'm on my knees feeling around for what's left, under the table, between the cabinets, in the corners.

The indecision over what to wear. I took out the few black clothes I could find and laid them on my bed, not wanting to bother my parents with such an insignificant chore. My mother borrowed a black cape from our neighbor at the last minute and I thought it strange to consider such a thing as we walked out the door, just as it was strange that I'd agonized over my outfit. But we were powerless that day, in control of absolutely nothing except the clothes we chose to wear.

The procession of cars driving at a snail's pace following the men walking slowly through our small town with the casket on their shoulders. Everyone knew us and everyone knew Charlie. People stopped and stared, their somber faces echoing ours. The constant rain, fat heavy drops, black umbrellas forming a cloak above us.

My father reaching up and touching the casket as the men carried it into the church, and me wishing he wouldn't do that. The workers from my father's grocery store attending and my father repeating, "He should have worked with me; he could have had the family business. I told him those cars were no good.

"He could have gone to college like our Beatrice," he said as if I weren't standing right next to him. "We told him we'd pay for it; why would he want to be a damn mechanic? I told him those cars were dangerous. He should have worked with me."

The church service was a blur, but I remember that we sat in the front row and it felt as though it were for someone else's family, not ours. At the cemetery, standing over the hole in the ground where they'd lowered the casket. My parents each sprinkled dirt on the wooden box and my mother buckled under the weight of it all, my father and I holding her upright and shuffling her back to her seat. I looked up and saw our old school directly across the street and I pictured Charlie and me passing in the hall and me feeling proud when he gave me a nod of recognition.

The absence of my best friend from elementary school. Her mother kept apologizing that she hadn't come back from college for the funeral. We were barely seventeen; we didn't know how to act or what to say in situations like these.

The cold unfriendliness of our house that evening, where we gathered after the burial. The darkness creeping in from the windows, the cheese sandwiches, the coffee, the lemonade, the bourbon, the awkwardness of trying to act like an adult, a lady, when all I wanted to do was to hide under the covers in my big-girl bedroom.

I didn't want to go back to the Manor and be alone, so we slept in the living room on opposite sides of the room as we had that first night when Thomas was injured.

"Why did you leave here and go to Pennsylvania anyway?" I asked. It was late and we'd already turned the lights out.

"I'd been thinking how solitary my life had become, how I'd be alone forever if I stayed at this lighthouse. So when my friend Hicks sent me a letter saying he needed someone to work at his repair shop I made a hasty decision to leave this behind. Someone's always after this job, so I let them have it, but the man who took over from me was a drunkard, sleeping through his shifts more often than not. They were begging me to come back days after I left. But I liked working with Hicks, especially when your brother and his friend started working with us. It made me think of my son a lot; he was just a little one then, but I thought about him growing up and me not being around him to show him how to work on a car engine and that sort of thing. Your brother was so eager to learn, he wanted to know everything. He didn't just want to know how to fix something; he wanted to really understand how it worked. He was such a smart kid."

"He could have gone away to college, you know," I said. "My father saved up enough for both of us to go to college, but Charlie didn't want to. That wasn't what the other boys in our town were doing. But what if he had gone, what if he had just been a little bit more interested in mathematics or literature? If he'd wanted to practice law, he'd be here with us now."

"You told me earlier that you can't keep going over and over all the what-ifs. You'll drive yourself mad."

I closed my eyes in the darkness and listened to the faint sound of the ocean waves rolling in and crashing, rolling in and crashing, one after the other like the ticking of a clock whose hands keep moving forward even when you want time to stand still.

23

The Manor lounge was abuzz with excitement about the End of Summer Masquerade Charity Ball. It was to be the biggest event of the summer and everyone wanted to be involved. I wavered back and forth about going or not going to the planning meeting that evening—in the end I decided it would do me good to get dressed and have a distraction.

The room purred with chatter and clinking champagne glasses and if you didn't know about the magnitude of the upcoming ball you might have thought this was the event itself. The women sashayed across the lounge in floor-length chiffon and silk. Even Dolly was dressed to the nines with a gorgeous lace headpiece.

A quiet ringing came from the front of the room. Jeanie was trying to get everyone's attention and call the meeting to order, but if they could hear her, no one took any notice.

"Ladies," *clink, clink, clink.* "*Ladies!*" she shouted, now standing on a chair in an ivory empire-waist dress. "Ladies, may I please have your attention? We are about to get started; please take a seat."

The women followed her orders and found seats at the round dining tables, turning their chairs toward her. No food would be served until business had been concluded, she had already warned us, so everyone drank the bubbly being passed around instead.

"As you know, the end-of-summer masquerade ball is just a few weeks away and there're lots of things to do and decisions to be made. In cases like this many hands make light work, so I'm asking each and every one of you to step up and help make this ball a raging success, not only for ourselves but for the local folk who will be joining us."

There was a halfhearted round of applause and light chatter started up again. I heard a few women question the reasons for inviting the locals and another wonder out loud if she should be worried about things being stolen from the Manor.

"This is our chance to thank the locals for making our summer so comfortable," Jeanie continued. "From the porters here at the Manor, to the lifeguards at the beach, to the tennis coaches." She fluttered her eyelashes and received a few giggles from her audience. I rolled my eyes; she'd used that line before and the same few women had laughed. "Dolly has so kindly offered to donate all the masks, she's having them made in the city and we will be handing them out to everyone who walks through the door, locals included, so it will be a true evening of elegance and equal footing, except of course for the staff who will be working at the event."

She went on. "As you know, this is a wonderful charity event and the proceeds will go to the Betterment of Montauk Fund. It's really important that we give back to the community that we have so enjoyed this year and will continue to enjoy for years to come. City folk will each be kindly asked to buy two tickets at the door, one for themselves and one for a local, and there will be an auction with some lavish prizes."

I felt as though I'd been walking around the room in a daze. I was thinking about my brother and reliving the accident all over again, but strangely relieved because Thomas had known him. And then there was the kiss. In the midst of all that I'd discovered, I kept coming back to the kiss. The thought of Thomas's lips on mine made my skin still tingle. It was ridiculous, but I fantasized about him attending the ball, brushing past him in the company of all these people, his hand catching mine; it made me feel light-headed.

"What I'd like to decide on tonight is what aspect of Montauk we wish to improve with the funds raised from the event." Jeanie's shrill voice brought me out of my daydreams. "We should be advertising it heavily to ensure participation and generous donations." She let those last few words settle across the room that she surveyed making sure that everyone understood they were expected to give. "And now I would like to introduce Clarissa Baxter, the head of the fundraising committee."

Everyone gave a round of applause as Clarissa approached the front of the room; they were expecting her to talk, but instead Jeanie gave her a nod and continued with her speech. Some women at our table started whispering loudly, clearly uninterested in where the money was going, more interested in comparing their ball gowns for the event.

"Shhh," I whispered at them across the table. They turned their eyes, starting up again almost immediately. I hadn't really been all that enthusiastic about charity work back in the city, but now that I had gotten to know Montauk and the people who lived there year-round I began to feel quite passionate about the whole affair and wanted it to be a success. I imagined how it might affect Elizabeth's family directly and the other kids I'd seen in the village and wondered if some of the money would go to preserving the lighthouse or fixing the erosion at the cliffs. This was far more appealing than some of the other causes Harry and I had supported over the years just for the sake of attending a fabulous soirée.

"Ladies, I can't hear," I said when the chatter didn't die down, so I got up from my seat and moved closer to the front of the room, taking Clarissa's empty seat.

"So after much discussion and deliberation we have narrowed our gift choices down to three options, and they are: a gazebo and a grand statue on the village green of a fisherman—with a sign above him that reads: 'Welcome to Montauk.'" I let out a little snort and the rest of the table turned and glared. I thought Jeanie was joking, but clearly she wasn't, so

I straightened my face. "A new tennis court near the boardwalk—that's my own personal favorite; how fabulous would it be to jump straight into the ocean for a swim right after a hot, sweaty tennis lesson." I began to feel my temperature rise and I raised my hand abruptly. This was some kind of joke, surely.

"Questions at the end please, Beatrice. And the third option is an additional row of docks at the yacht club so we can accommodate more boats into the harbor."

There were some oohs and ahs and the chatter began to start around the room again.

"Ladies, ladies, before you resume your chitchat we need to make a decision and take a vote on the best use of the funds raised at the ball."

I shot my hand up into the air again and when Jeanie took no notice I stood.

"Excuse me, Jeanie?" I said loudly. The room fell silent. "Is this a joke?"

"I beg your pardon?" Jeanie stared at me with disgust; suddenly everyone's eyes were on me, but there was no going back now that I'd spoken. "I'm sorry, but these are the most ridiculous gifts I have ever heard of."

"Well, excuse me—" Jeanie started, but I cut her off.

"These are not useful for the locals; these are useful for yourself and the rest of us. Why on earth would you think that Montauk would be improved by adding yet another tennis court? The one we have here is perfectly fine and how is that a gift for the local folk?"

"They'd be welcome to use it, too, especially in the off-season. And the addition to the yacht club means additional revenue potential."

"And the statue?"

"She might be right," I heard someone say quietly behind me, and feeling emboldened by the murmur of support I continued on. "Really, Jeanie, I'm sorry, but I can't sit here and say nothing and I'm sure others will feel the same way. That money should be donated to the local school, or the firehouse, or to build a playground, or to reinforce the cliffs up at the lighthouse or to improve the construction of the homes in the fishing village. There are so many better ways to use the money."

"Beatrice, that's not really the kind of thing we had in mind, dear; we are thinking something more long-term, something a little more sophisticated."

"Who cares if it's sophisticated? It should be useful." I turned to the rest of the room. "Surely some of you agree with me on this." I looked around for support, but many of the women averted their eyes.

"I agree with you, Beatrice!" Dolly called out from her seat toward the back of the room. "I didn't offer to have all those masks made free of charge so that you could put up a statue in the village green. Beatrice is quite right; let's improve the school yard, or give money to the teachers of these kids so they have a chance to improve their education, maybe get jobs in the city and pursue their dreams."

A few others piped in less aggressively but showing mild support for a more practical use of the money.

"I have to say, Beatrice," Jeanie called out, "if you were so interested in the Montauk betterment fund I wish you had contributed your time and thoughts at the meetings we've held instead of swanning off to, who knows where you've been swanning off to!"

I willed my face not to flush. "If I had known about the meetings I would have been there, but it seems this topic has been strangely secret until this point, and now we can see why, because you are trying to fix this fund to fall in with your summer activities." My face might have remained calm, but I could feel a rash of anxiety creeping slowly up my neck that developed anytime I was angry or worked up. I never spoke up like this, ever, but something had come over me. I felt strongly about this; I knew the people this could help and a newfound confidence rose up in me. My hands trembled, but I didn't back down. Somehow I knew I was doing the right thing.

"Well, maybe we should take a vote," Jeanie said.

"Okay, we can vote," I said. "But remember, ladies, many of the men and women work two or three jobs to put food on the table. They try to give their children the best opportunities, but for most of them that means they will learn to fish as well as their father or learn to launder as well as their mother and that will be their future and their children's future, because they won't be able to afford to do anything else. The school here is falling apart; some of the kids can't even go into their classrooms because the roof is falling in. Second graders are sitting in pews at the church trying to practice their handwriting on their laps because their desks are damp and rotten from leaks and mildew." I looked around the room and seemed to have the attention of a good portion of the room.

"Okay, Beatrice, we get it; you can get off your high horse now," Jeanie said, exasperated. "Anyone in attendance in this room has a vote; we cannot add anyone's vote who did not, for whatever reason, attend this meeting. All in favor of selecting one of the three options that Clarissa and I suggested, the statue, the tennis courts or the extra docks at the club, please raise your hand."

A vast amount of hands went up and Jeanie went around the room counting.

"Thirty-four," she said. I counted, too.

"Anyone in favor of dismissing all of the committee's hard work and pursuing one of Beatrice's rather un-thought-out options, please raise your hand."

The hands went up gradually this time and Jeanie started counting immediately, but I spoke up. "Hold on a second, Jeanie. Give everyone a chance to think through their decision; don't rush them, please."

She rolled her eyes and stood still, tapping her feet.

"Now may I count?" she asked.

"I'll count along with you," I said, feeling that the number of hands was substantial but perhaps not as many as thirty-four.

"Thirty-three," Jeanie said. "Well, that's that then."

"Hold on a second," I said, still counting. "I think we have an even split; I counted thirty-four."

"Oh, for God's sake. Let's do a recount," she said, before repeating the whole process, first counting the number of hands for her proposition and then the number of hands for mine.

"Well now, look what you've gone and done, Beatrice. We have a tie, and that doesn't help anyone. Would anyone from either group like to change her mind?"

"Or did anyone not vote?" I asked. "Please don't be intimidated; this is a very important choice. If you didn't vote, please do so."

A tiny voice came from the back of the room near the open double doors. "I didn't vote."

Everyone turned to see who had spoken so meekly. It was Elizabeth with five bags of laundry at her feet. "I hope I'm not interrupting, I was just passing through, but if my vote counts I would like to vote for Mrs. Beatrice's proposal."

I clasped my hands together.

"You can't vote," Jeanie snapped. "You're not part of this meeting."

"Whyever not?" I asked. "You said anyone in attendance, in this room, at this meeting could be counted in the vote."

"She's right!" Dolly called out, blowing a stream of cigarette smoke into the air as if it were a flag of victory. "You did say that."

The chatter started up and I heard a lot of agreements: "She's right, you know"; "she did say . . ."

"But she's a local, she's not staying at the Manor; her vote can't count."

Clarissa finally spoke up loud enough for everyone to hear. "I think Beatrice wins the vote," she confirmed. "It was a vote fair and square; everyone in this room can participate. I think you should take a seat on the betterment committee, Beatrice, and come to the next meeting with a few locally focused options that we can review as a group."

There was a round of applause much louder than from the thirty-five hands that voted in my favor, which made me think that those other thirty-four were just too scared to lose face to Jeanie.

"I would love to join the committee," I said, elated. I glanced over to the doorway where Elizabeth was gathering up her bags and we exchanged a quick smile; then she disappeared out toward the service entrance.

❈

I'd already had quite a few glasses of champagne when I got to the light-house, feeling free and liberated. I was so happy with the results of the meeting that I couldn't wait to get to work on my ideas and actually make sure that the money raised for this lavish party would do some good. I was excited and tipsy when I knocked on the front door of Thomas's house and let myself in.

"Good evening, sir," I said as I turned into the living room and found Thomas in his armchair reading, his sprained ankle propped up on the wicker coffee table.

"Bea," he said, glancing at the clock above the fireplace. "This is a nice surprise."

"How's the wounded soldier?"

"Not too bad." He looked at my gown and gave me a cockeyed look.

"I'm a little tipsy," I said as if the explanation were needed.

"I can tell." He smiled.

"Actually, I'm quite drunk."

"What good are you to an injured keeper if you're drunk?"

"Probably not much good at all," I said, laughing. "But maybe good entertainment."

"Help me up, will you?" he asked, reaching out his hands.

I held out my arms to pull him from the chair, but when he tried to get up I fell right into him. I burst out laughing, but he gasped as I landed on his chest.

"Sorry, sorry," I said. "Okay, let me try again." I kicked off my shoes to get a better grip.

"That's all right; just sit here with me," he said, and I sat on the arm of the chair.

"How was your dinner?" he asked, but before he could answer I hic-cupped loudly. I put both hands over my mouth, horrified. "Excuse me," I said, muffled. "It's the champagne. I didn't eat dinner; I left before it was served. I was celebrating my success tonight. I have to tell you what hap-pened; it was amazing. I am thrilled."

"Amazing?" He raised an eyebrow. "At the party planning meeting?"

"I know I've complained about those women, but tonight was different. We had a vote about the masquerade ball, and the funds, and I won. Well, Elizabeth helped me; she was there. But the look on Jeanie's face, you should have seen her. She's going to make me pay for it now, but it was so worth it. I've never been so bold or stood up for something like that before, and it was terrifying but so exciting all at once."

He smiled. "Elizabeth was at the meeting? Why?"

"Not at the meeting, she walked in halfway through—"

"Wait a minute; how did you get up here in this state?"

"George, the driver."

Thomas's face dropped. "Tell me you're pulling my leg."

"No, it's fine. I paid him; he won't say anything. I went out to look for Elizabeth to see if I could get a ride with her, but she had left already and then I just had my heart set on coming up here. . . ." I paused for a second. "I've gotten so used to seeing you. I wanted to tell you everything. Do you mind that I showed up like this?"

"Mind? Of course not, but you need to be more careful. I don't know what we've started here, but whatever it is it could get us both into a lot of trouble."

"I know," I said.

"I'm serious," he said. "Life-altering trouble."

"Do you want me to leave?" George was long gone and I was in no state to ride a bike home, but I certainly didn't want to beg to be there.

"I want you here," he said, "more than you know, but not like this."

"Why? Because I've had a few glasses of champagne?"

"Yes, and . . ." He brushed the hair back from my face and ran his finger along the neckline of my dress. He shook his head.

"And what?"

"Nothing, you're just . . ." He closed his eyes and took a deep breath. "You look beautiful in your pretty clothes, but you belong in this other life, not here, not in my life; it's like I'm taking something I have no right to even touch."

"Come to the masquerade ball as my guest," I said.

"I can't go to that," he said. "I'll be working and it wouldn't be right."

I stood up and walked to the desk in the next room. My head was starting to spin and I put two hands on the desk to steady myself, no longer wanting to feel the effects of the champagne. I checked the schedule and returned to the living room. "It's not your night to light up, so you can come to the masquerade ball. Everyone at the Manor is inviting someone from town."

"What about Elizabeth?"

"I would, but she'll probably receive twenty invitations. For some people she's the only local they know outside the Manor. Elizabeth and Patrick will both be there."

"What about your husband?"

"What about him?"

"Won't he be there?"

"I'm sure he will," I said, "for some of the time, at least." The thought of him hit me hard, replacing my champagne glow with a feeling of angst and unease. Thomas slowly pulled himself up from the chair to standing. He was building up strength day by day. As he walked toward the door I felt a sinking disappointment. I longed for him. I wanted to hide away with him at the light where no one else would find us. I felt like a character in a fairy tale and I wanted that feeling to stay forever, but Thomas was being rational, sensible. I watched him take a few more slow steps toward the door; then he turned toward me. Leaning on the doorframe with one hand, he reached the other hand out toward me.

"Want to follow me up?"

"To the light?" I asked. The thought of climbing 137 steps seemed impossible.

"No," he said, "to my room."

In his bedroom I stood nervously inside the doorway. He closed the curtains, turned back the bedspread, then rummaged in his chest of drawers.

"Here you go," he said finally, turning and handing me a neatly folded button-down shirt. "It's a bit big, but it's all I've got." I must have given him a bewildered look, because before he left the room he said, "You can change in here"; then he closed the door and I heard him make his way to the bathroom and start brushing his teeth.

I stood frozen for a moment; then when I heard movement in the bathroom I began to undress as instructed, folding my gown neatly on a stool by the door, removing my silks. I left on my step-ins, put on his shirt and sat on the edge of the bed and waited for my next instructions.

Harry had been my first and only lover and that whole experience had been more about the fear, the pain, the excitement and the accomplishment of becoming a woman. My girlfriends and I had spent years talking about it and when the time came I did as I was told and pretended it was enjoyable. I was the student and Harry was the teacher.

Thomas entered the room and smiled when he saw me wearing his shirt. He was in his jockeys and his undershirt. He folded his trousers and shirt and walked over to me, lifting my hands from my lap. He let out a sigh and I felt a rush go through me, feeling his breath, the magnetic pull of his body to mine, both of us half-dressed.

"We should get some sleep."

"All right," I said, feeling an irrational sense of disappointment.

"You've been drinking; I haven't. . . . I don't want you to feel . . ."

He stopped and looked at me, his beautiful eyes, his stare, pulsing through me, through my veins, like I'd known him my whole life. I never wanted to look away. He shook his head. "Oh, to hell with all this." He leaned down and kissed me, running his hands through my hair and tugging on it slightly, leaning my head back. I thought I might lose all control right there with the first touch. He began to unbutton my shirt. "My God," he said, letting his eyes move to my body as I slipped the shirt off my shoulders and let it fall onto the bed.

He took off his undershirt and laid me back. I reached up and touched his strong, smooth chest, his muscular stomach: then I pulled him down to me, pressing his body against mine. He kissed me, pulling me even closer, my breasts against his chest: we felt each other's skin.

He reached down and pulled off my step-ins, his kisses devouring my body, my neck, my shoulders, my breasts, my thighs. He ran his hands over every inch of me, all the way down my legs, up the sides of my body and along my arms to my fingers.

"I want you," I said, wrapping my hands around him and pulling him into me. I heard my voice echo around me, louder, climbing, my whole body heightened, touched in a way it had never been touched before. As Thomas kissed me, his muscles clenching and tightening, I had a strange thought that if I died at that moment I would be satisfied.

The bed suddenly seemed too small; he pulled me on top of him. Forgetting about his ribs for a moment, I leaned onto his chest, and he froze, moving me away for a second, then pulling me back.

"Did I hurt you?" I whispered.

"Don't stop," he said.

He held his hands tight on my hips, guiding me, and suddenly I felt a rising in me like the swell of the ocean building on the horizon. Our bodies felt as though they were made for each other, finally together, the missing piece of a puzzle, the triumph of everything merging. He pulled me tight against him one last time and I gasped, like a mermaid coming to the surface for air; then I collapsed onto him, my face to his, my hair falling around us.

"Good Lord," he said. "You are incredible."

I couldn't speak I was breathing so deeply. I kissed his shoulder and laid my forehead in the curve of his neck. We stayed like that for a while.

"I could die now and I would be happy," I said.

"That is not what I was hoping for."

"In a good way."

"I don't want to die," he said. "I want to do that again and again."

"How're your ribs?" I asked after a while, propping myself up on one elbow and lying on my side.

"They hurt," he said. "But I had a good distraction from the pain."

"Maybe you've been faking this whole injury business just to get me to your bed?"

"Yes." He laughed. "The whole falling into the trench, everything, it was all a big setup to get to this point. Worked quite well, actually."

I couldn't believe I had gone my whole life without this man, without kissing his lips, without seeing his face, without feeling his touch.

"Things like this aren't supposed to happen to people like me," he said.

"Then I suppose you just got lucky."

"I'd say."

I curled into him and he smoothed his hand along my hair.

We pulled the bedspread up from the crumpled mess it had fallen to on the floor.

"It's going to be difficult to fall asleep with a beautiful woman next to me."

I got up and put on his shirt and fastened two buttons, then climbed back into his bed. He lay behind me. He brushed the hair back from my neck and kissed the spot right under my ear; then he wrapped one arm around my waist, the tips of his fingers reaching between the two buttons on the shirt and ever so slightly touching my stomach. I could feel his heartbeat against my back and I thought I would lie awake until the sun came up.

Thomas was asleep next to me, shirtless, when I woke to the sound of seagulls squawking outside the window. My mouth was dry and I looked around the room getting my bearings. I reached over to the side table and sipped from a glass of water, moving as little as possible so as not to wake him. His shoulders were tanned and broad, his arms taut with muscles even in sleep. I wanted to run my hand across his wide chest.

The first glimpse of daylight was overtaking the night. It might have been past five o'clock. I reached over to the window and pulled the curtain open just a sliver. I could hear the steady rhythmic pull of the ocean, but a thick fog outside blocked the view. I was in the clouds, in some kind of daze, waking up next to this man and feeling at ease. I wondered briefly if anyone had noticed I was gone; what if someone had told Harry I left the Manor? But those fleeting thoughts were overpowered by a feeling of tranquility. Besides, I'd stayed at the lighthouse two other nights, that very first night after his fall and the night he told me about Charlie, and no one had noticed.

He turned his head toward me and smiled, stretching, then stopping abruptly, reminded of his injuries.

"Sleeping Beauty. How do you feel?"

"Happy," I said. "With a bit of a champagne headache."

"I'll make coffee," he said, but he didn't make it very far. Instead we made love again.

We started to drift back to sleep and somehow my eyes, my mouth, my heart, were all smiling. I wanted to stay in his bed, in his arms, forever.

"I feel as though I've known you for a long time," I said.

"I know." He kissed me. "Me too."

Nothing else mattered at that moment; everything else in my life felt like a distant memory, as if we were totally untouchable on top of Turtle Hill. No one knew we were there, limbs draped over limbs, my cheek on his chest, his fingers gently tracing the freckles on my shoulders. I must have started to dream, because we were on the cliffs, a section I hadn't seen before. The sun was beaming down on us, but the ocean breeze kept us cool, my skin prickling at the inevitable wind and Thomas pulling me into his body, keeping me warm. I was wearing a flimsy summer dress, not much more than a sheath of thin fabric skimming my body. I snuggled closer to him, feeling the warmth of his skin against mine under the covers, half-dreaming. The dress was something I could never wear in public, partially sheer, but on that hill there were no rules. I half-opened my eyes and sighed a contented sigh, catching a glimpse of my pale blue gown from the night before, folded neatly on the chair by the bedroom door.

There was nothing pressing I had to attend that morning, so I could slip into the Manor and nothing would look out of place. I could sneak in the back door or even right through the front door as long as it was a decent hour. And then I sat up quickly.

"What is it?" Thomas said with a start.

"What am I going to wear? I can't wear my gown back to the Manor! What if someone sees me? They'll know I've been out all night." I fixed my eyes on my dress by the door.

Thomas went to his chest of drawers and found some long johns and held them up. "This is probably the only thing I have that might work." He pulled a belt out of his closet. "And this," he said. "It's early enough that I could probably manage to drive the truck now and drop you at the back of the Manor. I'm not on duty until eight o'clock. Do you think any-one will see you if you go in through the service door?"

"There's a good chance I could make it without being seen, but I can't wear that," I said, suddenly feeling scared, not sure which was worse, show-ing up in a formal gown or a man's clothing at the crack of dawn. "If I wait any longer they'll all be coming down for breakfast. Can you man-age the clutch, though?"

"I think so. I'm starting to feel stronger now; it's those damn stairs that get me."

I slipped back into the gown and put the button-down shirt over it to keep me warm; then we rushed about and I grabbed my jewelry and shoes. Thomas, still limping slightly, went downstairs to get the keys for the truck and the garage.

"Tell you what," he said, "make a beeline for the pathway and I'll meet you at the bottom of the hill; we don't want to risk you running into Milton by the garage."

At the bottom of the hill I sat on the grass feeling disappointed. The magic of that morning was quickly dissipating; thoughts of the Manor and people I might see on my dash up to my room weighed me down. I wanted so much to stay in the haze of happiness that I'd felt when I awoke next to Thomas. I longed to stay in his bed, to watch the fog as it started to burn off the cliff tops, to see the seagulls dance in the sky, circling, to see Thomas dress in his uniform, but I knew that if I didn't leave now it would be too late.

He drove the truck toward the Manor in silence, then reached over and took my hand. "Are you okay, love?" he asked.

I nodded. "I wanted to stay." How fast things had moved from feeling intense pleasure, uninhibited, to feeling tense, fearful and anxious. In one moment I felt grateful for finding beautiful Montauk, which had led me to meet Thomas, and in the next I felt a pang of anger toward the Manor, all the people there I was afraid of seeing and Harry—the fact that he would be there in five days. It was unreasonable, I knew that, but these emotions rose up in me alternating between delirious happiness and fitful agitation. Here I was spending the summer in this beautiful place, essentially alone and free, yet imprisoned by the women, the gossip, the eyes constantly on me. Harry, though, could do whatever he wanted back in the city in broad daylight, at the well-frequented restaurants, even at the Manor apparently, and no one would bat an eye; no one would care. As a man you could get away with murder.

Thomas squeezed my hand. "Come back tonight if you can," he said. "If you can make it to the bottom of Manor Hill I can pick you up from there." I nodded. "Nine o'clock then," he said, and he pulled my hand to his lips and kissed it.

I made it all the way up to my floor without being seen, but as I was putting my room key in the lock a porter from the Manor walked past. "Good morning, Mrs. Bordeaux," he said as he passed, his eyes resting just a moment too long on my gown.

"Good morning," I said, head down, not looking his way, clutching my jewelry and shoes tighter to my chest. I opened the door and went inside, taking one quick glance at him as he walked down the hallway. As I did he turned and looked and I quickly shut the door.

24

Well, you sure look chipper today, Beatrice," Dolly said, peering over her newspaper. She was sipping coffee and smoking. I was dying to tell her everything, but I couldn't. For the past few days, I'd felt elated and it took everything I had just to wipe that look off my face before I faced the rest of the Manor in the mornings.

"I *feel* chipper," I said. My whole body felt alive, as if Thomas's touch had sparked the ignition and energized everything about me. I loved being in on a secret that no one knew, but when I saw Dolly I wanted to confess.

"Did Harry come out and you two manage a wild night?"

"Ha, no," I said flatly. "He stayed in the city again, for the whole weekend."

"Oh, I thought I didn't see you two at the golf tournament," she said. "You should have told me; I would have invited you to dine with us."

"It's okay; I just relaxed." I ordered a hot tea and some buttered toast. "Oh, and thanks for your support at the planning party. What a hoot that they thought they could spend all that money however they pleased. I'll probably be shunned by Jeanie now, though."

"You were right to stand up to her," Dolly said, her head in the newspaper. "Well, would you look at this." She turned the paper toward me. "Looks like the mothers out here have caused a bit of a stink." She laughed.

"Really?" I reached over to grab the paper from her, but she pulled it back toward her and read out loud, "'Diaper Explosion Reveals Montauk Visitors' Filthy Side.'"

I gasped at the title. I was going to be in even more trouble if anyone found out I'd penned this.

"I suppose Montauk is getting more and more popular if they are now sending city reporters to cover the goings-on out here; first they did the pig contest and now this!"

"Very fancy," I said, trying to suppress my grin. "Can I see it?" I tried to glance over the page. "Do you mind if I take a peek, Dolly?"

She was almost talking to herself and then seemed to move on to the next article. I couldn't sit still. I had to see it for myself, the second time my words had been in print, to see how it had been edited. Finally, I couldn't take the anticipation anymore and I got up to leave.

"Excuse me, Dolly, I'm heading to the ladies; then I have a few things to do," I said. "We'll catch up later."

"Bye for now," she said, barely looking up. I dashed out of the dining room to find my own copy.

After I read it I took out a piece of paper and began to write about the masquerade planning party, how it had been almost as glamorous an affair as the upcoming ball. I started with sparkle, writing of some darling headpieces, the extra long strands of pearls, the abandonment of gloves by most on that balmy evening and the standout gold sequin-embellished dress that Mary's guest from Hollywood wore with an open keyhole neckline and two daring front slits that revealed much of her tanned and toned legs—and for an all-women event no less. But then I segued into the main topic of the night, the funds and how the majority ruled that they'd be donated to the Montauk School. There was one way to ensure that Jeanie wouldn't back out of her agreement to dedicate the funds to the school, and that was to put it in print.

That night Thomas was waiting for me at the bottom of Manor Hill with the engine and the lights turned off. I looked around and climbed in, my heart beating fast.

"Go quickly before anyone sees us," I said.

"Not before I get a real hello."

I leaned over and gave him a quick kiss on the cheek. "Come on," I said excitedly. "Let's go." He started the engine. It was thrilling and nerve-wracking all at once. I just wanted to be in the safety of his house.

When we'd first met he'd been reserved, stoic, the kind of man who'd never show his true feelings, but now he trusted me with his emotions and the expression on his face told me that I'd made his day just by showing up.

As soon as we stepped through his front door I turned and kissed him properly. It was as if I'd never been kissed before. I had believed that Harry and I had been in love and passionate when we were first married, but it was hard to remember that; it seemed like someone else's life, someone else's story. Thomas's was the only kiss I could recall now, his embrace the only one I could feel.

He put his hands around my waist and pulled me into him. "Stay with me tonight," he said.

"I can't."

"I'll take you back early; I promise."

"It would have to be really early," I said, hesitating. "Harry might be coming out tomorrow on the early train, just for the day."

He straightened up and one hand dropped from my waist, then the other. "Midweek?"

"I'm not sure; he said maybe this week, maybe next. Some investment business."

He nodded, his face suddenly serious. "He's investing here?" he said, looking disgusted.

"He's looking into it. With some others, not just him."

He walked to the bar and poured himself a drink. "We need to talk about that at some point."

"About what?" I approached, touching his arm.

"You're married," he said. "Let's not forget that."

I poured myself a dram and knocked it back. He moved to the window and looked out, wiping some dust off the sill.

"Harry and I have an uncertain, difficult marriage," I said. He didn't turn around. "He's not in love with me anymore, and I'm not in love with him." He kept his back to me. "We are in a strange societal predicament in which, he has told me, and I am aware, it is all but impossible to get a divorce. I would be ruined, financially and socially. And now I'm stuck." I waited for some kind of response, but Thomas continued to look out the window. "And I had just sort of accepted that fact, even when I found out about the other women; that was, until now."

Finally, he turned. "So what does that mean?"

"Just that I thought he and I, the whole imprisonment, was my fate, a result of the choices I'd made and therefore the bed I must lie in, but knowing you, kissing you"—I walked up behind him and put my arms around him—"being with you. It has changed everything in me. I know I can't escape the marriage and him, but I'm no longer filled with despair; I feel filled with hope and excitement and love. . . ." I paused. Maybe I'd gone too far. What was the point in saying all this, really? "I'm just happy when I'm with you."

"And I am with you, but it doesn't make it right," he said. "And it doesn't mean anything's going to change." There was no good answer and no resolution, so I took his hands and looked up at him, asking that we just leave it for now, that we just enjoy what we had at that very moment, if nothing else.

"Show me something I've never seen before."

"You've seen it all," he said. I sighed. "You have—the light, the oil room, the house, the basement."

"I know there's something I haven't seen yet."

"Come with me," he said after a moment, taking my hand and leading me out of the living room, out the front door into the dark.

"Where are we going?" I asked, excited by the hope that we could turn things around.

"I want to show you the stars."

We lay on our backs on the grass. The sky was incredibly black and the stars were glowing.

"Can you imagine what it would be like to fly?" I said. "Like Lindbergh or Wrong Way Corrigan. I would be terrified, but it would be such a thrill. But how daunting to lose all sense of direction and end up in Ireland instead of California," I said. "Twenty-eight hours it took him; he would have been right up there with the stars at some point."

"He did that on purpose, Bea. He was Irish. He'd been trying to get permission to fly across the Atlantic to Dublin for months and they kept turning him down because his plane was a piece of junk he bought off a trash heap and they thought it was a suicide flight."

"Really? You truly believe Wrong Way Corrigan went the wrong way on purpose?"

"Of course; that man knew exactly what he was doing when he took off. He turned that plane around as soon as he got up in the sky. That was a bunch of baloney about the compass malfunctioning; he just wanted to be famous in his hometown."

I thought about that, what it would feel like to do something so astounding that no one ever thought you'd be capable of it. "He'll be remembered forever now."

"And I'm sure he'll take full advantage of his fame." Thomas laughed.

"I wish I had it in me to do something remarkable."

"You *are* remarkable."

"No." I laughed. "But to be a Hollywood movie star like Katharine Hepburn or Hedy Lamarr, or Bette Davis, where you'd be remembered."

"You don't really care about all that, do you?"

"Care about it?" I pushed myself up onto one elbow. "Who doesn't? How glamorous it would be to be a movie star, and your children and your children's children would see you in the films long after you were gone. Oh, come on; you wouldn't want to be Cary Grant if you had the chance?"

"You're already glamorous," he said, grabbing my chin in his hand and pulling me in for a kiss. "You, you're like a movie star who's walked onto the wrong set and into my life."

I laughed. "Well, I'd like to do something important, something meaningful, some unattainable thing. Would you want to build a plane? Fly across the Atlantic like Corrigan? Come on; what's your greatest dream?" I asked, looking over to him.

"I don't know." He kept looking up to the stars. "I'd like to be a proper father to my son. I dream about him a lot, you know."

I nodded and put my hand on his chest.

"I dream about him as a baby and a toddler mostly."

"You miss him."

"I should have fought harder in those early years; I shouldn't have just kept sending them money and let her keep him from me. At the time I thought I was doing the right thing, but now I regret it. Every day I regret it."

"But you're getting closer now." I brushed the hair back from his forehead. "You said he's showing more interest now that he's growing up." It pained me to see his hurt and regrets. I wanted to take it all away somehow.

"But, if I could do anything, make a wish come true," he said, turning to look at me, "I'd do it again. But I'd get it right this time. Love, companionship, a family. With you."

I felt my heart grow bigger in my chest just to hear him say it, a warmth, a truth, a feeling I'd never experienced before, but then he laughed as if it were a joke. He looked away and shook his head.

"Don't do that."

"What?"

"Don't say something like that, then laugh like you didn't mean it."

"You asked me what my long shot dream was. It's too late for me now anyway, but if I really could do anything and do it well, it would be that. To start all over again with you."

I wanted to make it true. I wanted to be free from everything I'd ever known so I could be with him.

"Do you see that over there?" He pointed down along the cliffs, toward town. "That little outline of a house?"

I nodded.

"You can't see much now, but that little yellow cottage is for sale. One day I'm going to buy that house. You and me, we could live there and you'd never have to go back to Manhattan again. You could just stay with me out here forever."

I smiled; the thought of it made me warm all over. "What about the house at the light?"

"This is a nice house and all, but if you were here and we had a family I'd want you to live in a proper house. I'd buy it, fix it up, paint it, put in a nice big bathtub and a kitchen with windows that look out toward the ocean, and a beautiful yard where the kids could play."

I smiled. "What color would you paint it?"

"Well, I'd have to get your approval of course, but I think I'd keep it yellow, a happy color."

I closed my eyes and pictured it for a moment, the house, us, the pitter-patter of little feet, our own little castle by the sea.

25

—✵—

The Montauk betterment committee took a beating in the paper.

"Another article about Montauk," Dolly said over breakfast, the same table in the corner. "Looks like we're getting quite popular." She read on and I felt my stomach flip with excitement again. "It's all about the funds from the masquerade ball and how they'll be going to the school. How fabulous." She looked up at me. "We'll probably get some big donations now."

"Wonderful." I tried to act normal, surprised and pleased with the news without giving anything away, but once again I was dying to see the article. Dolly held on to the paper and I glanced around the room seeing who else might be reading the same thing. A few men sat sipping coffee with morning papers stiff in front of them. To think that all these people and thousands more in the city might actually read the article and maybe even feel moved by it, compelled to donate or even just to consider for a moment what I was thinking.

I suddenly felt the need to tell Dolly the article was written by me, this one and the last one and next week's, too. This was just too much of a secret to keep. She would be thrilled with me, I was sure; she'd think I was awfully clever.

"Hold on a second. Oh my, you're not going to believe this; they've taken Jeanie to task."

I gulped. I had been so careful in the piece to remain stoic, report just the facts, I'd written and rewritten many times so as not to point the finger at anyone, and I'd crossed out lines that seemed incriminating many times before I submitted it. I certainly hadn't intended to hurt anyone.

"'Socialite Jeanie Barnes, head of the masquerade ball planning committee, had originally planned to pour the money, which is raised for the purpose of benefiting the Montauk community, into another tennis court, a bronze statue or another row of yachts at the yacht club, but in a close vote of thirty-five to thirty-four, fellow committee members, guests and one local, the majority ruled that the fund would be put to better use and be of far greater service to the people of Montauk if it helps renovate the school.'"

"Oh my," I said, picking up my teacup, then quickly setting it back down when I realized my hand was shaking. It did sound rather accusatory when Dolly read it out loud like that. "I wouldn't say that's slamming her, though," I said. "That's just telling the truth."

"Maybe so, but Jeanie won't see it that way. What a fantastically sharp slap in the face." She laughed. "It's about time someone put that woman in her place. I wonder if we have a mole among us; the Manor staff perhaps, maybe they're being paid off to snoop. What fun!"

The ladies were having a beach day and Dolly and I joined them. Dolly was particularly inspired to see Jeanie roil in her public humiliation.

"Morning, ladies," Dolly said, pulling up a lounge chair near the others. "Jeanie, looks like you took a beating in today's paper."

Jeanie slumped. "I don't know what you're talking about," she said, looking miserable. "It's good publicity for our event." Then she looked at me. "I don't know what you're looking at, Beatrice; you should feel responsible for part of this."

"Oh, Jeanie," I said. "I stand by my position on the funds going to the schools." I did feel a little bad for her.

"What about our children's schools? Maybe they need a little paint touch-up; I don't know why everyone's so concerned about the local folk here," she said. "We don't even know them."

"Yes, but it was your idea to create the betterment fund," I said; then Dolly linked her arm in mine and pulled me away.

"Okay, ladies, we're going for a dip," she said.

In my strawberry-red swimsuit, despite my straight up-and-down figure, I somehow felt more womanly than I had before, more confident. Harry crossed my mind for an instant. I wondered for a second what he was doing back in the city—it was habit to wonder—then I pushed him out of my mind.

"You look different. Something's happened; what is it?" Dolly asked as we took a dip in the ocean.

"What do you mean?"

"You're quite, I don't know, happy. And you're not letting Jeanie boss you around like before."

I dove into the water and under a wave, coming out the other side of it grinning.

"I'm just in a good mood," I said. "Can't a girl have a good day?"

"Sure, she can, but I want to know what you're having and where I can get some," she said, and I laughed. "Beatrice Bordeaux," she said. "Are you having an affair?"

I dove again and swam out to the ocean away from her.

"Beatrice." She splashed and swam after me. "You are. You've found yourself a lover. Good for you. Maybe that's just what you needed. Darling, I'm thrilled for you; this is going to be wonderful for your marriage."

"Dolly," I said. "I'm just happy to be out here spending time at the beach; that's all."

"Mmm-hmm," she said, grinning. "Well, either way, I think it's out-standing news."

Dolly was a daredevil, a breaker of rules, a pusher of buttons, but this affair, between a married woman in society and a lighthouse keeper, this one she might not be able to accept. I couldn't reveal the truth. Instead I told her something she could really sink her teeth into.

"There is something I've been meaning to tell you, Dolly."

"I knew it."

"The newspaper columns about Montauk, the ones you've been en-joying, the greasy pig party, the dirty diapers and today's masquerade funds . . ."

"Yes?" She seemed thrilled, as if I were going to predict what news would come next.

"I wrote them."

Dolly's eyes widened. "What do you mean, you wrote them?"

"I write them. That's me. Jonathon Hubert. It's a pen name; everyone assumes the author's a man."

She looked bewildered.

"Next time you're in my room, I'll show you my jewelry box. I have two checks for two dollars and thirty cents each and, after seeing this morning's paper, presumably another few in the mail. I get paid to write about Montauk; isn't that fun?"

"It certainly is." She was impressed; I could tell. "My, my, you are a quiet one, Beatrice, a quiet one with tricks up your sleeve, that's for certain."

"I've been wanting to tell you. I was just so scared that Harry would find out. He would be furious."

"Listen, there are quite a few women entering the world of journal-ism, not women of your social standing usually but women nonetheless. It's actually quite gratifying to see some females in this business. It's impor-tant that we are heard as well as the men."

"That's what Mr. Rosen said."

"Who?"

"Mr. Rosen, my editor." Just being able to say such a thing made me stand a little taller, feel a little more respected, even if the only ones respecting me were myself, Dolly and Mr. Rosen.

"Well, well, I always thought you'd be good at keeping secrets," Dolly said, "and boy, do you have some whoppers. Now we just have to figure out a way to put this column to good use."

26

Dolly was already chatting with George when I got to the car.

"Good morning, George," I said. "Can you take us down to the fishing village to pick up Elizabeth, just across the railroad tracks, then to the school?"

Elizabeth had arranged for us to meet the principal of the school and tour the facilities so that I could have an idea of what to propose for the fundraising meeting that week. Since handling money, making estimates and conveying these types of things to a not-so-friendly audience was not my area of expertise, Dolly had agreed to come along and help me focus on the school's most immediate needs and then figure out how to present them to the committee.

"Turn right at the bottom of the hill, George," I called over the purr of the engine, "and it's this house on the right, the one with the bikes out front."

I had been to Elizabeth's house, or at least in her front yard, so many times now that it had begun to feel normal, but I could see that Dolly and even George were taken aback at how comfortable I was in the village.

"How quaint," Dolly said. "Right on the water like that. At least the fishermen don't have a long commute."

"It is pretty, isn't it?"

"Yes, but that railroad track is literally in their backyards," she said.

Elizabeth was about to climb in up front with George.

"Sit back here, honey!" Dolly called out, moving over to make room. "Cute house," she said. And then she introduced herself and suddenly I felt relieved, remembering how Dolly was in the hat factory, treating everyone the same, whether they were a floor sweeper or a hat molder or a buyer from a luxury store. "Give us a little background on this chap before we get there, so we know what to expect."

"He's a wonderful man, Carleton Farrell. He's the principal but also teaches seventh and eighth grade," Elizabeth said, going on to tell Dolly what she had told me about the school and its need for a revamp.

Mr. Farrell was a short, round man with ruddy cheeks and very little hair. What he did have left he kept long and swept over the top of his head. He wore a waistcoat over a cotton shirt, a jacket with elbow patches and what looked like wool trousers, even in the heat. He looked as if he had been a teacher and principal since he came out of the womb.

"Lovely to meet you," he said hurriedly, opening our door as we pulled up.

"I'll be waiting for you right here," George said to Dolly and me as Mr. Farrell eagerly began the tour.

"I cannot tell you how grateful I am that you've chosen to raise funds for our school. It means the world, the absolute world."

"The problem is," Elizabeth chimed in, "that the school is just too small. We only have three classrooms, and the space that was going to be additional classrooms is damaged."

He took us through the front doors and into the classrooms. They were tiny and the desks were crammed in side by side.

"Each classroom has two grades being taught by the same teacher in the same room," he said. "So if your child is in fifth grade, he or she will come back to the same room, same teacher and slightly different curriculum for the sixth grade."

He led us to the auditorium. "We do Christmas plays in here," he said. "Every single one of our students has a role in the plays; the teachers and the mothers make the costumes. Mrs. Mulford, our fifth and sixth grade teacher, is also the music teacher, so she accompanies the students. Mrs. Parsons is our theater teacher; she's excellent and we are really hoping that one day we can manage to set up a stage in here. That would make it very special, wouldn't it?"

"The children performed an operetta in June at the end of the school year," Elizabeth said. "Can you believe it?" she said to me. "My Billy in an opera, he sung his little heart out."

We all nodded appreciatively, not daring to move on until Mr. Farrell was ready; it was as if he wanted us to appreciate the auditorium a little more before we saw the damaged areas.

"Anyway," he said finally, "along we go." He led us out of the auditorium, through a messy, unfinished courtyard and into an adjoining building that looked nothing like the parts we had just seen. It was partially built. Doorways without doors. The making of a classroom, but windows that had no glass. In one classroom the roof was only half-done; some greenery had taken root inside.

"What happened here?" said Dolly. "It's like night and day."

"Indeed it is," Mr. Farrell said sadly. "You know, the old school was torn down and this one was resurrected when Mr. Fisher bought Montauk. But then apparently he ran out of money or went bankrupt and the work just stopped. We were told it was temporary and that work would resume shortly, but it never did. We had a few bad storms over a few bad winters and these structures became unusable. I don't even think they are safe to repair, they essentially need to be knocked down now, but we don't have the means to do anything."

"That's why the younger grades are being taught in the church," Elizabeth said.

Dolly insisted that we had seen enough to come up with a plan and she took the lead in walking us back to the car, Mr. Farrell in tow.

"Back to the Manor please, George," Dolly instructed as we all piled in the car, Mr. Farrell up front with the driver.

"So, darling, tell me about your children," Dolly said to Elizabeth. "Beatrice tells me you've got a whole brood of boys."

"Oh yes," Elizabeth said. "Four of them, Billy's the oldest, then Gavin, Johnny and my youngest, Jake." She smiled. "They keep me busy."

Dolly kept up the banter with Elizabeth, but she mentioned nothing of the school until we were seated at a small cocktail table in the Manor barroom, close to the lobby, in full view of anyone who might come through. She ordered a round of mint juleps, despite Elizabeth's protests that she would have water.

"It's important that we be seen conducting our business," she said to me quietly. "And that we be seen and taken seriously in what we do, whatever that might be."

"All right," I said, never doubting Dolly's ease in society or her business smarts for a moment, just a little unsure if all this was necessary.

"Cheers," she said, raising her glass, Elizabeth and Mr. Farrell joining her a little sheepishly. "Okay, here's what we need to do," Dolly said, clasping her hands together. "We need to take pictures. I have a photographer friend who can come out from the city and take some pictures of these worn-down buildings. We'll ask him to develop the pictures back in the city and make them as large as possible, so we can display them at the next planning meeting."

She leaned in to Mr. Farrell. "Rich folk need visuals; I'm afraid some of them can be near blind when it comes to seeing outside their own situation." She turned back to Elizabeth and me. "Can we round up some of the school kids? Let's bring them along for the pictures. Then we'll get the images out there somehow." She fixed her gaze on me and smiled. "Out to the media perhaps, if we know of any editors or columnists who might be willing to write about the cause, and we'll generate a lot of interest and donations that way."

Dolly had been quiet for most of the tour, but she'd been taking it all in, absorbing, thinking, and now she was in action mode.

"Maybe we'll interview some of the teachers, some of the kids, just ask them a question or two about what they're wishing for, that kind of thing."

I was thrilled that I had brought Dolly along and for the look of gratitude and trust that Mr. Farrell and Elizabeth had on their faces, but I felt nervous about whether we could pull it off.

"Let's set a target amount we want to raise and we'll solicit donations, and perhaps promise some sort of plaque at the school with the names of the biggest donors." She leaned into the table again. "City folk love to see their names plastered all over the place; it's like pasting dollar bills around town with their faces on them."

"I know what my wish is," Elizabeth said. "It's for the kids to have a stage. They work so hard on those plays and concerts, I just think it would make them feel on top of the world to be able to perform on a stage like they hear about in the big city."

"Could we get them to perform at the masquerade party?" Dolly asked. "It could be our last push before everyone leaves for the city."

"Most of them are around here all year long," Elizabeth said. "Some might be working, but we can round up the majority of them, don't you think, Mr. Farrell?"

"It would be great," Mr. Farrell agreed. "But my wish starts small. We have half-pints of milk delivered to school every day and they are available to the kids for four cents each. Not everyone can afford that. Sometimes I see teachers buying milk for those kids. I'd like every child to be able to have milk every day, and then I'd like to get to work on these buildings so the first and second graders can get out of the church pews and sit in real desks where they belong."

As we chatted and sipped our cocktails a group of women walked in from the tennis courts, dressed in their whites, and headed for a table across the other side of the room.

"Ladies," Dolly called out, "you must meet our guests!" She introduced Mr. Farrell and Elizabeth and clued the women in on our morning, our mission and our need for donations. They all nodded and seemed open to the idea. "Great work, you two," one woman said. "I'll definitely get Geoffrey to donate."

"Oh, me too!" another called out, and then they were all chiming in, not wanting to be left out.

"The leisure photographer is here today, Dolly," one woman said. "Don't forget to put on your tennis whites and get your pictures taken."

Within minutes the group of women were settled at a table nearby and Dolly had left and returned with the hotel photographer.

"Right here is ideal," she said as she led him up to our table. "He's going to snap a picture or two for us, and perhaps we can get it in the newsletter. Remind people that there's work to be done and money to be raised."

Later that afternoon I walked down to the church where the first and second graders had class during the school year. I walked to the front row, pulled down the kneeling bench and rested my elbows on the pew in front of me. Inside the church was beautiful, the magnitude of it all making me feel small and that my secrets were not my own. It had been months since I'd been to church and I couldn't remember the last time I'd prayed. Harry and I only attended on Christmas and Easter, which I'd always felt guilty about, as if it were just for show. But I'd started questioning my beliefs when Charlie died.

I closed my eyes and waited.

"Charlie," I whispered into my hands. "I don't know if you can hear me. I'm sorry it's been a while. I miss you terribly and I have so much I want to tell you."

I waited as if I might get some sign.

"I've met someone, a wonderful, caring, good man, Charlie, and you're not going to believe it, he knows you! Or he knew you. It's Thomas Brown. He was a friend of Hicks McGowen at the repair shop and you worked for him, you and Timmy. Can you believe that? All these years after you left us and I meet someone who was your friend and teacher. Do you remember him? Of course you must. You can't imagine how it feels to have that kind of connection to you. I remember how much you loved your apprenticeship.

"But here's the thing, Charlie: I've been spending an awful lot of time with this man, and I know it's not what our parents would approve of; they don't know about any of it. I know I made my choice to marry Harry and now I have to live with that decision. But I was so young and it was so soon after you were taken from us. I think I was looking for something then, anything but the sadness that swallowed us up after we lost you.

"The thing is that I'm falling in love with this man; I am in love with him, everything about him. I can't help it. Now that I've met him I understand for the first time what that really means. Oh, Charlie, I wish you were here. We were so young before, we never would have talked about any of this kind of thing; we would have ignored each other or annoyed each other and talked to our friends but not to each other. What a waste, what a stupid waste, when we were under the same roof for all those years. I would do anything to have you here now. I know that once you saw Thomas again and once you saw how happy he makes me, you'd understand why I am saying all this. I think you'd approve of my feelings for him.

"But I don't know what to do. What would you do? Don't think badly of me, please. Harry doesn't treat me the way a husband should. He's not loyal to me and he's made me feel so awful, so inadequate, that I wasn't enough for him, that I somehow drove him to act this way. But I'm starting to think that I deserve to be happy, to be loved and appreciated, and Thomas loves me." I sighed and rested my head on my arms. "I just don't know what to do, all I can think about is escaping this life with Harry and starting over, but I don't know how I could ever untangle myself from my marriage—"

The large church door creaked open and let in a stream of bright sunshine. I looked back and saw a woman with a toddler enter the church. Suddenly I panicked. Had I been whispering loudly enough for her to hear? Was anyone else in the church? I gathered my pocketbook, made the sign of the cross and hastily exited down the side walkway hoping I hadn't been overheard.

27

I touched the water with my fingers, then slid my pointed toes into the scorching water like a hand into a tight leather glove. The skin on my calves turned pink, but I crouched down, dipping the rest of my body in slowly, methodically, my rear, my thighs, my stomach, my breasts. It burned for just a moment; then I acclimated to the sensation, steam settling on my face, perspiration forming on my brow. I leaned my back against the metal tub until the water almost reached the top, its rounded surface threatening to spill over with one hasty movement. I sucked in damp air, one sharp breath, but then the water around my body warmed my insides, and I melted into the water. I liked the flinching heat. I sank my body farther into the water, all the way to my neck, and the water rolled over the curved metal edge, pooling at the four feet of the tub; then I slid all the way under, my legs bent, back slightly arched, letting my hair fan out underwater as if it were a golden mane.

Harry hadn't come out the previous week—in fact, he hadn't been to Montauk since things had intensified with Thomas—and I was sick and anxious about seeing him that night. He was to meet with investors about buying out some of Fisher's share of Montauk. The man who had turned cattle fields into the Beach Club and the Manor into a Manhattanites' play-ground had lost a lot of his money a few years back and had been strug-gling ever since a summer hurricane had slammed Miami Beach, his other big development. The damage had all but ruined him.

Harry wouldn't spend the night, he'd conduct his business and head back to the city, and I thanked the stars for that. I hadn't told him about the break-in to our room, the lipstick on the mirror, I hadn't even spoken to him, but I certainly hadn't forgotten. His train had arrived a few hours ago and he was already at his meeting in town at the Fisher building, the tallest in Montauk. The penthouse was Fisher's and the street level housed a restaurant, but the middle five floors were vacant, intended for office space. Harry wanted to turn them into apartments. City-style living at the beach, he said.

While I was out at the school with Dolly and Elizabeth he'd left a mes-sage that I was to meet him at the Manor restaurant for a very early din-ner before he headed back to the city. I had hoped that our paths wouldn't cross. How was I supposed to act around him now? I was scared that he would take one look at me and know about Thomas and I was frightened of what he'd do if he did.

Thomas planned to pick me up at the bottom of Manor Hill before his shift started at six, since I had been sure that Harry would be gone by then. There was no way to get a message to him before dinner and it would be too dark to ride the bike by the time Harry left.

"Beatrice." Harry stood as I approached the table by the window, my hair curled and loose around my shoulders, my face powdered to its natu-ral milky tone, the pink flush from the hot bath gone or at least concealed. A long cream silk goddess dress, simple and elegant at once, flowed around my legs and trailed behind me.

"Hello," I said, giving him my cheek. "How were your meetings?"

"Quite good," he said. "Nothing settled yet, I think we can go lower on price. Fisher's hurting badly from the Miami blow; he needs some solid investors or he'll lose everything."

I nodded and we both looked at the menu for a very long time.

Harry snapped his fingers to the waitstaff and pointed to his bourbon. "And a champagne for the lady!" he called out across the almost empty dining room.

"If you're going to invest why not buy land and build a few houses, or even some small cottages, a lodge, a quaint version of the Manor, or buy a few existing homes? But nobody's going to want to come out here and stay in a high-rise building."

"Of course they will. That's what they know; it will be a taste of home for New Yorkers."

"Folks don't come out here for a taste of city life; they come here to escape that."

He flicked his hand in the air toward my face. "You're wrong. They think they want to escape it, but actually they want to put on airs just as they would back home and mingle with the people they know from the city." I looked away out the window to the silhouettes of trees, not caring to see him dismiss my suggestion.

"Just my two cents," I said, taking a slim out of my cigarette case and lighting it, blowing a steady line of smoke to the window like a tightrope between myself and the outside.

My casual clothes were already laid out on the bed upstairs and I thought about dropping my silk gown to the floor, stepping into my skirt and blouse and waiting for Thomas's truck to pull up on Manor Hill. I was discovering a capacity to make Harry invisible; he only had to do one thing, one flick of the wrist, one snide comment, and I could shut him out completely. I didn't hear his words as he spoke about return on investment and taxes.

"Sounds wonderful," I said, and I heard the way it curled from my lips, sarcastic, as if I didn't give one care. He looked up at me and shook his head ever so slightly, then looked back down to his drink. We ordered and he ate quickly. I picked at my food like a bird, distracted by my thoughts.

"I have to dash up to the room before I go," Harry said. I was wondering at what point I would let Dolly in on my secret until I registered what he had said.

"To the room?" I asked. "Oh, I'll go for you." I thought of my clothes on the bed, laid out neatly with an overnight bag on the floor next to my shoes with some other nighttime necessities. "What do you need?"

"Some paperwork," he said. "I'll go. I know where to look."

"Just tell me where," I said, pushing my chair back slightly. "No need for you to rush when you have to catch the train."

"It's fine," he said, getting annoyed with me, signing the bill, standing.

"I'll join you," I said quickly.

"Suit yourself." He started walking a little too fast for me to keep up in my dress, and he ascended the stairs one or two steps ahead.

In the room I watched him survey the space, trying to remember where he'd kept his paperwork, not even noticing the clothes I had on the bed, the clothes I'd be wearing for Thomas as soon as he left.

I couldn't help but linger on the slope of his shoulders; shoulders I'd once seen as powerful and manly now looked slim and angular. His long legs and lean build appeared lanky, even beanlike. Everything about him, from his chiseled jaw that I'd once found so attractive, to his pointy fingers, to his jolty movements as he strode across the room from one side to the next, seemed sharp and unwelcoming. He was a man I'd once admired; I couldn't even picture that now. I didn't want to and I blamed him for that. It was his fault that I'd found my way into another man's arms, I justified in my head. I was thinking this when I heard myself begin to speak.

"You know, you come here and you don't even attempt to make this marriage work, to spend any real time with me, to make love to your wife," I said, and my eyes widened. Thoughts had become words and the words were floating around in the air between us now.

He turned his head slowly and glared. "Excuse me?" He pulled open a drawer and closed it quietly.

I kept on. "What kind of man doesn't want time alone with his wife when he hasn't seen her for over a week?" I didn't know if these words were coming out of my mouth to assuage the guilt I was feeling or to justify out loud why I was having an affair. The absolute last thing I wanted was to be intimate with Harry, but it made me angry that he didn't want that either.

"What are you suggesting?" His voice low and cruel and bitter, I immediately regretted what I'd started. "I'm about to catch a train so I can get back to work, so I can support us."

"This room was broken into; one of your scorned lovers wrote on that mirror right there that you are a cheating liar, as if we didn't already know that." I had never spoken to Harry this way, ever, but I felt stronger than ever and I wanted to hurt him. "Perhaps if you had found more time for your wife and less time for your whores I'd have a child by now." I was speaking in vulgar terms and yet I couldn't stop myself. "It's your fault I'll never be a mother, God damn you! You haven't shown me any interest in months."

He turned and gave me a deep, penetrating stare, a menace in his eyes that I'd never seen. "How dare you? You ungrateful bitch." He strode over to me and took my wrist in his hand and clenched. A shot of pain ran down my arm, but I tried to act as if it didn't hurt.

"You want me to show you some interest?" he said, pushing my shoulders against the wall, my head knocking back against it abruptly. His hand was on my collarbone, close to my breast, close to my neck, pinning me against the wall, the other hand reached down and hoisted up the fabric of my dress, but it was too long, too full for him to grasp with one hand, so he ripped at the straps on both of the shoulders and with a tear the thin, wispy dress was at my feet.

"Harry," I said in a hoarse cry, "stop!" But he pulled at my undergarments, unhooking and ripping. I tried to pull away from his grip, but his hand went back to my collarbone, his thumb tightly pushing on my neck, and I found it hard to breathe. I grabbed at his shoulders but couldn't move him. With his other hand he unbuckled his belt and pants and within seconds he was slamming me against the wall, my neck still pinned, my toes barely touching the floor. I tried to scream, it felt like a knife between my legs, but I could only whimper. He kept at it; then he grabbed me under the arms and threw me on the bed, on top of the clothes I'd laid out for Thomas. He turned me on my stomach.

"Harry, stop this!" I cried, louder now. "Stop!" But he didn't stop. It was horribly painful, but I squeezed my eyes tight and stopped struggling, I just wanted it over, but that just seemed to make him more angry; he wanted me to resist.

"Is this what you wanted? Is this what you're missing?" he grunted, and he reached forward and yanked my hair back. "Is this what you want?"

He finished, releasing himself inside of me. I imagined his useless sperm pooling like a stagnant pond, everything inside of me closed off to him. I didn't move. Just lay there on my stomach, my face pressed into the sheets and clothes. I didn't care what he did next.

"Was that enough for you?" he said. I heard him do up his pants, open another drawer, find his paperwork and slam it shut. "Jesus Christ. And now I'm going to miss my goddamned train." The door slammed shut.

I emerged from my bed, disoriented, nauseated, in pain. I'd been curled in a ball, wrapped in the sheets, for what seemed hours and when I first awoke I assumed it was morning. I thought of Thomas, and then, in a flash, I remembered the ugliness of Harry's violence against me. I rushed to the bathroom and vomited, then crawled back to the bed, climbed back under the covers and lay there until morning.

28

Don't stand so close to the edge," Thomas said as I absently kicked some gravel and rocks over the edge of the cliff and to the water below.

He was fixing the emergency rope ladder that ran all the way down the cliff front to the shallow bay below. If someone were ever in trouble or in need, if a boat ran ashore and a crew cast off in a dingy, they would be able to get to safety.

I inched forward and shuddered at the thought of Harry, his face, his cruel eyes, chiseled jaw, tanned skin, like a Hollywood movie star, how I had looked at his face when we married and thought I was lucky. Disappointment and despair filled me. The wind picked up slightly and pushed at my back; I wanted to let it take me, carry me wherever it wanted me to go.

"Come on, Bea," Thomas said. "Come away from there." I heard his footsteps approach me. I was two steps away from a massive drop to the ocean below and one step behind me I could feel his breath on my neck.

"The ground is loose," he said. "The elements have worked havoc on this cliff." I inched forward a little more, feeling the magnitude of the drop right in front of me, feeling this man's presence close to me. If I stepped forward I would free-fall into the salty sky and the white-capped waves. If I stepped back I'd be against his chest; his arms would instinctively wrap around me. Both choices pulled at me. The briny air swept the hair back from my face, made my eyes water, and then I felt his arm close around my waist, pulling me away from the cliff and turning me around to face him.

"What are you doing?" he asked. "What's going on with you? You've barely spoken all day, you didn't show up last night, no explanation, and now you're acting strange." He pulled me toward him, but I was frozen.

"Nothing's going on; I couldn't get away." I wondered what my future looked like, a vague question I'd been pushing out of my head for too long but which was now shoved violently to the forefront. I couldn't imagine going back to the city after the summer was over and living out my life with Harry. Not now. How could I stay with him? I could never let him touch me again. I would never be able to look him in the eye, to smile or say anything nice. It would be a nasty life, filled with tension and hatred, a life I never wished for myself. All I wanted was to stay hidden up at the lighthouse with Thomas, but now I even flinched when he touched me.

"Is this about Charlie?" he asked. "I've upset you so much telling you everything, haven't I?"

I shook my head no, then nodded yes. Everything felt so overwhelming. "I do miss him," I said. I felt tears rising up in me, I couldn't let them out, so I searched the sky, forced to pull myself together. Thomas took my hands and squeezed them tight, but his touch weakened my will and the tears rolled down my cheeks. I didn't know what he would do if I told him the truth.

"It's nothing," I said, trying to smile, though my mouth wouldn't cooperate. "Oh, it's this school issue," I said. "It upsets me. Those kids should have a better chance."

"What? That's what this is about, the school?" He looked baffled.

"Did you know that some of those kids' parents can't even afford four cents a day for half a pint of milk?" The stinging sensation from holding back the tears finally left and I gave in completely; tears rolled down my face and I felt some relief. "And you know what they really want?" I took a deep breath and as I exhaled I was sobbing. "What those kids really want is a stage so they can put on shows."

"A stage?"

I couldn't see him through my tears. I knew he was watching me, but he wasn't about to question me in this state. He just pulled me into him and held me tight. How good it felt to cry, to really cry. How hard I'd been working to keep it all inside. Something about his touch, his strong body, his arms wrapping me up, made me lose all control, heaving big, heavy sobs, and he simply held me until I was ready to stop.

Harry ordered flowers sent to my room at the Manor and the next morning a letter arrived.

> *Dear Beatrice,*
>
> *I'm sorry for our abrupt meeting. You know I don't like to fight. I hope these flowers will help you move on from our little disagreement.*
>
> *Love, Harry*
>
> *P.S. I can't make it out there this weekend; I have business to attend to. Take some extra tennis lessons to amuse yourself.*

The note enraged me. I immediately took out a piece of paper from the bureau and wrote back:

> *Harry,*
>
> *It was not a "little disagreement." The flowers have not helped me move on. I am so upset by your violent actions that I am moving to a separate room until I can trust being alone with you again. You can tell the hotel staff whatever you want, that you need your room as an office for meetings, or some other pretense. We can go on in social situations as usual so as not to cause problems, but I cannot and will not sleep in the same room as you. I'm sure you understand.*
>
> *Beatrice*

I moved to a different floor immediately. I packed up my things. I couldn't wait to get out of that room and leave the hideous memory behind. I told the front desk what I needed and didn't care if they believed me or not. Let people talk. I felt a sense of relief and wished I'd thought of it earlier. Now I had a valid reason that allowed us to live apart. He knew it and I knew it.

Two weeks passed and I spent my days working on the masquerade ball charity project, writing the committee's proposal, working through the list of potential donors and writing letters asking them to give generously. I wrote an article for the paper explaining the situation at the school, telling readers how they could help. Interspersed was commentary on the luncheons and parties, what people wore and what people said. On the evenings that Thomas worked, I'd sit with him and we'd talk and work alongside each other.

Spending quiet hours with him allowed me to imagine us living a wholesome life, loving and being loved in this irreproachable way. I imagined helping with the duties of the lighthouse, cooking our meals, reading, writing, all the while being in the vicinity and in the arms of a man I trusted and adored. I daydreamed about this life constantly and when we were together I believed it was real.

One day, in the early evening, we walked all the way along the cliffs to the little yellow cottage that Thomas was convinced he would own one day and we joked about where I'd plant my vegetable garden and how he'd build a swinging bench where we could watch the sunset.

But even though we dreamed about what our life would look like together, I didn't really have the courage to make it real. Harry scared me. After the way he'd treated me, after seeing the look in his eyes as he pinned me against that wall, I feared what he was capable of. I wanted to be with Thomas, but even with the violence and the affairs, real reasons to leave, I didn't know if it was possible. I'd be disgraced and, worse, I'd disgrace Harry and I was terrified of what he'd do to me or to Thomas.

That night, after Thomas had fallen asleep and was breathing deeply, I lay awake silently conjuring up alternative plans. How could we be together? Maybe Harry and I would have an arrangement, living together but apart. Thomas would be my lover. I could stay married, go about my life in the city and come back to Thomas summer after summer. I'd find a way to visit Montauk in the off-season by convincing Harry I should be involved with his investment there, to help maintain the building he was considering buying. What if I learned to play the game the way that he did? I looked over at Thomas, sleeping peacefully, and felt sickened by my own thoughts. He didn't deserve to be loved that way. I turned to my side hating myself for being so vulgar—for thinking, even for a second, that Thomas would stand for that kind of disrespectful arrangement. But if I left Harry and he found out the real reason why, he'd be humiliated and that would fuel a fire of fury inside him.

In the morning Thomas brought me coffee and sensed my sleepless night.

"We can't go on doing this, Bea," he said.

"Doing what?" I said, feeling as though he'd read my thoughts.

"This." He stood up and wrapped a towel around his waist. "Us, making love, spending nights together, spending days together, as if you aren't a married woman. Pretending."

I felt insulted even though he spoke the truth. I was dedicated to Thomas and I cared nothing for Harry anymore—I had erased him from my heart.

"What are you saying, Thomas? Are you saying you want it to end?"

"I'm saying we can't go on acting as if this is normal behavior. We both know it's not."

"You don't want to be with me then?" I didn't have any answers. The idea of not seeing him anymore, of not being with him, sleeping by his side and waking up in his arms felt devastating.

"I think I've made my intentions pretty clear to you by now. I love you. I want to be with you," Thomas said. "I'd do anything and face anyone to make that happen. But you have to be willing to do that, too. You have to be willing to make the hard choices."

I sat up in the bed and pulled the sheet around me.

"I have a lot to lose," I said quietly.

"You also have a lot to gain." He turned away and put his hands on the desk. For a brief moment I wanted to tell him about the night that Harry had torn at my clothes and my body. I wanted to tell him that I feared Harry. "There's nothing else I can do or say to you, Bea. It's your decision."

When Thomas's shift started I walked to the beach below wearing nothing but a slip dress. The beach was empty and the air hot. No one came up this way to sunbathe. With the exception of the occasional surf caster, it was my own private hideaway, just the sound of the waves and the seagulls and nothing to disturb my thoughts.

I lay back and pressed my fingers into the warm, damp sand, my skin absorbing the sun's touch. The water reached up to my toes, then pulled back again, sinking me into the sand a little more each time.

I thought about those early New York days when I first met Harry. Was it just the contrast from my lonely life then that drew me to his dashing looks and fast-paced life: high society, dinners, lavish dos, champagne, diamonds? A world so different from mine. When he asked for my hand in marriage, I had barely even thought about it. It seemed impossible to me now, how I could have thought so little about the man I would spend the rest of my life with. But I had wanted and needed something different then and now what I wanted was to be myself again, to be free and uninhibited.

The tide came in, water reaching farther up my legs, wetting the edges of my dress. You can only go so long pretending, acting as if you're someone you're not. Eventually you must return to who you are, who you were born to be. You can stray from it, try on other roles, other personalities, other beliefs, other lives, but eventually it will catch up with you and you have to return to the only person you can be. As I lay there, eyes shut, hair loose on the sand, feet immersed, it came to me that some people must live their whole lives acting, only returning to themselves in the final moments on their deathbed. I didn't want to do that.

I felt as if I were peeling off an outer layer and my original self was emerging, with all my wants and desires and needs. I felt naked and vulnerable knowing that this decision was the biggest decision of my life, yet somehow I felt stronger and determined. I wouldn't be concealed by someone else's shadow again. My mind was full, churning and processing what had once been too impossible to confront.

The tide was rising. The water was up to my knees now, but I didn't move, too deep into the realization that my life thus far had been a series of missteps, decisions made to cure some other part of me. I sat up, opened my eyes and had to shield them from the sun. I knew what I had to do.

I climbed the zigzagged pathway back up the cliff. I crossed the grass and entered the engine room. Thomas sat on a wooden chair checking the oil levels. I stood at the door until I had his attention; then I shut the door behind me.

"Bea," he said, looking up, eyes wide.

"I want to be with you. I'm going to find a way."

He stood up, walked over to me and held me in his arms so tightly. "We'll find it together." He kissed my forehead and I felt him take a deep breath.

29

White-painted lettering spelled out "Dolores Ann & Friends" across the two large windows of the corner shop in town. As I crossed the village green I could see Dolly's silhouette in the store, hands on her hips, standing back, admiring, then moving in, styling, adjusting a hat, tightening a belt. She was in her element.

The trunk show at the Manor had been a raging success. She sold out of all the ready-to-wear within two hours and placed many orders. Following that, Dolly had taken over the lease for a corner shop for the month of August. It was right on the main high street, two doors down from Shagwong's Tavern across the street from White's Pharmacy, the post office and the liquor store. The corner building had been a fishing and tackle shop, but as Montauk's popularity had been growing and growing over the past few years, so did the rent for storefronts until finally the fishing and tackle shopkeeper just couldn't keep up. Now he sold his inventory out of a pull-along cart right down by the docks.

Dolly saw this shop as an opportunity to showcase and sell her hats but also a place to carry other designers, friends and acquaintances from the city who otherwise might be feeling the effects of the slower summer months when those who liked to shop left town. Though Montauk was full of women with plenty of time and money, there was very little in town to buy, except for the occasional trunk show. Until Dolly opened Dolores Ann & Friends there was nowhere to browse if it took your fancy. In fact, at this late stage in the summer many of the women around the Manor had started taking two-day trips into the city to get their shopping in. They were growing tired of what they'd brought out with them for the summer and missed the act of shopping and spending.

A bell rang as I opened the door. Dolly turned and winked. "Hi, honey," she called out of the side of her mouth, holding two pins between her teeth. Then she went back to her customer. It was an adorable shop. Clark had painted and put up shelving and Dolly and I spent the entire evening prior to the opening arranging the merchandise. It had a beach feel to it; driftwood and an assortment of shells were mounted on the walls, and the merchandise she'd selected was perfect for socializing, summering, Montauk, city women. The centerpiece was a table of her summer hats displayed on head forms. There were straw hats with wide brims, fascinators, navy small-brimmed straws with veils, a fabric bonnet, a straw cloche, a felt cloche, a boat hat, some with a simple hatband and a pin, and others so embellished with flowers and ribbons you could barely make out the hat itself. One even sported a small bird in a nest, atop a wide brim. It really was a stunning showcase.

Around the perimeter of the room, there were displays set up for each featured designer. Regine Brenner was one of those featured—because, as Dolly liked to say, who didn't need to refresh her lingerie drawer when her husband was coming out every weekend? Dolly couldn't keep enough lingerie in stock; the women were snatching up the merchandise as though they might never be able to get their hands on lacy delicates again. I held up a champagne-colored piece and wondered what Thomas would think if he saw me in something like it.

"Bea, there's nothing in your size left!" Dolly called out. "I have another delivery coming tomorrow, I hope. Apparently the ocean air is making everyone a little frisky."

"Oh, I don't need anything," I said, quickly setting it down and moving on to the next display case. Swimsuits by Claude. I picked up a suit; it had a halter top, black all down the left side and white all down the right, with a zigzag down the middle. Another caught my fancy, with a belted skirt bottom and a floral design climbing up one side.

"These are divine, Dolly," I said.

"Oh yes, Claude, he's amazing, isn't he? Those just arrived this morning on the Fisherman's Special. He's in the same building as my factory. I adore him. I have to introduce you to him when we are back in the city. You would love him."

"Can I try one on?" I asked.

"Of course," she said. "Fitting room is in the back. I'll come help you when I'm done here."

I browsed some more before I reached the fitting room. Bracelets, earrings, beach robes, parasols, straw handbags. She'd done a remarkable job of gathering the best pieces for a location like Montauk, a miniature version of the department stores that were beginning to crop up in the city and abroad.

I heard the bell ring and a new crowd of customers arrived, so I took my time in the fitting room, allowing Dolly to attend to them. I'd been considering telling her about Thomas that day. I held such a big secret and I desperately wanted Dolly to understand how my life had been turned upside down over the past month or so, but I needed to catch her alone. I stood for a while and looked at my face in the mirror. My hair was getting long; even loose and in curls around my face it was down to my chest and blonder from the sun than usual, only a hint of red. I stared hard, but I looked different somehow. I made eye contact, waiting for some sort of response, as though my own reflection might talk back and offer some words of wisdom. I wanted someone to tell me my next steps and I wanted Dolly to give me her blessing. As I removed my day dress and began to untie my undergarments I could hear the voices of the women in the store getting louder.

"These are darling, aren't they?" one lady said. "Vivian, you should get these earrings: they'd look good with your eyes." They must've been right outside the fitting room curtain eyeing the jewelry.

"I'll be with you ladies in just a minute," I heard Dolly call from across the room. "I just have to run to the stock room upstairs."

"No rush," someone called back; then they returned to their conversation.

"You can't get those earrings," another woman chimed in. "I've seen them on someone at the Manor."

"Beatrice Bordeaux has those earrings."

I froze at the sound of my name.

"Of course she does," someone said in a loud whisper. "She's best buddies with Little Miss Shopkeeper; of course she gets first dibs at everything." It was Jeanie's voice; I could pick it out a mile off. "Speaking of, did you hear she's not even sleeping in the same room as her husband anymore?"

"What? I didn't know that!" Someone must have stepped closer to Jeanie and to the fitting room, because the curtain separating me from them swayed and rippled. I felt as though I were in the huddle with them. I stepped away from the dividing curtain and pushed my back against the mirror.

"Apparently someone broke into their room," Jeanie said.

"And stole money, I heard." It sounded like Kathleen's voice.

"That's what they're saying; that's the story they're spinning." This was Jeanie talking. "But that's not what really happened. Apparently one of his lovers broke in and scribbled absurdities on his mirror in her lipstick."

The women gasped. "How do you know?"

"I have my sources." Jeanie laughed.

"Whoever the woman is, she's a fool." It sounded like Kathleen speaking. "If she'd kept her mouth shut she'd probably still be in his bed and he'd still be showering her with gifts and money."

"Well, what I heard"—Jeanie was back in charge of the conversation— "was that he told this girl he was going to leave Beatrice for her." More gasps. From me as well. I had to hold my hands over my mouth. Oh, the humiliation of hearing these women gossip about me like this with nothing but a sheet of fabric hanging between us. "And then the gal got angry because he hadn't done anything about it for months and apparently she found out she was one of many."

"Well, of course," someone said. "I'd be angry, too, but do these women really think these men will leave their wives?" A few of them laughed. "And risk the social humiliation?"

"And risk losing money."

I couldn't believe what I was hearing. I had to find out who this woman was who'd broken in and rifled through my personal belongings; how dare she have an affair with my husband and then insult me that way, and to think that Jeanie knew who it was. I was disgusted.

"Oh my," Jeanie said, "look how beautiful this silk chemise teddy is; it looks like pink champagne." The women moved away from the fitting room and began oohing and ahing over Regine Brenner's lingerie. "Oh, my husband would just die if I wore this."

"Buy it," one woman urged.

"That's the only one I have and it has a little tear on it right by the strap!" Dolly called out to Jeanie as she walked back into the store. "Your tailor could fix it, I'm sure, but Regine only sent one. Have you seen the way it crisscrosses in the back? And it snaps so you can take it off quickly." Dolly laughed.

"So alluring," Jeanie said. "It may be your last one, but it's in my size," she said. "Should I try it on, ladies?"

I was about to be exposed and humiliated. I should have gotten dressed and walked out long before I let them talk about me that way. Now I had to hope to stay hidden in the fitting room until they left or risk someone pulling the curtain back and seeing me. And of course Dolly would soon come over and blow my cover. I had no choice. I quickly put my clothes back on, touched up my lipstick, arranged my hair, took a deep breath and walked out of the fitting room into the store and over toward Dolly. I heard a gasp and the women went quiet.

"I'm so sorry, Dolly," I said, kissing her quickly on the cheek. "I have to go, but we'll talk later."

"Okay, bye, thanks for stopping in."

"By the way, it looks really fabulous in here," I said as I turned to the three women. "I imagine there's been a lot of gossip about me and Harry, and for good reason. Marriage isn't always what you expect it to be. Life can be so beautiful and then everything can change in an instant. It's not easy. But I am doing the best I can."

I wasn't going to walk out of there with my tail between my legs. I wanted them to feel ashamed of treating another woman that way.

"Oh, and Jeanie," I said, before opening the door, "you're right; that Regine Brenner does wonders in the bedroom. You should give it a try." I forced a smile and walked out the door. The silence that fell across the store was deafening. I didn't look back, but I felt their eyes on me as I walked out the door, crossed the street, turned right and kept going.

It was around noon and it was hot. I walked through the streets and out the end of town and began the ascent up Montauk Highway. It would take me an hour at least to walk all the way to the lighthouse, but I didn't care. I wouldn't go back to the Manor yet. I needed to clear my head. I had felt humiliated and embarrassed in that dressing room, but as I walked those feelings left me. Did it even matter who Harry was having an affair with? Did it even matter if he slept with the whole goddamned Manor? I didn't want him; I didn't want this life; he could have them all for all I cared. I was shedding my fears, my worries and the insults with each step. By the time I reached the bottom of the big hill with no more turns, no more diversions and roads to take me anywhere but the light, I was smiling. It was ideal, in fact, that the truth was getting out about Harry. It gave me more ammunition to leave him. It gave me a strange sense of hope and determination.

When I heard a horn honk and the engine of a car pulling up beside me, I was perspiring. It was Patrick.

"Get in," he said.

"Thanks." I climbed into the front seat.

"What are you doing walking all this way?" he said. "That's what the bike is for, isn't it?"

"I felt like walking," I said. "Although I was running out of steam. Are you picking up laundry for Elizabeth?"

"Nope." He shook his head. "I've been recruited."

"For what?"

He grinned but shrugged his shoulders. "Can't say," he said. "But looks like you're about to find out."

I saw Thomas first, on the grass, shirtless and sweating, hammering nails into a wooden post. Farther back toward the light was a team of five other men I didn't recognize, all hard at work, assembling and hammering and measuring.

"What on earth are you doing?" I asked Thomas as I approached.

"We're building something," he said matter-of-factly, looking up briefly, wiping away sweat from his brow, then going back to the hammer and the post.

"What do you mean you're building something? What are these guys doing?"

"Building a stage. You said you wanted one for the school, right? I recruited some men from Shagwong's. Told them I'd buy them a round or two of beers if they made this happen in time for your fancy party."

"But how do you know what size they need and what the school wants and all the details?"

Thomas nodded to the group of shirtless, sweaty men behind him. I strained to make out who anyone was in the bright sunlight, so I cupped one hand over my eyes. Mr. Farrell stood up and waved; hairy potbelly and all, it was more than I had wanted to see. I waved back, smiling.

"We're building a stage!" he called out.

"I can see that. Nice work!"

"We're going to put it up at the ball and get the kids to perform," he said. "Then reassemble it at the school in September."

"Amazing."

I turned back to Thomas. I wanted to kiss him and I had to squeeze my arms tight to my sides to stop myself from throwing my arms around him in front of all these men. "This is incredible, do you know that?" I said in a whisper. "You're incredible."

"You're the cat's pajamas yourself," he said; then he grabbed my chin in his hand and gave me a quick peck on the lips.

"Thomas!" I stepped back abruptly and looked up to see if anyone had seen, but everyone had their heads down or their backs to us. He laughed and returned to work.

30

<hr/>

That weekend, Winthrop Aldrick hosted an outdoor party at the Surf
Club. It was to be a casual affair, guests barefoot on the sand and
lighthearted, but "casual" was not part of Winthrop's vocabulary. The
gents had their trousers rolled at the cuffs and most of the women knew
to wear a shorter hemline, but Winthrop had tables set up on the beach,
candles everywhere ensuring a glow even as the sun went down, and a
staff of about fifty maids in black serving dresses and white aprons passing
hors d'oeuvres and aperitifs before dinner.

Harry and I entered the gathering walking stiffly, side by side, having
been driven there with another couple by George. I was pleased that we
weren't the first to arrive; I wanted our entrance together to be seen—to
let the few times that we were together be worth something and put on a
good show to keep gossip at bay. Harry led us immediately over to Winthrop. I hesitated at first, because Jeanie and her husband were part of the
group talking with him, but Harry barged in.

"Harry, my friend, so glad you made it." Winthrop shook his hand and
slapped him on the arm. Winthrop was golden brown from the sun, which
made his silver hair stand out even more, as well as his perfectly shaped,

gleaming teeth. I wondered if he had been an actor. "And what a pleasure to see your beautiful wife." He took my hand, squeezed it a little too tight and kissed it, his eyes not leaving mine. "Hello, Bethany."

"Beatrice," I said.

"Beatrice." He nodded and winked as if we were in on some kind of secret. He was handsome but much better looking from a distance. Close up, if you caught him off guard when he wasn't smiling you could see the crevices of fine wrinkles where the sun hadn't managed to tan.

I looked away and saw Jeanie staring. We hadn't spoken since the episode in Dolly's store. "Would you like something to drink?" I asked, turning to Harry, putting my hand on his arm.

"They're bringing drinks around," he said.

"I know, but I'm parched. I think I'll go to the bar."

"Suit yourself."

When I returned with an old-fashioned and a martini, the conversation had picked up. Winthrop and his wife, Gloria, Jeanie, her husband, Cecil, and Harry were all engaged in some topic that was more intense than before I'd left, and while Jeanie seemed excited, Winthrop's wife looked incredibly bored. Equally suntanned, yet slightly younger than he was, she seemed to have heard all this a hundred times before and was looking out at the other guests as if hoping for someone or something more interesting.

"If they would take me I'd volunteer myself to fight with the defenders of the Spanish democracy," Winthrop said. "But in general they want more youthful lads, a bit sprightlier."

Jeanie laughed loudly, her round bosom jostling as she did so, and she playfully tapped Winthrop on the shoulder. "Oh, I think they'd be thrilled to have you," she said. "Don't you think so, Cecil?" She was talking to her husband but didn't turn away from Winthrop.

"Sure, but you're better off leaving it to the young'uns," Cecil said. "They are really blasting the heck out of their own country; it's a damn shame."

"Well, somebody's got to stand up for them," Winthrop said. "I'm not afraid of being on the front lines. I mean Roosevelt going for neutrality, that's about as passive as you can get. I'm not a passive kind of guy. What kind of a leader is he if he won't get involved? What does that say about America as a country?"

"I agree wholeheartedly," Jeanie said, placing her hand on her chest as if she were about to sing.

Winthrop seemed to be boosted by her vote of confidence. "Maybe I should volunteer; maybe I should just show up. I know what war is; I've got some more fight in me."

Jeanie was giddy as if she'd been drinking all afternoon. Cecil didn't seem quite as enthralled by everything Winthrop suggested. I hated the way she turned into a completely different person around anyone with deep pockets who could help her out in some way. I hated more that others didn't find her insincerity as transparent as I did.

"Come on, Jeanie," Cecil said. "Let's go and find some of those deviled eggs you like; they're passing them around." He tried to pull her back from Winthrop a little, but she shook her arm free.

"I'm not hungry," she said. I didn't blame her husband; Jeanie was on the verge of embarrassing herself, throwing herself at Winthrop and his wife like that.

"Darling, did you know that Winthrop has been nominated by Mr. FDR himself to be the President of the National Foundation for Infantile Paralysis?" she said, again speaking to but not turning toward her husband.

"Oh," he said. "The March of Dimes?"

"That's right: actually, I just accepted," Winthrop said. "Although it wasn't the President who asked me to do it, Jeanie. It was one of his people; he's just involved." He laughed. "Now I've got the job of building the local chapters. I'm actually looking for someone to head up the New York City chapter, a really important one that I'll be pretty involved with." Jeanie locked eyes with him and I wondered what she had up her sleeve. "We're planning to have collection boxes on every corner this Christmas season, so if all those New Yorkers and their kids would drop a dime in the box on their way to and from work we'll make a lot of money for the foundation."

Jeanie stood a little taller and arranged her hair, then looked from Cecil to Winthrop, Winthrop to Cecil. When Winthrop turned to his wife, Jeanie glared at Cecil as if he'd just failed a test.

"And then, of course, there're the big parties we'll be throwing, grand events at the best spots in New York City."

Jeanie was smiling nervously, as if waiting to be invited.

"Of course, you'll all be at the top of the invite list," Winthrop said. "And Gloria and I will insist that you sit at our table, won't we, love?" He gave his wife a gentle nudge.

"Oh yes, of course," she said absently.

"Well, that's fine work, Winthrop," Harry chimed in. "Admirable. How are you going to do it all between this and your investments?"

"Well, I consider this an important investment, too, an investment in the children and an investment in the poor kids who are afflicted with polio and paralysis."

"Bravo," Jeanie said. "It's wonderful. They need someone like you at the helm."

"And what does Beatrice think, that's what I'd like to know," Winthrop said, startling me. "She's a quiet one today. Makes you wonder what's going on in that pretty little head of hers."

I knew it was part of his "charm"—he'd acted the same way on the yacht with Dolly and me—but I really didn't feel like playing along. Jeanie looked as if she'd just sucked a lemon. I wanted to tell her to compose herself; I was sure she had no idea her face was so contorted. And then she seemed to snap out of it and get back in the saddle.

"Well, Beatrice, what *do* you think?" she asked.

"About what?"

"Winthrop and his work with the March of the Dimes?" she said, exasperated.

"Oh, I think it's very important work."

Jeanie rolled her eyes at my vague response and changed the subject.

Once I began to feel the attention moving off me and onto something else I was relieved and about to excuse myself; that was, until Winthrop drew close to my side.

"Say, you should consider putting your name in the hat for the New York chapter," he said rather loudly. "It could be a lot of fun," he whispered this time, raising his eyebrows. "*We* could have a lot of fun."

For a split second I was flattered but then immediately was offended at his suggestion.

"Thank you for the . . ." I hesitated, trying to muster an appropriate response. "For the suggestion, but I'm working with Harry on his business a little and I just wouldn't have time."

"Really? It's for an excellent cause."

"I'm sure it is," I said, "but Harry and I—"

"I didn't think you two seemed all that entwined in business." He smirked and took a long sip of his drink but kept his eyes on me. "Don't look so surprised. You're a beautiful woman; any man in his right mind would want to spend time in your presence. You can't blame me for asking you to join the March of Dimes. Don't look at me like I'm a monster."

The interaction made me laugh. There was something oddly charming and ridiculous about Winthrop's blatant advances.

"Dear God, and now she's laughing at me." Winthrop put his hand to his head dramatically.

"I'm sorry," I said. "I didn't mean to laugh; it's just . . ." I shook my head.

Everything was starting to feel like a joke. Of course part of me still cared what other people thought of me and my marriage, it had become habit to care so much, but more and more I felt myself untying the obligation to give a damn.

Winthrop was looking at me waiting for a response.

"I didn't mean to laugh," I repeated. "I'm flattered, but Harry and I are *entwined,* Winthrop. For better or worse."

He shrugged. "Well, if you ever change your mind you know where to find me, out here or in the city."

He handed me a business card, then moved on to another circle. I was still amused; was everyone sleeping with everyone? Had I just been blind to it all this time? I thought of Thomas and immediately wanted to be away from all of this; I smiled just thinking of him. As I looked around the party I felt someone's eyes on me once again and I knew, before even turning around, that it was Jeanie.

Tensions between us were at an all-time high. Aside from her getting caught out at Dolly's store for her foul talking about me to the other women, she was beyond furious that I had taken such a prominent role in the charity efforts. The photograph that Dolly had arranged of the two of us with Elizabeth and Mr. Farrell at the Manor had appeared in *The East Hampton Star* with a headline about our dedication to raising money for the local kids. Dolly had managed to have the photograph featured prominently and Jeanie was enraged. She had been telling people that Dolly and I were trying to take all the credit for raising the money. I personally didn't care about getting recognition for it, but I had become passionate about raising money for the school. Knowing there was a deadline and that it would end soon and that the city folk would go back to Manhattan and forget all about Montauk until the next summer made me determined to solicit as many donations as possible before the ball.

After a few hours at Winthrop's party I found a seat away from Harry. A couple of men behind me were talking about publishing and a piece that had appeared in *The New Yorker* and I turned my head slightly to listen in. "I don't like that Parker woman as much as everyone else does; she writes for female readers." They must be talking about the most recent Dorothy Parker piece; I had loved it.

"I'm a fan of the magazine, though," another man said. "I've been talking to Raoul Fleischmann about some other opportunities in publishing," one man said.

"We subscribe, don't we, darlin'?" another called out to his wife. "It's very funny."

"Sophisticated too," the other man said. "It speaks to our crowd, I think, don't you? We don't have the same troubles as the rest of the country. We have our share of problems, but they're just not the same desperate struggles as the folks in the middle states. I mean there are some manufacturing plants that have shut down, but we don't rely on coal mines and steel plants; in the city we have diversified our labor. It's fun to have a magazine more in tune with our interests, something that speaks our language."

Harry's voice joined the conversation. "You're investing out here, too?" he asked. I stayed where I was sitting, with my body turned away slightly, close enough to hear but not obliged to participate.

"No, investing in *The New Yorker*. Why? What are you planning for Montauk?"

"I've got some ideas for Fisher's old office building in town," Harry said. "Not a bad spot for a full-floor vacation apartment, don't you agree?"

"I wouldn't turn my nose up at it, but how about a few hotels right along here, overlooking the ocean?"

"Like they did in Miami? Sure, we're talking about it," Harry said.

That was the first I'd heard Harry speak of hotels on the beach. They went on to talk about the opportunities to make Montauk even better, to pick up where Fisher had left off. I looked out to the vast sandy beach and the ocean, then out to the dunes that ran down as far as I could see, and I marveled at its beauty. How could we be looking at the same stunning vistas, unscathed by development and construction, but see completely different things? When they saw this serene open space, stretching out as far as the eye could see, all they saw were dollar signs popping up as beachfront hotels. When I looked, I saw freedom.

I was tired of this party. I told Harry I had a headache and asked George to drive me back to the Manor. As I climbed into the back seat of the car I saw Jeanie standing in the parking lot, smoking, watching me. I felt her glare even as we drove away.

I lay in bed and wrote about the party in a melancholy mood. It should have been a relaxed affair, our toes in the sand, the ocean waves breaking just a few feet from us, everyone leaving their work and worries behind for a few hours. Yet instead the mood had been filled with expectations, greed and entitlement and every time I entered a conversation with the men it was about changing the place we all claimed to love so much.

Someone should stop them, I wrote. Someone should ban them from lining the sandy beaches with tall, lavish hotels before it's too late. Someone should stop them from turning the pastures with cattle and wildflowers and winding trails into mansionettes and social clubs. If people wanted a place to escape the concrete city and enjoy nature then they should stop this compulsion to make money out of the untouched and unblemished. Once it was developed and ruined and turned over, there'd never be another chance to return it to its former beauty. There'd be other towns to fall into favor once Montauk was stripped of its unique charm, transformed into another "hot spot." Everyone would go through the excitement again of finding something new, someplace untouched, different from the rest, with places to walk, to get lost, to find people who are true and hardworking and forthright and kind. And then that too would change until everything became just an unrecognizable dot on the map.

I didn't put it in an envelope and address it to Mr. Rosen as I usually did when I finished a piece—it was too close to home, writing about Harry's investments. Instead I looked around the room and thought about where to keep it hidden, to be sure no housekeepers or, God forbid, Harry saw it if they snooped around. I folded it and slipped it into the side of my pocketbook.

31

---❦---

Thomas had left the subject of my marriage alone for a while. I supposed he trusted me to figure out a way to tell Harry at the right
time. I thought about it constantly but didn't know how anything was going
to work. I threw myself into the charity ball. I felt more invested than ever
and being busy agreed with me. My disappointment at being childless less-
ened and I didn't know if I had begun to accept it or if it was that I was
preoccupied and happy with other aspects of my life. I was so busy that I
almost didn't notice when my monthly bleeding didn't come. It wasn't until
that Monday when Dolly accompanied me on a bike ride up to the elementary school to drop off some paperwork that I noticed anything different.

We rode along, with me leading the way at first, our skirts tucked under
our legs, our head scarfs flapping behind us. Dolly was chattering on about
something, but I just couldn't pay attention to her voice anymore. I was
feeling utterly exhausted. I began huffing and puffing, wondering what
on earth was going on—after all, the ride to the lighthouse was much farther than to the school and I had made that ride at least twenty times. I
pulled to the side of the road when I saw a large boulder that would serve
as a resting spot.

"Sorry, Dolly, I'm going to have to take a little break. I'm a bit out of breath."

"Quite all right," she said, pulling a pack of Luckies from inside her pocketbook. "I'm happy to take a breather." She lit her cigarette and offered one to me.

"No, thanks." Suddenly the thought of smoking turned my stomach. "I'm actually a little dizzy," I said, sitting on the rock and steadying myself with my hands on my knees.

"Don't worry," Dolly said. "We're in no rush. It's quite warm, actually; maybe the sun is getting to you."

I lay back across the boulder, worried that if I didn't allow myself to rest for a moment I might faint. I gazed out to the pond with half-closed eyes and lazily let a man in a rowboat fade in and out of view. He pulled the oars gently and little ripples of water rolled out toward me, a simple lulling movement in an otherwise calm and flat water. I felt a ripple under my skin, a tiny flutter of nausea, and suddenly I thought I might vomit. I sat up with a start and leaned my head over my bent knees, retching, but nothing came out.

"Easy there, Bea," Dolly said, taking the last drag of her cigarette, stubbing it out on the ground and walking over to me, rubbing her hand on my back. "You're not pregnant, are you?"

"No," I said, feeling perspiration form on my brow. "Of course not, it's impossible."

"Impossible?"

"The doctor said so. I'm done. Past it." I could barely get the words out. Saliva gathered in my mouth and I tried to vomit again. I thought of my menstruation. I'd had no cramping, no tightness and none of the irritability that usually preceded my monthly flow.

"Well, either you've eaten some lobster past its prime or your doctor was wrong about you being past yours."

Barely opening my eyes, I counted the weeks on my fingers. It was late. It hadn't arrived. My God, I thought. Could it be? I looked up at her.

"Darling, Harry's going to be over the moon," Dolly said.

I reached up and grabbed Dolly's arm. "Don't." It was all I could muster. I looked pleadingly into her eyes, sweat dripped down my cheek and I felt positively faint. "You can't say anything to Harry."

Dolly's face dropped. "Oh dear."

"Are you going to the city this week?" I asked.

"I am now," she said, fixing her head scarf. "We'll go Wednesday. I'll make the arrangements."

"Thank you." Breathless, I vomited onto the dusty side of the road.

We sat on the train across from each other, bolt upright, dressed for the city, dressed for news. Dolly looked almost masculine in a short-brimmed straw hat, trimmed with a brown grosgrain ribbon, brown-and-white-striped silk dress with a collar and a matching brown silk necktie. I wore a wide brim, angled so that it covered half my face should someone see me entering the doctor's office, with a high-necked, buttoned-up navy belted dress to appear respectable.

If I could have gone the whole way into the city without speaking a word I would have. It wasn't that I didn't want to tell Dolly, I'd been dying to tell her everything about Thomas, about how he had changed my life in the course of a few short months, but this changed matters. Dolly had become a dear and close friend to me and I knew she would approve greatly of it all, she would absolutely devour all of this news and encourage me, but it was the "after" part I knew I wouldn't want to hear. Dolly's philosophy was to have your fun, pursue your dreams, indulge your desires, but go back home eventually, always maintaining your place in society.

I looked out the window and watched as we rode along the water's edge on Napeague Stretch, that narrow strip of land connecting Montauk to the rest of Long Island. It couldn't have been more than half a mile wide with the Block Island Sound on one side, the Atlantic Ocean on the other, and a railroad track and a two-way road running down the middle. It was the thread that linked my surreal Montauk life to my reality in Manhattan. Traveling down that stretch of railroad made my body tighten and clench, leaving me panicked in case I somehow couldn't return.

I had drifted so far out in thought that I had almost forgotten I had company.

"Good Lord, Beatrice, I am trying to give you some space, a little time for you to be ready to catch me up here, but what am I supposed to do, sit here all day and wait?"

"I'm sorry; I'm a million miles away."

"You've obviously got a lot on your mind. But my mother always told me, a problem shared is a problem halved."

"I don't know where to start."

"Start with the lovemaking, of course. Tell me everything, from the beginning."

Despite the fact that I knew she'd try to talk sense into me, I now felt a swell of relief, knowing I would finally confide in her.

"Oh, Dolly, I've had the most wonderful couple of months; it's just been divine. I feel alive again."

She clapped her hands and leaned onto the table between us.

"You know Elizabeth?" I asked.

"The laundry girl with the boys, of course I know her. Oh God, you're not in love with a woman, are you?"

"What? No, don't be ridiculous."

"I'm not opposed to that kind of thing, it can be quite freeing and wonderful if you are going through a creative spell, it can open up your artistic side, but that just doesn't seem to fit your current predicament." She nodded to my stomach.

"Dolly, no."

"That's good; you should save that for when you're a little older, when you know your body really, really well. It can be quite profound, and boy, do you have some tricks to take home and teach your husband. Anyway, go on."

I laughed. "I'll keep that in mind, thank you. Elizabeth has been very kind to me. I got to know her family, her boys; she lets me tag along on drives around Montauk."

"How lovely. I can tell you that some of the most stimulating parties Clark and I have hosted have been those we've had for the gents at the factory and their families: anniversaries, daughters' wedding receptions. Quite often more substance than what we get in our circles. Do go on."

"Well, through Elizabeth I've met the most wonderful man—loving, caring, thoughtful, handsome, a manly man." I told Dolly about seeing him in the fishing village, our run-in at the greasy pig contest and again at his house, his fall. I told her everything.

"I adore this story," Dolly said. "An affair with a lighthouse keeper! How thrillingly romantic."

"I was helping him at the lighthouse; we were around each other for hours at a time, sometimes with nothing to do but talk. He understands me more than anyone ever has. I've told him things I didn't even know about myself. He told me things about his estranged wife, his son—"

"An estranged wife? Ooh, the plot thickens. You know they're often more passionate when they've been denied something, don't you find? The men that have a beautiful wife, a beautiful home and beautiful children, they get bored of all the beauty and the availability of everything. The best affairs are with those who have been robbed of something, or who have to work hard to get it. They really know how to appreciate a woman, if you know what I mean. Oh my, I'm getting flustered just thinking about it."

I nodded absently; she spoke as if I'd experienced many affairs that I could compare this to. She was turning our love into a cliché, as if Thomas were of little significance, just someone to reignite the spark of my marriage. I urgently wanted her to understand how deeply I felt about him.

"He told me things he's never told anyone before, unfathomable stories about the war and how those times haunt him. He trusts me. He's taught me about wildlife out here and the ocean and the stars, Montauk before it was developed and how to run a lighthouse."

"How to run a lighthouse?" she said sarcastically. "How very salacious!"

"It was exciting, though; it is," I said, flustered. "He cares what I think and what I know, and I care about him, too—it's so different to actually have an intellectual connection with a man as well as physical."

"Yes, I can see that."

"But Dolly, the one thing that's so astonishing is that he knew my brother." I waited for a response.

Dolly raised her eyebrows. "Really?"

"Yes, he worked for a little while in my hometown. It makes me think it was my fate to meet him. I was meant to come here this summer and this was supposed to happen."

"I understand how that would mean something to you, Beatrice, but come now, it's a small world; it's not that uncommon."

"Dolly, you don't understand; I never thought I'd meet anyone else that I could connect to my brother." I could have gone on, but I wasn't able to convey how important it all was to me, and Dolly seemed to be getting a little tired of my story.

"I thought you were going to tell me about the whoopee!" she said loudly. "That's the whole point of all this, right?"

I put my face in my hands. "Dolly, will you stop!" I said through my fingers. "It's like nothing I've ever known."

"Go on."

"To have this intense combination of lust and passion, yearning and caring and wanting at the same time as a meeting of minds, to feel loved, appreciated, to have all of that in one person is something I've never experienced. And he's, how can I say this, very masculine." I laughed, a little embarrassed to be talking so openly, and yet picturing him and missing him at the same time. "I'm absolutely wild about him. I'm alive just talking about him." It felt surreal to talk to another person about all of this, after keeping it secret for so long.

Dolly nodded, but I could see the excitement draining from her face. "Okay, very nice." She sat a little taller and placed her fingertips together. "So you've had your fun; it's wonderful; I'm really quite proud of you. You deserve it. All the men do it until it bores them and they come back home again, so there's no reason why you shouldn't enjoy yourself, too."

She smiled but only with her lips; her eyes were serious. "So, now the fun is over you need to start thinking about what you'll do, if you are"—she raised her eyebrows—"you know, in the family way."

"What I'll do? I don't even know if I am," I said in a whisper, even though the first-class train car was empty. "This could all be a lot of talk about nothing, a few bad oysters."

"Be realistic, Beatrice." Dolly was taking a tone with me now and I wasn't sure I liked where it was going. "You need to think what you'll do if it's not Harry's."

I let out a loud, sarcastic laugh and shook my head. "It's not Harry's. There's no way in hell it could be Harry's. We've been trying for years and he hasn't impregnated me."

I thought about the night he had forced himself on me, the only time he could possibly have been responsible for my current situation. I cringed at the thought of a child, so pure and innocent and wanted, coming from something so vulgar and painful and full of hatred. There were a few times prior, much earlier, but I had had my monthly flow since then. I took some small solace in recalling what the doctor had told me, that the woman must climax in order to open up "the interior passages," and I clung to that detail, knowing with every part of my being that it could not be Harry's child.

"So you took up with a handsome lighthouse keeper and now you're very possibly with child," Dolly said.

"You make it sound like a terrible thing."

"It's not ideal, is it? It sounds like you've enjoyed yourself. I just wish you'd been more careful, used a diaphragm and considered the consequences more carefully. Now you have a 'situation' to deal with, you need a plan." She looked out of the window. I felt like a scolded child. "The way I see it you have two choices. Number one, you could get it 'taken care of.' I know someone who got herself into a difficult situation last year and she saw someone who handled things with delicacy and he was very discreet. He told her exactly what to say and do during recovery to make it appear as if she had been ill, a menstruation problem no man wants to know about."

"If I'm expecting then I'm having the baby," I said adamantly. "I am keeping the baby."

"Darling, darling, relax." She reached into her bag and brought out a silver flask. "I had a feeling we'd need this," she said, unscrewing the cap, taking a swig, then handing it to me. "Take a drink; you're getting your nerves up." The bourbon burned as it went down my throat but had an almost immediate effect.

I pushed it back toward her and took out a cigarette, lit it and inhaled deeply.

"Sweetheart." She took my hand in hers. "I'm not saying that's what you should do; I'm simply laying all the options on the table. A far better choice, and this is what I would do if it were me, you announce your pregnancy with sheer excitement and you and Harry live happily ever after."

"What? You think I should just play as if it's Harry's baby? Just go back to my marriage and let him believe, for his whole life, that this is his child and let the child believe that Harry's his father?"

"Well, yes, of course," Dolly said. "My only concern is those tests they can do now to determine the father. They can test the baby's blood once it's born and see if it's a match with the husband. What if Harry insisted? You'd be ruined, and so would the poor baby. But I suppose that's just a risk you'd have to take."

"Dolly, there are things that have gone on in my marriage that you don't know about."

She sighed. "I do know, darling. Unfortunately, that's the downside to the circles we run in; everyone knows everyone's business. It's more common than you think."

I felt disgraced all over again. Why hadn't she said something to me if she knew about the affairs all along? I sat a little taller. "I'm not just talking about his indiscretions. Dolly, there are things that you could not possibly know about." She didn't push me to talk more. "And besides, those tests are not even accurate," I said. "Anyway, I don't want to talk about this anymore until I get the results."

"Okay, love," she said, patting my hands. "You know I'll help you in whatever you decide. But Beatrice, darling, you need to think things through logically, before you find out, before you get emotionally invested."

I pulled my hand away and looked out the window, the brim of my hat turned to her. I couldn't go back to my old life. Not now. And I couldn't deprive Thomas of what was rightfully his and mine. The thought of expecting a child gave me the courage to build a new life for myself and for this child, no matter what the cost. This baby deserved a father like Thomas, a good man.

"I'm going to be with him, Dolly," I said quietly. "It's no use trying to persuade me otherwise. I've made up my mind."

She patted my hands. "Let's just wait and see what the doctor says before you go making any rash decisions."

I hadn't mentioned anything to Thomas before I left for the city. I wanted to see the doctor first. I had assumed, naïvely, they would be able to tell me right then and there at the doctor's office if I was in fact with child. I already knew the answer—my body felt different, my breasts were sensitive, I was dog tired and my monthly flow still hadn't come—but I wanted to confirm what I already knew.

Dolly had taken me to a different doctor, a friend of a friend of a friend, but still I had to provide my husband's name and information. I only gave my address at the Manor and told them we were both out there for the rest of the summer, just to be sure that there'd be no correspondence back to the apartment in the city.

While the doctor had been all business, the nurse looked at me with sympathetic eyes. "Mrs. Bordeaux, I know you are anxious and excited to find out, but the doctor is very strict about informing his patients of the news," she said as she helped me dress.

"But I'm not in the city, so a phone call would be the fastest way."

"One time the doctor relayed the news to a woman over the telephone that she was not with child. It must have been a bad line because she thought he said she was with child and she told her entire family and had a big celebration. It wasn't until two weeks later at a follow-up appointment that they realized there had been a miscommunication. The doctor has insisted on speaking in person or in writing ever since."

"But I'm staying at the Manor in Montauk; they have a very good phone line."

She shook her head.

"What about a telegram?"

"There is still room for error. It seems to me that your body is showing all the signs of a pregnancy; the doctor even told you that. Just be patient and you'll get the letter in the mail in a week or so."

"But could you at least ask him, see if he'll make an exception?" I pleaded, desperate to know as soon as possible so I could tell Thomas.

"He won't allow it," she said. "Be on the lookout for the mailman. I'll make sure he sends it out as soon as he gets the results."

It would kill me to wait another week to share the news with Thomas. But more than that, I was worried that the letter would get into the wrong hands and Harry might somehow find out.

This time the large doors of 820 Eighth Avenue didn't seem quite so intimidating. On impulse, I had decided to visit Mr. Rosen at his office while Dolly stopped at her factory, and when I arrived I was escorted straight up to see him. He had a modest office with a desk piled high with papers, a window looking west. His head was down and he was typing furiously. I knocked gently on the open door.

"Yes," he said, still typing, not looking up.

"I hope I'm not disturbing you."

He looked up and smiled. "Beatrice! What a pleasant surprise." He cleared a chair of newspapers and gestured for me to sit down.

"I was in the city and I thought I'd pay a visit before my train back to Montauk."

"I'm so glad you did. You know your column has been very well received. My publisher is happy with the response."

"I've been surprised anyone would want to read it."

"We've had a lot of letters commending the writing and the insight."

An unfamiliar flutter of shock and pride ran through me.

"Did you bring me something else to read?"

"Sorry." I shook my head.

"Too bad," he said. "We like the drama that's going on out there about the fundraising."

I unfastened my pocketbook and took out the article I'd written after Winthrop's party about greedy investors wanting to change the landscape of Montauk. It was rough and I hadn't planned to submit it, at least not without rewriting. I unfolded it and skimmed what I'd written, not really sure if it made sense, but out of obligation to present something I held it out toward him.

"I guess I have this."

He took it from me and read it while I sat awkwardly, trying not to shift in my chair. It felt like it took him forever. I began to feel queasy.

"That's what I like about you," he said finally, placing it on his desk next to his typewriter. "You capture how people connect or rather how they don't, with all their opposing motivations, all wrapped up in that quaint little town. It's really quite something."

It felt nice to be good at something, but I worried about how Harry would react if he ever found out I was behind the pen name.

"You don't think it's too much?" I asked.

"Well, you'll rattle the potential investors with this, of course, but that's what works. You don't beat around the bush; you don't let those rich folk scare you."

It was as if he were speaking about someone else. I'd always been scared of everyone and everything: scared if I did the wrong thing, said the wrong thing, scared of losing the people closest to me, of being all alone in this world. And yet I'd been knocking down every fear I'd confronted since I'd set foot in Montauk, and now I was almost definitely with child, I was going to have a baby that couldn't possibly be my husband's. In that moment I felt fearless.

32

―✦―

B ack in Montauk I waited. I tried to act normal. Every afternoon I walked down to the post office just as the train pulled in to deliver the mail. Nothing. I spent my days avoiding people, even Thomas. I made excuses about being busy at the Manor. It didn't seem right to tell him anything until I had official news from the doctor; I didn't want to get his hopes up or, worse, to make him panic.

And I kept having the same dream again and again. It always started walking out to the vegetable garden with a bucket and trowel to dig up some carrots and potatoes for dinner; it was autumn and chilly up on the hill. The sky quickly changed from a cool blue to a chilling yellow-grey as I moved farther away from the house and across the grass, as if a downpour were on the horizon. I hurried, gardening tools in the bucket in one hand, my other hand holding my protruding belly. But when I got there I was lost. I stood in the spot where the vegetable garden had always been, next to the sheds and directly across from the fog tower, and yet where the vegetable garden should have been, and had always been, there was the bird cemetery—a mound of dirt with a painted wooden sign that read "Geese" in Thomas's large, careful lettering. To the right were two crosses made from scraps of wood. One read "Bluey" and the other "Murphy," the former lighthouse dogs.

I circled the mass gravesite. It had always been farther away from the house, a real long walk to get to, a place I'd avoided. But the garden was where I'd spent many afternoons planting and weeding and chasing off the birds. I knew I wasn't going crazy; it had always been there. I got down to my knees and began to dig before the rain started. It took a while before I reached something that resembled potatoes, but they were shriveled and rotten; some were devoured by maggots, small hard and black, eaten through or mushy to touch.

The atmosphere grew heavier and the sky turned a deeper shade of grey. I dug some more, frantically, finding only the same hideous things. I threw them down the hill toward the cliffs. I wanted them to roll away into the ocean.

The rain started to come down in big, fat drops, slowly at first with a heaviness in the air. The heavens were about to open. I wiped a drop from my brow with the back of my hand and it was red, bloodred. The drops landed with scarlet splats on my arms. I looked up to the sky; mangled geese circled above, blood dripping from their wide severed wings, their limp hanging necks, their gashed breasts. Suddenly the sky was full of them, hundreds of geese flying above me only to reveal themselves as deathly and dripping when they got close. I ran back to the house, the thick, slick mud splashing up my legs. Wet, black dirt and red, bloody rain mixing together, forming a messy, earthy layer on my skin.

I'd wake up sweating and petrified and pull back the covers and check the white sheets. There'd be nothing and I'd rush to the bathroom and check again, just to be sure that there had been no bleeding. And then I'd go back to bed, my hand on my still flat stomach. I'd lie there until the sun came up and I'd swear that I wouldn't tell him, not yet, not until I was absolutely sure.

—❖—

One morning I found Thomas on the pier behind the lighthouse fishing. It was early, before eight o'clock, and the air was grey and hazy and chilled. You couldn't see more than fifty feet out in any direction. I didn't understand fishing in those conditions when you could barely see the water. It felt like a losing game. After having that dream one too many nights, I had to see him. I had to make sure I wasn't losing my mind. To remind myself of what we still had.

It had been several days since we'd spent time together and I sensed he might be upset with me, confused, maybe even angry, with no explanation for my sudden absence from what had become our customary routine. He might harden himself against me, expecting news that I'd changed my mind about not returning to the city with Harry. He must have heard me walking along the creaky pier, but he didn't stop what he was doing—pulling gently at the fishing rod, letting the line get taut, then slacken, letting the bait move, then settle, a dance, a game, with no idea if anyone or anything was playing.

I stood behind him and put my hand on his back.

"I've missed you," I said.

"Have you?" he said flatly, without turning around. He was angry with me, understandably.

"I have missed you, my love. I'm sorry I couldn't get away until now; it's been so busy." My words sounded like Harry's words and I hated myself for lying.

"Just a minute," he said, stepping away from me, reeling the bait and floater all the way in. "Damn thing just got his breakfast," he said, holding the empty hook in his hand, reaching down into a jar and pulling out a small, wriggling fish the size of his finger and piercing the hook through its body. "Watch out," he said as he swung the bait and hook out into the ocean.

I stepped back and leaned against the railing.

"The stage was delivered," I said.

"I know," he said, not taking his eyes off the nothingness in front of us.

"They're going to set it up. I still can't believe you got everyone to pitch in on that."

He seemed distracted or at least he was acting that way to let me know he was hurt. Just a few more days, I thought, then I could explain everything; he'd trust me again when he knew what I'd been hiding and that I'd just been trying to protect him. He'd understand.

He secured his rod in the holder, then reached into a bucket by his feet and took out a striper. It was medium sized and still alive, so he whacked its head on the gutting table that jutted out from the pier, then turned his back and began to gut the fish right there in front of me, throwing the unwanted parts into the ocean and causing a swarm of gulls to dive into the water. The whole thing made me sick and the salty, briny smell made me nauseous.

"It looks like you're busy," I said. "I'll try to get back as soon as I can."

"Sounds good," he said, not looking up.

I walked away disappointed, crushed. I had hoped seeing him would reassure us both and put an end to this recurring horrible dream.

"Bea," he called before I reached the end of the pier. I walked back to where he was. "What's going on with you?" he asked. "Tell me the truth."

I looked into his eyes and implored him to trust me, to give me just a little more time. "There is something, but I can't talk about it. Just give me another day or so and I promise I'll tell you. Everything will be okay; please believe me." I stood on my tiptoes and kissed him. I wanted to stay and tell him, but I forced myself to turn and walk away and go back to the car where George was waiting for me.

The masquerade charity ball would take place in four days. Dolly and I set up a table in the Manor lobby displaying artwork from the local schoolchildren and their wish lists. Dolly had come through on her promise to bring a photographer friend to Montauk to take a picture of the kids and she got that picture featured again in *The East Hampton Star*. I had written

again about the developing charity efforts for Mr. Rosen and the more
we worked to promote it, the more the donations came in, but we needed
more to make a significant difference at the school. I was sitting at the
table under a big sign Dolly and I had made that showed how much we
had raised and how much we still needed. If someone manned the table
people were more likely to give, and I didn't mind.

Jeanie came down the stairs in her tennis clothes, stared at the table
and grimaced. She walked straight past and then turned on her heel and
came back.

"Nice work, Beatrice," Jeanie said, running her hand along the edge
of the sign. "We really needed some worker bees to get on board with
this charity effort; it's just been wonderful having you assist me on the
committee, just lovely."

"Oh," I said, flustered though annoyed with myself for feeling this way.
Was she even on this committee anymore? I wondered. She wasn't; I was
sure it had been just me, Clarissa and Dolly had joined later, but what did
it matter? As long as we did good work, who cared if she thought she was
in on it? I didn't quite know how to speak to her. First she insulted me
and spread rumors about me in Dolly's store, then she glared at me as if
she were going to attack at Winthrop's party and here she was talking to
me in this insipid way.

She went on. "It's nice because, yes, we do need people with experience in these kinds of things, the brains behind the effort, people who
really know what they are doing, those who've been running society events
and charitable work for years for much bigger charities, but it's also important to just have workers, who are willing to do things like this." She
motioned to the pamphlets and the sign we'd made. "You know, sit at the
table, wait for donations, make signs. It's grand."

Was this about Winthrop asking me to work with him on the March
of Dimes? I wondered; it was as if she was jealous that he'd asked me and
not her, not that I was even considering it. I shook my head to myself
and forced myself not to lash out at her for belittling me after all the work

I'd put into this. Summer was almost over; I didn't need to be at war with Jeanie. I had enough to deal with. I organized some pamphlets on the table, willing her to walk away.

"But don't sit in here all day, Beatrice; it's lovely outside, a nice breeze. Good for a game of tennis."

"I'm just doing this for another hour or so; then someone else will take over," I said, not looking up.

"Wonderful." She smiled smugly. "You do get out and get fresh air quite a bit, don't you, up at the lighthouse?"

Just hearing the words come out of Jeanie's mouth made me freeze for a second; then I forced my hands to shuffle some papers and finally allowed my eyes to meet hers.

"It's beautiful up there," I said. "The best view of Montauk."

She nodded, not taking her eyes off mine. The blood pulsed at my fingertips and I tried to breathe normally. I thought I had been careful.

"I've never been up there," she said. "Maybe you could take me sometime, since you know it so well by now."

"There are some nice walking trails."

"I'm sure there are. So, think about it," she said, leaning toward me. Even from behind the table I could smell the hot coffee on her breath. "Maybe we can come up with some sort of arrangement." The corner of her lip curled into a self-satisfied grin.

As soon as she walked away I let out a huge sigh and instinctively, protectively, rubbed my stomach. I looked around to see if anyone had witnessed the conversation, but only the Manor workers were around and no one seemed to be paying attention. She knew something, maybe not everything, but she was definitely on to me. What kind of arrangement could she possibly mean? Suddenly a wave of nausea came over me and I thought I might be sick. I got up and walked quickly to the bathrooms next to the front desk and made it just in time.

This was normal, I had to remind myself, many women get ill in the first few weeks of pregnancy, so it was a good sign. My brow was sweating and I vomited again. Suddenly I felt filled with fear. The baby, as much as I already loved and wanted it, scared me because it created a deadline. I had to find out soon; I had to get confirmation. If Jeanie was going to threaten me or blackmail me or maybe even tell Harry that I'd been going up to the lighthouse, then I needed a plan. I needed to tell Thomas. Even if Jeanie thought she knew something she would dig and dig until she found out everything she could. I had to get her to keep her mouth shut for a little bit longer, until the ball was over, just through Labor Day, when the city folk would pack up to restart their lives in the city for the fall. I had to find out what she could possibly want from me now, and I had to find out fast.

33

It was the Thursday before the ball, the Thursday before Labor Day weekend, the last official weekend of the summer.

It had been a week and a half and still the letter had not arrived. Dolly knocked on my door and sneaked in like some secret detective.

"Any news?"

"Nothing yet," I said. "But I'm convinced it will come in the mail today. I'm going to the post office again this afternoon. I have a feeling that it's today."

I wanted her to be my friend no matter what, to be excited about the baby. She said the news was inspiring her to launch the baby bonnet line she'd been toying with, she even talked about having the baby be in the advertisements, but these assumptions all came with expectations. She expected me to do as she would, to tell Harry the baby was his.

When I arrived at the post office Patrick was leaving with a delivery.

"Oh, hi there, Beatrice," he said. "This is my colleague Samuel." He nodded to a postal worker also heading out.

"A pleasure," I said. "Say, are you two excited about the charity ball?"

"I sure am," Samuel said, grinning. "And my wife cannot stop talking about it."

"I'm so glad," I said. "We've been working on making it a really grand party. Can't wait to see the kids perform."

"The boys are nervous," Patrick said. "They will do the craziest thing in front of anyone—well, you know," he said, nodding to me. "They'll chase a pig into a swimming pool in front of a crowd of strangers, but they are nervous about singing in front of you fancy folk."

"Well, tell them we are very excited to see them sing."

"Will do," he said, and they headed out the door.

There was indeed a letter. I didn't even look, just opened my handbag and slotted it inside. It took all the restraint I had to walk, not run, back to the Manor. Everything that had seemed so terrifying before—social disgrace, money problems, Harry finding out—none of that mattered anymore. The future seemed clear now; it was as if I knew how it would all play out. I could see it like a picture show playing in my mind. I walked into the lobby, and when I got halfway up the staircase and out of view of any Manor guests I ran the rest of the way to my room, locked the door and sat on the bed. I'm not going back, I thought. I'm staying here in Montauk. I'm giving up my old life and building a new one. Thomas and I would have a child together. I took out the letter and looked at it for the first time, but with a sinking feeling in my stomach I recognized the familiar writing. It wasn't from the doctor at all. I slid my finger under the white envelope seal and took out a single folded piece of paper. Out fell a check for $2.30 from Mr. Rosen. I put it in my jewelry box with the others.

Though I hadn't received word, I knew the baby was real. The previous doctor had all but told me it was an impossibility and yet I knew there was a child, Thomas's child, growing inside me. I lay back on the bed. I had been so sure the letter would arrive and I'd hoped I could tell Thomas before Harry got to the Manor. I imagined, over and over, the look on his face when I would tell him. I would have a child with the man I truly loved, respected and admired. I knew he would be so happy. But then fear began to seep back in.

I began running over and over in my head what Jeanie might know. She could suspect, but was there any way she could know anything for sure? Once I was at the lighthouse Thomas and I let our guard down completely. During his time off we'd walk the grounds hand in hand. On the beach we had once gotten carried away and made love, telling ourselves no one was ever down that way. We took a picnic to the cliffs and drank wine and talked in the long grass. I had taken it for granted that when I was there I was safe, but maybe someone had seen us. Maybe one of the keepers talked at Shagwong's. Maybe Jeanie had convinced George to tell her about the trips to the light. Maybe the bellboy who saw me sneak into my room at the Manor early that one morning had talked. Suddenly it didn't seem I had been careful at all.

I had barely taken three full, deep breaths to pull myself together when there was a knock at the door.

"I'm sorry to disturb you, ma'am." It was the porter. "I have a message from Mr. Bordeaux. He has arrived at the Manor and requests that you meet him in the lobby at seven o'clock for dinner."

I closed and locked my jewelry box, splashed my face with water and began to dress for dinner. We continued to put on a show for everyone that our marriage was intact. When he was in Montauk he sent word for me to meet him and I met him, laughed when it was appropriate to laugh, smiled when it was appropriate to smile, and then at the end of the evening we'd go our separate ways.

It was a big dinner meeting with the Fisher investors and their wives. They were excited about the investment, their big plans for Montauk, about the ball, about the final weekend of summer. Many of the husbands had taken this last week off as vacation and would stay in Montauk through Labor Day Monday, when they'd pack up and head back to their city lives. There was a slightly drunken air about everyone even when we first arrived.

Harry immediately assimilated and I was glad. If anything looked different about me, my fuller face, my anxiety, my slightly larger breasts, he
would never notice

It was as if I weren't there at all, as if my body was there, present, but
my mind was at the lighthouse, finding Thomas engrossed in some task,
fingers oily, hair pushed back from his face, and me standing there smiling, beaming, bursting at the seams before he asked me, "What is it?" And
then I'd tell him, "I'm going to have your baby." My thoughts were anywhere but on that dinner, making small talk with people I knew I'd never
have to see again. I imagined myself back in the city on the Tuesday after
Labor Day, waiting for Harry to go to work, making a coffee, then as soon
as the door shut behind him I'd gather my belongings, only the things I
really needed, then leave a note on the bed telling him I wouldn't be coming back.

Harry summoned me again on Friday—an end-of-summer gathering at
the Lobster Shack. I thought I couldn't go one more day without seeing
Thomas, but Harry wouldn't let me out of his sight and I still hadn't received the doctor's letter. Harry was close to closing the deal and he wanted
to appear the perfect family man, loyal husband, trustworthy investor, just
the right man to hold the fate of Montauk's tallest building in his hands.

After the Lobster Shack a few different dinner groups joined and mingled at the bar in the Manor. Perched on a red velvet barstool, I leaned
against the long mahogany bar and lost myself to the sound of the band
playing an excellent rendition of "My Reverie." I sipped my martini, but
it didn't go down easy and the gin burned my throat. Then the singer
with the beautiful voice sang "It Had to Be You." I looked over to Harry
sitting two seats down with an investor in a thick bluish-white cloud of
cigar smoke.

"It's the Jews pushing for us to get involved, I'm telling you," the man
said to Harry.

"Could be, but we'll never do it; we're not going to fight another country's problems, not going to happen. We've got enough problems of our own." Harry laughed.

"It could happen," the man said, blowing another voluminous cloud of cigar smoke around the two of them. "There are seeds of war being thrown on fertile ground, my friend, very fertile ground."

"You don't think we'd really go to war, do you?" I leaned over toward them at the bar. I didn't really want to join their conversation, but it was the first time I'd heard someone say, so emphatically, that it could happen.

They turned, annoyed that I'd interrupted. "I keep reading about Europe in the papers," I said. "Seems like tensions are high. America will stay out of it, though, won't they?"

Harry shrugged.

"Look at Japan; they are hungry for it and it's like I said." The man looked irritated that he had to repeat himself for the sake of a lady, even if I was Harry's lady. "The only problem we'd have is if the Jews keep at it. They support war; they want us to go over there for the rest of the Jews. That's the issue."

"Do they? I don't think they do."

"Enough of all this miserable talk." Harry knocked back the rest of his drink and turned away from me, getting into another conversation. Jeanie was walking toward me and we locked eyes. I regretted ever taking my eyes off my martini.

"Hello, Beatrice," she said, sauntering toward me. She was wearing a black feathered cape around her shoulders that on anyone else might have looked astounding, but on her it looked severe and reminded me of the geese. "Nice to see you spending some time with your husband."

"Yes," I said. "He's been here for a few days." Harry was just steps away, engrossed in conversation with investors.

"Say, I stopped in and paid a visit to that nice lighthouse keeper the other day."

The palpitations began. I could reach out and touch Harry if I'd wanted to; that's how close we were. I was sure he wasn't listening, but Jeanie's voice seemed to go up a notch or two in volume.

"What a handsome man he is, lovely, just lovely." She gazed off into the distance and sipped her drink as if she was imagining some romantic moment they had shared. I knew exactly what Thomas would think of her. And lovely was probably not the first impression people got from him either—aloof, stoic, skeptical, maybe, but lovely was what you discovered only later if you were lucky. "Anyway, I asked him to present the stage at the ball." She grinned at me and I wanted to shrink inside of myself. I couldn't believe we were talking like this, about the man I loved, about the man whose child was a speck of life inside of me, the man who had been a secret, until now, and here we were speaking of him within ear's reach of my husband. "He agreed, of course."

He agreed? I could more imagine Jeanie repainting the outside of the lighthouse than I could see Thomas speaking publicly on a stage in front of several hundred dressed-up guests. "Of course I had to convince him," she said. "I reminded him how important it was that he be a good sport." I tried not to let my expression change. "And it's just popped into my head, perhaps you should present it with him—since you seemed to have a hand in the stage being built. Am I right?"

"Me? No, I mean I just mentioned it in passing and some of the local gentlemen built it." The words sounded rapid and shaky as they came out of my mouth.

"Anyway, let's meet tomorrow before the ball, the three of us, you, me and what's his name again? Oh yes, Thomas." She said it seductively, letting the name roll off her lips and down her bosom and out into the room. "To discuss the announcement." She winked and turned back to her husband, leaving me standing there alone, staring at the back of her dress.

"Well, actually, Jeanie." I grabbed her arm maybe just a little too firmly. She turned abruptly, looked down at my grasp with disgust and pulled her arm away. "I was thinking about the check we're going to hand to the school principal at the ball." She raised her eyebrows. "I know you've been busy with other aspects of the preparations, but if you wanted to present the check with Clarissa and me that would be fine."

Maybe if she felt more involved with the charity she could be buttered up. But she just laughed mockingly. "Oh, how generous of you," she said. "Thanks for the formal invitation. I was already planning on it." She turned and ordered another round at the bar.

She seemed tipsy and uninhibited. She could say something about me and Thomas at any moment, and I was grasping at anything I could possibly do to pacify her.

"I mean, maybe you could be the one to actually announce the amount we raised, it's quite significant, and since you've been coming out here longer and know more people."

"I sure do," she said.

"Well, then, what is it that you want, Jeanie?" I pleaded in a low whisper. "Seems like you want something from me, but I have no idea what."

She tapped the side of her martini glass with a red-painted nail. She looked away with a slight smile as if she had to consider this for a moment, but the silence was painful.

She took out a long, slim cigarette, placed it in her holder and waited. The bartender leaned over the bar and lit it for her. She inhaled deeply, then shot a column of smoke up to the high ceiling.

"I'm going to be the one heading up Winthrop's March of Dimes chapter back in the city. Not you, not anyone else. I'm ideal for the job," she said coldly. "I need to make sure it's clear to him, and you can help me with that."

"How on earth can I help with that?"

Jeanie took another drag of her cigarette. "How did you manage to get that photograph of you and Dolly in the East Hampton paper? And why is a New York City newspaper so interested in us all of a sudden?" She glared at me suspiciously.

"That was Dolly's doing, not mine; she knows the photographer."

She stared at me for what felt like a long minute and a drop of sweat trickled down the back of my neck. "Well"—she began to turn away— "if you're not going to help then I suppose I'll chat with the gents." She turned toward Harry.

"I'll tell you what," I said quickly. "I'll talk to Dolly about her friend who works for one of the papers in town."

She slowly turned her eyes toward me, but not a muscle on her face moved to give any indication if I was heading in the right direction. "Go on," she said.

"And I think Clark might also have some connection to the New York papers. What if I were to ask around and contact someone to ask if they'd write about your charity work, would that make you feel better?"

Summer was days away from being over. My writing about Montauk life was sure to end with it, and by the time anyone was able to put two and two together about my role in it I'd be out of that life for good and living a very different existence.

She raised one eyebrow ever so slightly. "A profile with a picture would suffice, and a mention that I'm considering taking the March of Dimes role," she said. "I can provide the photograph."

The thought of submitting something like this to Mr. Rosen made me cringe. What he'd liked was my honesty. I'd be betraying his trust and my own instincts, but I couldn't risk her ruining everything when I was so close to starting my new life.

"I'll let you get to work on that." She began to turn away again. "Oh, and it should happen fast, appearing in print immediately after Labor Day weekend so that everyone sees it as soon as they get home from the summer vacation."

"Jeanie, that's only a few days away."

"You're a smart girl, Beatrice, and you've already proven yourself to be very, very resourceful." She let out a taut, fake laugh and looked to Harry, then back to me. "I'm sure you'll figure something out." Then she turned and walked away to the other end of the bar.

"I Won't Tell a Soul" rounded out the band's set and I knocked back the last half of my martini in one gulp. I pushed my empty glass away from me, picked up my pocketbook and went up to my room.

34

---✺---

It was the day of the ball and the Manor was transforming. In the main room workers laid down a dance floor, set up tables and dusted the enormous crystal chandelier, making it sparkle more than ever. They placed huge bouquets of hydrangeas around the room and polished candelabras with long candles positioned on almost every available surface. Luscious greenery intertwined with ribbons and flowers was secured down the staircase, making the Manor look even grander than it already was. They decorated smaller rooms for entertainment—fortune-tellers, magicians and various other forms of distraction. The décor committee placed and replaced centerpieces and table cards, making sure that the right people were seated together, according to the seating chart. There was an excitement in the air like that for an elaborate wedding.

Teams of women moved in groups around the Manor with intense, focused expressions as florists brought in more arrangements so tall they required several men to carry them in.

Mary Van de Coop walked up to me with a huge smile, her hair in spring-lock Bobett curlers, her makeup pristine and her "working clothes" clearly thought out.

"Isn't this just fun?" she said, putting her face close up to mine. "And hard work, too," she added, dabbing her perfect brow with a tissue.

"Your perfume," I said instinctively; it was so overpowering I had to step back. My sense of smell had heightened and some smells, however lovely before, turned my stomach now.

"Vol de Nuit," she said, grinning big, as if it were some big secret. "By Guerlain, that perfume has gotten me many things in life." She ran her hand along her collarbone and rested her fingers on a cluster of diamonds that sparkled and dipped down into her robust cleavage, even on setup day.

"Oh, Mary," I said, trying to laugh.

"It's true, honey." She linked her arm in mine and began to walk me over to her station. "If you want I can drop a hint in Harry's ear for you. I'm telling you this perfume can change your life."

"That's okay," I said. I had to turn my head away as I walked with her. "Where are we going?"

"I want you to look at the greeting table," she said.

"Really?" I wasn't used to the women caring about my opinion about this type of thing, but a few of them had shown a little more respect since the fundraising efforts, or maybe it was since I stood up to Jeanie.

"We need a lot of space because we'll be handing out masks as the guests arrive." She led the way to the front door.

"Do you think people will actually wear the masks, or do you think they'll find it all a bit silly?"

She looked at me stunned, as if I'd asked if the guests might all arrive in the nude. "Well, of course they will wear them, honey; why on earth wouldn't they? This is going to be the most fun we've had all summer. Oh, and for the locals, it will be the most lavish party they've ever attended."

I couldn't wait to see Thomas in just a few hours and he'd be dressed up and handsome.

"Don't you think?" Mary nudged me. "They've never been to a party like this."

"I'm sure they know how to throw a good party themselves, Mary, especially in the off-season when they're not catering to us city folk all the time."

"I doubt it." She patted my arm. "So should we have the table here right inside the doorway, or back here, more in the main room?"

I looked at the space. "Probably right by the door, so that people can put on their masks." There was a short hallway that led from the dramatic Tudor-style front entry to the main room of the Manor. "In fact, if we could put up some sort of curtain here"—I pointed to the end of the hallway—"then we could ensure that everyone is properly disguised before they enter."

Mary clapped her hands. "Yes, red velvet curtains, great idea. Also," she hushed her voice to a loud whisper, "we want to see who they are before they put on their masks and enter the party, make sure we don't have any uninvited guests."

"Oh, Mary, I don't think we have to worry about that kind of thing."

She ignored me. "I've seen some curtains in the Manor somewhere; I'm going to ask if they can be set up here."

There was something thrilling about it all. I'd spent the entire summer with all of these people and then the thought of drinking and dancing and talking with guests we might or might not know felt very mysterious. To think of Thomas and me together in a room full of people, able to talk, to brush past each other, in full sight—I willed the hours to pass faster. But in the next moment my excitement turned to anxiety when I thought of Harry. Foreboding filled the space that had been warmth.

Outside, a few of the men directed the workers on the front lawn, where the party would inevitably expand. They pointed out where cocktail tables should be arranged and orchestrated where the bar should go. The stage was stacked in large pieces and more workers were beginning to assemble it on the lawn. None of the Manor folk were doing any of the heavy lifting. Harry was smoking a cigar, observing.

"Beatrice!" he called out as I walked out of the Manor toward Clarissa just a few feet ahead of me. "Darling." He waved me toward him. I looked from him to Clarissa, but she was getting farther away.

We were barely speaking to each other, Harry and I, except to put on a show in front of others at dinners. The only consistent communication between us was the envelope of cash he left for me at the front desk before he took the train back to the city on Sunday evenings. But for him to call me over when no one else was paying attention made me uneasy.

"Sweetheart." He was all smiles as I approached. I looked around uncomfortably to see who was watching us and whom he was trying to impress, but everyone seemed distracted. "We need to talk," he said. I hadn't seen him smile for a long time. His eyes were bright and his teeth gleamed, his mouth relaxed, not the clenched, false smile I saw during dinners and deals and lies. He put both hands on my shoulders and rubbed them. I wanted to shake him off; his touch felt intrusive. "Let's talk tonight before the party," he said, trying to get his eyes on my level, to hold my gaze.

"It's busy around here today," I said, glancing back to Clarissa. "There are things to do."

"Come on; let's have a drink, just you and me," he said, "before we make our entrance."

I pointed to the group of women standing on the other side of the front lawn. "I have to get back," I said. "But we can try, if there's time."

I walked briskly across the grass to check on the outdoor decorations. What could he want? If Jeanie had said something about Thomas, or even hinted, he would be furious, enraged. He wouldn't be acting like this. There had to be some reason for this sudden change of attitude. It was probably the Fisher deal, I tried to reassure myself. Perhaps he wanted to make sure I'd say the right things to the right people as it was coming to a close. Or maybe it was the end of the summer that cheered him up and he was hoping we could go back to our normal lives in the city, where I had complied with more ease, and we could leave this rough patch of our marriage behind in Montauk. The more I tried to reassure myself, the more my stomach clenched with uncertainty.

---❄️---

It had been a week since I'd seen Thomas on the fishing pier, our longest spell of time apart, and I was desperate to see him. I couldn't get the thought of our meeting out of my head and found myself playing out what it would be like to tell him the news, about the baby and our life together. I needed to tell him now. I had to see him first, before Harry.

Toward the end of the afternoon when everyone began to slip away to get ready for the evening ahead, I stopped at the front desk still hoping for a letter from the doctor's office, but depending on it less and less because I already knew the answer.

"I don't suppose I have any mail that came in late?" I asked the front desk clerk.

"Let me check, Mrs. Bordeaux," he said. "No mail, I'm afraid. The post office did deliver a telegram, but your husband already picked it up."

"Oh." I barely got the word out, trying to catch my breath. "A telegram?" I had begged the nurse to send word of my pregnancy by telegram, but she'd refused. Surely she wouldn't have done so now. The telegram would have to be something else, something to do with Harry's investment; that's all it could be, nothing to do with me. I took a deep breath, nodded and thanked him and began to walk away. Then I turned back. "You don't happen to remember who it was from?" I asked over my shoulder.

"I believe," he said, looking down to his message book and tapping his finger on the page. "Ah yes, it was from the office of Dr. C. Rosenberg in Manhattan."

I called the doctor's office from the downstairs telephone box and confirmed that they had sent news of my pregnancy by telegram.

"The doctor had clear forgotten to send the note in the mail," the nurse said cheerfully. "I was sure you'd be happy to get the news as quickly as possible by telegram."

I hung up the phone, and as I sat down on the stool a feeling of dread hit me.

After pacing my room, dressed, made up, trying to think where I could escape to, knowing it would be too risky to go to the lighthouse now, at this hour, dressed as I was, I decided to go to Elizabeth's.

I sat in the back of the car sick with fear, queasy with each bump in the road. I caught a glimpse of myself in the rearview mirror: bright red lips, perfectly waved hair, pulled back at one side with a crystal comb. But my face looked sickly, ashen grey skin, forehead furled with worry.

George tried to make small talk about the party preparations, but I couldn't speak. I looked out of the window and tried to calm the thoughts in my mind. The nurse must have sympathized with me after all and sent a telegram to make up for the doctor's delay. I ran my hand down the front of my dress, imagining a slight roundness that no one could possibly notice but me. But now Harry knew. If he thought the baby was his, it would explain the smugness, the smile, the talking. His slick grin and rubbing of my shoulders was his way of congratulating himself. He probably assumed it had been the night he forced himself on me. He was proud of himself for that. But I would never let him have the satisfaction.

Dear God, how would I escape him now? If he thought he had a child, a possible heir to his family name? I couldn't see him. I couldn't talk to him or tell him anything, not before I spoke to Thomas. I wished I hadn't waited. Thomas would know what to do.

"Here we go, ma'am," George said, coming round to my side and opening the door. "I'll be right here for you."

"Actually, George, I don't think they are ready to leave immediately. I'm a little early and I know you have others that you need to pick up for the party. Why don't you drive back over here in half an hour or so?"

He frowned. "But what will you do, ma'am, while you wait? You can wait in the car until they are ready."

"It's okay, George." I managed a smile. "They've never been to anything like this before and I promised to offer advice on what to wear."

"Oh," he said, "my wife would have loved to have your nod of approval before coming tonight."

"Please introduce her to me later. I'd love to meet her."

It occurred to me that not a day had passed that summer when George hadn't been standing at attention or polishing the car at the front of the Manor or chauffeuring guests around town. I'd seen him as a permanent fixture at the Manor and suddenly I realized we might soon be neighbors. His wife and I could become friends. I had thought of Thomas and me and our baby tucked away at the lighthouse. I hadn't thought so much about making friends, buying groceries in town, sending our child to school with the other local children when he or she was older.

Walking among the lobster traps and soccer balls and crushed shells, pressed and trodden into the dirt, and up to Elizabeth's doorway, I smoothed my elegant lavender silk dress down. Tiny violet rosettes formed cap sleeves just skimming my shoulders. I felt a bit ridiculous in this dress at this house, with this huge secret inside of me. Soon everything would change.

Elizabeth had tiny white feathers in her hair when she opened the door.

"I sent the boys out to find them," she said. "They came home with a handful of seagull feathers, long and stiff." She laughed. "So I sent them back out to find smaller ones. Kept them busy long enough for me to finish off the hem of this dress."

She wore a white gown she had made herself, intricate and delicate, layered with various textured fabrics. You couldn't tell that this was the result of not being able to afford a full four yards of any one fabric, instead piecing together scraps that her dressmaker friend had given her. But it looked as if it was meant to be.

"You look angelic," I said.

"Oh no," she said. "It's going to be so different from everyone else's."

"That's good. People pay a fortune to have a unique design. We must show your dress to Dolly! She'll love it." I wondered if Dolly and I would remain friends or if it would be impossible to continue that friendship after making the drastic change I was planning. I wasn't sure if there'd be a way to merge the old with the new.

"Most nights she's been falling asleep mid-stitch with a needle in her hand," Patrick said, coming into the living room dressed in a waistcoat, white shirt and trousers.

"Do we have to leave now?" Elizabeth asked, concerned.

"No, we've plenty of time. George is coming back in half an hour. Why? What's the matter?"

"Oh, it's nothing." She shook her head.

"I brought you some lipstick," I said. "And a few other things." We sat down at the kitchen table. I draped a kitchen towel around her neck and shoulders and powdered her face slightly, blending a little rouge onto her cheekbones. I ran a soft powder puff across her brow. "Why are you frowning?" I asked. "Are you nervous about the ball?"

"No, no, it's not that."

"What is it?"

"It's just that I got a new laundry job, someone recommended me to him and he's paying really well, four times the amount that most pay me for the same job, except I pick up the laundry from his boat, so I suppose it's a little more work to get there."

"Well, that doesn't sound like a problem."

"No, but I washed his clothes this week, they were mostly fishing and sporting clothes, dark colored, and they were quite grubby, so I let them soak overnight in the bathtub."

She looked like she might start crying.

"Elizabeth, surely you are not going to sob over some dirty laundry." I set the makeup down. "What's upsetting you so much?"

"Oh, it's silly. It's just that I didn't realize there was some beautiful delicate lace lingerie in with the clothes, it looks terribly expensive, and I soaked it with the rest of his clothes and now it's a horrible greyish-green, brown color. It must have cost a fortune and when he sees it I'm sure he's going to make me pay for it."

A tear actually fell from Elizabeth's eye and she quickly wiped it up, apologizing for ruining the makeup. "It's just that I'm sure I'm going to lose the job and it was really good money and we told the boys we were going to buy them each some new shoes this weekend. They start school on Tuesday. But now I reckon I'll have to give the money back to pay for the damage."

"Show me," I said. "Maybe there's something we can do to get the color out. I'll bet it's not nearly as bad as you think."

She nodded and walked me out to the back where she had a maze of washing lines running back and forth across the yard. I'd never seen so much laundry in one place. There must have been seven families' loads hanging out there, blowing gently in the breeze. We ducked under a few rows of trousers, shirts, undergarments and sporting vests until we came to the offending piece.

She was right; it was hideous. There was no way that a woman would intentionally buy a piece of lace lingerie that beautiful in that color. Elizabeth unpegged it from the clothesline and held it up.

"And the thing is, the first few times it had only been men's clothing, hunting gear, I was washing for him. I assumed he wasn't married, so I wasn't on the lookout for more delicate pieces. I would always wash those separately."

"You tried baking soda? My mother using baking soda for everything."

"I already tried it."

I took the sludgy grey-green teddy from her, an all-in-one. Suddenly the ground began to shake, a loud horn sounded and the train rushed past us just a few feet away from where we were standing. The clothes flipped up in our faces and we had to swat them away. I'd almost forgotten, while standing in the maze of washing lines, that the train track was so incredibly close to her house. I cut my way through the clothes to take a look at the train as it sped past me about a foot and a half from my face.

"My God, that scared the heck out of me; it's practically in your backyard!"

"I know," she said. "We're used to it."

I inspected the lace in my hands a little more, racking my brain for the methods my mother used, but they refused to come back to me, and besides, Elizabeth would know twenty times as many tricks and nothing had worked so far. I turned the lingerie over admiring the back.

"It is very beautiful; at least it would have been." I tried to get Elizabeth to smile. The straps on the back crisscrossed all the way down in a very sensual manner and it reminded me of the all-in-one teddy I had purchased at the beginning of the summer with Dolly at Regine Brenner's showroom. I looked inside and sure enough it was a Regine Brenner design, her subtle label sewn into the side.

"Wait a second," I said, turning it to the front again and noticing a small rip of the top left where the strap met the bust. "I know this piece; it's the Regine Brenner that Dolly had in her store. I remember looking at it when it was a very pale champagne color. That would explain why it absorbed so much color."

"And I tore it, too." Elizabeth pointed to the small tear. "I can't believe I was so careless."

My mind was ticking, I had seen the piece, with the slight rip, and then someone else had bought it. Jeanie.

"So is your new laundry customer Mr. Barnes?"

"No, his name is Mr. Aldrick. He's kind, but he seems very particular about his clothes."

I examined the teddy. It was definitely the one from the store: Dolly had said the new designs had snaps between the legs. When I had bought mine at the beginning of summer she only had step-ins. And Dolly had said there was only one.

"Winthrop Aldrick?"

"Yes, that's him. Oh God, is he a friend of yours?"

"Not really," I said. "So this was already in the bag with Mr. Aldrick's clothes?"

"Yes, all the way in, tangled up with his clothes; otherwise I would have seen it."

"Listen, I don't think he knew it was in there. Don't return it. Just drop off his clothes and don't mention the lingerie. And if he does ask you for it, we'll ask Dolly to get you a new one. We'll figure it out."

"But that's stealing."

"No, it's being kind."

"How so?"

"Mr. Aldrick is married and I'm almost one hundred percent sure that this does not belong to his wife. So actually you are doing him a favor, because if his wife found it then he'd be in real trouble."

"Oh, gosh!" Elizabeth put her face in her hands. "This is too much for me."

"You'll smudge your makeup." I pulled her hands away from her face. "Would you mind if I held on to it?" I asked. "I might need it for something."

Elizabeth gave me a strange look.

"Please trust me."

I was asking her to trust me and I knew she would, and yet I still hadn't told her, explicitly, about my involvement with Thomas and I certainly hadn't told her about the baby or my plan to leave Harry. In my heart I was sure that she and Patrick knew about Thomas and me and that their silence was a hushed blessing. Thomas's injuries hadn't been hindering his work for many weeks now and I still went up there regularly. They had to know.

It was just us, two women in a cocoon of white sheets and shirts. I felt safe, as though I'd escaped the part of my life that didn't fit me anymore. This fit—this friendship, this life, this truth. I could tell her now. I trusted her completely. But then Patrick called.

"Ladies, the car is here; we'd best get going."

I folded the silk lingerie into a tiny square and placed it in my pocketbook.

35

By eight o'clock Ella Fitzgerald's voice spilled through the open windows and filled the night sky, pouring down to what must have been a desolate town. Everyone, locals and summer visitors, and even some who'd never been out this way before, descended on the Manor that night. The driveway was lined with parked cars, four deep extending down Manor Hill and parked in haste. The main hall and verandas were ablaze with chiffon and silk and glittering with masks. Smoke and conversation curling from unknown lips below beautiful and mysterious disguises. Some were so extravagant they extended twenty inches high like flames rising up from the woman's eyes. Others were adorned with feathers, emerald green and cobalt blue and jet black, so that the masked women had to walk sideways through crowds so as not to tangle their feathered feelers in another's crystalline disguise. Dolly's were smaller, made with felt and velvet, but still stunning in a variety of styles, most attached to a decorated stick that the women could hold to their face while the men's could be tied on.

There were performance dancers and musicians. There were party dancers to get people in the swing of things, and a full jazz band and sopranists. Beauty and music were everywhere and there was wine. And champagne. And every imaginable cocktail being passed indiscriminately by tuxedoed waiters. Two bars were set up, each lined with gins and liquors and cordials, but we had no need to approach them; instead trays of cocktails floated throughout the crowds, constantly replenished.

My dress caressed the floor as I walked. It hugged every part of me and I knew in a few weeks I wouldn't be able to wear a dress like it. Soon my figure would really curve and I'd be resigned to sailor collars and loose bodices. I wanted to lunge forward to those days. All style aside, I longed for my body to change.

While I was still stick thin, the masquerade was anything but. It was a voluptuous scene. Lanterns hanging from the ceiling, tables of strawberries and chocolates and smoked salmon roulade, just to whet the appetite. There would be two dinners, one near the start of the party and another after midnight. No one would go hungry or thirsty.

The Manor's transformation made me feel slightly disoriented, as though we'd been transported into an unknown place and time. Where usually the lower level of the Manor was one enormous room, encompassing the lobby, the dining hall, the breakfast room, and divided in some areas into reading "rooms" or smoking "rooms" only by lounge chairs and armchairs and buffet tables, that night everything had been rearranged and divided into several separate and distinct chambers.

Temporary structures formed walls at strange angles so that when you were in one room you couldn't see into another and you'd turn one corner and almost lose yourself in a space that you thought you knew so well, a space that you had wandered all summer long. Decorators from the city had used the large Tudor windows to orient each room. Many of the rooms had some form of entertainment, a gypsy psychic, a magician, a card table. The farthest room, out back by the service entrance, was draped with scarlet fabric and accents of red—a strange choice I thought, but maybe it was to be a sultry room, the passionate room, the place where lovers would meet at the end of the night to make promises that would never be kept.

——✳——

My mask was enormous and even more extravagant and wild than Dolly had promised. The face was intricate gold filigree that perfectly fit the contours of my face, set with a sparkling blue gem, the color of a Ceylon sapphire. Masses of deep purple feathers about twelve inches long all curved forward to frame my face. Delicate lavender feathers were interspersed, picking up the color of my gown. It was a Venetian splendor, an exquisite creation of whimsy that only she could have imagined. I tied it on and it had a transformative power. My hair was pulled back from my face and when I looked in the mirror I was unrecognizable. I just hoped that Thomas would find me before Harry.

Once Elizabeth and Patrick received their masks they stuck together and walked around the perimeter of the room, taking it all in. They seemed excited but a little anxious, as if they weren't supposed to be there. When trays of canapés were brought around and held in front of them to make their selection, Elizabeth didn't seem to know what to do, looking to Patrick to take the lead. Patrick was less shy, heaping four onto a napkin.

Within fifteen minutes they were on the edge of the dance floor, moving hesitantly to the music. They looked happy together even in their uncertainty, and I always felt that about them, that no matter what situation they were in, they were in it together. I wished I could enjoy the moment like them, instead of worrying so much, just hoping to get through the night.

Scanning the crowd as best I could through the slanted eyes of my mask, I searched for Thomas. Many of the men wore simple masks in black or silver. I looked for height and then I looked for pants and shoes, but the main room was already so crowded it was hard to pick out one man from another.

My eyes darted from one man to the next. I wondered if I'd keep a respectable distance from him when I eventually found him, or would my hands go instinctively to his? Would all logic leave me, knowing what I was about to share with him? I looked from one mouth to another. I would know his lips, no doubt about that, his kind smile. I was desperate to explain my distance from him, to change the stories he'd made up in his mind about why I had stayed away, but I knew with just a few words he'd understand everything. A sudden panicked thought intruded: What if he didn't come? What if he thought my absence from him meant I'd had a change of heart? I had to find him.

The jazz quartet grew louder and livelier and several couples began dancing. One couple seemed so connected, so in tune, anticipating each other's every move, as if they were made to be together, that I stopped and stared; others did, too. They were mesmerizing.

By the bar I heard a loud roar of laughter and recognized Harry's voice. I stopped in my tracks. He already sounded a little drunk. I pressed myself against the column out of sight. How could he be drunk already? The night had barely begun. I stood for a moment and listened. The usual banter.

"Another round!" one of the gents called out. "To celebrate."

There was a clinking of glasses and some "hear, hears." "To Harry!" someone shouted out. "To Harry, you old bugger," another said. "We didn't think you had it in you!"

"To Harry," another called out, "and to the kid!"

I almost doubled over. He had told them already, without even waiting to speak to me.

"And to your wife!" someone called out as an afterthought.

"To my wife," Harry repeated. "She's around here somewhere."

It would only be a matter of time before the women would know about the pregnancy and start congratulating me, too. I had to find Thomas.

I quickly walked by the dining room where the tables were set up and then I went into the powder room so I could take off my mask and think. Kathleen and Clarissa were in there, powdering their noses, and I looked around for Jeanie.

"Don't worry; she's not here," Kathleen said.

"What do you mean?"

"Jeanie, she just left. Ever since you told her off at Dolly's store she seems to have it in for you, Beatrice, but you must have done something else to rock her boat."

"Oh, for goodness' sake," I said, "I haven't done anything to Jeanie; she seems to be quite capable of rocking her own boat." I glanced at Clarissa, who was eyeing me as she pushed another cigarette into her holder and lit a match.

"Really?" Clarissa said. "How so?"

I took a deep breath, relieved that I had Jeanie's lingerie in my pocketbook should I need to urge her to keep quiet about anything she might know. But this was not the time to be creating more strife with Jeanie, or any of the women for that matter; I had my own trouble to deal with.

"Never mind."

"No, go on, tell us. We'd love to know, wouldn't we, Kathleen, just how Jeanie might be rocking the boat."

Kathleen giggled. Maybe they knew about her affair with Winthrop, but I didn't want to get involved, unless I had to.

"How are you liking the ball so far?" I asked.

"Quite nice," Kathleen said, "but I thought I'd love seeing everyone in their masks and talking to tall dark handsome strangers, not just our husbands for once, but I'm realizing I don't like to talk to people unless I know who they are and what they look like."

"Me too." Clarissa continued looking at herself in the mirror. "What if he's a beast under that mask and we spent half an hour chatting, and what if he's a local? I mean it's fine, but there are certain things that are appropriate to discuss and certain things that are not. I don't think the masks were a good idea for this type of ball."

"I was talking to one man, he looked quite dashing from afar, but he got a little too close and his breath smelled like fish!" Kathleen and Clarissa burst into fits of laughter.

"Must have had his dinner at the docks," Clarissa said. "Maybe he didn't know there'd be two dinners tonight and enough canapés for a small country!"

I couldn't listen to them anymore, so I left the powder room, scanned the dance floor area one more time and checked that Harry was still installed in the back bar drinking. I was about to head to the front of the room and check with the welcoming committee to see if Thomas had checked in when I felt a hand grab mine.

It was him.

Finally, I could breathe and the relief I felt took over. I wanted to fall into his arms. All the tension, worry, fear, that I'd been carrying dissolved with his touch. I held his hand a moment longer and squeezed, fingers interlocked with mine and my whole body warmed. This, being with him, however inconvenient, however ungraceful and life changing it was going to be, was the most real thing I'd felt. Slowly I turned toward him.

"Hello, beautiful," he said quietly, lifting the back of my hand to his lips and kissing it gently.

"I didn't know if I'd recognize you."

"I'd know you anywhere." He lightly touched his thumb to my collarbone. I wanted to kiss him right there in front of everyone, but I stepped back slightly, reluctantly.

"I've missed you," I whispered. "Let's get out of here before someone sees us." I glanced back to the bar in the corner of the room, but they were out of my line of sight.

The music ended and everyone turned toward the stage and clapped. The singer brought the microphone to the center and looked down to the floor. The bass strummed a few notes and he began to sing slowly, softly. His voice was beautiful and the dance floor filled up and people began to sway, mask to mask and chin to shoulder, gentlemen's hands between their partners' shoulder blades, guiding their way. Each couple began to form one gliding body, moving in time with the singer's smooth voice.

"Just one dance," Thomas said, whispering into my ear. He could have been any one of them at the Manor. His body looked powerful and elegant in a tuxedo jacket, his shoes polished, his shirt white and pressed. I was bursting with the news of the baby and wanted to tell him right away, but I'd waited this long, I could wait one more song. He took my hand

and held it in his, putting his other hand on the small of my back. I leaned into him, closed my eyes and took his lead.

When the song was in its final notes I looked to Thomas, then whispered in his ear, "I have something to tell you."

"Tell me," he said, our bodies pressed against each other's in front of all these people. "Will it explain why you haven't been coming 'round lately?"

"We should go," I said, but really I didn't want to move. To be held by him in this room full of people who knew the other me, who knew nothing of the life I was so close to living, I stretched up on my toes and put my lips right next to his ear, the words already on my tongue.

"I love you, Thomas, and I'm having our baby." I felt his body stop for a moment; he moved away slightly so he could see my face, but of course we were masked. He pulled me back into his arms tightly.

"I thought you couldn't," he whispered.

"That was before I met you," I said.

He held me close to him. I could almost hear the questions spinning in his mind.

"Are you sure?" he whispered.

"Absolutely sure now; I just got word from the doctor."

"But . . ."

His hesitancy scared me. "But what?"

"Well, is it mine?"

I began to pull away, horrified he'd ask.

"Wait." He held me. "I'm sorry; I didn't mean—"

"Why would you ask such a thing?" I said. "You know my situation. You are the only one; you've been the only one ever since I met you." That horrific night with Harry ripping at my clothes and shoving me against the wall flashed through my head and out again. That didn't count. That was repulsive and hateful. Life is not created through acts of hate and violence. And knowing that truth, thinking of Harry hurting me that way, would crush Thomas. I could never tell him.

"Why didn't you tell me sooner?"

"I was waiting for confirmation, I didn't want you to get your hopes up if it was a false alarm, but I could tell all along," I said. I looked up at him.

"Promise you'll stay and be with me," he whispered in my ear. "I want you to stay with me forever. We'll be a family."

"I want that more than anything else in the world," I said, and as I did I felt the tears fill my eyes. "There is absolutely nothing that could make me change my mind."

Nothing had ever felt this right. We weren't even dancing; we were just holding each other, completely entranced and in our own world. I knew we should move. The music stopped and the other couples turned to give a round of applause. I snapped to attention. "We've got to get out of here," I said. We couldn't risk being seen like this, not yet. Harry was too close.

I let go of him and stepped away; then he hooked my finger, very lightly, onto his as he led me through the crowd away from the dance floor, away from the jazz quartet, away from all of it.

"Where are we going?" I asked.

"Anywhere." We walked past the beautifully decorated rooms to the very last one, blue in color, where it was quiet and private, or so we thought.

A bored-looking fortune-teller looked up from her table. The creases in her skin were so deep they looked as if they'd been drawn on.

"Welcome," she said, her face suddenly animated. "Please sit and I will tell you your future and your fortune." She ran her hands over an imaginary ball with a flourish.

"No, thank you," I said.

"Don't you want to know what the future holds?"

I smiled at Thomas.

"We don't need to," Thomas said, and he took my hand and led me back out of the room and down the long corridor.

I felt giddy like a schoolgirl trying not to get caught. I stopped him in the hallway and kissed him quickly. He led me into the next room, took off my mask, and we kissed again. I wanted to leave the party. None of this mattered anymore. I began to feel careless, reckless, excited. Now that he knew, I didn't even care what Harry thought, but that was just the elation of the moment making me senseless.

"We need a plan," he said, turning serious. "Do you want me to get all of your things out of your room tonight? I can get someone to help us, and I can ask Patrick to meet us with a car in back and just get it all done."

"Wait, I think we should wait it out just a little longer," I said. "Until all the city folk head back to the city. I'll leave as planned right after the weekend."

"But why?"

"So as not to raise suspicion. I'm scared of what Harry will do when he finds out. I need to go back to the city as planned and then the minute he leaves for work the next day I'll gather a few belongings and come back on the train."

"I'll come and get you," he said.

"You don't have to do that."

"I want to. And besides, I have to make sure you don't change your mind, once you get there." We kissed again. It all felt like something out of a fairy tale. "That means you have to keep up this act for another week?"

"I can do it," I said. "I've been doing okay so far, but Jeanie knows something, and I'm really scared of what Harry might do if he ever finds out."

"Okay, we'll do whatever it takes." He took my face in his hands. "I've been wanting to go to Connecticut to see Tommy; I could go this weekend and remove the temptation for us to see each other. I've got a few days' leave I need to take."

"That's a wonderful idea."

"I'm going to take your advice and give him the knife I made for him in person. I made him a leather holder for it. He might not get my letters, but at least he'll see that I think about him all the time, when I'm up at the light."

I felt so full of love for Thomas and for this boy I hadn't even met.

He smiled. "And I'm going to tell Tommy about you. I'm going to ask him to come and visit once we're all settled."

"I would love that." I felt my world falling into place, a real family, however unconventional.

We heard heavy footsteps making their way down the hall, so we stepped inside a little more and pressed ourselves against the wall. Then the footsteps stopped and a man popped his head 'round the door. I recognized his large, red face but couldn't place him.

"Here she is!" he called out, and two other men walked into the room. As they entered, Thomas instinctively stepped in front of me, his arms protecting me, to shield me. Except that what he didn't know was who he was shielding me from.

"Harry," I said, stepping out from behind Thomas.

"Where have you been?" he asked. "I was looking for you everywhere." He stumbled a little, then found his footing.

"Goodness, I've been looking for you, too. I had to come down early to arrange the presenters," I rambled, but Harry looked from me to Thomas and the expression on his face spelled confusion and building rage. I couldn't see Thomas's face, but he must have had that same sinking feeling I had, that his one, instinctive action to shield me could have revealed too much.

"Who the hell is this?" Harry spit; his breath smelled of bourbon.

"This, this is Thomas Brown. The lighthouse keeper," I said. "From the lighthouse. He's presenting the stage."

Harry scrunched up his face. "What stage?"

"The stage for the school. I told you about it; I thought I had."

Thomas would want to confront this head-on, tell the truth, face the facts and take a punch in the face if he had to, but I knew that wouldn't solve anything, not now, not seeing the frightening reality of Harry in front of me.

"Thomas," he said, holding out his hand. "Thomas Brown." Harry just looked at his hand until Thomas lowered it and the two men stood and stared at one each other for what felt like a long while. Finally, Harry broke away from Thomas's gaze and grabbed my wrist hard.

"Beatrice, let's go," he said. "We need to talk." And he pulled me toward the door.

"Wait," Thomas said, grabbing my other wrist. "Just hold on a second." I felt myself getting pulled in both directions.

Harry stopped in his tracks, dropped my wrist and turned slowly toward Thomas, carefully lifting his eyes from Thomas's hand on my wrist, to his chest, to his face. They stood face-to-face, almost the same height. "No, you hold on a second," Harry growled. "That's my wife's wrist you're hold-ing, and if you don't let go I'm going to have you arrested."

I stood in the doorway. Harry's back was to me and Thomas's eyes flashed to mine.

"It's okay," I said, willing my voice to be strong and not to quiver. "We've gone over all the arrangements. Jeanie will let you know what time you're needed onstage. Probably soon, right after we donate the check, so the children can perform and then everyone can get drunk," I tried to joke. "Best to get the kids back to their beds before the real party begins." No one was laughing. Thomas's face looked pained, as if I were asking him to do the impossible and just let me walk away. It's just a few more days, I told myself, hoping he could somehow read my thoughts.

Harry clenched my wrist again and we walked into the now heaving, swelling party, along the edge of the dance floor and toward the bar. He grabbed a martini off a tray as we passed it, and knocked it back. Then he grabbed a second. From the corner of my eye I saw a masked man with horns, who'd clearly become a little too familiar with the bar, tumble into Harry's side, hard, sending the contents of his drink, olives and all, down the back of the woman standing next to him.

"Watch where you're going," Harry said, and he shoved the guy back off the dance floor. The man mumbled some apologies and bumped his way out of our view and most likely into some other poor soul.

"What?" Harry said to the woman who was searing her glare on him.

Her gown was also silk, pale blue and now doused in gin. "It was that drunken fool, not me," he said, pointing in his direction.

"I'll get you something to clean it up," I said, eager to make an exit, but Harry shook his head. "She'll be all right," he said, and pulled me to the center of the dance floor. He held me stiffly and began to attempt the steps of a slow fox-trot to "Night and Day" but he wasn't listening to the music. I felt claustrophobic, my stomach against his, all these people around, laughing, having fun, his strong alcoholic breath inches from my face. This was the closest I'd been to him in weeks. He firmly held his right hand against my back and had my hand clenched in his as we took the steps, but I wanted to push away, create distance between us. Nothing felt familiar anymore.

"So we have some news to discuss," he said matter-of-factly. "You're carrying our child." A lump the size of a rock was in my throat, my mask started to itch and I began to perspire.

"It was going to be a surprise" was all I could manage to say. I'd been concentrating on finding Thomas so much that I hadn't prepared for any of this. I wanted to take the mask off, but I didn't want him to see my face. We slowed almost to a standstill on the dance floor and he dug around in his inside pocket, finally taking out a piece of paper and unfolding it, large blue Western Union letters on the top of the page.

MR. AND MRS. BORDEAUX

YOUR VISIT AND SUBSEQUENT TEST FOR PREGNANCY ON AUGUST 28

REVEALS THAT YOU DO SHOW SYMPTOMS OF PREGNANCY IN THE FIRST

TRIMESTER. IMMEDIATELY START TAKING MEDICINAL IRON PILLS,

JAYNE'S TONIC PILLS—

The next few lines began to blur into a jumble.

"Yes," I said. "The telegram. Okay, I will go to the pharmacy tomorrow. Actually, I'm a bit dizzy all of a sudden," I said, trying to turn and get off the dance floor completely.

"I'll come with you," he said, grabbing hold of my arm. "So when were you going to tell me?"

"I didn't know for certain until today and I looked for you earlier," I lied.

He cleared his throat. "Well," he said, his face as straight and expressionless as could be, "it's good news. My parents will be thrilled, a grandson I hope, to carry on the name."

I nodded. "Yes, of course, that would be nice." It was all I could say.

Harry nodded, then released my arm from his grip. When he did so I rubbed the red imprint where his hand had been.

"I think it's time to present the check," I said, and I walked across the huge room to the front doors to get some air. With each step I felt his eyes on me. It seemed as if I were walking in slow motion; I couldn't get to those doors fast enough.

Once outside I put my hands on my knees and gasped for air. I tore off my mask. In the background I heard the band play, the singer's voice penetrating the air in a low and serious tone. When the song ended he made an announcement that the party would be moving out to the great lawn for the next portion of the evening and the shuffle of feet grew louder as the crowd filed out onto the lawn. An instrumental rendition of "Summertime" began in the background; trumpet or saxophone, I wasn't sure. I stood up and tried to regain my composure.

"Are you quite all right, darling?" It was Dolly and I was so relieved to hear her voice.

"Hi, Dolly," I said, and I wrapped my arms around her. "Great to see you."

"If I took a guess what you're all flustered about I think I'd get it right."

I looked up at her and nodded.

"Harry told Clark that you're with child. Clark said he was drunk as a beast. So I suppose that means you had the conversation."

"We did," I said. "But he didn't get the news from me; the doctor sent a telegram and he got to it first."

"Oh, Lord."

I shook my head, wiping my brow.

"Don't look so dismal about it all, Bea. Clark said Harry seemed really happy, drunk as a skunk but happy." She gave my shoulders a squeeze. "You're doing the right thing, Bea." I looked up at her, seeing the reassurance in her face that I was doing what she expected of me and letting Harry believe he was responsible.

"I wasn't even going to tell him, Dolly. Now he's going around telling the world it's his."

"Shhh," she said, frowning as if I should know better. "Keep your voice down, for God's sake." She looked around. "What do you mean you weren't going to tell him? You're not going to be able to hide it soon enough."

"I told you, Dolly, I'm not staying with him; the child is not his."

"But Harry's been telling everyone—"

"Harry doesn't know what he's talking about."

"Oh God, Beatrice." Dolly began to massage her temples. "I worry about you so much when you start talking like this. I thought you had taken my advice; I thought that's why Harry knew."

I hugged her hard. "You're such a good friend to me. I appreciate your advice and your concern, but I have to choose my own way."

"I know you're going to make up your own mind, but please think it through. Until then, you need to be smart about this. Don't put you, your baby or even that lover of yours at risk. One wrong move here and Harry could blow his wig. He has a wretched temper and he's also a sharp businessman. He can make things happen in an instant if he wants to; don't be naïve about that."

There was a loud *tap, tap* on the microphone. "Good evening all," Jeanie's loud voice came over the great lawn. "Hope you are all having a wonderful time." Everyone was still talking, ordering drinks, finding spots on the lawn.

"What are you saying, Dolly?"

"You know exactly what I'm saying, Beatrice. Play your cards right, be smart and don't be a fool."

Jeanie tapped the microphone again with her fingertips.

"Now, now, everyone, settle down; we are about to begin the main part of the evening, where we'll reveal how much we've raised for the Montauk community and we'll unveil the generous gift to the Montauk School. Could I have Clarissa, Dolly and Beatrice join me onstage?"

I took a deep breath to calm my nerves. Dolly linked her arm in mine. "Now come on, Beatrice. Put on a brave face." And we walked to the front of the crowd and up onto the stage.

Jeanie directed us to stand off to the right, toward the back of the stage. She stood front and center and talked and talked. As I looked out at the crowd that had filled the entire lawn, everyone began to blend together. I couldn't believe that just three and a half months ago I had never even set foot in Montauk. To think that I hadn't known Thomas, that I'd been blind to Harry's infidelities and that I'd expected my whole life to go on as it was.

Most of the guests had their masks off now that they were outside and held them in their hands. I forced my eyes to focus and on the right side of the crowd about halfway back I picked Patrick out from the sea of faces; he had his arm around Elizabeth's shoulders and Thomas stood next to them. They were talking; they looked happy.

Toward the front of the crowd and closer to the outdoor bar, Harry was with a large group of men and a few women. Some had their backs turned to the stage. As I looked out at everyone, at Thomas, Elizabeth, Patrick and Harry, it felt as if I were in a dream, floating above them, watching them. At the beginning of the summer Harry's crowd was my crowd. I didn't belong with them anymore.

Thomas's group had grown slightly. I saw faces I recognized, people I'd seen around town, but I didn't know their names. They looked kind, or maybe that was just me hoping they'd be as warm and friendly as the three I'd gotten to know so well. Standing alone was Mr. Rosen. He looked a little out of place and uncomfortable. It was hard to tell, but he seemed to catch my eye and nod. I kept glancing back and forth between Thomas and Harry; everyone else seemed to melt away.

Jeanie finally got around to presenting the oversized check to the Mayor of Montauk, and then she called Dolly, Clarissa and me to join her. As she called our names she announced which husband we each "belonged" to and she seemed to intentionally get her mouth close to the microphone as she spoke, "Harry Bordeaux." When she said his name I was watching him and he quickly looked to the stage. And, once she had his attention, she called Thomas to the stage as well as a few of the other local gents who had helped build it and provide materials. They received a big round of applause and Harry didn't take his eyes off me. Every time I looked over he was staring and every time I glanced to Thomas I felt myself being scrutinized.

"Beatrice, why don't you give the scissors to Mr. Brown so that he can cut the ribbon and officially dedicate the stage to the children of Montauk School?"

Reluctantly I took the scissors from Clarissa and walked them over to Thomas, feeling hundreds of eyes on me.

"Thank you," he said, and with the men by his side, he cut through the ribbon, everyone cheered and the children filled the stage. Jeanie ushered them into place while taking a second to smile at me. She was loving this.

First the youngest children sang "Oh Little Playmate"; then the older kids sang an operatic piece from *Romeo and Juliet*. It was quite impressive. I kept thinking of Elizabeth's boys kicking around that soccer ball in their front yard, these same boys who played on the train tracks and down by the docks and ran home just in time for dinner scruffy and laughing, cheeks red and foreheads sweaty, and here they were singing like angels. The audience was captivated. Toward the end, though, people began to get restless, eager to get back to the party.

Later, after dinner had been served, devoured and cleared away, some of the men moved to the card tables. I began to stand and hoped to find

Thomas again while Harry was preoccupied, but Mr. Rosen came over to my table and offered me a cigarette.

"How are you, Beatrice?" he asked. "This is quite some party."

"It is indeed."

"I'm sure there's a story here."

I smiled. "Oh, there's a lot your readers would like to know about."

"I'd love to have an end-of-summer piece, something dramatic and powerful to wrap up the season. What do you say?"

I inhaled my cigarette. If he knew what I knew. We all had our secrets.

"It's not my intention to gossip," I said.

"You're not a gossip; you're tasteful and always truthful. That's why our readers like you."

"I'll see what I can do," I said, but I couldn't imagine what I would send. I was so focused now on returning to the city, then escaping back to Montauk. And then what? Would Harry come looking for me? He wasn't just going to let me walk out of his life. I had to think. I looked around the room for Thomas.

"I'll let you get back to the party," Mr. Rosen said.

I spotted Thomas talking to some friends near the card tables and I walked toward him. If the plan had been for the locals and the city folk to mix it had failed miserably—everyone stuck to their own kind. When he saw me coming he fixed his eyes on mine and gave a subtle shake of his head, then averted his eyes over to the card tables. I looked over and saw Harry sitting, looking drunker then ever, clearly not involved with the cards. I changed course and joined Mary Van de Coop, who was talking about her plans for the fall season in the city. Dolly's runway show at Berg-dorf Goodman was the topic of conversation and I realized I wouldn't be there to support her. My life would be so different by the time of her show.

Thomas and I kept our distance for the rest of the evening, exchanging occasional quick glances, almost imperceptible smiles, a slight pucker of the lips to send a kiss through the crowd to his cheek. But constantly keeping an eye on Harry and feeling under his watchful eye became too much. I stayed as long as I thought would be socially acceptable; then I approached Harry and informed him I'd be retiring.

"I've-had-my-things-moved-to-your-room," he said, slurring all the words together. "Given-the-news, it's-the-right-thing-to-do."

"Oh." I tried not to look startled.

"Is-that-a-problem?"

"No, fine." I nodded. "Starting when?"

"Tonight." His eyes began to close to half-mast.

"Oh, but we should wait until I see the doctor one more time in the city before we tell anyone else about the baby," I said.

"No need," he said, with a shrug of his shoulders. "Night, Beatrice." He leaned over and tried to kiss me on the cheek, but it was more of a bumping of his nose against my cheekbone.

As I walked to the stairs I felt Thomas's presence. Our eyes met, but I had to force myself to look away once again. Just a few more days, I told myself, then all this pretending would be over. I went to my room and prayed the days would fall away.

Harry's belongings felt intrusive. A trunk pushed against the wall in the corner, some suits in the closet. His nightclothes folded on the bed. The Manor staff probably knew more about the guests and the "goings-on" than anyone else. Seeing his things made me feel anxious and unsafe. Dolly's words echoed in my head and suddenly I wasn't tired at all. I longed for the security of being at the light with Thomas. I was probably being naïve, of course. I didn't want to think about the logistics of divorce or how I would attain one, but I would face all that when I had Thomas by my side.

As I walked across the room to the bathroom to get ready for bed I heard someone try the door handle and I stopped in my tracks, startled, my stomach clenched. The door handle moved again and instinctively I rushed to the closet and pulled out Harry's shotgun. It was an impulse I didn't know I had. A ridiculous impulse perhaps, but I had a baby inside of me, a life to care for and protect, and I wouldn't let anyone or anything jeopardize it. I had no idea how to use a shotgun, but I felt a tiny bit safer knowing I had something in my hands. Someone tapped at the door.

"Who is it?" I said, standing to the side of the door. The person tapped again and tried the door handle.

"I said who is it," I said louder this time.

"It's me, Bea."

Hearing Thomas's voice, I opened it immediately. I looked down the corridor both ways and saw no one, so I pulled him inside and shut the door, locking it and putting on the safety chain.

"What are you doing here?" I said, excited but scared. "You saw the way Harry looked at you. This is dangerous."

"Dangerous? You're the one holding the shotgun," he said.

I leaned it against the closet door. "I'm wound up right now. Harry knows about the baby and he's going around telling everyone it's his. How can he think that?"

"Shh," he said, putting a finger on my lips. "I know; I heard some men talking. It's good that he thinks the baby is his, at least for now. It will keep you safe. But I didn't come here to talk about him." He looked around the room. "So this is where you've been living all summer long." He ran his hands along the ruffled edges of the cushion on the armchair.

"It's just a room." It occurred to me that he'd probably never stayed in a hotel like this before.

He walked over to the dresser and picked up a long necklace and matching earrings that I'd left out. "Did Harry buy you these?" he asked.

"He did; he's bought me everything I own except for a few pieces my mother gave me." He picked up a few other things, a silver pen resting on the bureau, a silk shawl hanging over the back of the chair.

"You have such nice things, Beatrice. . . ." He paused. He was confident, strong-looking and completely comfortable in his own skin, but I knew what he was going to say. "I can give you a nice life, Bea, I can make you happy, but I can't give you all this. You know that, right?"

"I don't want any of these things. They mean nothing to me." I went to him.

"I just want you to know what you're getting when you walk away from this life."

"I only want you." I wrapped my arms around him and kissed his chest.

He turned me so my back was against the door and stared into my eyes. To be looked at that way, to feel so wanted, loved, to know that no matter what came next we would face it together. I wanted to feel him, to connect. He held my face and kissed me.

He ran his hands down my breasts and over my stomach.

"I can't wait to see your body again, your beautiful body that is making our child."

"You will," I said, drunk with anticipation.

We moved to the bed and he felt my body, my thighs. I closed my eyes and I tried to enjoy being with him in my room, but I was scared about Harry's return.

"You should go," I said.

"I love you, Beatrice." He kissed my lips, my breasts, my stomach. "Stay strong over the next few days. I'll be waiting for you." He kissed me one more time and left. Everything in the world felt right again, at least for now.

Somehow I managed to fall asleep. I didn't think I could. I was watching the door, covers pulled up to my chin, for what felt like hours. I couldn't imagine sleeping in a bed with Harry again, but I had to play along for a few more days until summer was officially over, everyone would go home and we could go our separate ways. Eventually I couldn't keep my eyes open anymore.

The sound of fumbling and clicking woke me and I sat bolt upright but couldn't see a thing except the white curtains illuminated by moonlight, my eyes wide until they adjusted to the dark. A click and another stumble over by the closet.

"Harry?" I whipped off the covers and sat on my knees staring in the direction of the movement. My eyes were focusing now and I could make out a shape. I felt my throat tighten and my breath tremble as I reached for the lamp on the nightstand, but in my haste I knocked it over.

"Harry, is that you?"

I stood up and managed to get the lamp upright and switched it on. Harry was sitting on the edge of the unopened trunk he'd had moved to the room; he was swaying slightly but staring straight ahead at the door-way in a daze, eyes fixed but dull, almost dead-looking. Lying across his lap, clenched tightly with both hands, was his shotgun. He was tapping the barrel with his thumbnail.

"Harry, what on earth are you doing?" I instinctively wrapped my arms across my stomach and inched backwards away from him, glancing up at the door and noticing the dead bolt. He started mumbling something that I couldn't make out. I'd seen him drunk before but not like this. It was as if he didn't know I was there.

"Harry, sweetheart," I tried, softer this time. I was petrified. "What are you doing over there?"

"We're having a baby," he said quietly, almost whispering. "It's the most wonderful news." He sounded delirious. He picked up the gun and began looking at it closely, examining it. My God, I thought, what if he's already done something? What's if he's hurt Thomas? What if he saw him leave my room and he went after him?

"Put the gun down, Harry," I said. "You must be tired; you should try to sleep." I had backed myself up against the chest of drawers.

"Harry," I said again, and this time he looked at me, piercingly, as if it were the first time he'd realized I was in the room. His stare startled me and I didn't know what to say or do next. I stood there frozen. For the first time I thought he might actually turn the gun on me.

"It's not mine, is it?" His voice was dark and low. He didn't even blink; he just kept his eyes on mine. I didn't dare breathe, let alone move.

"What?" I managed to say something, the word leaving my mouth as if of its own accord.

"Is the baby mine, Beatrice?" All of a sudden his words were clear. Dark and terrifyingly somber but clear and precise.

"What are you talking about, Harry? How could you ask me such a thing? I'm your wife." I started to put one foot in front of the other and move toward him. My whole body trembled, but I kept moving forward.

"You've had such a long day," I said, my shaking hands reaching out toward him. "The hunt isn't for a few more hours." I placed the palm of my hand on his cheek and left it there for a moment, taking a deep breath, trying to remain calm. He felt cold. Then I put both my hands next to his on the long metal shotgun and I lifted it out of his lap. He didn't let go and we held it between us, equal weight, neither one having a firmer grasp than the other, but as I kept lifting it away from him he gradually loosened his grip, until eventually he uncurled his fingers completely and let them drop into his lap. His head followed, dropping into his hands, curling into himself completely, and he began to sob. I stood a few feet away from him now, startled and in shock; then I walked the gun over to the other side of the room and put it under my side of the bed. He wept, the sounds only muffled by his hands, and I approached him once again.

"It's all right, Harry," I said. "It's going to be okay." I put my hand on his head and felt him shaking. I couldn't bear to hear him cry. It was all just terribly sad and too much to fathom. I smoothed his hair down the back of his head and when I did he wrapped his arms around my thighs, his cheek pressed to my stomach, his tears soaking my nightgown. I stood there, motionless, letting him cry until he seemed to run out of energy. When his sobs gave way to deep breaths, then more subdued breathing, I inched away from him slowly and he began to sit up.

"Go to bed, Harry; you don't want to miss the hunt in the morning."

He nodded and made his way toward the bed, head down, as if ashamed. Then he climbed under the covers and closed his eyes. His face was red from crying, but he still looked handsome, lying there, that same chiseled chin and jawline, the golden skin and hair. The image of a man. Within minutes he was breathing shallowly, already caught in the warm and healing arms of sleep.

I sat in the chair in the corner of the room most of the night. I couldn't bring myself to turn off the light. I wanted to know what had gone through his head, what his intention had been. He had sat on that trunk with a shotgun in his hands. He was just drunk, I told myself; he didn't know what he was doing. But then I remembered how clear his words had been toward the end. My hands began to tremble at the thought of Harry knowing the truth.

Finally, around 4:00 a.m., my body ached from sitting upright, so I lay on top of the bedcovers and allowed my eyes to close.

The next morning I forgot, for a second, that my room wasn't my own. I stretched and thought about Thomas in my arms the night before. Harry's hunting gear and the shotgun were gone, his tuxedo thrown over the chair, so I stayed in bed, slept on and off and got up only to bathe, letting myself soak in the hot water for what felt like hours. When I got out, dressed and walked into the bedroom Harry was back. I just about gasped out loud to see him.

"Good morning," he said almost cheerfully. "How did you sleep?"

"Fine," I said, but I could barely speak. My throat felt dry and raspy. I stood still and watched him unbutton his jacket and place it on the back of the chair. He ran his hands through his hair, looking ragged and regretful, but he kept on forcing a smile when he looked over to me. "How about you?" I said. "Did you manage to sleep?"

"I did. I'm a bit tired, but the hunt and the fresh air helped a lot."

"Good." I kept watching his face for signs of what to expect next, or what he might say.

"To be honest, I barely remember the end of the night," he said, glancing at me a little sheepishly.

"Did you win anything?" I asked, trying to sound normal. Was that something I would have asked before? I could hardly remember anything from before. He looked confused. "You were playing blackjack."

"I'm sure I lost a hell of a lot of money. Absurd to play when you're not in tip-top shape. Absurd of me really. But I had good reason to celebrate." He smiled cautiously as if asking permission. Something in him had softened and I couldn't tell if he was just pretending that last night hadn't happened or if he really couldn't remember it.

"You're going to be a fine mother," he said.

"Thank you." I managed to press my lips into something that resembled a smile.

"Are you scared?" he asked.

I watched him for a moment and he watched me, waiting.

"Yes," I said. "A little."

"You'll be fine, Beatrice. Just fine." He walked over and awkwardly patted my arm, took a deep breath and rubbed his eyes. "Listen," he said; then there was a knock at the door. "Oh, I ordered breakfast."

A waiter delivered a tray of eggs, toast, a selection of preserves and coffee on a wheeled silver tray.

"I thought you'd prefer breakfast in the room."

"Thank you." We sat down. He didn't continue his train of thought and I didn't encourage him to.

"So we'll need to start looking for a nanny," he said. "And we should plan a trip to see my parents as soon as we get back so we can tell them the news. Have you told your mother and father?"

"No," I said, keeping my eyes on the breakfast cart.

"Of course my mother will want to be greatly involved, but you know her. She doesn't change diapers; she said she was finished with that decades ago!"

"I remember."

"You should talk to Jeanie; she's got an army of nannies; the children don't seem to interfere with their social life too much," he said. "Talk to her, get some tips."

"I'll do that."

Harry poured some coffee and gulped it down. "I'm going up by old Fisher's mansion for archery after breakfast. And this afternoon we're going to sign the papers on that building in town. What do you have on the books?"

We had barely spoken, let alone told each other our whereabouts, all summer long and it seemed strange that I should have to tell him my plans now. I was taken aback. Yet somewhere, in the very back of my heart and in the corner of my mind, I acknowledged that he was doing the best he could, given the circumstances. He ate a few bites of toast, waited a moment, then stood up, put his hands in his pockets and looked at the floor. I felt I owed him something.

"What am I doing? A walk perhaps, to get some fresh air."

"Okay," he said. "It's supposed to rain this afternoon, or at least it looks that way, so best to get out there soon." I nodded. "Make sure you eat something." He took off the silver dome keeping the eggs warm. The smell turned my stomach.

"I'll start with toast," I said, placing the cover back over the eggs.

"All right." He hovered a little at the door as though he might say something else. But what was there to say, really? The trying, the hint of kindness, after everything, after he hadn't cared for far too long, after I'd fallen in love with someone else—it was all too late.

"I'll be back for lunch then," he said, and he left the room, closing the door quietly behind him.

I did walk, hashing my way through brambles and long grass and over fences. It was as if I were looking for something to fight with. Anything I could wrangle with so I could get my mind off the Manor, my marriage and even my pregnancy, just for a little while. I needed a break from it all—a few moments when I wasn't turning it over in my head again and again. But I couldn't escape, no matter how far I walked or how aggressively I pushed through the nature that seemed to be telling me not to go farther. A thorn scratched all the way up my forearm and beads of blood rose to the surface, but I didn't slow down. I didn't know if it was pity, if it was guilt or if it was just that I felt Harry's hurt, but suddenly things didn't seem as simple as I'd played them out in my mind. When I reached an open cattle field the cows started objecting loudly, protecting their calves. I kept on. Harry had made his choices. I didn't want to hurt him, I just wanted to be free, I wanted the chance of happiness, but the guilt managed to seep in anyway.

36

Everyone congratulated us about the baby on Sunday night. Harry linked my arm through his and proudly paraded me around and stopped to thank everyone for the kind words and wishes. It felt awful.

Dinner was at the Trail's End Restaurant and our group took over the entire place. The men were particularly jovial and heavy-handed with the drinks from the get-go. Ordinarily, around that time on a Sunday evening they'd be getting off the train back in the city and starting to think about Monday morning at the office, but since this was the last weekend of summer, most of them stayed in Montauk with their families. The waiters had rearranged the tables in the small, home-style restaurant from several two- and four-tops to three long tables that stretched down the entire length of the place. Our dinner companions were basically everyone we knew: Dolly and Clark, Jeanie and Cecil, Clarissa and Mitchel and the rest of Jeanie's crew. Winthrop and his wife and a handful of their boating friends were there as well as the Fisher investors, a group that had grown since I'd seen them last. Fisher's luck was reported to be taking an even more ominous turn. He was not only bankrupt, he was now sick as well and quite a few others wanted in on the action. They smelled blood and wanted to get their hands in the pot.

"I heard that Fisher is so ill he's given up on traditional doctors and is seeing a veterinarian," one of the investors said.

"Apparently he's suffering from cirrhosis and has to have twenty pounds of fluid drained from his body a week," said another.

"Sure, because he's drinking that much in alcohol."

"If someone had twenty pounds of fluid drained from his body every week there'd be nothing left of him."

"There would if he kept replenishing." They all laughed.

"Honestly, he's so desperate, he's seeing a veterinarian!"

"My God," Harry chimed in. "What a pathetic end to a wealthy and successful man. Just about ten years ago he was worth one hundred million dollars."

"Before he built up Miami there was no way in hell anyone would have bought land down there. You couldn't give it away."

"It was the hurricane that ripped the place to shreds—that's how he lost all his money."

Harry spoke again: "That's when he started building up here, borrowing against the places he had down there."

"The crash didn't help him."

"Lucky us." The investor next to Harry laughed.

Here were these rich men from the city who'd been reaping the benefits of Montauk all summer long. Hunting its fowl and game, lying on the beautiful beaches, swimming in the pools, ocean and lakes, feasting on its cattle, sailing its waters, mooring their boats in the bays and yacht clubs, all of which would have been impossible if it hadn't been for this guy, and they were mocking him for a lifetime of investment and vision. Unlike some of the other beaches we'd visited in Miami and even in France, where large, ugly hotels had been constructed, ruining the coastline, obscuring the view, Fisher had developed Montauk without ruining its beauty. He had enhanced it and made it more accessible, but there were still vast untouched beaches, acres and acres of land that were preserved for hunting and hiking, and the fishing village.

"Don't you think you're all being a bit crass about a man who's on his deathbed?" I said.

"How awfully sympathetic of you," Jeanie chimed in from the other end of the table, joining a conversation that she hadn't been part of before I piped up—as if she was waiting to pounce the moment I spoke. "Do you always have a soft spot for the dead and dying?"

I turned back to the offending men. "We should all just remember that we wouldn't have had this summer if Fisher hadn't developed Montauk."

"I still would have had this summer," Harry's investment partner said. "It just would have been in Newport or Cape Cod instead." His jowls shook with laughter and he pounded the table with his hand, sending his drink spilling over the edge of the glass.

"Perhaps we should all be a bit more grateful," I said.

"Steady on, Beatrice," Harry said, glaring at me. "Who are you to complain? You've been out here all summer long sunning yourself."

"It's all right, Harry," the man said. "I am grateful, Beatrice; I'm grateful that he's drinking himself to death and that he's desperate to sell up all of Montauk for a cheap dime. I'm very grateful because he's making us all very rich men—and women." He tipped his hat to me.

"Hear, hear." The table all raised a glass. "To Fisher!"

These vultures devouring the carcass before he was even dead struck me as disgraceful and ugly. Lies were everywhere. Jeanie patronizing Cecil, smoothing down his hair, while her lover sat opposite with his arm casually draped around his wife's shoulder. Harry intent on taking credit for a child who couldn't possibly be his. Jeanie blackmailing me to get her name in the paper so that Winthrop would add to her prestige with the March of Dimes appointment. And me. Sitting there with a child growing inside me, a plan to leave my husband, all the while giving off false pretenses that I'd be returning to the city along with the rest of the city folk, when all I could really think about was sneaking off to the lighthouse so I could climb into the bed and arms of my lover. It was all lies. Deceit.

I excused myself to go to the powder room and splashed my face with cold water.

"Are you quite all right there, Beatrice?" Jeanie followed me in.

"Fine, thanks, Jeanie," I said, dabbing my skin dry.

"Say, I believe congratulations are in order. I heard you are in the family way. Harry must be thrilled."

"Yes," I said, not looking at her. "Thank you."

"You know, I haven't heard from you about your progress with the newspaper profile," she said. "As you can see, we are quite close with Winthrop and the choice to select me for the March of Dimes is going to be very clear. But I need that profile to appear in print as soon as possible. Do you have something for me?"

I looked at her stone faced. I had given a lot of thought to the piece I was supposed to write and I'd halfheartedly attempted to put pen to paper about her for Mr. Rosen, but I couldn't bring myself to say anything nice. She was beastly to everyone and didn't deserve the favor.

"Do you have something for me or not, Beatrice? Because I just don't know how much longer I can keep your little lighthouse escapades a secret." She threw up her hands. "It's quite a lot to keep to myself. Especially now that there's the baby to think of. I'm just wondering how Harry would take it."

I thought I might explode. I could have slapped her right across the face, but I managed to regain control of myself, crossing my arms over my chest and glaring instead. "I have something for you, Jeanie; I do. I'll be sure to leave it with you before the end of the night," I said, and then I walked out and returned to my seat at the table.

I barely touched the dinner of scalloped potatoes and lamb chop and I couldn't eat the dessert either.

"Are you not feeling well?" Harry asked at the end of the meal, a crease of concern on his brow. "I thought you loved lemon syllabub."

"I'm nauseated," I said, and wasn't lying for the first time in ages. "Very nauseated, actually. I think I'll get George to drop me back at the Manor."

Most of those at the table had moved to the bar area while the waiters cleared away the plates. Harry got up to go over to join them. "I'll see you back in the room then," he said.

I walked down to Jeanie's end of the table where her shawl was draped over the chair back. I felt in the bottom of my handbag for the folded lace lingerie. I'd kept it with me, sure that I'd need it at some point before the week was out. I placed the lingerie on the seat of her chair, then unfolded it, just to make sure she didn't miss it. And then I returned to the Manor.

Once in my room I grew despondent. The way everyone had acted at dinner was disgusting and I had thought of myself as so different from them, but maybe they were right and I was just like them. I had spent all summer at the Manor, being waited on hand and foot. I wore expensive clothes and jewelry. I had eaten at all the best restaurants in Montauk and most of the best ones in the city, too. I'd only found Thomas because I had the luxury of doing nothing all summer long in one of the most desirable summer spots of the day. Was I just as bad as Jeanie and Harry and Winthrop?

I took out a piece of paper and wrote down the truth I knew about every lie the Montauk city folk were telling themselves and one another, including my own. I did not spare Harry, or Jeanie or Winthrop, the investors or myself. Let it all be known. By the time this scathing piece was published everyone would be back in the city living their lives and I'd be in Montauk. I didn't care what anyone thought of me anymore.

I walked to the post office in the black of night and dropped the letter in the mailbox outside the main door; then I took the long way home, walking back through the fishing village along the water's edge. I passed Elizabeth's house, small and fragile, and yet what was inside, four boys and a couple sleeping in their beds, was complete and sturdy. It felt within my reach.

When I got back to my room I was exhausted.

I dreamed I was watching Thomas from a distance. He was hammering a nail into a piece of wood. The knocking of the hammer on the nail became louder and louder. And then I heard Dolly's voice.

"Yoo-hoo. Beatrice, it's me." *Knock, knock, knock.*

I looked around the room completely disoriented. The sun was streaming through the gap in the curtains. It was morning, Harry had apparently been and gone—his hunting clothes were no longer on the chair in the corner—and it seemed as if I'd been asleep for days. I slipped on my robe and opened the door.

"Darling, get dressed," Dolly said, walking in and opening the curtains, pulling the bedsheets up, then rummaging through my chest of drawers.

"What are you looking for, Dolly?" I sat on the edge of the bed rubbing my eyes.

"Your swimsuit! Have you looked outside? It's a gorgeous day! The indoor games morning has been called off because it's clearly not raining." She held back the sheer netting that covered the window for privacy and it was in fact the bluest, clearest sky I'd seen all summer. Everyone had been complaining that rain was expected for the last weekday of summer.

"We're all taking picnics down to the beach and the gents are going to meet us there after the hunt."

Reluctantly I began to dress, and Dolly followed me around trying to hurry me up.

37

The picnic hampers had already been delivered to the Beach Club when we arrived. Our wicker basket included a joint of cold roast beef, chicken and leek pies, asparagus with vinaigrette and watercress and beet salad, as well as a bottle of champagne and a bottle of white wine. There were crackers and butter wrapped in lettuce leaves to keep it cool, cookies and a fruit tart for dessert. The Manor kitchen had prepared our hamper for Harry and me and Samuel, one of his investment partners, but we had enough food to feed the entire club.

The Manor staff had been scrambling that morning helping guests pack up to return to the city, but it turned out to be such a beautiful summer day, one of the clearest and warmest we'd seen, that almost everyone decided to enjoy one last beach day and leave later in the afternoon instead. No one seemed ready to bid Montauk farewell.

The cabana boys brought a low table to our chaise longues on the boardwalk and dressed it in red-and-white-checked linens. This picnic was far from the sort my mother used to bring to the beach—hers were more like a tub of egg salad with crusty bread and a limp salad—but I had always loved dining outside like this, no matter how simple the food.

We had a prime spot right in the middle of the boardwalk, at the front, with a view of the pristine beach.

"It's a beauty, isn't it, Beatrice?" Harry said, stretching out on the chair, hands behind his head. "Samuel, I was telling Beatrice it's a real beauty today," he said to the overweight man.

"That it is," Samuel said, rubbing his hand on his solidly fat and hairy stomach. I wondered if his wife had ever been attracted to him. "You know what?" he said, sitting up and putting his feet on either side of his lounger, his round paunch hanging down between his legs. "We are damned smart to have found this place, and to think that when these deals go through we'll have our hands on a nice-sized portion of Montauk."

"We've got the beaches; we've got the hunting; we've got the fishing and the boating. It's got everything we need and it's so close to the city. Say, Beatrice, maybe we'll be staying in one of the new apartments next summer." Harry reached over and squeezed my thigh. "What do you think?" he persisted.

"I always liked the idea of a little cottage," I said.

"Sure, but if we could get those apartments done in time it would be far more luxurious."

In the two days since the ball I had been in a constant state of flux, alternating between total calm and peace of mind, anticipating only a few more days before Thomas and I could be together, and then utter panic that Harry would find a way to stop me or that I would be too frightened to go through with it. That day, though, on the beach, warm from the sun in a cloudless sky with just the gentlest breeze, I felt at peace. There was something about having a baby growing inside me that made me feel less lonely when I was with Harry and this crowd, as if I had a constant companion and a purpose in life that I'd never felt before.

Thomas would be in Connecticut now. He had taken the ferry that morning to see his son, then would stay with an old friend for the night so he could spend time with Tommy the next day, too. I knew he'd been discouraged by the boy's mother from seeing him or even contacting him, she'd given Thomas the feeling he wasn't wanted or needed, but what boy didn't need his father? And what father could live without his son? Knowing he was with him now comforted me. I thought of Thomas as a father, as the father he always wanted to be, and I ran my hand across my stomach. All the pieces were starting to pull together like magnets, drawing themselves to where they should be.

After the picnics had been devoured, the drinks had flowed freely, the hampers removed and our lounge chairs moved down to the sand; the Beach Club was in a hazy siesta. The gents were all mostly sleeping in the sun, tired from the early hunt, full and fat from lunch. The women dozed or flicked through the weeklies and some of the children played by the water's edge with their nannies. Roosevelt recently announced that some 10.5 million Americans were out of work and he'd declared the beginning of the "real drive on the depression," and yet here in Montauk, all of us lazing about in the afternoon sun, it seemed no one had a care in the world.

The white sand was dotted with striped umbrella after striped umbrella as far as the eye could see, and all around us were long, lean legs on lounge chairs, strong and tanned from all the summer activity. Contentment, though no one was really content. This wasn't enough for anyone really; nothing would ever be enough, it seemed. No matter how perfect all these lives might have seemed from a distance, so full of possibilities and promise, we all wanted more.

Around two thirty that afternoon the wind picked up slightly and I put an extra beach towel around my shoulders. Within minutes everything began to take on a sickly yellow tint. The sky changed from the brightest blue to a cooler, almost eerie grey-yellow color, and as I looked up and out to sea it looked more and more jaundiced. Some of the cabana boys and other beachgoers walked to the water's edge and looked out to the horizon. Harry was snoring in the beach chair next to me. I got up and walked down.

"Look at the fog rolling in," a young waiter pointed out with an empty silver drinks tray.

"That is a dense wall of fog coming our way," said a dad to his two small children. "Go and tell your mother to start packing up," he told his son. "Let's go to Johnny's and get ice cream." The kids ran off shouting about what flavor they'd get and who would get the bigger scoops.

The group of spectators grew and soon twenty or thirty people stood at the water's edge watching the fast-moving grey sky coming closer. I heard the foghorn blare from the lighthouse, and even though I knew Thomas wasn't there, just hearing it made me feel closer to him. We hadn't seen fog like this all summer long. Even from Connecticut, Thomas would see it and start thinking about boats navigating their way around Montauk Point.

The air cooled quickly and the wind picked up even more.

"It feels like it's going to rain after all," I said to no one in particular, and after a few minutes I began to walk up the beach to the club. I felt a smattering of rain and looked back at the horizon. The fog now looked like a black wall closing in on us.

"That's not fog at all!" one of the men called out as he ran back up to the club. "That's rain. It's going to be one hell of a storm."

As the wind sent towels and newspapers flying, everyone scrambled to get their things together. The cabana boys closed the umbrellas and brought them in along with the beach chairs and tables. Some guests relocated inside to the covered bar to wait it out while others had their belongings carried to their cars.

"George, take the women first and then come back for the rest of us," Harry said, and we all piled into his car, Dolly, Clarissa, Mary Van de Coop, Winthrop's wife and two others and me. We were just about on top of one another, cramming in as fast as we could as the rain was starting to come down in fat drops.

"I'll wait with the gents," Jeanie said after she eyed Winthrop's wife, Gloria, climbing in without her husband. "I'm not afraid of a bit of rain. It's quite exciting really."

"Come," Dolly said as some of the women battled for a seat, and she reached for my hand, pulling me to sit next to her. "We may not be heading back to the city today, after all, if this rain keeps up."

By the time we got up the hill to the Manor the pelting rain was coming down in sheets—hard and heavy and drenching—and the wind was so strong that we had to link arms and hold on to one another just to make it to the door and get inside. One minute it had been the most beautiful day of the entire summer; next it was the greyest, darkest, most ominous weather any of us had witnessed in years, or ever. The Manor staff brought us towels to dry off, but we didn't even go up to our rooms to change. We just stared out the windows, some arms still linked.

The wind hammered against the windows, making them rattle and us jumpy.

"That tree's not looking so good," the restaurant manager from the Manor said, approaching the windows with a busboy. We all got closer to the windows and crowded around him to see what he saw. "That oak is about a hundred years old," he said, pointing at the huge tree in the corner of the great lawn. We had spent many afternoons out there under the shade of the tree that summer. Knitting socials, decorating committee meetings, lemonade breaks from playing croquet in the hot sun. The kids spent a lot of time under that tree, too—story time, nap time—or the nannies would take shade while the children played on the lawn. Though the enormous trunk looked sturdy, the tree limbs were waving about frantically. One whole section in particular, a full third of the tree, seemed awkwardly out of synch with the rest. It was being tugged and thrown in all unnatural directions and then in an instant it cracked, ripped off and flew toward us at the window. We all gasped. "Get back!" someone shouted. Half the people ducked where they were, while the rest leapt to the back of the room. There was a thunderous thud against the exterior wall, but luckily it didn't hit the windows.

The crash left us all shaken and any hint of nervous laughter about getting so drenched immediately ceased. The men weren't back yet and there were many, many others staying at the Manor who were out somewhere in the storm.

My mind kept going to Thomas. He'd be distraught now, since he wasn't at the lighthouse. He knew exactly what to do in times like this; this was what he lived for and lighthouses were made to withstand the worst kind of weather. The walls of the tower were thick and it was high up on Turtle Hill. Milton's family would be safe there. I wished there were some way to contact Thomas in Connecticut, to let him know what was going on here and that I was out of harm's way.

"I can't believe this," Mary Van de Coop kept saying. "I just can't believe it; this storm came out of nowhere!"

When George pulled up to the front of the Manor and let out a carload of men, they muscled through the winds to get inside. Winthrop's wife ran to him and they held each other, relieved, it seemed. They looked as they should, the two of them together. But Clark was bleeding and the side of his face was covered with tiny slivers of glass.

"My God! What happened?" Dolly said, rushing to him. "Get us some water and a washcloth."

"Oh God, Dolly, we saw the rooftop peel off Shagwong's Tavern," Clark said. "It just lifted up on one corner, then peeled right off, and the whole side of it flew into the middle of the street. People could have been killed."

"That's terrifying," someone said standing behind Dolly.

"What happened here?" Dolly said, starting to pick out some of the tiny splinters of glass from his cheek.

"A slate shingle flew straight into the car's window and smashed it in, right where I was sitting. But it could have been worse. Geez, it could have been a lot worse."

"Where's Harry?" I asked.

"He got into a different car with some others," Clark said. "There wasn't time to wait for George to come back; the wind was throwing things around. Maybe they went somewhere closer to wait out the storm."

I nodded, feeling a shot of worry and concern for him. I didn't want harm to come to him. The lights flickered and went out. The women gasped. Someone began to cry.

"We'll be all right here at the Manor," one of the men said. "This building is sturdy and we're on high ground up here in case of any flooding."

"What about the fishing village?" I asked, suddenly panicked, the thoughts forming in my mind after the words. "Oh my God, what about the village?"

Dolly looked up from tending to her husband's face. "They could be in trouble if the water rises," she said.

"We need to get help to Elizabeth and the boys!" I cried, the severity of the storm suddenly sinking in.

"George!" I called out to him across the Manor lobby. I'd never seen him look so afraid and I rushed over to him.

"I need to get to my wife," he said.

Chilling sounds of sirens screamed in the distance and the thunderous roar of the wind beat against the Manor walls. Harry, Elizabeth, Patrick and their boys all out there somewhere in this horrific storm, and Thomas unreachable. The foghorn blasted over and over again and my body ached for him. It could be Milton or Worthington working the foghorn, but I envisioned Thomas. They'd be working up a sweat, searching the sea for boats, keeping the light and the horn going. Everyone had retreated from the windows and huddled in the center of the room. I glanced outside and saw George about to leave again in the car.

"I want to go with him," I said, rushing frantically toward the door.

"You can't go out there," someone said. "You'll be blown away!"

With great effort, I pried open the heavy wooden front door and tried to run to the car. The driving wind was like sheets of glass pressing against me and the pounding rain so heavy it stung my skin. I couldn't even see my hands in front of me, but I tried to force through toward the car. I wanted to help. I wanted to go to the village. I wanted to be at the light; I wanted to be there when Thomas returned. All reason left me.

A tremendous gust of wind slammed against me and almost threw me to the ground. I covered my stomach with one hand and reached my other out to break my fall, but someone grabbed me under the arms and pulled me upright, then backwards. When I managed to regain my footing I turned to hold on to whoever had suspended my fall. It was Winthrop.

"What on earth were you thinking?" he barked at me when, dripping and shivering, we were back inside.

"I wanted to help."

"You'll get yourself killed and that won't help anyone," he said.

Once we were inside, his wife, Gloria, rushed to me and took over. "Think of the baby, Beatrice," she said, guiding me into the lobby, my clothes clinging to my body, drenched with rain and a pool of water at my feet.

"Let's get you changed," she said, leading me up the stairs to my room.

"Be quick!" the manager called out. "It's safer down here in the main room. Some windows have blown in up there."

I realized my stupidity as I climbed the stairs. If I'd fallen, if Winthrop hadn't caught me, I could have hurt the baby. The thought was unfathomable. I needed to be more careful, smarter and safer. But I felt so helpless inside the Manor.

"I know you're upset and worried about Harry, but he's going to be all right," Gloria said. "He's safer waiting it out somewhere else." I nodded. They were all empty reassurances. None of us knew what was going on. None of us knew what was happening in the fishing village, in town or at the lighthouse or across the water in Connecticut. I wanted some assurance that Thomas was okay.

After what seemed like hours, several carloads of folk from the fishing village made it to the back door and assembled with us in the Manor lounge.

"We were told it was safe up here?" one man called out as he came in with his family. "Is it?" We all assured him that it was. Then George's car pulled up and everyone raced to the window to see who he'd managed to bring to safety. His wife staggered out of the car and two men from the Manor ran to bring her into the lobby. Elizabeth was with them, too, holding baby Jake in one arm and gripping little Johnny's hand with the other. Five more men fought the wind to get outside where they formed a tight circle around them and escorted them inside. Both boys were crying hysterically when they arrived.

I ran to her and hugged her and when I did she started sobbing. "The boys are at the school," she said. "A whole bunch of the older kids went in today to volunteer and paint. I couldn't get to them! I had to get the little ones to safety."

"Oh God." I felt my stomach flip and thought again of my own baby. "They are going to be okay," I tried to reassure her. "They have to stay where they are; they'll be safer there." More empty promises when all we could do was hope.

"Patrick's delivering mail today; he could be anywhere." She began to sob again.

I picked up Johnny and walked him over to the chairs, trying to soothe the little boy, but he was too worked up.

"The houses in the village are coming apart like sheets of paper," Elizabeth said. "We were all in Gerry Dock's house because it's bigger and stronger, but I dread to think what we'll have to go back to."

Another woman from the fishing village had arrived with her husband; she was delirious, soaked to the bone and walking around in circles, pulling at her hair. "My house was swept out to the Sound!" she wailed. "A huge wave of water hit my street and the house just slid right into the water!" Her husband sat at the bottom of the staircase with his head in his hands. "It's gone; everything we had is just gone. We've got nothing. Nothing."

I wanted them to stop. It was horrible, just horrible, for them, but I wanted the woman to calm down so that Elizabeth would be calmer, too. Several people went to the woman and tried to get her to sit down, but she couldn't; she kept pacing, ripping at her hair.

"There were other houses, too, that just slid away and crumbled."

"You're safe now. You're here with us and your husband's here," one of the Manor staff was telling her.

"If we'd stayed five more minutes we would all be underwater right now!" she shrieked.

"Yes, exactly, but at least you got to safety."

"We have nothing; everything is gone." It was as if she couldn't hear anyone. "We don't even have a fork, or a cup, or a pencil or a pair of socks. . . ." She began listing every mundane item from her house that she would no longer have and it made everything so real and devastating. I wondered if by the end of all this Elizabeth would have anything left either. I just wanted the woman to stop talking so we could all pretend this wasn't happening.

George's wife clung to him and didn't let him go. She hadn't spoken a word since she arrived, but she was clearly shaken up. George had his arms around her tightly.

We passed whiskey around in mugs to calm our nerves, but when a chicken hutch, its chickens and debris flew past the window, followed by what looked like part of the roof from the maids' quarters, which slammed into one of the cars and then off the side of the Manor, we knew whiskey wasn't going to be much help. There were about sixty of us at that point, including the Manor guests, the staff, the fishing village folk and everyone else who'd been smart enough to come up there early for safety. We all took swigs and passed the mugs on anyway.

Around 6:00 p.m. the wind abruptly died and the air grew cold. Clark organized teams of men who went out to survey the damage and look for those who hadn't made it back yet. The first team went to the school. By that point, baby Jake and Johnny were sleeping in chairs and it was all we could do to get Elizabeth to stay with them and not join the rescue teams to find Billy and Gavin. A doctor gave the hysterical woman from the fishing village and Elizabeth each a pill to calm their nerves, but this just seemed to make Elizabeth more anxious.

"I'm not taking a sleeping pill; my boys and my husband are missing!" she shouted.

"It's not a sleeping pill; it's a barbiturate," the doctor said in a soothing voice. "It will stop you from being so upset and you will be able to concentrate more on getting your family back." Eventually she gave in and took the pill, which seemed to make her lethargic but no less upset.

I couldn't stand being in the Manor lobby a minute longer waiting helplessly, so I went outside and walked around the property. It was an ugly mess. Smaller trees running along the side of the Manor had toppled like bowling pins. The lawn, usually so neat and perfectly manicured, was thick with debris, branches, leaves, a huge wooden beam and planks of wood that must have been ripped from someone's barn or home. The fence surrounding the tennis courts was flat against the ground as if it had been steamrolled and the tree near the service entrance where I'd so often sat and waited for Elizabeth to come up the hill to collect the laundry had been ripped from the ground, its roots exposed and raw like hair pulled from a scalp. The tree had landed in the middle of the picnic bench where we always ate lunch after tennis, slicing it in half, right down the center.

Around 8:00 p.m. a pale and half-dressed man in a state of shock stumbled into the Manor.

"It's all gone," he said as he entered the room. "The fishing village is washed away."

People from the village began to cry; one man fell to his knees and wept. Elizabeth sat with her boys and covered her face with her hands. We still had no news of her two older boys or Patrick and now she had no home to go back to.

Slowly, others trudged into the Manor in various states of shock, many of them with injuries. Bedroom windows in the Manor had been left open that morning and many were ripped off their hinges by the wind, leaving several rooms severely flooded, so the women made beds on the floor of the Manor's lounge area out of sheets, towels and bedspreads.

Clarissa, Mary Van de Coop, Kathleen and I set up an assembly line of sorts. Clarissa and Mary received the injured and brought them to a "hospital" area where we had also set up makeshift beds. There Kathleen and I helped people out of ripped and bloody clothes; we cleaned and wrapped their wounds if they were minor and sent them to the doctor's corner if they were more serious. The doctor was a guest from the city and the only one at the Manor, so we sent the most serious injuries to him and tended to the others ourselves. One man walked in supporting his arm at such an unnatural angle we all knew it was badly broken, but when we tried to remove his shirt he passed out cold, so we padded the floor for him and gave him a cold compress until the doctor could see him.

While we recorded who had arrived safely, Clarissa's husband started a list for all those who were missing family members, including possible places they could be so the rescue teams could be more efficient in finding loved ones. People crowded around him shouting out names. "My Andrew was out on the boat with five other men; they went out for striped bass. Oh God," one woman sobbed. "My boy was working the kitchen at John's Pancake House; please go there. Please go and get my boy and bring him back."

"Jeanie's not back yet!" Kathleen called out. "Jeanie and Cecil."

"They'll be with Harry; I'm sure of it," Clark said.

I had a horrible thought that Jeanie might be in trouble; she had been so adamant about staying at the Beach Club when all the other women piled into the car.

By ten o'clock I was physically and emotionally exhausted. It was as if my body and my mind were already asleep and I was forcing my eyes to remain open.

"You need to get some rest," Dolly said. "We all do." She took me by the hand and made a little bed of towels and pillows from the chair. "Just lie here and close your eyes. It's the baby taking up your energy."

"But what about everyone who's still missing, Dolly? Harry's still not back and I'm worried about Thomas; he went to Connecticut this morning," I said.

"He'll be fine; Connecticut will be just fine," she said. "Anyway, you should be worried about your husband."

"I *am* worried. I'm just so tired."

She brushed my hair back from my face and as soon as I let my eyes close I must have fallen asleep, because when I woke I heard Harry's voice.

"Beatrice." He was crouching down next to me. "Beatrice, are you okay?"

I instinctively sat up and put my arms around him. He was cold and wet and shaking and he held me tight. "Thank God you're okay," he said. "Thank God the baby is okay. It was all I could think about!"

I looked around. It was black out and the place was lit with candles; people were sleeping on the floor or in chairs, wrapped in blankets or towels. If Harry was here then everyone else should be here, too, the kids, Jeanie, maybe even Thomas would have come back early, but I didn't see anyone else.

"What happened?" I asked. "Who else came with you?"

"We got as far as the church when the car stalled." He was shivering as he spoke.

"Who?" I stood up and led him to a pile of dry towels.

"Me and the rest of the guys."

"Jeanie and Cecil weren't with you?"

"No, they went a different way, I think; it all happened so fast. The water was up past the wheels of the car. It was so deep on Main Street we had to fight our way out and waded over from the car to the church and we climbed up to the highest point we could get to, the choir balcony."

I wrapped a towel around Harry's shoulders, noticing the familiar small patch of hair in the center of his chest.

"How did you get back?" another woman asked, bringing more rags and clothes.

"We walked over the golf course and through the cattle fields to get here. There are too many downed power lines and flooded roads in town," he said.

"I'm glad you're okay," I said once he was in dry clothes.

Elizabeth was sleeping with her two kids, thank God. She was frowning in her sleep and had her arms around both boys.

Word seemed to have spread that the Manor was a safe haven and there was food and drink available. Maybe a hundred people made their way there. They came in throughout the night and we fed them, gave them dry clothes and blankets and updated the list of the missing, and as the men came back, bringing the wounded and the scared, we learned more about the devastation that this storm had caused.

"All the windows are blown out of Dick White's store and the front wall came down," one of the men in Clark's group said.

"Main Street is a river," someone else said. "Office desks and restaurant tables and living room furniture were all bobbing down the street. There are abandoned cars everywhere caught in the flood; we saw one with its headlights shining up from underwater—it's really eerie." We listened entranced and devastated, all the while we had our eyes on the door waiting for others to walk in.

At some point in the early morning about thirty kids came through the Manor doors looking for their mothers and fathers and falling into their arms or the arms of strangers. Billy and Gavin ran to Elizabeth and clung to her. Except for scrapes and bruises, all of the kids from the school were fine. When the rains started pounding the rooftop and the first window shattered Mr. Farrell had made sure all the children in the school filed into the auditorium and instructed them to climb onto the stage that had been assembled that very weekend, to wait it out. They were on higher ground, and though many of the classrooms suffered damage and one wall collapsed, the auditorium held up fine. They had left as a group, though, looking for home, and that's why it had taken them so long to make their way to the Manor.

"It was so scary," Gavin said.

"I wasn't scared," Billy said, but the look on his face gave him away. He put his arm around his mother's waist and didn't leave her side. "Do you think Dad's safe?" he kept asking.

"He'll be fine, Billy," she said, some of her strength back now that she had all four boys around her. "You know him; he'll be helping people right now; that's just how he is."

But Patrick was still unaccounted for and none of us would be at ease until he walked through the doors. Elizabeth and I kept going to the window, opening the door, seeing if someone was walking up the driveway.

I should have felt a small sense of relief knowing that Thomas was in Connecticut, but until I heard from him I couldn't rest easy. What if he had gotten caught in the storm on his way there? The ferries probably weren't running if the damage was as bad as they said, and the roads sounded like they were undrivable, so he might be stuck out there until the mess was cleared up. I imagined different scenarios over and over in my head all that day, longing to get any word of his safety.

At sunrise the next round of men had gone out, Harry included. Two cars were sent to East Hampton, the nearest town with sufficient resources, to bring back supplies and much-needed medicine, including morphine, but when they reached the narrow Napeague Stretch they had to turn back; it was completely underwater and Montauk had become an island. No emergency vehicles or supplies could get in, and no one could get out.

That day the school auditorium became the morgue. Five bodies were taken there, laid out and identified. Later in the afternoon the news came that one of the Manor guests, a female, had been brought into the school. We all gasped. Jeanie was the only woman from our group unaccounted for. Cecil had made it to the Manor in the early hours of the morning, frantically looking for Jeanie, and since then he'd been out repeatedly searching for her. He had returned briefly to the Manor for water before heading back again when the news came. He let out a loud wail and collapsed to the floor sobbing. We all tried to reassure him that it couldn't possibly be Jeanie, that she'd be smart enough and strong enough to make it, but he just kept shaking his head.

"You don't understand," he said. "She wouldn't leave; she was acting like it was all going to blow over; she was being very brave about the whole thing." He sobbed again, then took a deep breath. "Then this wave just came out of nowhere, this huge wave hit the beach and everyone started running and we made it only as far as the next street and I pulled her into that little lunch place, it was raised up off the ground, and we ran straight up the few stairs. It was the stupidest thing we could have done because then we were trapped inside."

"No," I said, holding his hand, trying to calm him. "No, you did what you thought was best." He was shaking and freezing cold. "Can we get more blankets over here?" I called out to no one in particular.

"There was an explosion of water; it knocked the door down behind us and chased us inside. I told her we had to grab something that might float; we were getting pulled by the flooding water." He sobbed again, loudly. It was all so awful. "She wrapped her arms around this floor-to-ceiling beam as if it would keep her safe, keep her grounded, but the water was rising. She was so frightened. I started to climb out the window and I thought she was right behind me, but when I turned around she hadn't let go. I held on to the window shutter and reached for her, but it ripped off its hinges and we were pulled apart!" he cried out, and we all kept saying the same thing over and over, but even as I tried to reassure him I didn't believe it myself. I was terrified of the truth.

He looked up at me with a strange expression of surprise. "She was talking about you when the rain started to pour," he said.

I looked around uncomfortably, hoping he meant someone else. "Me?" I said.

"Yes." He took my hand, hopeful almost, as if I might be able to provide some insight into her whereabouts. "She said she had something to tell me, that it was something about you and her, and that's when everyone started running." He dropped his head and began to sob again.

I didn't know what to say. "She's going to be fine, Cecil," I said, releasing my hand from his grip and placing it on his shoulder. "She's going to be just fine."

Later Cecil returned from the school ashen. A few of his friends led him directly upstairs to one of the dry rooms. We had all been wrong with our fake assurances. It was as if he had died himself. Jeanie, we were told, was brought in with just shreds of clothes and full of seawater. No one could believe that she hadn't made it. People began to cry quietly for a woman who many disliked, but others looked up to, even idolized. At that moment it didn't matter what anyone thought of her, it didn't matter what had happened in the past, because it was all over now. Nothing could be taken back, fixed, smoothed over. Jeanie Barnes was gone.

Elizabeth joined the other women and me; we all rolled our sleeves up and got on with it, side by side. I think she was trying to distract herself. Every few moments she'd stop and look out the window. I kept telling her that Patrick was probably helping others, I repeated back to her what she had told her boys, but the more time passed the harder it became to reassure her.

Harry worked with the rest of the men, city folk and locals working side by side, coming back briefly with updates, then trekking back out, sorting through debris and rubble to find those still missing. The list was constantly amended.

Someone reported that the post office had been torn from its foundation next to White's Pharmacy and ended up in one piece all the way at the other end of town by the grocery store. The mailbox and all its contents had been seen bobbing through town in the flood. The spiteful letter I'd mailed to Mr. Rosen would be drowning, too, thank God. The thought of my vengefulness, exposing people and their secrets and lies, now seemed so despicable. I felt ashamed for ever writing it. And now, Jeanie gone. The fragility of human life laid out on the floor of the school auditorium.

That night Patrick walked through the front door of the Manor with cuts on his face and arms and tears in his eyes. He wore drenched, ripped, filthy clothes, looking as if he hadn't slept for days, searching for his wife and his boys, and when he set his eyes on one, two, three, four, all five of them he crumbled.

He'd been on his way out of Montauk toward East Hampton when the storm hit. Strangers leapt into his car from the beaches when the waters started rising, but it soon became clear that the car wasn't going to guarantee anyone anything, so they drove uphill on the outskirts of Montauk as far as they could until trees whipped across the road. They pulled into an empty garage attached to a house, closed the heavy metal door and waited it out inside the car. They could hear the wind pounding the garage on all sides, but miraculously they had made it to high enough land and didn't get washed away. After the storm, he and the strangers in the car went into the house and checked on the residents and stayed there until it was safe enough to leave.

Seeing Patrick take his wife and boys into his arms made me weak. Just seconds before, her life was at a near tragic crossroads. Loss and devastation, or a family complete and reunited. Suddenly I was breathless. Watching them, trying to wrap their arms around one another even more, even tighter than they already were, their closeness not enough, it brought tears to my eyes. This was family. This was love.

A feeling that had been in the pit of my stomach rose up, a feeling I'd been pushing down, willing it to go away. What if the baby is Harry's? I thought. I tried to ignore it; it couldn't be. I knew in my heart that it was Thomas's child, but I couldn't prove it. Thomas deserved to know about that horrible, hateful night with Harry. It could change everything, but I had to tell him.

38

On day three Manor guests with undamaged rooms had moved back upstairs and the lobby and dining rooms now served as living quarters for stranded locals. The city folk were anxious to return to the city, which, we heard, had suffered heavy rain but no significant damage. They waited eagerly for the railroad service to be back up and running at regular speed so they could leave the mess behind. In the meantime Harry put in a decent effort with the rest of the men in town, helping to recover merchandise from the stores, throwing water out onto the street from storefronts by the bucketload.

In the kitchen a group of women began washing sheets with a few of the Manor staff who hadn't been able to get home. The pile of towels and muddied clothes grew taller and taller. In a pile of clothes we saw a shirt soaked in blood.

"Throw it away," the maid said. "It will never come out."

"What can I do to help?" I asked.

"I'll grab some of Clark's shirts from upstairs," Dolly said. "Bea, can Harry part with a few shirts, too?"

"Absolutely," I said. "I'll go up after we hang this pile of sheets to dry."

Some of these people didn't even know if they had anything to go back to. It was some small consolation to be able to give them the dignity of walking back to their homes with clean shirts on their backs. Patrick had been to see the damage at the fishing village and their home. Though not flattened like some, it was severely damaged and too dangerous to move back into. But they'd be able to salvage some of their belongings.

"What will you do, Elizabeth?" Dolly asked.

"I don't know," she said. "Patrick said we could maybe go and stay with his parents in New London, but they don't have space for us. We would be lined up like six sausages on their living room floor. It could be a temporary solution, but I don't know how we'll survive down the road."

"You could come to Manhattan," Dolly said. "You could work for me in the hat factory. I'd give anything for a hard worker like you. You could work on my women's line and if it works out you could help me with my kids' line, too."

"Thank you, ma'am. It's really nice of you, but I don't know anything about working in a factory."

"I'd teach you. And Patrick could work there, too. He'd start as an apprentice, but he'd learn the ropes and work his way up. My business is growing. I'm looking for good people."

"Thank you, it's so kind; I just don't know. Patrick's never worked a job like that before; he's always been an outdoors man, out on the boats. The post office was the most civilized gig he's had, but still he's outside; that's the way he operates."

"Well, he could look for work at the docks, I'm sure there would be something for him, but this might be an easier life and I could train him with a real skill where he'd make decent money as he gets the hang of it."

"But where would they live, Dolly? They can't afford Manhattan," I said. The offer sounded generous and possibly the best thing they could wish for, but I felt a pang of possessiveness. I had dreamed up all kinds of scenarios in which Elizabeth and I would spend time together and I would ask advice about the baby. Now to think of her gone, living in Manhattan, working with Dolly, made me uneasy. I should have wanted what was best for her and her family, but I wanted her to stay.

"Well, she certainly wouldn't be living on Park Avenue, but if she's willing to live on the outskirts, you could find a place," Dolly said. "And I haven't tried them myself, but people say the underground trains are working quite well; they can take you all over the city. And her boys could go to school."

Elizabeth looked at me for approval, or guidance.

"It's not a bad idea, Elizabeth," I said. "It'd be a very different life from what you're used to, but you'd adjust."

"I don't know if Patrick will do it." Elizabeth added more soap to the sink and began scrubbing. "He may just want to rebuild here, not leave."

"But how can you do that with the kids?" Dolly said. "Come for a year, build yourself up again and then you can rethink things."

Elizabeth nodded. "You're really very kind," she said. "I'll talk it over with Patrick."

"Of course," Dolly said.

"Let's take this lot out and hang it to dry," I said after a while. Dolly and I picked up the sheets and made our way outside.

"That was a little odd back there, you trying to tell Elizabeth not to go to Manhattan."

"I didn't tell her not to," I said.

"Well, you weren't very enthusiastic. Do you know how many men and women here are going to be out of work now, and homeless? They need to get out of here."

"It's just that this is her home; I think they'll want to start over." The thought of telling Thomas about Harry and the idea of Elizabeth leaving Montauk left me grasping for this new life I'd planned; fear of losing it before it had even begun sent a frantic, desperate feeling through my body.

Dolly looked at me as if I were a child. "We don't always get what we want, Beatrice. So what's your plan, anyway?" she asked.

I kept my eyes on the ground. So far Dolly hadn't wanted to hear about my plan.

"Well, out with it."

"I've already told you, Dolly, but you don't want to know. I'm going to go back to the city to get my things and then I'm coming back here to be with Thomas."

"Oh, Beatrice." Dolly threw the sheets down on the lawn near the washing line we'd set up across what used to be the tennis courts. "You're being ridiculous."

"I'm not being ridiculous; it's what I'm going to do."

"For one thing, you haven't even heard from him since the storm hit. You haven't heard a word and neither has anyone else. He could be dead for all you know."

I threw my pile of wet sheets down, too. "He's in Connecticut!" I shouted back at her, then looked around to see if anyone else was there. "Don't say such an awful thing."

"I'm just saying you don't know anything about his current situation. Anything could have happened. Just look at poor Jeanie."

I took a deep breath and began to pick up the sheets and shake them out.

"And what if things don't work out, Beatrice? What if he doesn't want the child after all? You won't be able to waltz back into Manhattan and pick up where you left off; you'll be disgraced."

"That's not going to happen. It's not like that."

"You hardly know him, really; it's just a love affair. What if he doesn't respect you? Then what would you do? You'd be stuck out here with a child and no money. What are you going to do, become the first female lighthouse keeper?"

"I know him, and nothing like that is going to happen. Anyway, I've been making a bit of money writing for the paper."

"Not enough to live on. I don't think you've thought this through. Give yourself a chance; give the child a chance."

"I am," I said adamantly. "I'm giving him or her a chance to have a normal, healthy life, to be raised with strong, solid morals, with people who love him. Not with people who think that just because they have some money in the bank they can do whatever they want."

"You're still sore about all the affairs."

"Honestly, I don't care about the affairs. I've experienced something that's true and real, and I won't give up on that. I refuse. You don't understand."

"I do understand, but you're thinking with your heart, not with your head." We began to hang the sheets over the washing line and I was grateful for the temporary divider between us.

"Let's just drop it, okay?"

Suddenly I was desperate to see him and desperate to tell him the truth about that night. He had to know. This could change everything, but I couldn't go through with this without telling him about that night. Dolly had me all worked up. I left her on the lawn and made my way back inside. As I did, Elizabeth came running toward me.

"He never left, Beatrice," she said in an excited whisper.

"Who?"

"Patrick just got word that Thomas never left the light to go to Connecticut, he was there throughout the storm and he's sent word for you. He wants you to go if you can."

"Oh thank God!"

"Oh, and Beatrice," she said with a big smile. "I'm happy for you." She hugged me.

"Thank you, Elizabeth." I squeezed her hand. "I have to see him."

George was nowhere to be found. I saw Winthrop and his wife heading down the stairs and toward the door.

"Where are you going?" I asked.

"We're trying to leave," Winthrop said. "We may not be able to get through the Napeague Stretch, but I'm going to try. Our driver's waiting out front."

"Can you drop me somewhere?" I said.

Winthrop frowned. "Where could you possibly need to go? This is the safest place for you," he said. "At least until Harry gets back."

"No, really, I must. I need to check on someone." I felt desperate. "Please," I said. I was willing to say anything.

"How will you get back?" Gloria asked.

"I'll leave a message for George to collect me when he's back; don't worry."

Reluctantly they agreed. I asked them to wait while I dashed off a note for George, told Elizabeth to make sure he got it, and climbed into their car.

The road to the light had already been cleared—the bigger fallen branches were pulled to the side of the road and we only had to dodge the smaller debris.

Winthrop seemed uneasy as I got out of the car at the bottom of the hill to the light.

"Harry would agree to this, would he?" Winthrop asked.

"Yes," I said, trying to say as little as possible. "I hope you get back safely."

Walking away, I could hear the engine idle behind me, but I didn't look back. Eventually, once I was halfway up the hill, I heard them drive off.

I spotted Thomas by the equipment sheds. They were damaged, crooked, with one side blown in, but somehow still standing. He was retrieving rope and equipment and pulling it out to the grass. I walked closer and after a moment he looked in my direction, stood up straight and rushed toward me, picking me up and kissing me.

"Thank God," he said. "I've been trying to get word to you. I'd given myself an hour and if you didn't show up I was coming down to get you."

"I'm fine," I said, throwing my arms around him and holding him tight. "Elizabeth told me."

He kissed me on the lips, then on the forehead, then pulled me into him. I held him tightly, terrified of what I was about to tell him. Then he released me as we heard Milton emerging from the shed with tools clanking.

"Oh, Milton," I said. "Everyone at the Manor was concerned about what happened up here at the light, so they sent me to check on you all and report back."

"Very nice of you," Milton said. "We're okay." He looked from me to Thomas.

"How's your family?" I asked Milton. "Where were you during the storm?"

"Oh, we're all fine. We rode it out at the base of the lighthouse. The walls are six feet thick down there, you know. Probably no safer place to be."

"I'm so glad." I tried to keep the attention on Milton.

"This fool, though, he's a different story." He nodded to Thomas. "He was running between the beach and the light tower. I'm surprised he didn't get himself killed."

"What the hell was I supposed to do, leave Ted down there to drown?"

"You didn't need to do it alone."

Thomas turned to me. "Ted London was out fishing when the storm hit," he said. "We saw his boat run ashore on the rocks. Thank God we saw him and were able to get down there to help or he could have been in real trouble."

"True, he'd have been a goner," Milton said. "Thomas saved his life."

Thomas shook his head, wound up the rope and threw the reel over his shoulder.

"Is he okay now?"

"He was banged up pretty good, but we got him out of there," Thomas said. "He's resting in the house; I'm about to see if I can salvage his boat. His house is gone. The boat might be the only thing he's got left."

"I'll finish up with this mess," Milton said, nodding toward the sheds. "Then I'll head in to see how Ted's doing."

"Thanks, Milton," Thomas said.

We made our way toward the pathway that led to the beach. When we were out of sight he stopped and took me in his arms again.

"That was one hell of a storm," he said. "I was worried sick about you.

I almost came down to the Manor last night, but Ted was in bad shape and after the way Harry acted the night of the ball I thought it might cause more trouble for you."

"I'd say."

"I hope Patrick got word to you?"

"He did. What happened? Why didn't you leave for Connecticut that morning?"

"We got a letter from the inspector that morning announcing an imminent inspection, so I stayed longer to prepare and make sure everything was in order. By the time I was ready to set off we saw the clouds rolling in and I knew it meant trouble—I'd never seen the sky like that before. No one was expecting that weather; it came out of nowhere."

I wrapped my arms around his waist. "It was terrifying, Thomas; two of Elizabeth's boys and Patrick were missing for hours. And Jeanie, remember Jeanie? She didn't make it."

"Good God," Thomas said.

"I can't believe it; it just makes you realize how insignificant everything is and how important everything is all at once." Tears welled up in my eyes.

"Bea." He held my face in his hands. "You're safe now."

"That night, remember the night I didn't show up here, and the next day you said I was acting strange out on those cliffs?"

"What are you talking about?"

"I have to tell you something about that night." He looked at me, the concern spread thick across his brows. I tried to imagine what could be going through his mind that could possibly be worse than what I was going to tell him. The tears started to run down my cheeks.

"Did something happen to you? Tell me."

"Harry, he . . ." I looked down, ashamed, and began to sob. "He forced himself on me that night."

Thomas put his hands on my shoulders, the look of horror on his face made me think it was ending, but I had to go on.

"It was as if he had to prove something. I said some horrible things that pushed him to the edge. I provoked him."

"You didn't deserve that," he said.

Thomas turned away to the ocean and ran his hands through his hair. I watched him, wondering if I was watching it all dissipate, the life I'd dreamed of swept away with the ugly truth. Then he turned toward me. "You can't go back with him. There is no way that I will let you be alone with that man for a second."

"But the baby," I said in a whisper.

"I love you and I love this child no matter what, and I will never stop, but you cannot go back with that man." He took my hands in his. "Stay here in Montauk; this is your home now. You, me and the baby."

I collapsed into his arms, the relief pouring out of me.

"You're going to be fine now, Bea." He took my hand and we walked along the beach slowly. Everything was right; everything was as it should be. I felt a tremendous sense of calm.

It was high tide and the waves were crashing hard on the pebbled beach. The sky was bright blue, as if nothing had changed. But there were mountains of seaweed washed up onshore and the pier was severely damaged. Ted's boat was pretty mangled, tied to a post that had separated from the rickety pier, and was now way too close to the shore where the waves were breaking. With each set of waves that crashed on the beach, the boat pulled and smashed against the stakes of wood that shot up from the ocean in jagged spikes.

"Stay here," Thomas said. "The pier could collapse. I want to see if I can get the boat up onto dry land."

I sat on a boulder near the edge of the water and watched Thomas cautiously walk down the damaged pier. He balanced himself between two posts, lay down on one of the remaining planks and reached into the water to untangle the ropes that had wrapped around themselves and the posts of the pier.

Thomas worked and I leaned back on my elbows, watching him.

Shirtsleeves rolled up, sun catching his muscles, his skin glistening. There was nothing that I wanted, nothing I needed. I'd never felt such clarity and certainty that this was where I was supposed to be.

Half an hour passed, maybe longer, and I heard shouting and scuffling from behind me. I jumped up and as I turned I saw Harry hurtling toward us.

"Thomas!" I shouted as I stood. But Harry was running at full speed. I tried to stop him, rushing toward him, but he pushed me down to the ground and kept on running out onto the pier. He lunged toward Thomas.

"Harry, stop!" I screamed, hearing my voice, high-pitched and frightened.

Thomas barely had a chance to get to his feet before Harry punched him squarely in the face.

"No!" I cried desperately. "What are you doing, Harry?"

Thomas almost fell backwards into the water, but he managed to catch himself and find his balance. Harry swung at him again. Thomas ducked and as he recovered he punched Harry in the jaw. Harry stumbled backwards and toppled straight back and off the other side of the pier. The ocean must have been twenty-five feet deep where they were and he splashed and went under.

"He can't swim!" I shrieked, running toward the pier. "Thomas, he'll drown!"

"God damn it!" Thomas shouted. "Stay where you are," he called to me. There were gaping holes in the pier under his feet where planks of wood had fallen into the ocean. Harry was clinging to one of the single posts sticking up out of the water, but the waves were curling over him and he gasped for air with each break until the next wave rolled in. Thomas wiped blood from the side of his face, tore off his shirt and jumped in. I ran into the water, but the waves were breaking hard onto the beach now and they forced me back. I got up and tried again, my dress now heavy with water and seaweed, wrapping around my legs.

Thomas swam to Harry and dragged him toward part of the pier that was somewhat still intact. He pulled himself up, then reached down and hoisted Harry up, who struggled, crouching and coughing, before finally coming to his feet. He started swinging again.

I ran out onto the pier where they were standing.

"Bea, it's not safe for you here." Thomas reached for my hand, sending Harry into another fury.

"Get your goddamned filthy hands off her," he spat, lunging again at Thomas, shoving him in the chest, but Thomas just stood taller.

"You're going to get off this pier right now," Thomas said, taking steps toward Harry, nearing the edge of the pier. "Then you're going to walk off this beach, and leave us here, and you're never going to look back, do you hear me?"

"Like hell I am."

"Beatrice!" There was shouting on the beach. "Beatrice!" It was Winthrop and his wife. "Stay back!" Winthrop shouted. "He's got a gun."

"What?" I gasped.

Harry reached in his pocket and pulled out a pistol. "That's right." He waved it from me to Thomas, back and forth. "You son of a bitch, you don't get to walk into my life and take my wife and take my child."

"You know it's not yours, Harry!" I cried. Fear spread over my body like a sea creature, wrapping its way around my legs, my body, up to my chest. I could hardly breathe.

Thomas stood in front of me, holding me behind him. "She's staying here with me, in Montauk. She's not going back with you. We're going to walk away now. And then you're going to leave Montauk and never come back."

Harry's face contorted as he pointed the gun at Thomas.

"Fire that gun and you might as well turn it on yourself. Your life will be over. Go on and live your life and let us live ours," Thomas said as we started to back away.

"You think I want to be with her?" He spat onto the pier. "I never want to see her again, that dirty whore." I was shaking behind Thomas, petrified of what Harry would do.

"Go, Bea," Thomas said, still facing Harry while I turned and got off the pier to the shore. Thomas followed behind, took my hand, and we began to walk up the beach, leaving Harry on the pier and Winthrop and Gloria stunned at the water's edge, witnesses to all that unfolded.

We walked fast, not looking back, gripping each other's hands, yet it felt as if we were moving in slow motion, the distance from the beach to the cliffs an eternity.

"Thomas, I'm scared," I said, tripping on my dress, weighed down with water.

"We're almost there, my love. Soon this will all be over."

Then I heard a shot, loud and thunderous. I turned to look but felt Thomas's hand drop from mine and he fell to the ground.

"Thomas!" I cried, falling to my knees, seeing a wound and blood spreading on his back. "God, no!" I screamed. His face was pained and I struggled to turn him to his back. There was more blood on his chest. "Help him!" I cried out. "Please."

Winthrop ran to us and knelt by my side. He pressed his hand on Thomas's chest. "Get me something to stop the bleeding," he demanded. Gloria gave him the wrap from her shoulders and he held it on Thomas's wound.

"Thomas," I said, but the words didn't leave me. "Oh God."

There was a second crack, not as loud, then a crashing sound in the water. The pier had collapsed. No one turned around.

"Milton!" I screamed, though he was all the way at the top of the cliff and there was no way he'd hear us. "Someone help us." Thomas looked at me, his piercing blue eyes pleading with me as he tried to speak. He was sweating and breathing heavily.

"Don't, Thomas, don't say anything; just breathe, please, please." Tears streamed down my face. "Please."

"Go and get help," I said to Winthrop, pressing down on the wound on Thomas's chest. Winthrop looked at me, as if he knew it would be too late. "Now," I begged. "Please." I was desperate, willing to do anything, helpless.

"It's too late," Winthrop said quietly, taking his blood-soaked hands off Thomas's chest.

Thomas's eyes looked up to the sky and suddenly he didn't seem in pain; he didn't seem to know what was going on around him.

"Stay, Thomas!" I cried. "Stay with me."

39

<hr>

The next spring I bought the small yellow cottage on the bluffs with a pathway that led to the ocean. It had been damaged in the storm, just like everything back then, but I got it fixed up enough for us to be comfortable. On the warmer days I'd open the windows in baby Charlotte's room so the sounds of the ocean could lull her to sleep. From a tiny window at the top of the stairs, you could catch a glimpse of the lighthouse. If our child wasn't to know her real father or who he was, I at least wanted her to know and love Montauk the way Thomas had and the way he'd taught me to, through the ocean and the lighthouse and its natural beauty. She should be surrounded by all its goodness the way we had been that summer.

In those first unbearable months after what was ruled an accident, since Harry wasn't there to bear the guilt of Thomas's murder, I went through the motions of mourning in a state of numbness. "She's in shock," people whispered. "I'm worried for the baby." The only relief I had was when they said, "She's exhausted; she needs to rest," because those were the times I could be alone and succumb to the gripping, gut-wrenching and perpetual grief that took over whenever I thought of Thomas.

I could never love anyone else the way I had loved Thomas, and now he was gone from me, from his daughter, from his son, from all the people who loved him, all because of Harry's hatred and jealousy. But sometimes, at unexpected times, I mourned for Harry's wasted, misguided life, too. I was overcome with remorse for my role in the loss of both men. After Harry fired the fatal shot into Thomas's heart, the pier collapsed under him and he drowned while we tried to save Thomas. If I hadn't gone to the lighthouse that day they would both still be alive.

I told myself the baby inside me needed me to keep going and stay strong for her sake. And once she was born she brought me a joy and a love that I didn't think I'd feel again. I had my writing still, which I knew I would continue, but what filled my heart and mind with purpose, love and duty was my daughter. Letting her fill my life with light left slightly less space for sadness and grief.

She was baptized at the church in Montauk—the same church I'd visited to talk to Charlie. It was only Elizabeth, Patrick, my parents, Dolly and the priest, and I was grateful that the press had finally stopped following the story, that this moment was private for me and the small circle of people I had left.

"In the name of the Father, the Son and the Holy Ghost, I baptize you Charlotte Olivia Holmes."

I gave her my maiden name. I closed my eyes and took a deep breath when the priest said her name slowly and deliberately. The cold water trickled down her forehead between her bright blue eyes. She looked startled, then began to cry. The priest dabbed her head with a folded white towel, then passed her back to me, and the crying stopped, turning to a soft whimper.

I felt the presence of something or someone surrounding us, holding us, and I knew it was Thomas. I could feel his strong arms around me and our tiny baby and I felt the strength and courage that I'd felt when I was with him. In that moment I knew that while this was terrifying, this new